Also by Jonathan Kellerman
Available from Random House Large Print

ALEX DELAWARE NOVELS

Breakdown (2016)
Motive (2015)
Killer (2014)
Victims (2012)

The Murderer's Daughter (2015)

HEARTBREAK HOTEL

JONATHAN KELLERMAN

HEARTBREAK HOTEL

AN ALEX DELAWARE NOVEL

RANDOM HOUSE
LARGE PRINT

F
Kell-h

Published in the United States of America by Random House Large Print in association with Ballantine Books, an imprint of Random House, a division of Random House LLC, a Penguin Random House Company, New York.

Cover design by Eric Fuenticilla and Scott Biel

ISBN: 978-1-68331-262-8

Printed in the United States of America

This Large Print edition published in accord with the standards of the N.A.V.H.

To Masha

Special thanks
to Doreen Hudson
and
Laura Jorstad

HEARTBREAK HOTEL

CHAPTER

1

I lead a double life.

Some of my time is spent using the doctorate I earned: evaluating the mental health of injured, neglected, or traumatized children, making recommendations about parental custody, providing short-term treatment. My own childhood was often nightmarish and I like to think I'm making a difference. I keep my fees reasonable and bills get paid.

Then there's the other stuff, initiated by my best friend, an LAPD homicide lieutenant. Once in a while my name leaks into a news story. Mostly I keep out of public view. I doubt any of the families I see are aware of the murders I work on. They've never commented on it and I think they would if they knew.

When my invoices finally make their way through the LAPD bureaucracy, I may get paid at an hourly rate far below my office fee. Sometimes those bills are ignored or rejected outright. If my friend finds out, he makes noise. His success clearing homicides is first-rate. Getting me paid for my time, not so much.

Business-wise, the other stuff doesn't make much sense. I don't care.

I enjoy seeing bad people pay.

What began on a Monday morning in early June seemed to have nothing to do with either half of my life.

Go know.

The answering service operator was a new hire named James, with a shaky voice and a way of turning statements into questions that implied self-esteem issues. Either he hadn't been trained in handling non-emergency calls or he was a poor student.

"Dr. Delaware? I've got someone on the line, a Ms. Mars?"

"Don't know her."

"That's her name? Mars? Like the candy bar?"

"Is it urgent?"

"Um . . . I don't know, Dr. Delaware? She does sound kind of . . . weak?"

"Put her on."

"You bet, Dr. Delaware? Have a great day?"

A faint voice as dry as leaf dust said, "Good morning, Doctor. This is Thalia Mars."

"What can I do for you, Ms. Mars?"

"My guess is you don't do house calls but I'll supplement your fee if you see me at my home."

"I'm a child psychologist."

"Oh, I know that, Dr. Delaware. I'm well aware of the wonderful work you did at Western Pediatric Medical Center. I'm a great fan of the hospital. Ask Dr. Eagle."

Ruben Eagle worked with Western Peds' poorest patients as head of outpatient services and was routinely ignored by hospital fundraisers because the day-to-day maladies of the uninsured couldn't compete for headlines with heart surgery, kidney transplants, and whiz-bang cellular research.

Had he sent this woman to me as a way of stroking one of the few donors he had? It wasn't like Ruben to politick without asking me first.

"Dr. Eagle referred you to me?"

"Oh, no, Doctor. I referred myself."

"Ms. Mars, I'm not clear about what you want—"

"How could you be? I'd explain over the

phone but that would take up too much of your valuable time. Once we get together, my check will include whatever charge you decide is appropriate for this call."

"It's not a matter of billing, Ms. Mars. If you could give me a basic explanation about what you need—"

"Of course. Your work suggests you're an analytic and compassionate man and I could use both. I'm not a nut, Dr. Delaware, and you won't need to travel far. I'm at the Aventura Hotel on Sunset, a short drive from you."

"You're visiting L.A.?"

"I live at the Aventura. That's a bit of a tale, in itself. Would an initial retainer of, say, five thousand dollars set your mind at ease? I'd offer to wire it directly to you but that would require asking for your banking information and you'd suspect some sort of financial scam."

"Five thousand is far too much and there's no need for a retainer."

"Don't you take retainers when you work for the courts?"

"Sounds as if you've researched me, Ms. Mars."

"I try to be thorough, Doctor, but I promise you there's nothing ominous at play. The hotel's a semi-public place and the front desk knows me well. Is there any way you could meet me today, say at three P.M.? You'd avoid rush-hour traffic."

"What if I told you I had a prior appointment?"

"Then I'd request another time, Doctor. And if that failed, I'd beseech you." She laughed. "There is an issue of time. I don't have much of it."

"You're ill—"

"Never felt better," said Thalia Mars. "However, on my next birthday I will be one hundred."

"I see."

"If you don't believe me, when we get together I'll show you my last active driver's license. Flunked the test when I turned ninety-five and have depended, since, on the kindness of others and their internal combustion engines."

My turn to laugh.

"So we're on for three, Dr. Delaware?"

"All right."

"Fabulous, you're analytic, compassionate, **and** flexible. The front desk will direct you."

CHAPTER

2

As soon as the line cleared, I phoned the Aventura.

Miss Mars is here. Would you care to be put through?

No, thanks.

My next call was Ruben. At a conference in Memphis. The Internet had nothing to say about Thalia Mars. No surprise, I supposed. She'd lived most of her long life before techno-geeks decided privacy was irrelevant.

I spent the rest of the morning writing reports, broke at one P.M., slapped together a couple of turkey sandwiches and brewed iced tea, brought a tray out to the garden. Pausing by the pond, I tossed pellets to the koi, continued to Robin's studio.

Two projects occupied her workbench, a gorgeous two-hundred-year-old Italian mandolin restored for the Metropolitan Museum of Art and an electric contraption that resembled a giant garden slug.

The grub-like thing was part cello, part guitar, and dubbed the Alienator by the aging British rocker who'd commissioned it. Forced to learn classical violin as a kid, the invariably drunk Clive Xeno wanted to try his hand at bowing heavy metal. Per his insistence, the instrument was finished in metal-flake auto paint the color of pond sludge. An enamel-tile portrait of Jascha Heifetz protruded below the bridge, showing the maestro looking skeptical.

Robin, hair kerchiefed, wearing a black tee and overalls, was holding the monstrosity up to the skylight and shaking her head.

I said, "The customer's always right."

"Whoever coined that never met Clive. Ah, lunch. You're a mind reader."

Blanche, our little blond French bulldog, rose from her basket, waddled over, and rubbed her head on my ankle. I put the sandwiches on a table and fetched her a stick of jerky from the treat bag.

Robin gave the slug another look. "Five hundred hours of my life and I end up with **this.**"

"Think of it as an avant-garde masterpiece."

"Isn't 'avant-garde' French for 'weird'?" Washing her hands, she kissed me, tossed a drop cloth over both instruments, untied her hair, and let loose a cascade of auburn ringlets. "This is **after** I convinced him to tone it down."

"No more penis-shaped headstock."

"That and Heifetz doing something gross. How's **your** day going?"

"Finished some reports and heading out in a couple."

"Milo beckoned?"

"I'm going to see a woman who claims to be nearly a hundred and wants to talk."

"Claims to be? Like she's only ninety-eight and is being pretentious?"

I laughed. "No reason to doubt her."

"She introduced herself that way? I'm almost a hundred."

"She worked it into the conversation."

"Why not?" she said. "Last that long, you'd want to strut your stuff. My great-aunt Martina lived until ninety-eight and advertised it in every conversation. 'Canned green beans, anyone? Been eating them for ninety-eight years and **I'm** still breathing.'"

She picked up a sandwich, nibbled, put it down. "Delicious, you're the perfect man . . . so why would a hundred-year-old chick call **you**?"

"She didn't go into details."

"But you agreed to do a house call?"

"She's one of Ruben Eagle's donors."

"So you do a good deed and get to escape the office. It **has** been a while since the Big Guy called. I've been wondering when it would get to you."

"I've been restless?"

She kissed my nose. "No, darling, but I know you. The crime rate falls, good for society, boring for you."

She took another bite of sandwich. "A hundred years old, huh? Imagine the things she's seen."

When you've lived in a city for years, there's no need to know much about hotels. Robin and I sometimes ate or drank at the Bel-Air and back in my hospital days I'd attended fundraisers at Hiltons and such. My exposure to the Aventura had been driving west on Sunset and passing a directional sign staked at the mouth of an entrance framed by palms. First time for everything.

The opening fed to a cobblestone drive. The palms were overgrown, bordering on unruly. A second sign legislated **5 MPH**. Speed bumps placed every twenty feet enforced the rule. Combined with the cobbles, that made for a kidney-thumping crawl.

Beautiful, sunny L.A. day. Isn't it always? But when eucalyptus joined the vegetative mix, branches dense enough to form a roof created an artificial dusk. Ten spinal concussions in, I reached a fork marked by a clot of massive banana plants. Valet and self-parking to the right, hotel entrance to the left.

I pulled the Seville into a surprisingly shabby asphalt lot boxed on three sides by pale-pink stucco walls and backed by fifty-foot Canary Island pines. Out-of-state plates and rental cars predominated. A couple of golf carts in **Reserved** slots. No valets in sight.

I parked, walked for a while, finally arrived at a structure that might've been designed by Clive Xeno during a bender: two stories of tile-roofed hacienda in the same pallid pink, attached to a four-story steel-and-bronze glass cylinder.

Cracks had formed in the older building's stucco where it merged with the tower. Spanish Colonial mama struggling to birth a giant alien baby.

The only indication of the hotel's identity was a rusty iron **A** above glass doors centering the newer addition. When I was two steps away, the panels hissed open, creating a maw that led to a three-story atrium—a tube within a tube. Background music was a brain-eroding electronic mantra flicked with random bird peeps. The ceiling was matte black embedded with starry-night LED bulbs. What might have been actual constellations, but I'm no astronomer.

To the right, thirty-plus feet of waterfall trick-led down a pebbly glass wall. A scatter of leather deco-revival chairs dyed a strange liverish red were sided by chunks of resin pretending to be boulders. Empty chairs but for a hipster couple in their thirties facing each other as they worked separate iPhones. A girl around five stood near the woman, limp doll in her hand, thumb in her mouth.

Ranchero Revival meets Missile Silo meets twenties Paris meets Fred Flintstone via Beijing.

With an overhead tribute to the Griffith Park planetarium.

Maybe dealing with that on a daily basis helped a hundred-year-old brain stay in shape.

To the left, a pair of chrome elevators preceded glass doors leading to the older wing. At the center, **Reception** and **Concierge** shared a poured-concrete counter. Three pallid, ponytailed people in their twenties were on duty, a woman and two men, each the same five-six or so and wearing Asian-style tunics colored the hepatic hue of the chairs.

No name tags, no notice of my approach as thirty fingers continued to tap laptops.

When I reached the counter, one of the men

smiled with astonishing warmth while continuing to type. "May I help you?"

"I'm here to see Ms. Mars."

"Thalia," said the woman. Now three wan faces found me fascinating.

"We **love** Thalia," said the other man.

The woman said, "You're her doctor. She said to send you right over."

"She's in Bungalow Uno," said the first man.

The woman eyed the glass doors. "If you go through there, you'll be in El O-ree-hee-**nal.** Just keep going and go outside and you'll see a sign leading to The Green."

I said, "O-ree—"

The first man said, "Ori-hi-**naaal.** Spanish for 'original.'"

Second said, "What's left of the old hotel. The Aventura believes in preservation and synthesis."

The woman said, "Uno's the last bungalow."

First said, "We **love** Thalia."

On the other side of the glass was a rose-carpeted hallway lined with numbered oak doors. The first few rooms had been converted to computerized card-slot entry. The rest retained heavy cast-bronze knobs and keyholes.

Partially ori-hi-**naaal.**

The corridor emptied to an echoing loggia that led outdoors. The air smelled like freshly cut grass. **The Green** was a wide stone path swathing through more palms, plus ferns and bromeliads. Like the entry drive, dimmed by overgrowth.

The first bungalow appeared fifty feet in, white clapboard, tar-roofed, swaddled in green. A sign over the door read **Ocho: 8.** The count-down continued with a series of identical struc-tures through **Dos: 2.**

Then, a traipse through jungle until a larger building backed by a high pink wall slipped into view.

Uno: 1 was set on a raised foundation with three steps leading to a screened porch. A roof pitched higher, a brick chimney, and black shut-ters set it apart from the other bungalows. Paint flaked from boards, the roof was patched with tar where shingles had come loose.

Once upon a time, the VIP suite?

The location afforded privacy, the high wall security. But the distance from the parking lot would mean a serious hike for an older person. Maybe Thalia Mars was one of those super-specimens.

The porch door was open. As I climbed the steps, the arid voice I'd heard over the phone said, "Dr. Delaware! Who knew you'd be so handsome?"

Eighty or so pounds of vintage humanity in a

Ming-blue dress sat in a rattan peacock chair and smiled up at me. The chair looked identical to the throne Sydney Greenstreet had occupied in **Casablanca.** The actor had been four times that weight and overflowed the cane. The current occupant evoked a toddler playing grown-up.

"Ms. Mars." I extended my hand and received a quick, firm shake by fingers that felt like chopsticks. A ring set with a huge amethyst collided with my knuckles.

Thalia Mars's wide amused mouth was augmented by meticulously applied coral lipstick. Her eyes were clear brown. Shoulder-length hair tinted the ivory of old piano keys had been whipped into a meringue of waves. Nearly a century of gravity had done its inevitable thing with her jawline, but a dagger-thin face below the cloud of hair retained enough integrity to suggest a once-firm chin and prominent cheekbones.

The blue dress was silk with long, tapered sleeves defining pipe-cleaner arms and a knee-length hem that revealed brief segments of seamed stocking. Yellow kitten-heeled sandals dangled well above the floor. Red toenails, silver manicure, diamond chips in her earlobes, a pearl necklace dangling from the dress's high neckline well past the waist of an attenuated torso.

She took a deep breath, said, "Thank you for

coming," braced her hands on the sides of the chair, and took a while easing herself upright and planting her feet. She tottered and I moved toward her but she laughed softly and waved me off.

Inhaling again, she drew herself up.

Maybe five feet tall, including the heels. Despite her attempt to straighten, her back remained humped, her head pitched forward. She swung her arms a few times and announced, "Hup two march."

No movement at first. Then she began obeying her own command.

I followed her trudge across the porch and into a small living room enlarged by clever layout and natural light. The ceiling was white beams, the floor wide-plank pine burnished the color of old whiskey where it wasn't concealed by a threadbare lilac-and-olive Persian rug.

A plum-colored mohair chair faced a limestone fireplace. Perpendicular to the hearth, gray velvet love seats faced each other across a black lacquer Chinese table. Silk throw pillows were scattered with a pseudo-randomness that requires care. Petite occasional tables were topped by glass-shaded lamps, one of which sported a dragonfly motif and might have been Tiffany. A floor lamp to the left of the fireplace, its base green enamel, its dome studded with bubbles of red glass and crowned by a faceted red finial the size of a cocktail olive, looked crude by comparison and probably wasn't.

The scant remaining square footage was taken up by a two-chair dining table and a bare-bones kitchenette. A rear doorway suggested a dim hall.

Thalia Mars settled herself in the mohair chair and motioned me to the left-hand couch. "Thank you for indulging me, Doctor. Something to drink or a snack, perhaps?"

I said, "No, thanks," just as a soft rap sounded on the front doorframe and a pretty young Filipina in a liver-colored frock entered wheeling a tray on a cart. "Teatime, Miss M. For two, like you asked."

"Punctual as always, Refugia. Thank you, my dear."

The tray was set down on the Chinese table. Crustless sandwiches, scones, chocolate wafers, cheese, grapes.

The maid snuck a look at me. "Bon appétit, Miss M."

"Take a scone for yourself, dear."

"Oh, no, thank you."

"Indulge, dear, you're perfectly trim. Take it from me, darling: Enjoy your appetite while you still have one. I can barely smell or taste, food has become hay and straw."

"Oh, I'm sure you're fine," said Refugia.

"Fine, but insensate, dear." Brown eyes drifted upward. The tiny body swayed. "Sometimes I dream that I can taste mussels in France, tomatoes in Italy. Then I wake up with a tongue made of felt." Soft laugh. "At least I wake up."

"Oh, Miss M, you'll always be okay."

"Thank you, Refugia. That's all, for now."

"When should I come back to collect the tray?"

"Let's say two hours, dear."

Stripped of cargo, the cart rattled all the way to the stairs. When silence returned, Thalia Mars said, "Can't taste tea, either, but I'm diligent about hydration. Would you please pour me a cup, Doctor? One lump but only half full, my wrists aren't what they used to be. And take something for yourself. If that doesn't violate a professional regulation."

"I'm fine, Ms. Mars."

"Fair enough but would you mind dispensing with half the formality? I promise to stick with 'Doctor' but I'd prefer you address me as Thalia. My parents were vaudevillians who had high hopes for me and named me after the comedic muse. To their great disappointment, I rebelled and became an accountant, but I've always liked the moniker."

"Sure, Thalia."

I poured and handed her the cup. She used

both hands to guide it to her lips, lapped like a kitten and smiled over the rim. "Hearing my name on a young man's lips is rather a kick—was that inappropriate? If it was, please forgive me. I've never had a personal experience with a psychologist."

"What changed your mind?"

"Have I experienced a nervous breakdown?" The smile enlarged. "Not as far as I can tell."

Slowly, painstakingly, she lowered the cup to the table. "So why **have** I imposed on you? I suppose honesty's the best policy, so I'm going to come right out and admit my lack of complete candor over the phone."

Patting her hair, she crossed her legs at the ankles. "When I said I was aware of your work at the hospital and admired it, that was sincere. However, that's not why I called you. I became interested in your involvement in . . . less savory matters."

I sat there.

"You don't understand what I'm getting at, Doctor?"

"Why don't you tell me."

She reached for the teacup, missed, lost her balance. I took hold of her arm and stabilized her.

"Drat," she said in a choked voice. "The thing that used to be my body has turned traitor."

"May I hand you the cup?"

"Seeking permission?" She grinned. "You're worried I'll fly off the handle at some perceived slight."

"Some people prefer doing things for themselves."

"Old people."

"All kinds of people."

Brown eyes aimed at mine. "Yes, please, pour."

I filled another half cup.

She said, "Done with finesse, Doctor. Is there someone at home for whom you regularly pour—" A hand shot to her lips. "Oops, that was a **definite** faux pas. Gad, I feel the fool."

"You're not being tested, Thalia."

"Really?" she said. "Are we sure of that?"

"I am."

"Well," she said, "that's kind of you to say—I suppose at this point you're wondering if I **am** an utter fizzy-head. Perhaps I should dig up that driver's license to prove I haven't fibbed about my age."

"I'll take it as fact," I said. "Though you do look considerably younger."

"Always have. Not that there are standards for how artifacts are supposed to look. But vanity aside, have you met any other gals of my vintage?"

"I haven't."

"I suppose novelty counts for something." She frowned. "Why am I going **on**?"

"It's a new situation, Thalia."

She stared at her lap. "This is harder than I thought it would be."

"Why don't we start with why you think I can help you."

"Well," she said, "I'm a big reader, always have been. Always been a fan of the public library. Harder to visit there, now that I don't drive. Refugia and some of the other infants who work here prod me to give the computer a try. I'm sure it would've proved helpful back in the Pleistocene era, when I had a job. But now?" She stuck out her tongue.

I said, "What kind of accounting did you do?"

"Nothing impressive, Doctor. I kept the books for a number of government departments, ended up at the county assessor until I retired."

"How long has the hotel been your home?"

"A while," she said. Lifting her cup with both hands, she sipped silently. The pinkie of her right hand extended. Nails perfect, every hair in place. A slight tremor had taken hold of her hands but she managed to put the cup down. "Would you be so kind as to hand me one of those chocolate biscuits?"

I complied and she nibbled twice before shaking her head. "Like eating lint. I used to love chocolate . . . anyway, how I found you. Sans the library, I have occasional copies of the paper delivered to me by the staff. Mostly when the yen to work a crossword or a Sudoku takes hold."

She swiveled toward the partially open door. "Back in my bedroom, I've got a sixty-inch television, high-definition, the works. I record movies and that show about the Alaskan crab fishermen—have you seen it? Poor men taking their lives in their hands simply by going to work each day—what I'm trying to say, Dr. Delaware, is that I'm not a total Luddite. I enjoy being in **touch.**"

I said, "You came across my name in the paper."

"More than once, though I wouldn't call it often. Unrelated criminal cases but no explanation of what your involvement was. I found it intriguing."

She recrossed her legs. "This is the point where I confess that I wasn't totally accurate with regard to the Internet. Once you piqued my curiosity, I did have one of the infants look you up—what do they call it, Googling a search? What emerged was your work at the hospital, and that intrigued me further. Crimes **and** helping kiddies? I thought to myself: This is an interesting person. Western Pediatric really is an institution that I admire—would you mind helping me shift position? Just grab and pull me forward a smidge."

She extended both hands. Her skin had turned icy. Using me as a counterweight, she inched forward, finally let go, breathing hard.

"Thank you. Now I have a question for you: What's the current psychological wisdom with regard to guilt?"

"There really isn't one."

"Why not?"

"For some people, guilt can be crippling. For others, it's helpful."

"Hmm . . . how about an example of when it's beneficial?"

"People with no capacity for self-examination are capable of terrible things. Guilt helps society sustain itself."

"What kind of people are we talking about?"

"The extreme example would be psychopaths."

"Crazy people."

"No, psychopaths are sane but they're selfish, lack empathy, and can be cruel and impulsive."

"What we used to call bad eggs," she said. She went silent, looked to the side. "Can total scoundrels be changed? Or at least channeled into something productive?"

"If it suits their purposes."

"So, not really. Do bad eggs inevitably exploit the **good** eggs?"

"Again, Thalia, if it's in their best interests."

"Big dog eats little dog when hungry."

I nodded. "Psychopaths are good at sniffing out victims. Psychopaths with brains and charisma can succeed on a grand scale."

"You could be describing politicians."

I smiled.

She said, "I worked for the county, don't get me started. All right, another question: When looking for their victims, is there a type they go for?"

"Whoever they sense will fulfill their needs."

"Predators with a nose for prey."

"Exactly."

"Do they specialize? Thieves running with thieves, burglars with burglars?"

"Criminologists used to believe they did. Now we know that's not true."

"Bad is simply bad."

"There's a psychopathic range of behavior, but it's narrower than for morally normal people."

"But theoretically," she said, "any miscreant is capable of anything. Violence, for example."

"Smarter psychopaths tend to avoid violence because it's usually a losing strategy. But in the end, it depends on whether their goals can be achieved nonviolently."

"If push comes to shove, nothing stops them." She drew a hand across her gullet.

"Are you asking about someone in particular, Thalia?"

"Oh, no . . . what a disheartening picture we've drawn of humanity, Doctor. I suppose I was hoping for better. Would still like to think of our planet as an evolutionary gem rather than an orbiting hunk of waste material. Several years ago when I saw photos taken from that faraway telescope—the Hubble—I was cheered. The universe seemed beautiful. Jewel-like. But I suppose one needs to be light-years away to see it like that."

I said, "Thalia, context is important. Psychopaths can be disruptive but they're a very small percent of the population."

"Most people are morally sound."

"I believe so."

"You believe?" she said. "What does the science of psychology have to say about it?"

"It's not a topic that's been studied well."

"I see . . . this has been most helpful, Dr. Delaware. Is our time just about up? I don't wear a wristwatch anymore, too heavy. And the only clocks I have are above the stove and on my bedside table, so if you don't mind—is that a vintage Rolex on **your** wrist?"

"Girard-Perregaux." Gift from a great-uncle,

a Battle of the Bulge hero who'd bartered it for candy bars in postwar France and came home wanting to forget.

"Very **chic**, Doctor. What time does it proclaim?"

"We've got a quarter hour left."

"Really?" She suppressed a yawn. "Excuuuse **me**, so sorry. Would you mind terribly if we kicked in early? I'm flagging."

"No problem." I stood.

She reached out a hand. I gave her mine. She held on.

"Will you come see me tomorrow, Dr. Delaware? Perhaps a bit earlier in the day, so I can conserve my energy, say eleven A.M.? Oops, I nearly forgot. Your fee. You'll find a check over by the blue Tiffany, the one with the dragonflies. Aren't they lovely creatures, so ephemeral. Would you mind fetching it yourself?" Patting her knees. "The hinges are creaking."

I walked to the lamp. A cream-colored paper corner peeked from under a bronze base molded into the stalk of a lily.

Bracing the lamp, I pulled out a seven-by-five envelope, heavy stock, no personalization. Inside was a check drawn on the personal account of Thalia M. Mars, made out in a gracious but shaky hand.

Six thousand dollars.

"This is way too much, Thalia, and as I said over the phone, a retainer's not called for."

"Consider it an account to be drawn upon."

"That's the definition of a retainer."

"It is when advance payment is for the convenience of the **payee**," she said. "However, in this case, you're helping me keep things simple."

"Even so, Thalia, six thousand—"

A coral grin livened her face. "Are you doubting I'll last long enough to deplete the full amount? If so, what's the big deal? You'll reap a windfall."

"Thalia—"

"Just joshing, Dr. Delaware. Look, the check's already made out, let's not haggle. By doing it my way, you really are helping me avoid constant calculating, writing, recording."

She blew a raspberry. "Ledgers were my life for decades, I saw them in my dreams, have had quite enough of **that**, thank you. And **should** you come out on the plus end, nothing will stop you from donating any overage to charity. I'm sure Dr. Eagle would appreciate that."

I said, "Payment aside, I'm still not clear about the purpose of our sessions."

"You're not? I thought I was being lucid as a diamond. All right, allow me to sum up: What I want from you is exactly what you just provided.

Clarification of questions that arise, plus open ears and an open mind."

She yawned, covered her mouth. "**Excuse me**—I really am running out of steam. Tomorrow at eleven?"

Before setting out, I'd checked my calendar. Open-ended conference call on a three-child custody case at nine A.M., new evaluation at twelve thirty.

"I'm not free for most of tomorrow, Thalia."

"No, of course not, why would you be, you're a man in demand. All right, is there **any** time you could squeeze me in?"

She winked. "As I mentioned, I do have a rather momentous birthday coming up."

"I can probably be here between ten and ten thirty but if an earlier appointment runs late, we'll have to reschedule."

She clapped her hands. "Wonderful! Ten it is!"

"I'd still like to know more about your goals for our sessions."

"My immediate goal is breathing, Doctor."

"Seriously, Thalia."

"Oh, **must** I be? I thought I wasn't being **tested**." She wagged a finger. "Gotcha!"

I fought laughter and lost.

"Aha! I've **amused** you!" she said. "And just to

show what a nice gal I am, I won't even ask for a discount."

I drove home knowing I'd been played by a tiny, wizened person. Why didn't it bother me?

Because I found the hints she dropped interesting? Guilt, criminal patterns, victim selection, incorrigibility.

The universe as a jewel, not junk.

Despite what she'd said, people don't see psychologists for theoretical discussion. So the past half hour had been all about self-defense and possibly denial.

Something personal she wasn't ready to discuss?

A woman with a past? Nearing the end of her years and seeking atonement?

Putting all that aside, she **was** eons out of my patient range. Did open ears and an open mind constitute valid use of my professional time? Was any sort of payment justified, let alone a six-grand retainer?

I'd give her another session, take it from there.

Meanwhile, I'd hold off cashing the check.

Robin knows better than to ask me about patients. But when I got home and found her in the kitchen feeding Blanche supper, she said, "Have fun with your new girlfriend?"

"It was different."

"After you left, I did a little cybering. Did you know that a third of centenarians live independently? Superior protoplasm, I guess."

I poured myself coffee, offered her some, but she said, "No, thanks, there's enough caffeine in me to go rock-climbing blindfolded."

She portioned out the last bit of canine cuisine and sat down across from me. "I asked about fun because you looked kind of chipper when you came in."

I smiled and shrugged.

She ran a finger over her lip. "No more nosygirl. But anything that lifts your spirits is okay with me."

CHAPTER

3

The next day's morning call ended at nine thirty-five. At five to ten, I pulled into the Aventura parking lot. A valet sat smoking in a golf cart. Two black-suited drivers chatted near their Town Cars.

I headed for The Green. The path was blocked by a mass of red.

Red L.A. Fire Department paramedic truck. A couple of hotel maids and one of the ponytails from the front desk stood watching but no one said a thing as I made my way around the vehicle and hurried up the walkway.

Nothing at Ocho, Siete, Seis.

Maybe at Cinco, Cuatro, Tres. I could hope.

Ninety-nine years old; hope seemed absurd.

◆

Just outside the steps to the screened porch of Uno stood the young maid who'd served tea yesterday—Refugia. A wadded tissue was pressed to her mouth. Her eyes were wet and her chest heaved.

When she saw me, she shook her head violently.

I said, "How long ago?"

"I found her just now. Brought breakfast at nine like always but her bedroom door was closed and she didn't answer. I thought maybe she wants more sleep. Then I thought, she's always up early but I still didn't want to wake her."

She gulped air. "I left and delivered to Cinco and they asked me also for a paper so I went to get that, then I came back here. Nine thirty-four, I looked at my watch, figured I should maybe check. She was in bed, looking so peaceful. But then I couldn't wake her."

A rush of tears. "I know she's old but there was a lot of life in her. It's stupid to be surprised. But I was. I called 911."

A blue-uniformed paramedic appeared in the bungalow doorway. Tall, muscular, young with a shaved head and narrow eyes. As I approached, he said, "Sir, you can't go in there."

R. Barker on his tag.

"I'm Dr. Delaware. Ms. Mars and I had an appointment."

"You're her doctor?" he said. "Sorry, too late."

"What happened?"

"She passed, probably in her sleep. She looks pretty elderly."

"In three weeks, she'd have been a hundred."

"Really?"

Refugia sniffed and Barker glanced at her. "Too bad, that would've been a milestone. Anyway, Doc, we're finishing up."

He descended the porch steps. "I'm heading to the john over in the hotel. My partner's in there keeping watch till the coroner's van arrives."

After he left, I climbed the stairs to the porch. Heard murmurs and glanced back.

Just within vision, Barker and Refugia stood on the pathway, talking. Call of the bladder notwithstanding, he looked mellow. She stared up at him, a rapt pupil. He patted her shoulder. She'd stopped crying.

I went inside.

A breakfast tray sat on the Chinese table, coffee cup and orange juice glass roofed by paper doilies, plates concealed by silver domes, toast in a rack. The door to the rear of the bungalow was ajar.

Ten feet of gold plush squelched my footsteps. Floral prints on the wall; shutter closet doors to the right, then an old white-tile bathroom.

The bedroom door was wedged open. A portable defibrillator and an emergency kit sat on the floor. A second paramedic stood at the foot of a canopy bed, wide enough to block most of the view.

I said, "I'm Dr. Delaware," and he swiveled. Tall as Barker, half again as broad, with the moon-face of a well-nourished toddler. His eyes were black. Spiky hair was peroxided yellow. **C. Guzman.**

"Hotel called for a doctor? Nothing you can do anymore, sorry."

"I had an appointment with the deceased. I'm a psychologist."

"Huh," said Guzman. "She had mental problems?"

"I met her yesterday, don't know much about her."

"What did you say your name was, sir?"

"Alex Delaware."

"No offense, but would you mind showing me some I.D.?"

I fished for my wallet, sidestepping so I could see around him. He was a wall of flesh but a few details registered.

Mahogany bed, oversized for the room, the canopy's underside pleats of gold silk. Barely enough space for a night table. A black silk duvet was patterned with tiny Asian figures. Black satin pillows created a berm against the head-board.

Thalia's body remained out of view.

I gave Guzman my state license card and my LAPD consultant clip-on. As he read the card, he shifted a bit and I took in more of the room. South wall: floor-to-ceiling books; nothing on the north wall but a plain maple dresser. Atop the dresser, a mirrored tray, an onyx-handled manicure set, lotions, powders, perfumes.

Big bottle of Chanel No. 5. Corresponding aroma mixed with something sour.

The TV that Thalia Mars had described proudly was off in a corner, resting on an old Vuitton trunk.

Guzman switched to the clip-on, shifted his weight again, exposed the center of the room.

Thalia lay on her back, her body so small it barely tented the duvet. The covers shielded her to mid-torso. Her eyes were shut, her mouth half open. Piano-key-colored hair spread atop a black pillow. Twig-fingers rested atop her abdomen. The digits looked rigid. Maybe rigor; dead for a while.

No obvious disruption. The amethyst ring was in place and glints of jewelry radiated from the nightstand. I thought I saw some pinkish mottling around her nose but otherwise death's hue—that green-gray that marks the retreat of cells—had taken ownership of her skin.

Guzman said, "You're with the cops? Some-one suspects something?"

"I consult to the cops but mostly I work privately. Thalia was a private patient."

"Starting yesterday."

"That's right."

"Huh." Guzman tapped a foot. The floor-boards vibrated. "Listen, Doc, I'm not sure what's going on, so I have to ask you to leave. I'm sorry if that's offensive but I need to amend my first call-in."

"How?"

"Sir, really, I can't discuss. I'm calling the cops—real cops, no offense, sir, but procedure has to be followed."

I said, "There's some evidence of homicide?"

He didn't answer.

I said, "From here it looks as if rigor has set in. What about livor mortis? Any pooling below the waist?"

"Sir!"

I took out my phone and speed-dialed.

Milo mastiff-growled, "Sturgis."

"Lieutenant, this is Dr. Delaware."

"Alex? What's up?"

"Yes, Lieutenant."

"You in some kind of fix?"

"I'm at a death scene, Lieutenant. A patient I came to see turned up unexpectedly deceased.

The first responder has some suspicions, let me put him on."

I held out the phone. Guzman stared at it.

I said, "Lieutenant Sturgis is the senior homicide detective at West L.A. We're cutting out the middleman."

Guzman took the phone. "Sir, this is LAFD paramedic Guzman . . . yes, sir . . . no, sir, I'm not saying definitely, that's not my area of expertise, sir, but I couldn't help notice . . . yes, I do believe so, sir . . . would you like me to tell you why . . . sure, that makes sense . . . the Aventura Hotel, sir, Sunset and—you do? Great, yessir, I will totally preserve it but are you saying no need to go by procedure . . . sorry, sir, yessir, right away. Oh, yeah, about Dr. Delaware . . ."

He listened some more, returned the phone and my I.D. His face was an odd mixture of resentment and reverence.

"Man, you must have **something** going on with the cops. I'm supposed to tell you **everything**."

Handing me latex gloves, Guzman found another set for himself before motioning me to the right side of the bed. "I'm sure I don't need to tell you not to disturb anything, Doctor. But . . . anyway, take a look at this."

Two huge fingers tweezed Thalia's right eyelid open, then its mate. Both sclera were rosy with broken blood vessels.

I said, "Petechial hemorrhaging."

"Didn't notice it at first, Doc, 'cause when we got here the eyes were just a smidge open and you figure someone her age, in bed, no struggle, why shouldn't it be natural? But after Rob—my partner—left, like a second before you got here, I was finishing up and I bent down and got closer to her eyes and saw the red and checked."

I said, "Asphyxia or strangulation."

"No strangulation I can see," said Guzman. "By that I mean her neck looks clean. But I'm no doctor and someone this old, maybe the body can do things, right? Like something bursting in her brain and the blood goes into the eyes? But then I saw **this,** check it out."

He pointed but I'd already noticed. The redness I'd seen around the nostrils. Up close, discreet rosy spots.

"Again, Doc, maybe nothing, but combined with the eyes? So, now I'm **real** curious."

I bent closer, breathed in Chanel No. 5 and a rising must. "The bridge of her nose is swollen."

"I don't know what her nose looked like before, Doc."

"I do. There's definite swelling." I jiggled the

cartilage softly. "Doesn't appear to be broken, more like a pressure mark. Maybe someone squeezing both nostrils."

"Oh, boy—okay, there's this, too."

He lifted Thalia's head with one hand and pointed with the other.

An oval bruise marked a spot beneath the chin, less than an inch long, purplish.

I said, "Thumb-sized. Someone forced her mouth and her nose shut."

"That would sure do it," said Guzman. "Poor old thing. If something was done to her, I hope she slept through it."

Yesterday's questions about criminal tendencies clanged in my head. Incorrigibility. Psychopaths.

Someone specific in mind? Someone she'd let into the bungalow, despite her suspicions?

Guzman said, "Maybe I'm wrong and there's some explanation, Doc. I'd sure **like** to be wrong. What do **you** think?"

"I think you did the right thing by paying attention."

He shrugged, ripped off his gloves, tossed them onto the floor where they landed like dead moths. Thinking better of it, he retrieved them, crushed them into a ball.

"This is pathetic, Doc. She reminds me of my great-nana."

CHAPTER

4

Guzman lifted his gear and the two of us went outside. Rob Barker and Refugia stood in the same place. Now she was talking and he was listening. Both of them looked relaxed.

Guzman shook his head. "There he goes."

I said, "Socializing."

"He's got a really nice girlfriend but he's a dog."

"Time to tell him your suspicions?"

"Probably should, but what's the point? All he wants to do is pick up chicks. He thinks I'm a wuss because I don't cut corners. But he's a good partner, real good at CPR— Doc, can I ask why you came to see the decea—Ms. Mars?"

"Sorry, I can't say."

"Oh. Sure. What I'm getting at, was there a serious mental problem? Not that you could explain it with that."

"Explain what?"

"Well," he said, "we see a whole lot more suicides than homicides but I guess that doesn't apply here, I shouldn't run my mouth." A moment later: "I mean, you couldn't clamp your own nose and mouth shut long enough, right? It would be like trying to hold your breath, you'd have to give up."

"This wasn't suicide, Chris."

"No, of course not. But if she had problems, maybe she knew someone else who was willing to help her."

"Assisted suicide."

"It's legal in some places, Doc. Some people don't think it's wrong."

I said nothing. Guzman was one of those people with a low tolerance for silence. It didn't take him long to say, "The thing is, the maid—the one Rob's chatting up—told us she found the door unlocked. So she—Ms. Mars—probably let someone in that she knew. Didn't seem to me there was any struggle and with all that jewelry in there, those antiques, it sure doesn't look like robbery. So it makes me wonder, Doc. She was old, needed a shrink, I'm wondering if maybe some psychological thing was going on."

I flipped back to yesterday's session, probing my memory for allusions to suicide. Anything remotely depressive.

Just the opposite, she'd seemed ebullient.

But anyone could be fooled.

This time the silence led Guzman to move a few feet away. He looked at his watch. Barker's and Refugia's hips edged closer as they continued to chat.

Guzman said, "We **do** see some bizarre suicides. You probably have, too, working with the cops."

"You bet."

"What I mean, Doc, is you get a scene you're sure is a murder then you find out it isn't."

"Something staged."

"Exactly. Like this woman we had last year, must've really despised her husband's guts. She ties her hands behind herself with duct tape but only after she positions the handle of his hunting knife so the blade's sticking out between the slats of a chair. Facing out, you know? Then she gets down on her knees, right in front of the knife, and stabs herself in the head."

He winced. "**Big** blade, heavy duty. Goes right through the bone into her brain, talk about pain. The impact makes her jerk back, she falls hard enough to take the knife with her, we find it like that, sticking out of her. Top of that, she made sure to direct attention to the husband by writing in her diary that he was out to kill her and leaving the diary on a table where you couldn't miss it."

"Too obvious," I said.

"That's the first thing made the cops suspicious. But there was also physical evidence. Dust on her knees, and the shape of the bloodstains didn't fit someone chopping her from above. What clinched it was she used gloves when she touched the knife so that only his prints would be on it. But she forgot about the inside, the only DNA there was hers. Also, the husband had a total alibi. Screwing his girlfriend in a motel."

I said, "All that trouble for nothing."

"Exactly, Doc. Though I guess she got what she wanted, which was obviously to be dead. You see something like that, you start to doubt your own reality. But I guess that's not what happened here, right? You're not saying Ms. Mars was seriously depressed or disturbed."

"I'm not saying much of anything, Chris."

"I know, I know, sorry," said Guzman. "But if she **was** depressed and afraid or too weak to take her own life, she could've had someone else do it for her in a painless way."

"Forcing her mouth and nose shut?"

"Okay, yeah, maybe it's ridiculous, why not

just swallow some pills?" He shrugged. "That's the way I am. Too curious."

"That's how you learn, Chris."

"Maybe I **should** tell Rob, 'cause I don't think lunch is on the schedule, anymore." He took a couple of steps toward Barker, changed his mind, returned to my side. "Nah, he'll just rag on me. If he gets antsy, let **him** come **here**."

He cracked his knuckles. "You like working with the cops?"

"I do."

"I've been thinking about applying, myself. Maybe, end up a detective one day."

"Curiosity's a good trait for a detective."

"That's what I figure. Problem is the fire department pays great and my wife doesn't want me carrying a gun. Plus I like what I do. Sometimes I even get to do a little psychology—seeing people in all kinds of stress."

"I'll bet."

"Like last week—oh, man, look at that **dog**."

Barker had fished out his phone and was taking a selfie of himself and Refugia. Then another. A whole series of shots ensued, his arm snaking around her shoulder, hers circling his waist.

Guzman said, "You wouldn't believe the stuff he's got on his phone. One day, Tonya, that's his girl, she'll get suspicious and check it out. When that happens . . ." He ran a finger across his throat.

Same gesture Thalia had made yesterday.

Guzman rubbed his wedding band. Gold, etched with two hearts. "How long do you think it'll take for Lieutenant Sturgis to get here?"

"He's usually prompt."

"I'm asking 'cause if we get another call it'll be tricky, we'll have to explain to the dispatcher . . . so you treat mostly older folk."

"Actually, I specialize in children."

His brow knitted. "Are you saying she was in some kind of second childhood?"

"Do you have kids of your own, Chris?"

"One. Anabella, eight months old, she's crawling like crazy."

"Got a picture?"

"Long as you asked." Big grin. "My phone's G-rated."

He'd scrolled through the first two dozen shots of a chubby blond baby when movement up the road drew us away from the tiny screen.

Barker and Refugia had shifted closer to each other, no air between them. They moved apart as a big, wide figure in a gray suit headed their way.

The man's stork legs appearing too flimsy for the watermelon-shaped trunk they supported. Long arms swung loosely with each rapid step.

Barker and Refugia moved to opposite edges of the stone path. The convex belly that was

Milo's opening act asserted itself as he loped toward them. His big, black-haired head was carried low and thrust forward, as if battling a headwind.

The same stance you see in rodeo bulls itching to inflict pain.

Drawing himself up to his full six-three, Milo looked at each of them, flashed his badge, and began talking. Refugia had the tissue pushed up against her mouth, again. Barker looked stunned. Milo said something that made Barker turn toward Guzman and me. He gave his partner a palms-up what's-the-story signal.

Guzman ignored him.

Milo continued his march.

"That's him?" said Guzman. "Is he kinda ticked off or something?"

"That's his thing."

"Being ticked off?"

"Making people wonder."

Milo's greeting was a nod-grunt combo followed by taking out his little notepad. Daylight enhanced the acne scars and lumps decorating his face. Up close, the gray suit was unpleasantly silvery. Pretending to be sharkskin but ending up closer to mullet-belly. The collar of his white wash-'n'-wear shirt rode up on one side and curled on the other. A skinny strip of olive-green polyester necktie ended well above his belt. At the bottom of the stilt legs were the ritual desert boots, this pair, tan soiled to brown, with red rubber soles.

Barker and Refugia were watching us. He cocked a head at Guzman and held his hands out, again. Guzman pretended not to notice.

Milo said, "Good morning, Firefighter Guzman. What does 'C' stand for?"

"Christopher."

"So, Christopher. You're the one who first suspected something out of the ordinary."

"Yes, sir."

"So how come your partner over there is clueless? Downright surprised to see me."

"Paramedic Barker and I haven't conferred yet, sir."

"Because . . ."

Guzman flushed.

Milo said, "You're all business, he's monkey business, huh? He seems real eager to get out of here. Any particular reason for that?"

"Sir, Paramedic Barker's probably a little hungry because we've been on since five, it's coming up on our lunch hour. If we don't get another call."

"Hungry? Yeah, that's not a fun feeling. All right, let's see if we can get you out of here in time for a burrito or something." Out came a pen. "What exactly tipped you off this might not be a natural death, Christopher?"

"Like I told the doctor, the first thing was ocular petechial hemorrhaging, sir. That got me looking for other signs of asphyxia and I found suspicious facial bruising around the nose and under the chin. Dr. Delaware agrees it's suspicious."

"Clamping the airways shut."

"That's what it seemed to me, sir. Want me to show you?"

"I'll see for myself. Who's the victim?"

"Name's Theda Mars, sir. Hundred-year-old white female."

Milo stared at him.

I said, "Thalia Mars."

"Oops," said Guzman. "Sorry, yeah, Thalia."

Milo's bright-green eyes shifted to me. "A hundred?"

I said, "She would've been, in three weeks."

"And she was **your** patient?"

Guzman studied my response. Back in Mr. Curious mode.

I said, "I saw her once, yesterday. Got here for a second appointment just before ten A.M. and found Paramedic Guzman with the body."

Guzman frowned. I hadn't answered the question. But Milo said, "Ah," as if that explained it. "That maid over there said she discovered the body. Either of you pick up anything iffy about her?"

I shook my head.

Guzman said, "Me neither, but I guess anything's possible."

"Want to make a guess as to time of death, Christopher?"

"That's not my expertise, sir—"

"That's why I said 'guess.'"

"Well, sir, rigor's set in and the room's not particularly cold."

"So probably three to eight hours," said Milo. "Makes sense, if I was up to nasty, I'd do it in the dark. I didn't notice any cameras on the path. You see any security in the bungalow, itself?"

"No, sir. But I wasn't looking."

"Maybe I'll get lucky and the hotel conceals them." The notepad tapped his thigh. "All right, Christopher, if there's nothing else you want to tell me, I'll take it from here, go get some nutrition."

"Thank you, sir." Guzman lifted the case and the defibrillator and headed toward Barker. Barker greeted his arrival with a rapidly moving mouth. Rudimentary lip reading clarified the greeting: "**What the fuck?**"

Guzman kept going. Barker took a final look at Refugia and followed his partner out of eyeshot.

Refugia started to leave. Milo curled a finger and she hurried over.

When she got to us, he slumped a bit. Making himself smaller, the way he does when he's trying not to intimidate. From the look in the young maid's eyes, not successful.

He said, "Thanks for sticking around, Ms. Ramos." As if she had a choice.

She managed a sad-looking smile. Dark eyes had misted.

Milo said, "It had to be tough walking in and seeing that."

"Oh, God, **so** terrible, sir. She was a beautiful person. Here, I mean." Tapping her left breast.

"You knew her well."

"Oh, yes. I've done her cleaning and her room service since I started working here."

"How long is that?"

"Three years, a little more," said Refugia.

"She's been here that long?"

"Longer. She lives here, sir."

Milo looked at me.

I said, "Her description was 'forever.'"

Refugia Ramos said, "I got her by accident—they sent me here with her breakfast and she liked me so she asked for me the next day. They didn't do it right away but she kept asking and the schedule worked out so they put me on permanent breakfast and high-tea delivery to The Numbers."

"The Numbers?"

I said, "The bungalows."

"Uno," said Milo. "But it's not Los Numeros?"

"No, sir, we're instructed during orientation that it's The Numbers. 'Continental breakfast at Cuatro.' 'Cocktails at Ocho.'"

"So she's been here forever."

"Everyone says that, not just her. She used to say, 'I'm a fixture, Refugia. Like one of the faucets.' Then she'd laugh. She liked to laugh."

"Happy person."

"Oh, yes."

"Is longtime residency pretty common for the hotel?"

"No, sir, she's the only one."

He turned and peered up the pathway. "No other longtimers in The Numbers or anywhere else?"

"The Numbers don't get used much," said Refugia. "They don't have air-conditioning and they're far away from the parking lot. No WiFi, everybody wants WiFi."

"Ms. Mars didn't care."

"She liked to read and watch regular TV."

"The rest of the hotel has WiFi?"

"Not in all of El Ori-hi-nal—the older wing— just some. Mostly people stay in The Can."

Milo smiled. "That sounds like an outbreak of intestinal flu."

"Pardon—oh, no, no, sir, The Can's the new wing. The big tower, looks like a can? The hotel doesn't call it that but the staff does because of the shape."

"Bungalows, Spanish, The Can. Interesting place," said Milo.

"El Ori-hi-nal's what's left of the old hotel, most of it fell down in an earthquake a long time ago. I guess they kept it because . . ." She frowned. "I don't know why."

Milo said, "With The Numbers not being popular, Ms. Mars would have had plenty of privacy. Was she happy being by herself back here?"

"Very happy, sir. It's her home."

"How much did that cost her?"

"I don't know, sir."

"Who's the hotel manager?"

"Mr. DeGraw," she said. "Should I get him?"

"In a minute. What time do you come on shift?"

"Seven A.M."

"And you go off . . . ?"

"If I'm working a single, at three. If it's a double, I stay till eleven."

"You do a lot of doubles?"

"Maybe five, six a month."

"Pretty full schedule."

"I like to work. I came to **America** to work."

"From?"

"Manila."

"Any family here in L.A.?"

"Oh, yes, my sister and her husband. They're registered nurses. I live with them."

"Where, Ms. Ramos?"

"North Hollywood." As Milo took down the address, Refugia's mouth screwed up. "Where I live is important, sir?"

"Probably not, but just a few more questions. How long have you been in the U.S.?"

Refugia blinked. "Four years. First I worked as a health aide at a retirement home, then I got this. I like this better."

"More enjoyable."

"Working with healthy people is better, sir. That's why when I got assigned to Miss Thalia, her being so old, I wasn't so . . . but she was great. Not like the people in the home."

"In good shape."

"She had a little trouble moving around but her brain was young, she was smart and funny."

"Almost a hundred," said Milo. "Pretty impressive."

Refugia sniffed and dabbed her eyes. "May I ask a question, sir?"

"Sure."

"Are you here because you think someone did something to her?"

"Don't know, yet."

"Rob—Mr. Barker told me his partner's got a crazy imagination, sees bad stuff everywhere."

"Could be," said Milo. "So all the other Numbers are currently unoccupied?"

"No, there's a couple staying in Cinco, from Europe somewhere—the Birken-somethings—Birkenherr, Birkenharr, something like that. This morning I brought them coffee then they called for a paper but they must've gone back to sleep because they didn't answer. So I rang the bell and left it in front of the door."

"Cinco," said Milo. "No one else."

"There was a family in Dos. Tourists from Korea, but they moved out two days ago. Seven people. They used the couches for sleeping and they put sleeping bags on the floor. They complained about the A.C. not working and I told them there wasn't any and they started talking in Korean. Next day I had to clean the whole place."

"They left instead of transferring to The Can?"

"I don't know, sir, I only work the ground floor of The Can, if they were on a higher floor, I'd have no idea." Tears formed in her eyes. "She looked so peaceful but then I couldn't wake her."

Milo said, "Sorry you had to go through that. Did Miss Mars leave her front door unlocked?"

"Just the porch door."

"But not the main door."

"No, sir."

"Did you find it locked?"

Wide eyes. "No, sir, it was open."

"That didn't bother you?"

"I figured she opened it, like she usually did."

"Okay," said Milo. "Anything else you want to tell me?"

"**No,** sir." Tight voice.

"Then now would be a good time to get Mr. DeGraw."

"His extension is—"

"Would you mind going over and telling him in person?"

"Okay. Sure." She took a few steps, stopped and pivoted. "If someone **did** hurt her, it's not **fair.**"

She hurried out of view.

I said, "Those background questions. You're wondering about her?"

"She found the body and she's been on duty for four hours, which could be within the time frame. Sometimes the ones who get emotionally involved get **involved,** right? She bother you?"

"Not at all. When I got here she was pretty broken up."

"She didn't seem broken up when she was flirting with Barker."

"Good point."

"Am I saying she's a sociopath with shallow

emotions, Alex? Like you always tell me, insufficient data. But yeah, I'll check her out for a criminal history."

He scanned the surrounding greenery, then the high wall behind the bungalow. "The Numbers. Sounds like a racket—so what were you doing treating a hundred-year-old?"

I told him.

He said, "Impressed by the stuff we do? Not just a bored shut-in wanting to make small talk with a suave shrink?"

"That might've been a reasonable assumption, yesterday," I said. "Can we go inside?"

He laughed. "This is a switch."

"What is?"

"You getting to a scene first."

CHAPTER

5

I waited by the bedroom door as he gloved up and entered. He scanned the space, inspected Thalia's eyes, then the bruises around her nose and chin.

"Yeah, this is wrong. Gold star for ol' Chris. Though any C.I. would've spotted it—Jesus, she's a **twig.**"

Lumps the size of cherries formed along his jaw. "Anything out of place from yesterday?"

"I wasn't in here yesterday. Talked to her on the porch and in the living room."

"Ramos said she had trouble moving around. I don't see any cane or walker."

"She managed," I said. "Halting but mobile. Lost her balance a few times and I helped her."

"A hundred years old in three goddamn

weeks," he said. "And some asshole decides to ruin her birthday."

"Guzman wondered about assisted suicide."

He looked at me. "Do you?"

"Not from what I saw. She was in good spirits."

"But now you're wondering because . . ."

"Just being thorough."

He gave the room a second scan. "Neat and clean, everything in place. Makes it creepier . . . maybe she did pay someone to off her painlessly. Let's see what comes up after the C.I. clears the body and the techies toss the room. Meanwhile, let's get some fresh air and you can give me the details of your one and only session with my victim."

Out in front of the porch, Milo assaulted fresh air with a cheap panatela. He does that when bodies reek, but no serious odor had polluted Thalia's bedroom other than the slight sourness backing up French perfume.

I told him everything I could remember, wondered out loud if Thalia had a specific psychopath in mind.

He dropped the cigar to the dirt, ground it out. "Her not being ready to spill everything at once could mean someone she cared about. Like a relative. But if we are right about it happening in the middle of the night or early morning, you see her opening the door for anyone? Particularly if she couldn't move well."

I said, "Someone with a key?"

"Ergo my interest in Ms. Refugia and everyone else who works here."

"Or someone Thalia gave a key to because there was a closer relationship."

He said, "As in potential heir with an obvious motive."

"Maybe **that's** why she called me. At her age, the issue of inheritance wasn't theoretical. She was concerned about leaving assets to a lowlife."

"Maybe serious assets, Alex. We're talking someone able to live full-time in a fancy hotel. First thing I'm going to look for is a will."

We stood in silence for a while.

I said, "Any time my name appears in the paper, you get ink. If she was worried about criminal kin, I could've been just her stalking horse and her real goal was making contact with you."

"Why not contact me directly?"

"A centenarian phones and tells you she's worried about a nasty psychopathic heir? What would you have done?"

"Suggested she hire security . . . Okay, if there is some reprobate behind this, it gives me somewhere to look . . . at her age, a son or a daughter would be in their seventies, late sixties at the youngest. Why wait that long and then snuff Mommy?"

"Circumstances change," I said. "Seventy-year-old son marries a younger woman, she wants bangles. But sure, we could be looking for a middle-aged grandkid."

"Hell, Alex, we could be talking about an evil **great**-grandbaby. Go all the way: great-**great**." He frowned. "Or just a sweet little maid who's been cleaning up after her for four years and knows where the goodies are stashed."

His eyes swung past me. "Here's our manager, why do they wear that stupid color, reminds me of old blood."

A man in a liver-red blazer and gray slacks walked our way, hands laced in front of him, as if stretching sore wrists. Middle height, thin and pigeon-toed with a limp, sandy hair and a goatee, he had the round-shouldered posture of someone laden with too much responsibility.

That made me think about Thalia, hunched by a century of responsibility. What had her good cheer concealed?

The sandy-haired man reached us. "Officers? Kurt DeGraw." Slight accent, hard-edged, Teutonic. The beard was neatly trimmed, shaped to a point.

Milo handed him a card, introduced me as "Alex Delaware," with no explanation.

DeGraw didn't crave one. Corporate-savvy, he kept his attention on the boss.

"Lieutenant, may I assume Miss Mars is deceased?"

"You may."

"The maid who came to get me told me something bad happened, the police had been called, but when I asked her for details, she ran out, crying." DeGraw looked at the bungalow. "Sad but not surprising. Are you aware she was a hundred years old?"

"In three weeks," said Milo.

"We'd have baked her a cake," said Kurt De-Graw. "As we always do. Now, if you could tell me when we'll be able to clean the unit—"

"Not for a while, Mr. DeGraw."

"Oh? Is there a problem?"

"There's reason to believe Miss Mars's death wasn't natural."

DeGraw stared. Plucked at his necktie, stamped a foot. "Unnatural in terms of . . ."

"Possible homicide."

"You can't be serious."

"Nothing but serious, sir."

"She was a **hundred** years old, Lieutenant. Why would anyone bo— Why would they do that?"

Why would anyone bother?

Milo said, "Why, indeed?"

"For what reason do you believe it wasn't natural?"

"Can't discuss that, sir, and I imagine you don't want rumors to circulate."

"No, no, of course not." DeGraw glanced at the bungalow again. "All right, do what you need to, but if you could give me a fairly accurate estimate as to when we'll be able to begin—"

"How long did Miss Mars live here?"

"A long time, Lieutenant."

"Could you be more specific?"

"Well," said DeGraw, "I've been here two years and she was well established by then. My predecessor told me about her. The unique situation."

"Permanent residency."

"Exactly, Lieutenant. We don't normally allow it."

"Why'd you do it for Miss Mars?"

"She had a contract."

"Stating?"

"I'm not familiar with the details," said DeGraw.

"You don't keep records?"

"With regard to current data we keep excellent computerized records, but there have been informational changes."

"Meaning?"

"Updated systems. Information gets deleted."

"No old ledgers in a storage room?" said Milo.

DeGraw's expression said Milo had suggested he pierce his own scrotum. "Dust, mold, insects? I can't imagine we'd want **anything** like that."

Milo flipped a notepad page. "Who owns the hotel?"

"The Aventura is in transition."

"From what to what?"

DeGraw sighed. "I'm not at liberty to discuss but a sale is currently being considered."

"Who's selling?"

"The parent company is Altima Hospitality."

"Where's corporate headquarters?"

"Dubai."

"Who owned it before Altima?"

"Another corporation," said DeGraw.

"Which one?"

"Franco-Swiss Château Limited."

"And before that?"

"I couldn't tell you."

"How much did Miss Mars pay to live here?"

"She got a bargain," said Kurt DeGraw. "Whoever agreed to it originally must've been—" DeGraw shook his head. "She was flat-rated with cost-of-living increases but she still got a bargain. One hundred ninety-six dollars and some change per day. With tax added, she paid a little over seven thousand dollars a month and that includes full board and maid service."

"Eighty-four thousand a year, give or take."

"A **bargain**," said DeGraw. "Full board **plus** afternoon tea if she wanted it? And she always did. The current per diem on a deluxe bungalow is four hundred and eighty dollars."

"No air-conditioning is deluxe."

"Lieutenant. Many guests, particularly our sophisticated Continental travelers, prefer fresh air, and Miss Mars never complained."

"You have no idea who she signed the original agreement with?"

"It was decades ago."

"Have you tried to get her to move?"

DeGraw looked away. "There was an initial suggestion when we took over that she might be more comfortable somewhere else. With compensation for moving tossed into the package."

"She turned you down."

Nod.

"The deal was iron-clad," said Milo.

DeGraw looked as if he'd swallowed a glass of warm spit. "Apparently."

"When was the hotel built?"

"The Aventura was erected in 1934."

"El Ori-hi-nal," said Milo.

DeGraw blinked. "What's left of it. We'd love to tear it down but preservationists . . . our priority is The Tower."

"How many guests can you accommodate in total?"

"The Tower handles a hundred forty-five, the old wing, around forty."

"Plus The Numbers."

"Occupancy in The Numbers is at a far lower rate than the rest of the hotel. In fact, it's not uncommon for it to be zero."

"Except for Miss Mars."

"Her situation was unique."

"People opt for A.C."

"People opt for everything electronic. WiFi, Bluetooth," said DeGraw. "Today's traveler demands instant connection."

That sounded like an ad line. I said, "Speaking of technology, where are your surveillance cameras?"

"We have no cameras."

Milo said, "Really."

"You are surprised," said DeGraw, with the glee of a magician unfurling his trick. "Franco-Swiss had begun installing a system. When we took over, an executive decision was made to de-install."

"Why?"

"We choose not to rely on the false sense of security provided by electronic surveillance. Instead, we employ a top-notch security team."

"Guards patrol."

"Security personnel are aware."

"How often do the bungalows get patrolled?"

DeGraw's fingers fluttered. "When there's a reason for coverage, it occurs."

"No formal schedule."

"Lieutenant. We pride ourselves on the human touch. Decisions based on actual need, not mechanics. We've never had a problem."

Milo cocked a finger at Uno. "Time to amend that claim."

DeGraw blew out a long gust of air. Mint fought a losing battle with garlic. "Our mission is based on discretion and privacy. An inviting home away from home where a traveler can stay without fear of being harassed."

"Harassed by who?"

"Unwanted observers."

"Paparazzi?"

"This is L.A., Lieutenant."

"Cameras wouldn't help with that?"

Theatrical sigh. DeGraw licked his lips. "If I tell you something in confidence, will it remain that way?"

"If it doesn't relate to Miss Mars."

"Can't see that it does, so please be discreet." DeGraw's eyelids shuttered and opened repeatedly, an out-of-control camera. He leaned in closer. "One of our specialties is surgical aftercare."

"Get a little tuck 'n' roll then get tucked in."

"We've developed a specialty, Lieutenant, have accommodated numerous highly important individuals during their time of physical need. Physicians are here frequently, nurses as well, but no one wears a uniform nor is medical equipment carried openly."

"How's it transported?"

"In luggage."

"Covert clinic," said Milo.

"You can see why cameras would be unwelcome, Lieutenant."

I said, "You've got no gate or guard booth. It's pretty easy to enter the property."

"Superficially it is," said DeGraw. "That's part of the illusion."

"Meaning?" said Milo.

"As your assistant just said, **apparent** ease."

I hadn't.

Milo said, "Explain."

Another sigh. "The tighter you close something up superficially, the more inviting it becomes to **those** people."

"Security staff peek behind the trees."

DeGraw inched closer. "I'll give you an example and hopefully you will understand. An obvious sentry, a guard booth, both would scream vulnerability. Instead, there's always a triad of staffers at the front desk, one of whom is a highly trained security **specialist**."

I thought back to the ponytails. No clue as to which one was the eyes-and-ears.

"Subtle," said Milo.

"Exactly, Lieutenant. Even a room maid could be one of our security staff."

"Is Refugia Ramos one of your security staff?"

"Normally, I wouldn't be at liberty to tell you," said DeGraw. "But given the circumstances, no, she isn't. What I'm trying to get across is that our guests deserve harassment-free healing and we see that they get it. For surveillance cameras to be effective they'd need to be computerized and computers can be hacked."

"No nose jobs uploaded to Gawker."

DeGraw let out a garlic-mint gust. "I'm glad you understand."

"What about WiFi opening up electronic doors?"

"We set our system up so that each traveler has his or her individual link to cyberspace. Once they're logged in, several firewalls go up. We have no way of learning our guests' connection patterns, nor do we wish to."

"But you do know when they order room service."

"That's an entirely different thing. Extremely limited."

"How many of your guests are post-surgical?"

"I'm not at liberty to say."

"Do they ever stay in The Numbers?"

"Never," said DeGraw, "always in The Tower.

Security covers every floor regularly. And please, Lieutenant, no implication that whatever happened to Miss Mars—**if** something did—can be linked to us. She was happy here, had every opportunity to leave if she changed her mind."

"Got it, Mr. DeGraw. You're sure there are no old ledgers, anywhere?"

"I'm afraid not." Kurt DeGraw smiled crookedly. "Though obviously, we've held on to an old lodger."

Milo and I stared at him.

"Well," he said, "that may have come across wrong—but don't you **people** do the same thing? Try to lighten up a sad situation? Now please tell me what's going to happen."

What happened was the arrival of the death army.

Six cops in three patrol cars were charged with maintaining the scene.

A coroner's investigator named Gideon Gulden agreed the bruises pointed toward a suspicious death and got to work.

Enjoying the fresh air, a pair of burly crypt drivers killed time with their phones and waited to transport.

The lab squad was on its way.

Milo and I walked back toward the hotel, checking each bungalow, getting no response.

Yellow tape had been strung up at the mouth of the pathway. A fleet of official vehicles was parked where the fire van had sat, blocking the exit from the Spanish wing's loggia.

Curious absence of onlookers, just Kurt De-Graw on his phone and the ponytailed woman I'd seen yesterday at the desk. This morning, she had appraising eyes and a harder expression.

I pointed her out to Milo and she walked away.

He said, "The expert, I'll check her out later."

"Kind of quiet, considering."

"Weird-quiet. Guess they **are** good with the prying-eyes set."

"Or maybe everyone in The Tower is sedated while recuperating."

"Clinic masquerading as hotel," he said. "Terrific business model, when you think about it. Liquid diets at an inflated rate, no wild parties. Still, you'd think some gossip-monger would catch on."

"Despite what DeGraw claims, getting in **was** easy. Maybe because The Numbers and Thalia are considered nuisances. She refused to leave so they gave her the minimum."

"She give you any indication she was unhappy with the accommodations?"

"No," I admitted. "Just the opposite, she seemed at ease."

"Except maybe when she thought about a reprobate heir. Which leads me to another question: If getting hold of her dough was the goal, why wait so long? Circumstances change, but still."

I had no answer for that.

Milo said, "Eighty-four grand a year. A bargain to DeGraw but it's still serious dough. How did a public-sector numbers cruncher have the means to pay it year after year? Plus those Tiffany lamps, her jewelry, whatever else she had stashed in the room."

My phone buzzed in my pocket. Answering service text passing along a message from an especially meticulous family lawyer. Mr. Bunyan wanted to confirm my evaluation in fifteen minutes. Two kids, five and seven, tied up in a custody battle. Both had lived in France for most of their lives until their mother decided to move them away from their father. Very little English. A translator would accompany them.

If I left now, I'd make it in time. "Gotta go, Big Guy."

Milo said, "Things to see, people to do? Have fun, something turns up, I'll let you know."

CHAPTER

6

As I neared my house, my service called. Mr. Bunyan letting me know today's consult was canceled, the parents had reconciled.

I'd be paid for a day's work.

My karma was shaping up strangely; at this rate, I should go looking for a subsidized crop not to grow.

I got home, drank coffee, walked to the studio and told Robin about Thalia.

She gasped. As a child, she cried a lot, does her best to avoid it now. But now the tears flowed and she tried to distract herself by brushing sawdust from her bench.

She put her whisk away. "That was stupid, I never met the woman. Milo's sure it was murder?"

"That's what it looks like."

She shuddered, took hold of my arm, rested her head on my shoulder. "No life's worth more than another. But shouldn't there be extra credit for endurance?"

I returned to my office, opened a drawer, found Thalia's uncashed check.

Getting paid not to work doesn't sit right with me. I'd figure something out.

Meanwhile, time to learn about the Aventura.

The Web had plenty to say. Built in 1934 by a consortium of private investors who'd managed to make money during the Great Depression, the hotel had been conceived as a "Spanish Revival masterpiece that would rival the 23-year-old Beverly Hills Hotel, the relative upstart Beverly Wilshire, built in 1928, and the venerable Bel-Air occupying 60 acres two miles east of the former bean farm where the four-story, three-hundred-room structure was erected."

The finished product featured three swimming pools, one a "therapeutic lagoon" filled with salt water trucked in from Santa Monica, plus half a dozen tennis courts. Llamas, ostriches, and exotic parrots were caged in a private zoo. The Aventura Slim, a since-forgotten cocktail based on absinthe, was served up at the Agua Caliente Bar.

An old black-and-white photo depicted an imposing structure with "El Ori-hi-nal" little more than an appendage leading to "tropical gardens and secluded meditation spots."

Soon after the Aventura's construction, the business plan faltered, leading to dissolution of the consortium and sale to a "shadowy group of investors reputed to have ties to organized crime, including former bootlegger and mobster Leroy Hoke. Hoke was also rumored to have been a member of the original group who'd taken control by exerting pressure on his partners."

Under new management, the hotel acquired a reputation as a place where illicit lovers could expect to enjoy privacy, gamblers could operate one-night casinos, and rich girls could undergo illegal abortions.

The surgeries were reputed to have taken place in a series of bungalows tucked into the western edge of the property. Known as The Numbers, hidden from view by thick vegetation, and reached via a guarded footpath, the outbuildings served as a hotel within a hotel, ideal for clandestine activity.

Origin of the name inspired debate, with some chroniclers guessing a literal reference to the numerals on the doors of the clapboard structures and others claiming it reflected the operation of numbers and other rackets.

Everyone agreed that by the late thirties the Aventura was a favorite of the demimonde, and the absence of police raids suggested cozy connections to those in power.

On December 14, 1941, a week after the U.S. entered World War II, Leroy Hoke was convicted of racketeering and tax evasion and sent to San Quentin. The Aventura was shut down and loaned to the U.S. Army as officer housing, and after the war served as a short-term military psychiatric hospital specializing in "shell shock."

By 1948, ownership had shifted to a third syndicate, this one announcing intentions to demolish the structure and build low-cost housing for workers servicing the burgeoning upper class of Bel Air and Brentwood.

That plan ran headlong into protests by the intended utilizers of domestic service. Drawn-out legal battles were followed by complaints that the hotel's abandoned grounds had become a "haven for vagrants."

On August 9, 1950, William Parker became L.A.'s new police chief, ushering in an era of iron-fist law enforcement. One of Parker's first directives was to raid the now squalid Aventura acreage and "convince" the transients to vacate.

Parker might have played a part in the city's demand that the still-litigious owners clean up their mess within days or face criminal prosecution. A December 1950 sale transferred the property to a St. Louis hotelier named Conrad Grammar, who promised speedy rehabilitation and return to "the glory days of luxuriant hospitality."

Grammar kept his word but his profligate spending saddled the Aventura with crushing debt. Unable to shake its unsavory reputation, the hotel proved unable to compete with its high-end rivals and ended up offering package deals to road-tripping families.

The burgeoning upper class groused about a "trailer park totally at odds with the new face of Brentwood."

In 1957, Grammar got out of the hotel business, switching to the manufacture of recreational vehicles, and the Aventura began decades of revolving-door foreign ownership.

A British group tried to make a go. Then Italians, Franco-Italians, Franco-Swiss, Franco-British, all-Swiss.

On February 2, 1971, an Icelandic corporation announced plans for the world's largest "health-oriented spa," including forty prefab authentic Icelandic saunas scattered around the property for "thermal rejuvenation on impulse."

The neighbors began grumbling.

On February 9, 1971, the earth shrugged.

Tremors originating in the foothills of the San Gabriel Mountains blossomed into a 6.5-magnitude disaster. Most of the Sylmar Quake's damage was concentrated in the Valley, but older structures throughout the L.A. Basin suffered as well, including four dangerously sagging stories of Spanish Revival stucco resting on an unbolted foundation set atop soft earth that had once nourished beans. Strangely, several wooden cabins on the property survived intact.

By the time the aftershocks ceased, the Icelanders had cut bait and a Macao-based concern had taken the property at a poorly attended auction. A grand scheme to build the world's most luxurious six-star hotel was thwarted by the necessity of demolishing the main building running up against the demands of preservationists that "any structurally sound components of the historic locale be left in place."

The result was years of additional litigation, yet another forfeiture, and a rushed-through statehouse decision to use taxpayer money to fund demolition of all but "a stable western wing plus loggia plus supplementary outbuildings."

That took half a decade to accomplish, after which a young Dubai-based sheik with a penchant for totaling seven-figure supercars scored the site at an even lower price. He hired a "cutting edge" architect who designed a "postmodern tower merging with the psycho-structural suggestion of the original wing as an exemplar of stylistic incest."

Nothing since then.

How much of the parade had Thalia witnessed? Kurt DeGraw claimed she'd scored a bargain and maybe she had. But living through the changes only to end up smothered in bed seemed a steep price to pay.

Milo phoned at four twenty-three P.M.

"I'm here at the scene, just went over the bungalow. No evidence she kept a safe but I did find a little under three grand in cash in her underwear drawer, so it doesn't look like burglary. She wasn't sexually molested, either. I'm open to suggestions about motive."

I said, "Maybe someone enjoys beating God to the punch."

"A psycho with a thing for the elderly? Crossed my mind so I checked for similars over the past ten years. Nothing remotely like Thalia. Every elderly vic was either collateral damage in a drive-by or dispatched to the next world by a loving relative. A lot of the family cases were arguments that escalated, the rest were rotten kids trying to inherit early. The money crimes tended to be staged burglaries. This one's just the opposite, everything peaceful, no misdirection, not even a drawer pulled out. With those bruises, the murder would have been detected soon enough. Why not try to mask it as a burglary?"

"Maybe the bad guy was overconfident, felt he'd masked it as a natural death. Or showcasing the murder was the thrill."

"Like one of those trusted nurses, turning off respirators or shooting crap into I.V. lines? You know where that leads."

"Refugia or another staffer."

"Refugia," he said, "is judged honorable by everyone she ever worked with. More important, she's alibied for last night until six in the morning, when she left for work. Per her sister and brother-in-law, but there's nothing to say they're lying. I asked DeGraw how many other people had regular contact with Thalia and he said he had no idea. I suggested he do everything in his power to speed up the investigation because the media would love to do an ironic story about the murder of a helpless old woman. He thought I made an excellent point and promised to get back to me. Obviously, we need to know about a will, if she had one. I found a checkbook in her nightstand drawer with two business cards clipped to the cover. Lawyer and money manager, put calls in to both. Her balance is impressive, Alex. Over four hundred thousand."

"Five years of rent in reserve. What else did she spend on?"

"Not much for the past year except a check written to you, dated a coupla days ago."

The day before I'd met her. Confident woman. "Six-grand retainer."

"Why so much up front?"

"No good reason," I said, "that's why I haven't cashed it. I told her it was way too much and inappropriate. She claimed I was doing her a favor by keeping her bookkeeping simple. Then she joked that if she didn't live long enough I'd profit and if that bothered me I could donate the overage to charity."

"You're sure she was joking about not making it to the end?"

"It seemed that way but now I'm not sure."

"Well," he said, "don't see why you shouldn't get paid for your time. Especially now since we know how generous the department is."

"I'll think about it."

"Meaning mind my own business." He laughed. "What else . . . I had our locksmith install padlocks on the porch and the door and one of our carpenters is due any minute to nail the windows shut. DeGraw tried to talk me out of all that, promised to 'maintain vigilance.'"

"The way he looked out for Thalia."

"Exactly. I've got uniforms stationed for a day or two but my captain says that could end if he needs personnel. I've put in the order for Thalia's stuff to go into storage at the crime lab, director's doing me a favor but that's also time-limited so it'd be nice to find out if there are heirs."

I said, "I picked up a few factoids," and recapped the Aventura's history. "The earliest she moved in is probably '50 or '51, after the squatters were evicted and it became a hotel again. She'd have been in her thirties, rates had dropped, she took advantage of it. But even good deals come with escalator clauses so eventually it climbed to eighty-four thou a year."

"Deal or no deal," he said, "if she could come up with that kind of dough, why not invest in a nice full-service condo? Instead, she bunks down in her little slice of heaven even while the ground's shaking and everything around her is crumbling?"

I said, "Let's hear it for clapboard. She was clearly a woman with her own personal vision, manipulated me so skillfully that I didn't mind."

"Because she was old and adorable," he said.

"That plus people skills she was probably born with."

"Well," he said, "I'm glad she had her moments in the sun, watching them take her away was pathetic. One of the crypt guys made a crack about wishing they were all so light—hold on, someone trying to call in."

Seconds later: "Thalia's lawyer, all broken up and ready to see me. I'm gonna give the carpenter another fifteen and if he doesn't show, I'll head over. I'm assuming you'll want to join me."

"Name and address."

"Richeline Sylvester, calls herself Ricki. Olympic Boulevard west of Sepulveda."

The building was eight stories of suntan-colored glass, the three bottom levels, parking.

A smooth, silent elevator rocketed me to Richeline Sylvester's office on the seventh floor. Her name only on the door.

Milo sat in the waiting room checking his phone and drinking something dishwater-colored from a frosty glass. Minimal waiting room; white walls, charcoal carpet, no windows, a single blotchy blue flower print.

A bearded man in his twenties wearing a plaid shirt and a red tie sat at a clear plastic desk. He smiled as if he knew me and pointed to a pitcher resting on a tray. "Iced jasmine tea? Freshly brewed."

"No, thanks."

Milo said, "Try it, it's delicious."

The young man beamed. His phone beeped.

He picked up, listened, said, "Sure." To us: "Boss is ready for you, to the right, guys."

A right turn was the only possible route to twenty feet of hallway. Doors to the left were marked **Supplies, Restroom, Library.** The right wall conceded a couple of windows but the tinted glass blurred an already hazy eastern panorama.

Like viewing the world through murky pond water.

The last door was held open by a well-padded woman in her fifties with curly blond hair shaped into an unflattering bowl. She wore a rust-brown mock turtle over a knee-length tan skirt and flat white sandals. Turquoise in her ears and around her neck, no makeup, reading glasses on a chain.

She examined both of us, settled on Milo. "Lieutenant? Ricki Sylvester." He introduced me and she gave me a longer look. "You're also a detective?"

Someone curious enough to ask. Or maybe I just wasn't giving off a cop vibe.

Milo said, "Dr. Delaware is our consulting psychologist."

"There's something psych-y about what happened to Thalia?" She grimaced. "I'm not sure I want to hear about that."

"Nothing gruesome, Ms. Sylvester. With certain cases, we try to be extra thorough."

"What constitutes 'certain'?"

"No obvious motive. Can you think of one?"

"I wish I could." She motioned us inside. "I'm glad you're being thorough, Thalia deserves your best effort. Not that everyone doesn't. But she was . . ." Her voice caught. "No, I **can't** think of a motive. What kind of monster would destroy such an **amazing** person?"

The dimensions of her office made up for the skimpy prelude, an easy six hundred square feet with a wall-of-glass view of a city squirming with activity. A massive carved rosewood desk old enough to be worn at its gilded base spanned a healthy section of the space. A vintage red leather tufted couch looked as if it had come with the desk. A cheap-looking black tweed sofa with three matching chairs didn't. Same for the round, fake-wood conference table in a corner.

As if the room had been slapped together using valuable hand-me-downs and cheap close-outs.

Two other walls were blank. The one behind the desk sported the expected paper: bachelor's from Penn, law degree from the U., specialty certificate in trusts and estates. No photos of loved ones, nothing personal on the desk but a file folder thick as a dictionary, an empty drinking glass, and an identical pitcher of jasmine tea that hadn't been touched.

Ricki Sylvester said, "Either of you want some of this? Jared used to be a barista, I humor him."

She sat down behind the desk. "I still can't get over this. Do you have **any** idea who?"

Milo said, "Not yet, that's why we're here."

"I'll do anything to help." She patted the file. "This is a copy of everything I have on Thalia, it's yours to take."

"Appreciate it, Ms. Sylvester. How long did you handle Miss Mars's affairs?"

"For my entire professional life. My grandfather ran an estate and trusts practice and I began working for him right after I passed the bar. My initial contact with Thalia was small assignments—notarizing, drafting forms. When Grandpa died three years later, I inherited the practice. So thirty years ago, if you're asking when I actually began operating as her attorney. Most of the clients from back then are deceased but Thalia hung on. You do know how old she was."

"Nearly a hundred."

Ricki Sylvester shook her head. "The woman seemed immortal. She was never sick, I can't recall the last time she ran up a medical bill. I remember asking what her secret was. She laughed and said, 'Stay healthy.' One time I told her, 'Thalia, disease lost and you won.' She said, 'Lucky roll of the genetic dice.'"

"Speaking of which," said Milo, "what can you tell us about her family?"

"When I took over she hadn't gotten around to writing a will—Grandfather said he'd suggested it several times but she'd put it off. When I suggested it, she agreed. Maybe because she was already seventy. I inquired about heirs and she said there were none, she had no family at all. When I expressed surprise, she laughed and said, 'How do you know I was born? Maybe I sprouted like a mushroom.'"

Milo said, "What kinds of legal issues have you handled for her?"

"Not much, really. The will, making periodic changes to keep up with the law. She was a CPA so she handled her own taxes back when she was working. By the time I took over, she was retired and her taxes were minimal."

"Was she involved in any lawsuits?"

"You're wondering if someone bore a grudge against her? Absolutely not. She's never sued anyone or been subject to litigation."

"Going back to your grandfather," I said, "is there any particular reason a civil servant would need an estate lawyer?"

Ricki Sylvester's eyes rose and fell. She fooled

with her eyeglass chain. "It's a common misconception, Doctor, that only the extremely wealthy need estate counseling. Anyone with assets to speak of benefits from counsel."

"They must've turned into pretty big assets by now," said Milo. "How did a retired civil servant come up with eighty-plus thousand a year to live in the Aventura?"

The chain jangled as Ricki Sylvester gave a small start. Her eyes yo-yoed again. "I can understand your confusion but it all boils down to simple math. Read the file."

She nudged it closer. Milo took it.

"I'll definitely be reading it, Ricki, but if you don't mind summarizing?"

"All right, I'll keep it simple. When I took over from Grandpa, Thalia was already a woman of means, with a net worth just shy of four million dollars. By then, most of her money was in municipal bonds and she was earning over two hundred thousand per year, tax-free. She plowed the bulk of the interest back into munis, making her money work for her. As of this morning, per Joe Manucci, her broker at Morgan-Smith, she was worth a little over **eleven** million and earning close to half a million a year."

She smiled. "How did she accomplish that working in the public sector? If you're thinking dishonestly, guys, think again. Thalia Mars did it the old-fashioned way: rising through the ranks quickly so she earned a respectable salary, living responsibly, and making sound investments over a **really** long time. It's like building a quality art collection, people who bought Picassos when he was cheap. Start with good taste and get old."

Milo said, "What kind of investments?"

"Every penny she didn't need to live on went into quality stocks and real estate. As an example, she was able to cash in a whole bunch of IBM that had split a gajillion times. Joe Manucci can give you more details but from what I understand most of her equities were the bluest of the blue chips. The shift to munis began around fifty years ago. She sold all her properties, paid her capital gains taxes dutifully, and began a new phase of her life clipping coupons."

"What kind of properties did she own?"

"Mostly vacant lots and foreclosures. Her position at the assessor and other agencies gave her access to information. Back then, acreage in the Valley and Santa Monica could be had for a song. She held on until she got an offer she liked, then traded up—what we call 10–31'ing, so there was no tax burden or depreciation payment until she cashed out completely. She was no trust-fund tycoon, we're talking small steps. But it adds up if you live within your means and last nearly a century."

She put a fingertip to the pitcher, drew a ragged circle in the frost. "If I were still teaching trust law, I'd use her as an object lesson. It's not what you make, it's what you keep. That was Grandfather's philosophy and he passed it along to me."

She waved a hand. "I practice what I preach. Like this place. I could pay three times as much to be a couple of miles east in Beverly Hills, not to mention an exorbitant monthly for parking. I could lease an ostentatious suite in order to feed my ego, hire staff I don't need. Who needs the complication? That was Thalia's forte. She knew how to focus on what was important and she kept things simple."

Including writing a far-too-generous retainer check.

Milo said, "She seemed to be living pretty stylishly."

"I'm not saying she was a skinflint. When she wanted something, she bought it. And she appreciated quality. But she never shopped for shopping's sake. She told me a few years ago, 'Live long enough and everything becomes vintage.' She also said, 'Live long enough and your interests narrow.'"

"What interested Thalia?"

She frowned. "I suppose doing what she felt like."

Milo said, "She had half a million a year coming in, spent a sixth on room and board. Where did the rest go?"

"Back into munis with some left over for charity. And charity's where her entire estate is bound, as you'll see when you read that."

I said, "Where she was born?"

"Somewhere in the Midwest—Missouri, I think."

"My home state."

Ricki Sylvester said, "You're a show-me guy? I guess that would be helpful for a psychologist. What exactly do you **do** for the police?"

Milo said, "He has an interesting brain and we like to tap it. So no idea at all about Thalia's roots?"

"Lieutenant, asking the same question repeatedly won't change the answer."

"Got it, ma'am. It's just that knowing the victim is a big part of closing a case and after all these years, I was wondering if something slipped out."

Ricki Sylvester drew a triangle on the pitcher. "Let me clarify my relationship with Thalia. I adored her and I believe she liked me. But we didn't interact much. With some clients, you need to adopt a more hands-on approach, get involved in their personal lives. Some even want you hovering. Not Thalia, she glided along just fine."

Her lips trembled. "Until now. Who would **do** such a thing? And what exactly happened? All you said over the phone was you suspected an unnatural death."

"Can't discuss details, yet. I can tell you there wasn't any significant pain involved."

"Significant? So there was some?"

"No reason to think there was any," he said.

"Well, that's a relief."

"How about her social life?"

"I wasn't aware that she had one," she said. "But as I said, our face-to-face contacts were infrequent. There wasn't much to do on her estate, period. She never mentioned friends or acquaintances. She used to travel but stopped. Had no interest in joining clubs or associations. She told me so in no uncertain terms when I suggested she might want to get out once in a while."

"When was that?"

"Years ago . . . around ten?"

"You were concerned about her."

"As I said, I rarely saw her but when I did I was taken by how much time she seemed to spend in her suite. Lying like a pixie queen in that giant bed of hers, going nowhere other than walking from her bungalow to the front desk and back. It wasn't always that way, she used to take luxury cruises all over the world. Then she just stopped. When she turned ninety—I guess it was exactly ten years ago."

"Any idea why she stopped?"

"She said she'd seen everything she wanted to see."

I said, "Did she cruise alone?"

"Always. Booked a cheap room, said it made no difference for sleeping."

"People can make friends when they travel."

"Are you asking if she met a silver fox at sea and recreated a bit? It's a nice thought." She coiled her eyeglass chain around a finger. "But as far as I know, no lasting relationships developed."

Milo said, "No man's an island but Thalia was."

Ricki Sylvester shook her head. "I get where you're going with these questions: Did someone she know end her life? I just don't see it. Yes, Thalia was basically a loner, but not in the sense of being timid or antisocial. Just the opposite, she was friendly, had a great sense of humor. She simply preferred her own company. So why not investigate other avenues, Lieutenant? What would stop some burglar or random **nut** from breaking into her bungalow? She did keep cash for tips and whatever and if you don't find it, there's your motive."

"Anything else that might've attracted a burglar?"

"There was some jewelry—diamond earrings, a ring set with a gigantic amethyst. It's a semi-precious stone but one of those junkie lowlifes would go for anything flashy, right?"

Her eyes rounded. "I just **thought** of something. A few years ago she ditched her old TV and bought a humongous flat-screen. She was quite proud of it. If **that's** gone—"

Milo said, "It's still there, Ricki, and so is the ring and her cash."

"Then I don't know what to tell you."

"Which charities get her money?"

"The primary recipient is that children's hospital, Western Pediatric. Helping kids was her priority, everything else goes to agencies who work with them."

Milo tapped the file. "You're her executor."

"I am indeed and have been paid well for such, as you'll see from my bills. From here on, I'm going to do it pro bono because the estate's so simple. No liens or debts, no squabbling claimants, no estate tax. So why shortchange sick kids? Now, if there's nothing more, I do have some more complicated clients to tend to."

"Just a few more questions, if you don't mind."

Forced smile. "Sure."

"Why did Thalia choose to live in a hotel?"

"Good question, I haven't a clue. I asked her about it once. She said it was what she preferred."

I said, "With her experiences as real estate investor, why not buy a condo where she could build up some equity?"

"Maybe that was the point. She'd spent her entire life working and wanted to kick back and not worry about investing. If you're suggesting she put herself in danger by living there, that **really** upsets me. Because I admit, it concerned me, that bungalow of hers was so secluded and she was finding it harder and harder to get around. A couple of times I arrived after dark and I found it downright spooky—oh, no, do you suspect someone on the **staff**?"

Milo said, "We have no leads at all. Did anyone on the staff give you a bad feeling?"

"No, but I felt there wasn't much in the way of security—no alarms, no cameras, and there were times when I showed up and both doors were unlocked—the porch and the main one. Now, it's true Thalia had been expecting me, but still. I said something and she pooh-poohed it. With Thalia you didn't nag."

"Strong-willed."

"Titanium-willed. It seemed to be working for her. Now if—"

I said, "You didn't see her often but when you did it was face-to-face."

She flushed. "Precisely. Quality, not quantity.

I felt Thalia deserved it. She was such a doll, I never believed anything like this could happen."

"Despite the lack of security."

She blinked. "I should've insisted?"

"Sounds like it wouldn't have mattered."

"No, it wouldn't." Her shoulders rose and fell. Her eyelids fluttered. She sniffed, twisted her nose as if working to suppress a sneeze. Grabbed a tissue, covered her eyes and whatever face remained below.

When she looked up, a sick smile had taken over. "I believe we've touched all bases. I really must get back to work."

We breezed past Jared, drinking his own tea.

In the elevator, Milo said, "Eleven-million-dollar estate, per her. What if it was actually more and Thalia found out?"

"Embezzlement?"

"Or just egregious overbilling."

"Thalia doesn't sound like someone you could con."

"Again, per Sylvester. Thalia discovering she'd been conned fits that chat she had with you. Not a felonious relative, a lawyer she'd trusted for years. Yeah, it's cynical. Then again, I just saw an old lady being carted away."

The elevator door rattled open.

As we walked through the parking tier, Milo said, "Let's see what the money guy—Manucci—has to say." He scrolled to the broker's number. "Dead zone, no bars."

A few steps later, he tried again. "Here we go . . . voicemail. Guess bankers do keep bankers' hours."

I said, "Meanwhile you could check the bar association for complaints against Sylvester."

He ran the search right there, frowned. "Nope, clean. I'm heading back to the hotel, bug De-Graw about that employee list. I also want to talk to whoever passes for security."

I said, "Let's start with that front-desk woman."

He looked at me. "You never turn it off."

"Do you?"

"Occasionally when I sleep. Maybe."

"One more thing: The bungalows aren't high-occupancy, so anyone who did pass through would be conspicuous."

"Like Ricki making an unscheduled visit. Okay, let's ask Ponytail."

"Refugia said the only other guests were in Cinco. Europeans with a long name, Birken-something. They might also be able to tell us something."

"Us. The old team spirit."

I said, "Rah rah."

CHAPTER

8

He followed me home, where I dropped off the Seville, and we continued to the hotel in his unmarked.

The lobby was empty. The same trio worked the front desk.

The woman saw us coming and knew why. Before we'd crossed half the lobby, she retrieved a large black purse from beneath the granite counter and motioned us outside.

Once we got there, she continued to the parking lot, ended up in a rear corner shaded by palms in need of trim. Unclasping the purse, she pulled out a pack of Marlboros and a clear plastic lighter half filled with fluid. When we shook our heads at her offer of cigarettes, she lit up, took a deep drag, and untied her hair.

A dense brown sheet flopped onto her shoulders. Handsome woman, with knife-edge features, a freckled nose, and narrow dark eyes. In daylight her skin looked more weathered and I recalculated her age as late thirties.

She smoked hard enough to create a sizable ash, flicked it onto the ground. "What can I do for you?"

Milo said, "You're security."

She smiled. "I blew my cover, huh? Or did DeGraw tell you?"

I said, "When it became a crime scene, you were observing."

"Ah. Okay: name, rank, et cetera. Alicia Bogomil, **alleged** security consultant here." She spelled it. Milo wrote it down.

She said, "I used to have one of those—the little pad. Spent seven years with Albuquerque PD, four on patrol then special assignments to vice and gang violence. I thought of going for detective but ended up following my boyfriend out here. He does location scouting for TV, the show he was working in New Mexico dried up, he had no alternatives so we moved."

"Nothing like loyalty," said Milo.

"And sometimes he even appreciates it. Anyway, a homicide here is the last thing I expected."

"When did you find out it was a homicide?"

"When you got here and stuck around. Then you talked to DeGraw and he told me. He's pretty freaked out."

"Generally, it's a safe place?"

"To the point of being boring," said Alicia Bogomil. "My job is ridiculous, basically standing around. Yeah, there's towels and hangers getting ripped off, once in a while someone puts a hole in a wall with a doorknob, but how much trouble can softballs get into?"

"Softballs?"

Bogomil's smile was crooked and knowing. "Lumpy things, all stitched up?"

I said, "Plastic surgery patients."

"Exactly, softballs. That's what we do here, it's ninety percent of the occupancy. DeGraw said he told you about it."

"He didn't give a number."

"Well, that's the number, ninety," she said. "This place isn't really a hotel, it's an aftercare facility for vain rich people. Not that I'm dissing anyone who wants to improve themselves, it's your money, your pain threshold. What I'm getting at is we're supposed to turn a blind eye to anything short of a serious felony. Like a patient freaking out and destroying property because they're on too much dope. Until now we never had a serious felony."

She smoked some more. "Is it definitely a homicide?"

Milo nodded.

"Too bad it was Thalia, she was a really nice lady." To me: "When I told you that the first time you showed up, I meant it. My only contact with her was when she'd take a walk, see me and talk. She was fun, great sense of humor. You could tell she had class."

"How often did that happen?"

"When I first started, little over a year ago, it was once, sometimes twice a day. She had an exercise routine, stroll in the morning, then in the afternoon. But recently—few months ago— it started tapering off. Probably because she was getting weaker and her balance was off. Occasionally, I'd see her stop and hold on to something. Guess she could've used a cane but didn't want one. One of those proud ones."

She looked at her cigarette. "My best guess is she became a total shut-in like a month ago."

I said, "Great sense of humor."

"The best." She flicked a liver-colored lapel. "Like this stupid thing. The color sucks, Thalia called it bilious. Said the word came from 'bile' and according to the Greeks or someone, bile was a nasty body fluid, the original bad humor. She said if they kept making us wear it, we'd become incurably cranky."

More tar entered her lungs. She took a deeper drag.

Milo said, "Ten percent of the guests aren't softballs."

"Once in a while you get some sucker who found the place online and is expecting luxury for a bargain price."

"Rates are low," I said.

"And getting lower. The rooms in The Can are boring, basically boxes with a round wall. Give me a choice, I want corners."

"The softballs are medicated so they don't notice."

"They arrive totally out of it," said Alicia Bogomil. "Mostly at two, three A.M. No check-in, it's all prearranged."

Milo said, "Who brings them?"

"Sometimes it's an ambulance but never with a siren, sometimes it's a limo or a private car. There's always a nurse dressed like a civilian but they rarely stay more than the first night. You can always tell when they're getting better and ready to leave because the attitude kicks in."

Milo looked at me. "Therapeutic obnoxiousness, there's a diagnosis for you."

Bogomil grinned again. Fine lines formed at her eyes and mouth. "Hey, maybe I can be a doctor." To me: "What kind are you? Never saw Miss Mars sick."

"Psychologist."

"Really? She was the last person I'd peg with an emotional problem."

Milo said, "It was a consultation."

"Okay," said Bogomil. "So why's he with you now, Lieutenant?"

"Long story. What else can you tell us about Thalia?"

"Just that we all liked her. And I never called her Thalia, always Miss Mars—same way I'd treat any old person, I was raised right."

"She ever have problems with the staff?"

Narrow eyes became slits. "Never." She studied Milo but knew better than to probe.

I said, "We've heard there's very little security back in The Numbers."

"There's **no** security back in The Numbers. DeGraw made it clear, we don't go there, not worth spending time or money on. Maybe that's why he's so freaked out. My guess is he'll close The Numbers down, now. The softballs can't use them because they need temperature control and wireless links to their doctors in case of an emergency."

Milo said, "DeGraw considers The Numbers a nuisance."

"Exactly," said Bogomil. "He's a world-class prick. Made a crack once about wouldn't another earthquake be nice, everything except The Can would fall down."

"Did he resent Thalia?"

"You think he could've done something? Really?"

"Not likely?"

"He's a prick but I never picked up any big-time anger. And he wasn't losing money on her, she paid her way. And it's not like people are beating down the doors, you ask me, the whole hotel will eventually close down."

"Why do you say that, Alicia?"

"Because the Arabs who own it always look super-unhappy when they show up. DeGraw gets calls from Dubai, he looks like he just swallowed vomit."

"How often do they visit?"

"Twice since I've been here, second time was like . . . four months ago. Some prince or emir, whatever, with an entourage. A kid, looked like he didn't shave, drove up in an orange Lamborghini followed by a bunch of limos, walked past us, had some face-time with DeGraw. Afterward DeGraw was like he just dropped the soap in the prison shower. He waited like an hour and went home. Called in sick the next day."

"Job insecurity and mistreatment," said Milo. "That could make someone resentful."

"He's always resentful, probably born that way," said Bogomil. "Do I think he'd off Miss Mars? Honestly, I don't see it. He's a wuss, not big on taking action, period. And what would be his motive? With or without her, the place is still going to struggle."

"What's your take on Refugia Ramos?"

"Quiet, goes about her business. She was Miss Mars's regular so I can see why you're asking. But sorry, nothing weird about her. I assume you ran all the checks."

"We did. Clean."

"Doesn't surprise me," said Alicia Bogomil. She ground out her cigarette. "I wish I had something juicy for you guys but this place is mega-boring, only thing you ever see is softballs and nurses coming and going, only thing you hear is moaning behind doors up in The Can. Not the kind of moaning you get at other hotels, I'm talking the pain meds ran out."

"Anyone on the staff twang your antenna?"

"My antenna." She smiled. "I like that, gonna use it from now on. Nope, no one stands out, people are just putting in their time. Was there a burglary?"

"Doesn't look that way."

"But maybe?"

Milo smiled.

"Got it. Anyway, with no burglary, I can't see

the point of anyone on the staff doing something. Not much of a staff left, the Arabs keep cutting costs. But no new hires and I think I know everyone pretty well and I never saw anyone pull a hissy."

Milo flipped a page. "What about Miss Mars's visitors? Anyone stand out?"

"Never saw a single visitor."

"She had a lawyer who came by, a woman named Ricki Sylvester."

"Don't know her," said Bogomil, "but that doesn't prove anything. I'm either at the front desk or patrolling The Can or having a room service meal, it all comes from the kitchen, now, no restaurants anymore. Tastes like hospital food, wish there were trucks coming by, nothing like a street taco. What does this lawyer look like?"

"Middle age, a little heavy, curly blond hair, maybe glasses around a chain and a briefcase."

"You know," said Bogomil, "I think I did see someone like that, like a week ago. Had no idea she was headed for Miss Mars. I was right here, taking a smoke break before going off-shift at seven, meaning four thirty in the afternoon, give or take. The lot was mostly empty, per usual, even the livery drivers are giving up. This crappy old Buick drives up, out comes a woman who fits that description. I figured her for a nurse or some rich person's gofer, delivering meds, we see that plenty. She's a lawyer, huh? Doing a house call? Guess that makes sense."

"How so, Alicia?"

"Personal service for a client with bank."

"Miss Mars had big bucks."

"That would be my bet. Living here full-time and the way she carried herself, the way she spoke. She reminded me of the rich old women I'd meet when I used to waitress at a country club when I was in high school in Cincinnati. Ladies who lunch, you know?"

"Anything else you can think of?"

"Nope."

Milo handed her his card.

"This reminds me of Albuquerque," she said. "The job sticks with you even after you leave it. If I ever want to try LAPD, maybe you could give me a recommendation—just kidding."

She pulled out a second cigarette. "Or maybe not."

Alicia Bogomil said, "I'm heading back to the desk." We stuck with her. A uniformed man waited outside the glass doors in a two-row golf cart.

Bogomil said, "Matt."

"Alicia."

The doors opened discharging two people.

The thirtyish hipster duo I'd seen in the lobby. Where bandages didn't cover the woman's face, her skin was inflated and glossy, the color alternating between eggplant and banana peel. She tottered and clutched the man's elbow. He looked triumphant.

No sign of the little girl. I wondered what she'd been told.

The woman struggled to get into the back of

the golf cart. The man sat up front and the vehicle putt-putted away.

Alicia Bogomil said, "Eye tuck and neck-lipo at her age? By the time she's fifty she'll have eyes on the side of her head like a goldfish."

Milo said, "The things we do for love."

"Love, huh? She's up there on painkillers, he's coming down to the lobby, telling me he's a hot-stuff record producer and suggesting we meet sometime."

I said, "Talent scout."

She laughed. "I can't carry a tune. Anything else you guys need?"

Milo said, "Where can we find DeGraw?"

She punched a four-digit code into her phone. Seconds later, it bleeped a digitalized "I Love Rock 'n' Roll" and she picked up. "Police are here for you."

She clicked off. "He said he'd be down when he's done. But no sense you guys wasting time. He's checking out a room on Floor Three."

The elevator stopped on Floor Two but no one got on and we got a brief view of beige walls, doors, and gray carpeting plus an earful of silence. The setup on Floor Three was identical.

One door, wide open. Before we got to it, Kurt DeGraw stepped out.

"I told Alicia I'd come down."

Milo said, "Thought we'd save you the trouble. How're we doing on that employee list?"

"Oh," said DeGraw. "Soon as I can, you have my word."

"We also need the names of anyone terminated during the last couple of years."

"Really? You're not thinking—oh, no, I can't see anyone taking out an employment issue on a defenseless old woman."

"Being thorough, Mr. DeGraw."

I'd sidled closer to the doorway. The room was the same bland hue as the corridor, probably the result of market research. A hospital bed was propped up forty-five degrees. Used bandages, mattress pads, and paper towels littered the floor, along with rubber tubing that looked like hormonally enhanced pasta. Much of the paper was splotched with blood and other body fluids. Human leakage worthy of a crime scene.

Nothing like that in the pristine room where Thalia had been murdered.

Kurt DeGraw saw me looking. "Another successful recuperation. This will be perfectly sterile within a couple of hours."

Years ago, I'd seen germ counts taken from "clean" hospital rooms. No such thing.

He got on a phone and told someone to have "three sixteen processed," then cocked his head toward the elevator.

Milo said, "We also need to speak to the family in Bungalow Cinco."

DeGraw said, "Pff. Good luck with that."

"What's the problem?"

"They're gone, Lieutenant."

"Since when?"

"As far as I can tell, yesterday."

"You're not sure?"

"People are free to come and go. What they're not entitled to is a free room." He pushed the elevator button. "An outrageous example of Penal Code Five Thirty-Seven."

"Defrauding an innkeeper," said Milo. "How'd they do it?"

"False passports and credit cards," said De-Graw. "This day and age, anyone can get anything. Our medical guests are prepaid and they are **sterling,** I keep telling **them** we should stop trying to attract anyone **else.**"

" 'Them' being the folks in Dubai."

DeGraw's tongue glided between his lips before tucking back in and swelling one cheek. "I wouldn't call them folks. They're nobility."

"What name did the defrauders give?"

"I don't remember—Birken-something."

"Where were the passports from?"

"Austria. No doubt to look **respectable.**"

"Austrian people are respectable."

"Isn't that the Teutonic image, Lieutenant?"

He smiled. Small teeth, big gums. "I'm from Switzerland, everyone in Switzerland believes they have inherited respectability. My father was a tax collector, he knew otherwise."

"How long did the Birken-whatevers stay here?"

"Are you saying you will help me recover the money? Excellent! How long were they here? Three nights."

The elevator arrived. DeGraw held the door open as we boarded.

Milo said, "Did they ask to be put in The Numbers?"

DeGraw's eyebrows arched unevenly, the right climbing higher than the left. "You can't seriously be thinking there's a connection. Really, Lieutenant, what a dreadful thought. An **illogical** thought. If someone was up to no good, why would they call attention to themselves by defrauding me?"

"If they gave you real I.D. and we wanted to talk to them, what would be happening now, Mr. DeGraw?"

"Ah, I see. But no, I **don't** see it. What connection could there be?"

"Maybe none," said Milo. "But I'll need copies of the passports and the credit cards."

"We don't make copies, we list numbers."

"Why's that?"

"Security of our guests."

"Why would copies get in the way of security?"

"It's our policy," said DeGraw. "The less information we have on our guests, the happier they are."

"I can see that working for patients but it's kind of sloppy, no?"

DeGraw drew himself up. "I'm sorry you don't approve of our protocol, Lieutenant. We have never had this problem before."

"When did you discover you'd been ripped off?"

"The maid went to clean this morning and saw the room had been vacated. Vacated rooms require a different protocol than daily freshening. The maid notified the front desk and they pulled the bill. There was no reason to worry at first, guests often leave without a formal checkout, we simply charge their cards. But when the front desk tried that, they learned the Amex on file was invalid. I was then notified and of course my next step was verifying the passport number with the Austrian consulate." DeGraw threw up his hands. "I should've followed my father's advice and become a civil servant."

"How many Birkens are we talking about?"

"Hmm," said DeGraw, "I believe three."

"Parents and child."

"Three adults. A woman and two men. One of the men was a personal assistant who slept on the living room foldout. His name we never got. The assumption was that his employers were footing the bill."

The elevator landed on the ground floor.

DeGraw said, "No more guests in The Numbers. As soon as you allow me, **her** unit will be put out of commission."

He exited, striding ahead of us.

Milo said, "Are any of the front-desk people who checked in the Birkens on-shift?"

DeGraw stopped and studied the two men behind the front desk. Neither was among the clerks I'd seen with Alicia Bogomil. On the left, black hair, brown skin, and a luxuriant ponytail, on the right, a colleague whose head was all skin. I imagined a corporate rule book. **In cases of insufficient follicular supply, employees may opt for total shaving of the cranial region.**

DeGraw said, "That's Malone, no, he wasn't here—Bretter . . . maybe."

He wagged a finger at the bald clerk. "The police have questions for you regarding the situation in Number Cinco."

The clerk said, "Okay," as if that was the last thing he meant.

Milo said, "Mr. DeGraw, thanks for your time, we'll take it from here."

"Good luck, Lieutenant. I have a cousin in Zurich, a police officer. Extremely unhappy man."

He walked away. The bald clerk stood there, tapping a foot.

Milo motioned him to a seating area in a corner of the lobby. Out came Milo's pad. The bald clerk's Adam's apple jutted.

"Full name please."

"Max Edward Bretter. Is he blaming it on me? I followed regulations."

"No one's blaming anyone."

"They make the rules," said Bretter. "We do what we're told."

"Rules like not holding on to passports."

"Stupid," said Bretter. "He's like, Privacy is what we sell."

"But you do copy down numbers."

"What's that going to do if they're scamming? Same with keeping the damn things, for that matter."

"What name did the scammers give?"

"Birkenhaar. Two a's."

"Was there any sort of bad vibe when they checked in?"

"If there was," said Bretter, "don't you think I'd call DeGraw?"

"I understand—"

"I barely remember, we're **also** instructed not

to make a lot of eye contact. Because of the softballs—" He faltered. "The patients. We're not
supposed to make them feel self-conscious."

"What do you remember about the Birkenhaars?"

Bretter rubbed his head. "They had the accent. Had an assistant to carry the bags. I was
ready to put them in The Can but they wanted
The Numbers."

"They requested The Numbers."

"They called them bungalows. I told them no
A.C., it was far from the lot, service could take
longer. They didn't care."

"Who did the talking, the man or the
woman?"

"Hmm," said Bretter. "Him I guess—yeah,
him, I didn't hear her at all. She just stood there
looking . . ." He colored. "Nice-looking woman."

He'd made enough eye contact for that judgment. Milo said, "Blond, brunette?"

"Brunette."

"What else?"

Bretter shrugged. "Good body."

"How old?"

"Hmm . . . I'm gonna say forty? I really wasn't
looking."

"How about him?"

"Didn't notice him, much," said Bretter. "Or
the pudgy one with the bags."

"Hair color?"

"No idea."

"What were they wearing?"

Bretter shook his head.

"The assistant was pudgy."

"Shorter, kind of heavy."

"Age?"

"No idea, maybe the same as them," said Bretter. "Don't hold me to any of this."

"Routine check-in."

"Totally. Name, passport, and card numbers for copying."

"What time of day?"

"Night. That I remember because it's dark, hard to find. I offered to have someone show them to the room."

"Who showed them to the room?"

"No one," said Bretter. "They said they'd find it their-self."

"Did they arrive in their own vehicle?"

"Couldn't tell you."

"No driver came to the desk with them."

"Nope. You think they hurt Miss Mars?"

"We're just starting out."

"Maybe they did," said Bretter. "Asking for The Numbers? Never happens. And then they scam? This tops it for me, soon as I find something, I'm outta here." He glanced in the direction of DeGraw's exit. "I'm sure they're going to sell it anyway, let all of us go."

"Why do you say that?"

"They keep shutting down services—no restaurants anymore. It's a feeling, you can just tell."

"Good luck," said Milo. "You told DeGraw they had German accents."

"German-ish," said Bretter. "One of my grandmothers came from Germany, what I said to DeGraw when he started questioning me is he sounded like that. But I'm no language doctor."

Milo scanned his pad. "He's got an accent, she's a looker, assistant's a chub."

"That about covers it," said Bretter. His mouth formed an O. "Sorry, I was wrong about something, I **did** hear the assistant. He said something to her, the woman. I didn't hear most of it but I did hear 'Frau.' So they have to be German, right?"

CHAPTER
10

M ilo and I walked through the old wing and into the loggia. At the end of the passageway, Alicia Bogomil smoked and harassed a potted palm with ash-flicks.

He asked her about the Birkenhaars.

She said, "No idea, never met them."

"You have a key to the bungalows?"

She dipped into a pocket. "Got a master. Something off about these people?"

"They requested The Numbers, presented false passports, and paid with a bogus credit card."

"That's pretty criminal," said Bogomil. "You think they could've been stalking Miss Mars? **Was** there a burglary?"

"So far we can't verify anything was taken.

The front-desk guy who checked them in didn't seem to know much about them, either."

"Who's that?"

"Max Bretter."

"Max," she said, "is an okay guy but a drooling green chimp could walk right by and he wouldn't notice. I'll find out who he was working with that day and let you know if it's an improvement."

"Thanks, Alicia. Could I borrow that key?"

"Sure."

"Where'll you be so I can return it?"

"Don't bother, keep it," she said. "There's a drawerful of masters in the security office. Which is basically a closet on the first floor of The Can."

"Really," said Milo. "Tight system."

"Worse than that, Loo, you probably won't even need a key, the bungalows have crappy old locks, a hairpin'll do the trick."

"Wonderful," said Milo.

"Yeah, we ain't Fort Knox, I told DeGraw he should beef up." She made angular motions with one hand, spoke like a robot: "Words. Hit. Wall. Bounce. Off. These suspects, they bring their own wheels?"

"Bretter didn't know."

"I'm asking because if they used one of the drivers who hangs around, there's a specific guy who might be able to help you. Leon Creech, he did MP work in the military back in the day, likes to think he's sharp-eyed."

"He's not?"

"Well you know," she said. "He's kind of old. He used to drive Miss Mars back when she wanted to be driven, so that could be a bonus."

"Any idea where he took her?"

"Never saw any shopping bags but she'd bring dessert back for the staff, so dinner. Sweet woman, whoever did this should be strung up by the you-know-whats."

I said, "Why'd she stop going out?"

"She didn't look depressed if that's what you mean," said Bogomil. "Maybe she just got tired, you know? Anyway, Leon liked Miss Mars so if he saw something hinky about your suspects he'll tell you."

"Where can we find him?"

"He used to be here regularly," she said. "Lately, he comes and goes because there isn't much business. But I did see him a couple days ago. That's why I'm thinking maybe he drove your suspects."

"Does he work for a company?"

"Uh-uh, independent, drives an old-school Town Car, got to be thirty years old but he keeps it up nice. I'll go see if I can find a number for him."

"Big help, Alicia. You want that recommendation, it's yours."

She grinned. "Who knows, maybe I'll take you up on it, Loo."

As we approached Cinco, Milo gloved up. No hairpin required, the door was unlocked.

"Hundred-year-old woman with doors that can be opened by a kid," he said. "For all we know she left hers open. Guess she felt safe."

I followed him inside. The layout was similar to Thalia's but on a smaller scale, with half a chipped Formica counter in lieu of a kitchenette, no fireplace, cheap-looking furniture from the seventies, and a low, dim bedroom barely able to accommodate a queen bed.

The feel of a budget summer rental gone stale. But the smell was anything but stale: acetone after-bite augmented by fake pine essence.

Some whiz-bang, industrial-strength deodorizer/ cleanser favored by the hospitality industry, who knew what toxins were bouncing around.

The bed was stripped. The toilet was banded with one of those paper things that's meant to imply hygiene. Milo opened the pull-out sofa; nothing inside. He searched drawers and cabinets. "Nada. No prints other than Thalia's and Refugia's in her room and they zapped this place, but let's see if anything comes up."

He made the call to the lab. No availability until later today.

"What a dump," he said. "My eyes are watering, let's get outta here."

The walk to Uno was brief and I said so.

He said, "The better to stalk, murder, and rob you, Red Riding Hood? Let's say she was the target. How would these alleged Austrians know her?"

I said, "One or all of them could've had a personal connection to Thalia."

"That's what I'm thinking, except she said she had no family."

"She might not have wanted to acknowledge a black-sheep relative. And if one or more showed up, that could've worried her enough to call me."

"You, not us, because we'da told her to get a security system and a noisy dog or just move the hell out."

"Or," I said, "she wanted reassurance that there was nothing to worry about. Unfortunately, she was wrong."

"Nasty kin," he said. "If it's the Birkens, could be one, two, or three of them."

"Teamwork would've made it easy," I said. "Whoever wasn't smothering her could look for the money."

"Someone that frail, not a chance in hell she

could defend herself. Too bad she didn't put a name on whoever worried her."

"She probably intended to," I said. "We were just beginning."

No uniform stood guard at Uno but the yellow tape hadn't been disturbed. Milo yanked it free, tried the door to the screen porch, found it locked and used the master key. Ungraced by Thalia, the peacock chair looked shabby, the cane splintering and stained.

Milo unlocked the bungalow door and stood on the threshold. Thalia's furniture and lamps were wrapped in thick plastic tarps secured by duct tape.

I said, "If there's time, we could check her reading material."

"Why?"

"It could tell us something about her."

"Sure, do it. I'm gonna start here, with a re-check of the cabinets, her fridge, all that good stuff."

Thalia's taste in reading was mostly nonfiction. Travel, fashion, landscaping, food and wine, music, biographies of historical figures with an emphasis on presidents and notable women.

Several additional shelves were given over to city accounting and zoning manuals, volumes on real estate law, curling copies of a magazine aimed at landlords called **Apartment Age.** Below that was a small fiction section. Several of the classics but mostly a collection of crime novels from the forties and fifties. Not just Chandler and the other usual suspects. The authors Thalia had read—Horace McCoy, David Goodis, Jonathan Latimer, Fredric Brown—suggested a depth of interest in the genre.

Or memories rooted in that period?

Either way, she seemed to have no taste for real-life evil; not a single volume of true crime.

Perhaps her concerns about an actual psychopath had been recent.

Or nonexistent.

I'd read the spine of every book, was standing near the bookcase unable to conjure the merest what-if, when Milo charged in breathing audibly.

"Nothing."

He began searching behind and under nightstands, flipping corners of rugs, peering under the canopy bed, checking the carved posts to see if they rotated, lifting the mattress.

Emptying drawer after drawer only to snuffle and proceed to the next futile step.

Some cops toss a room with the abandon of deranged adolescents. My friend's grooming may come across as hastily assembled but he puts things back exactly as he found them.

Considerate detective. The dead get most of his respect.

His industriousness spurred me to reexamine the books, removing each volume, fanning it open and shaking to dislodge anything secreted between pages.

No hidden treasure but as I neared the end of the mystery section I spotted handwriting on the title page of a small leather-bound book.

Small because it was the original edition—a cheap paperback, still bearing its lurid covers behind panels of tooled black morocco.

Robber's Destiny by a writer named Alden Smithee.

The inscription was blue block letters, ink laid down unevenly by an unsteady hand.

TO MIDGET HEY THIS GUY
GOT IT LOVE MONARK

I'd read a lot of pulp fiction, keeping busy between sets when I worked my way through college playing guitar in pickup wedding bands. All had been borrowed from an old, rheumatic sax player. Stan something, a recovered alcoholic who sidestepped the other musicians' methods of killing time—smoking weed and emptying airline vodka bottles.

I'd come to enjoy the fist-in-the-face syntax, overwrought plots evoking the late-late-night TV movies my father watched when his own booze addiction got in the way of sleep.

But I'd never seen this one or heard of the author. I ran my gloved finger over the leather. Robust and pebbly, bordered in still-bright gold. Someone taking the time to give a dime novel a fancy re-bind.

I began paging through the tough, urgent prose and the anything-but-subtle story line took shape: jewel heist gone bad, the usual noir combo of seduction, betrayal, and violent death.

Did the inscription have anything to do with Thalia? For all I knew, she'd picked the book up in a secondhand store.

I had a third go at every other book in her collection. No additional leather or inscriptions.

Midget. Easy to see someone her size acquiring the moniker.

If so, who was Monark?

I showed the message to Milo, who was rubbing his back and looking ready to spit.

He said, "A king who can't spell? When was it published?"

I turned to the copyright page. "'Fifty-three. Probably not long after she moved here.'"

"Yeah, well, I was hoping for something more recent. Let's try to find that driver, Creech."

As we neared The Can, Alicia Bogomil hurried toward us waving a bright-green Post-it. "No address on Leon but here's his number, he's listed."

Milo gave her a quick hug that made both of them blush.

DMV gave up Leon Creech's address on Wooster Street just south of Olympic, and when Milo phoned, Creech answered.

"Alicia told me. I was wondering if you folks would call. Seeing as I knew Miss Thalia pretty darn well."

"We'd appreciate talking to you, Mr. Creech. Could we drop by your home right now?"

"Why not? I'm not going anywhere. You over at the hotel?"

"We are."

"Twenty-three minutes on a good day," said Leon Creech. "Longer if people are driving like idjuts."

CHAPTER
11

Only a few idiots; we made it in twenty-nine minutes.

Leon Creech's mint-green stucco traditional was one of the few remaining single homes on a block of duplexes and apartment buildings. Most of the front yard was concrete. A car covered by a custom-fitted, all-weather navy-blue cover luxuriated in two parking spaces.

Milo lifted the cover. Waxed navy-blue paint, chrome polished to mirror-brightness, the rounded butt of a Lincoln Town Car. A blue-and-gold plate from the late seventies read **I DRYV U.**

The front door opened. A tall stooped man in his seventies wearing a brown cardigan over a red golf shirt said, "That's my baby. Ford had a lock on the market and stopped making them, corporate idjuts."

"Mr. Creech. Milo Sturgis and Alex Delaware."

"Sirs. Come on in."

The living room was crammed with cut-glass lamps, souvenir plates, fleecy throws, and over-stuffed seating. Mementos from Disney World, Graceland, Carlsbad Caverns, Mount Rushmore. Calendar landscapes favored Bambi-deer in autumn-red forests. A black-and-white photo showed a young couple on their wedding day.

Like Thalia's bungalow, unmodified in decades. Lower-budget than Thalia, but just as meticulously maintained.

Creech's complexion was pale with sallow borders. Same color scheme for hair thin enough to fly away on a low-breeze day. He motioned us to sit, settled with care on the other side of a hexagonal coffee table. The table hosted a bowl of mixed nuts, a pitcher of water, and three drinking glasses. Slices of lemon floated in the water.

"Unsalted, hope you don't mind. The blood pressure."

Milo said, "Probably a good idea for me, too."

Creech appraised him. "Can't hurt to be careful."

Milo picked out a Brazil nut, molared it to dust, and crossed his legs. Creech crossed his, too. Brown-and-tan argyle socks, black New Balance walking shoes.

"Thanks for taking the time, Mr. Creech."

"Got plenty of it, sir. It's hard to believe someone would do that to Miss Thalia. If anyone was class, it was her. Can you tell me what happened?"

"Afraid not."

"I get that. Used to work criminal apprehension in the army."

"CID?"

"No, just plain MP in Seoul, South Korea. The base was huge, right in the middle of the city. Twenty thousand young bucks, always someone in trouble. Anyway, I understand about keeping it close to the vest. But you definitely think someone killed her?"

"We do, Mr. Creech."

"Damn," said Leon Creech. "That's just obscene."

"How long did you drive her?"

"Approximately two years, sir. Started a career of driving eight years before that when I retired from the unified school district—used to supervise maintenance in some tough neighborhoods. I began with the big companies—CLS, Music

Express—decided to reduce my hours and work for myself. The Aventura was perfect, I knew I'd be taking it easy."

"Not much business, there."

"Place is always struggling. You know what they mostly do now, right?"

"Surgical aftercare."

"The fancy hotels didn't want to deal with it. Too much liability and I imagine there'd be all kinds of unpleasant stains on the upholstery and whatnot. The fancy surgeons want to keep all the money to themselves so they mostly handle transport but sometimes they don't or can't. Perfect for me, I wanted part-time. I bring my lunch, listen to big bands on the Sirius, somebody needs a lift, I take them. They don't, I don't, who cares, I got my pension."

"How often did Ms. Mars want to be driven?"

"Not often," said Creech, reaching for an almond. He studied it for a moment before nipping off a corner and chewing slowly. "Less as time went on and then it stopped."

"When?" said Milo.

"Two or so months ago. Out of the clear blue she came out to the parking lot and said, 'Leon, I'm sorry. No more excursions for me, I've seen everything I want to see in this world.' She was walking real slowly, I guess I hadn't noticed because she always seemed like she was okay. Then she shook my hand and handed me an envelope and left."

Creech's sunken cheeks vibrated. "I figured a nice tip, hundred bucks if I was lucky."

He placed the partially eaten almond on the table. "It was a five-thousand-dollar check."

Milo whistled.

"I wondered if she'd made a mistake, so I walked back to her bungalow. She was out on the porch in that big chair she liked. Smiling like she expected me. Before I could say anything, she said, 'Leon, don't argue. It's a retainer in case I change my mind and want to resume excursions.' I said did she realize how long it would take to chew down five grand with fifty bucks per hour of driving? She said, 'Leave the accounting to me, Leon.' Then she said she was tired and went inside. Never saw her after that."

Creech picked up the almond, looked at it, popped it in his mouth and chewed rapidly. His eyes were watery and brown, his brow pale and surprisingly unlined. "I deposited the money. It didn't feel exactly right but she wasn't open to argument."

I said, "Did she make large gifts to anyone else?"

"I wouldn't know, sir. Only thing I did see

her do regularly was come back with desserts for the hotel people. She'd usually bring me a burger or a sandwich. The only other person took care of my stomach like that was my wife and she passed twenty-one years ago."

"Nice person."

"The best."

"But no other money gifts you ever saw."

"You're thinking she put herself in a situation by flashing cash?" said Creech. "If she did, I never saw it."

Milo said, "She eat by herself or with company?"

"Always by herself. Always in Beverly Hills. Cheesecake Factory, La Scala Boutique, Spago, E Baldi."

"And then she stopped going out, period."

"People get tired, sir. I'm seventy-two and there's days I don't want to do a thing."

"Know the feeling, Mr. Creech. In two years of driving her, what did you learn about her background?"

"Nothing. She never got personal. A lot of times she slept. Which was fine with me, I like to concentrate on the road."

I said, "So no mention of family or other people in her life?"

"No, sir."

"We're asking, because as you know from your MP experience, the most important thing is to understand the victim."

"The victim," said Creech. "It feels terrible using that word for her. I know she was real old but she was also real **alive**. I knew I'd never live close to as long as her, fact is with my family genes, I'm doing great making seventy-two. But however much I lasted, I said to myself, Learn from her. Enjoy each minute. Tell you one thing, I enjoyed driving her. This city, a stranger gets into your car, they want you to be a psychiatrist."

He shook his head. "Fifty bucks an hour don't cover that."

"Speaking of strangers," said Milo. "We hear you were at the Aventura a couple of days ago."

"Got restless, so I figured what the heck?"

"Did you happen to drive people called the Birkenhaars?"

Creech's jaws clenched. "You saying they had something to do with—"

"Not at all, Mr. Creech. They were the only people staying near Miss Mars's bungalow so we'd like to ask them if they saw anything. So far we haven't been able to locate them."

"Them. That's exactly the type I was talking about."

I said, "Wanting psychotherapy."

"With them it was more like **sex** therapy,"

said Creech. "Disgusting. I came this close to pulling over and telling them to call Uber or something." He shifted in his chair. "I was raised Mennonite. Don't practice anymore but it sticks with you."

I said, "A moral code."

"You bet, right and wrong. And those people were just **wrong**." He looked down at his lap, tugged up his trousers.

I said, "They got sexual in the back of your car?"

"Not actually . . . doing it. More like playing around?" Sallow edges had turned pink. "Laughing, like it was a joke. She pulls out her you-know-whats and they're both . . . disgusting." Head shake. "It's not like I was out to watch, when I'm driving, I'm driving."

"But that kind of thing is hard to ignore."

"Exactly, sir. Someone's making those noises you're going to check the rearview to make sure it's not getting crazy back there. Which it was, I came this close."

He created a slit of space between thumb and forefinger. "Maybe they figured out they needed to behave because they stopped. But they kept laughing and every so often one of them would sneak in a touch of her."

Milo said, "They talk to each other in a foreign language?"

"Why would they, they were Americans."

"They told the desk they were Austrians."

"Then they lied."

"What names did they use for each other?"

"Never heard any names, everything was whispers. Didn't take them long to . . . do what they did. Like wanting to be in a limo so they could show off. Even the other guy, I got to admit, that surprised me."

"The other guy."

"The good-looking ones I pegged as a couple. They looked like they went together. Slick, you know? Like actor-types. The other guy was shorter and heavier and had a face like a warthog. Him I figured for the guy who tags along. But then she—he also got—I **really** don't want to talk about it, it's the kind of thing I forgot when I stopped working for the big companies, crazy proms, kids acting crazy."

"No prob," said Milo. "Where'd you take them?"

"House of Blues on Sunset," said Creech. "What I hear is there's no seats, you have to stand up, talk about getting a backache."

"Who was playing?"

"Search me, sir. I didn't look. I just wanted to drop them off and go home."

"They didn't need return transportation."

"Not from me. I'd have said no if they did. On top of everything else, no tip."

"How'd they pay?"

"Cash," said Creech. "But just the fifty minimum. No class, whatsoever."

Back in the car, Milo said, "Backseat threesome, some personal assistant."

"Americans," I said. "They lied about everything."

"And now they get **hunted**." He placed a second call to the crime lab, said the need for a print tech in Bungalow Five was urgent. That moved the ETA to early tomorrow morning.

I said, "We could try the House of Blues, maybe someone remembers them. If not, there are the restaurants Thalia frequented."

"Creech said she ate alone."

"He's out in the car, could miss something."

"Thalia had dinner with them?"

"Long-lost relatives get in touch, she's curious, agrees to meet up, but something bugs her so she doesn't invite them to her home."

"But they got there, anyway. Okay, let's find out."

The House of Blues had been reserved for a private party that night. Small VIP gathering, record-business honchos and their significant others. The manager was absolutely certain no one matching the frisky trio had been there.

At the Cheesecake Factory, La Scala Boutique, Spago, and E Baldi, we found hosts and servers who knew and adored Thalia. A regular. Not weekly but maybe once a month. So nice. The word "classy" kept coming up. Her preferences ran to white wine or a Sapphire Martini on the rocks with a twist, olives on the side, followed by some kind of salad and a seafood entrée that she barely touched. Never dessert for her, but always to-go packages of sweets for her "friends."

Seeing the hotel staff as her social circle. Living in an increasingly narrowing world, two rooms her universe.

Doing fine with that until the worst aspects of humanity oozed over her threshold.

CHAPTER
12

Discouraged by no sightings of the Birkenhaars with Thalia, Milo dropped me back home at seven twenty P.M.

I said, "Thalia was big on retainers."

"Probably just what she said, keeping it simple. Thanks for your time, enjoy your nice life."

I said, "Come in for a bite."

"No, thanks, too much homework." He glanced at the backseat where Ricki Sylvester's file on Thalia sat.

"Happy to split the job with you."

"Against regulations."

I laughed.

He said, "True, but like I said, it's homework, ergo I'm taking it home." He revved the engine.

"Something comes up from the print tech, I'll let you know."

"Regards to Rick."

"He's on-shift, perfect opportunity for me to plow through."

As I got out of the unmarked, the front door opened and Robin stepped out onto the terrace. She waved and danced down the stairs, hair loose, face scrubbed and gorgeous.

"That's a vision," said Milo. "Ergo your nice life."

"Hi, guys. Long day?"

Milo said, "Fun and games. I brought Romeo back in workable shape."

She kissed me. "He doesn't require much work. I threw together some pasta with a bunch of random leftovers. Why don't you stay for dinner?"

"Ouch," he said. "That's the sound of my arm being twisted."

"Random leftovers" meant veal roast, Genoa salami, artichoke hearts, cherry peppers, mushrooms, onions, fennel, chicken. Accompanied by a bottle of Barolo, and Blanche begging at Milo's feet.

Robin said, "No chicken for her, please, Big Guy. Her tummy doesn't like it."

"The rest is okay?"

"Not onions, either."

Blanche reacted to that with a head-cock. Milo fed her a piece of veal, ate, wiped his mouth. "This is fantastic. What do you call it?"

Robin said, "Use it or lose it. Thanks for helping."

He beat his chest. "Public service. Along those lines, pass the bowl, please."

Robin went to take a bath, I washed the dishes, Milo dried.

When we finished, I said, "Go get the file and we'll divvy it up."

"I told you: homework."

"This is a home."

Milo split the massive three-ring binder into two approximate halves, gave me the top, and took the rest for himself. Most of what I ended up with was decades of monthly brokerage statements recording Thalia's wealth, and February 1 reminders from Ricki Sylvester to provide state and federal tax information so she could file in April on Thalia's behalf.

Between Thalia's training as a CPA and the bulk of her money coming from tax-free bonds, the short form had been a cinch. The only other income since Sylvester began handling the estate were two county pensions that had risen to around fifty thousand a year, plus eighteen K from Social Security, with deductions for Medicare.

A note from Sylvester every March 1 confirmed Thalia's continuing intention to donate every cent of her taxable income to charity, "per your goal of obviating the need for burdensome accounting."

Everything had been CC'd to Joseph A. Manucci, Certified Financial Planner, at Morgan-Smith's Encino office. No personal correspondence from Manucci but the statements bore his name on top, as did stacks of boilerplate stock-market analyses from the brokerage house's home office in New York.

Given the size of Thalia's account, he'd probably sent holiday cards and calendars, too. She'd probably tossed them.

No records from the time when Sylvester's grandfather had been in charge. Probably in Milo's batch.

I kept going, came upon pages of photocopied pension and Social Security checks along with letters from Sylvester confirming direct transfer of yearly donations to Western Pediatric Medical Center of Los Angeles and the Shriners Hospital for Children. Subsequent letters listed smaller donations to St. Jude's Children's Research Hospital in Memphis and other pediatric institutions in Orange County, San Diego, Boston, Houston, and Philadelphia.

On the last page, a blank, white business-sized envelope resting in a plastic pouch. When I pulled it out the paper felt starchy and stiff.

Inside was a letter dated December 14, 1950, typed on the embossed stationery of

John E. McCandless, Esq., Attorney at Law.

McCandless had run a one-man operation out of an office on Green Street in Pasadena. No address listed for the recipient.

Dear Thalia,
Enclosed is the contract with Grammar. I trust you find the terms agreeable.
Betty sends her best.
Yours, as always,
Jack
JEM: tg

Paper-clipped to the letter was a plain white sheet specifying a rental agreement between Miss Thalia Mars and The Conrad Aventura Grande Deluxe, to take effect January 1, 1951. The hotel's parent company was Conrad G.

Grammar, Inc., St. Louis, Missouri, doing business in California and Arizona as Conrad Hotels and Banquet Services, Ltd.

Ricki Sylvester had told us Thalia was from Missouri. Had a personal link between tenant and hotelier enabled the sweetheart deal bemoaned by Kurtis DeGraw?

The terms of the contract blew that guess to bits.

Occupancy fees for "Deluxe Bungalow VIII" had been set at one thousand dollars a month, with service charges added to create a yearly rent of $12,667.67, plus a three percent escalator every anniversary to be applied "at the discretion of the property owner."

Twelve grand had to be huge money in '51, far beyond the reach of an unmarried municipal clerk.

I logged onto the Internet and confirmed it: U.S. median family income that year had been thirty-seven hundred dollars.

Somehow Thalia had come up with nearly four times that amount for the privilege of living in two rooms on a property recently cleared of vagrants.

Perhaps she'd already stockpiled cash from real estate deals. Maybe those records were also in Milo's share of the file.

I told him what I'd found.

He said, "Yeah, all the property transfers are here, but if this is all of 'em, she didn't start wheeling and dealing until '53. Her last transaction was in the seventies. She sold six hundred acres of desert near Palmdale to a film ranch. Paid five grand and raked in six hundred twenty-five K. Not bad, huh? It's all like that, huge profits for years."

"But not in '51," I said. "Did Jack McCandless handle the deals?"

"Yup."

"Ricki Sylvester reminds her to file taxes. Same for him?"

He said, "Nope. You're thinking she wasn't paying taxes back then?"

"Or someone was handling them for her. Handling more than taxes."

"A kept woman," he said. "Fronting someone else's dough."

"How else could she come up with twelve grand a year? No need for a front if you're legal. Maybe that book inscription's important. Monark financed Midget, put her up in a secluded hotel bungalow because she was his fun on the side."

"Little Miss Moll," he said. "Sure, why not. But it's a big leap from that to murder seventy years later."

"Unless Midget and Monark got together and

made a little Monark or two who didn't turn out so well. Thalia never acknowledged any descendants. But that doesn't mean they don't exist. Maybe as she neared the end of her life, she decided to make sure they didn't get a cut. Is the will in there?"

"Not yet." He pawed through the rest of his pile, did a lot of head shaking, finally drew out another white envelope. The single page inside this one was dated earlier this year and printed on Ricki Sylvester's letterhead.

Brief document, as uncomplicated as Thalia's approach to taxes. Half of her estate was bequeathed to the Western Pediatric Medical Center, specifically to the Outpatient Division run by Ruben Eagle, M.D.

"Your buddy makes out like a bandit," said Milo. "Hey, maybe I should look **into** your buddy."

I said, "Feel free but on the morality scale he's somewhere between Mother Teresa and the Dalai Lama."

The rest of the will listed another twenty percent going to the Shriners Hospital, the remaining thirty to be divided up equally among the remaining institutions she'd long supported.

Milo said, "She had a soft spot for kids."

"And left nothing for any relative."

"So, what, a bunch of reprobate descendants

sneak in, suffocate her, and make off with some loose cash? Another stash, not the three G I found?"

"They got a bigger stash, were in a hurry, missed the three."

"What, ten, twenty, fifty? Compared with her net worth, we're talking chump change. Wouldn't it be smarter to try to butter her up and score big?"

"You take what you can," I said. "Beyond that, you get to express your feelings."

"Also, how would they know they were excluded?"

"Good question."

"Got plenty of those," he said. "Enough for tonight, I'm getting heartburn—not the dinner, my fragile emotional state."

After he left, I got on the computer.

Monark turned out to be a popular brand-word attached to bicycles, boats, golf equipment, auto parts, and beer. Lots of bands, also, many from Scandinavia.

Pairing the keyword with **gangster** caused the search-engine gods to inquire if I really meant **gangsta** and sent me back to the bands.

Monark and **midget** brought up a few sites specializing in vintage toys. Monark bikes tended to be grouped with midget cars, but never had the twain met.

An hour plus produced nothing. Milo was right. Enough for tonight.

◆

The following morning, I reached Ruben Eagle at the hospital and told him about Thalia.

He said, "Oh, no! She was a **wonderful** person, who the hell would **do** that?"

"How did you meet her?"

"She walked into the clinic one day and asked for me. I was swamped and had no idea who she was. It took a while to get to her but she waited patiently. I come out, see this cute little old woman, she smiles and hands me a check for ten thousand dollars. I was stunned. Getting Development to pay attention is always a challenge and a donor just walks in? She didn't ask for a tour, didn't want to be stroked like most of them. Someone **killed** her, Alex? Grotesque. What a screwed-up world."

"How much contact did you have with her?"

"We invited her to affairs but she never showed up. Once a year, before Christmas, she'd bring bags of toys for the kids and give me a check. The second one utterly blew me away. **Fifty** thou. And that's what it became for the next few years. It changed our whole budgetary setup, basically she became our patron saint. Now she's—who the hell would **do** something like that? She was almost a hundred, for God's sake, next month was her birthday, we were going to surprise her with a cake."

"Are you aware of anyone she had problems with?"

"No one here, that's for sure," said Ruben. "My staff adored her. This is repugnant, Alex. I know bad things can happen to anyone but someone lasting that long, and then . . . it's fucked **up**."

First time I'd heard him swear. "Any idea how she found out about you?"

"When she gave me the second check, I walked her out to her limo and asked. She told me she was referred by Belinda Wojik. Know her?"

"I don't."

"She was one of my residents, stayed for a few years on staff then went into private practice. When I called Belinda to thank her, she seemed surprised. Said she'd talked about her work but didn't push for a donation. But gift horse and all that. I really can't **believe** this, Alex."

Milo phoned at 11 A.M., sounding shockingly happy.

"Print tech came by early this morning. The place was wiped clean but she pulled up a couple of latents on the doorjamb and there was an AFIS match, scrote named Gerard Waters. History of money crimes but no violence. Physically he's a match for Mr. Pudgy. Got a driver's license last month, actually lived where he said he did. I just spoke to his landlord. Waters cut out a few days ago, owed rent. West L.A., not your zip code socioeconomically, but not that far geographically. I'm going over there, up to you, but if you feel like it—"

"You know the answer."

"Not really," he said. "Mostly I'm still trying to figure out the questions."

The address was minutes from the West L.A. station so I left the Seville in the staff lot and Milo drove. As he turned onto Butler Avenue, he handed me a sheet of paper. "This is who we're looking for."

Gerard Brian Waters was forty-three years old, five-seven, two hundred four pounds, with gray hair and brown eyes. Daffy Duck tattoo on his left calf, crude rendition of crossed sabers on his right shoulder blade. Inked in places where viewing would be optional.

Not a face the camera loved, even accounting for the indignities of arrest and booking. Broad, pouchy, the skin rough and grainy, an off-kilter nose, spiky hair, a skimpy chin-beard devoid of mustache.

The mugshot was seven years old but Gerard Waters looked closer to fifty than thirty-six. Living in confinement can do that to you, and he'd spent a quarter of his life in various penal institutions. Charges ranged from shoplifting to drug possession to larceny. Most of the lockups were local jails but Waters's most recent stint had been four years at a federal prison in Colorado for passing bad checks.

"No blood and guts on his record," said Milo, "so they put him in minimum security. Model prisoner until he walked away from a work detail raking leaves in a park. That doubled a two-year sentence."

"How close was he to getting out?"

"Six months."

"For the sake of half a year, he loses two," I said. "Impatient fellow. Any idea what he's been up to since?"

"Other than defrauding an innkeeper and cutting out on his rent? Nope. He got full release, no parole, so he wasn't reporting to anyone."

I thought of Thalia's question about criminal specialization. My response that it was a misconception.

"No blood and guts in his background," I said. "But you know how it is."

"Oh, yeah," said Milo. "A few they get caught for, a bunch they get away with."

Gerard Waters's last known address was a block east of Sawtelle and the same distance north of

Olympic. A neighborhood of modest one-story houses where elegant Japanese nurseries had once thrived along with the hardworking people who ran them. Sparse reminders of that time were a few sushi bars on Sawtelle and a scatter of landscaping niceties: topiary conifers, beds of Zen grass, bamboo peg border markers. But most of the front lots had regressed to weedy grass and uninspired planting.

The house we were looking for sported no Asian elements but it had been maintained well, with a lush lawn, thriving roses, long-established birds of paradise and hydrangea.

A man stood in front, hose in hand, watering grass that couldn't get any greener. Sixties, medium-sized and narrow-shouldered, he was completely bald with a sun-spotted pate and a white croquet-wicket mustache that right-angled past a thin lower lip. Dressed for outdoor chores in a **Catalina Jazz Club** T-shirt, cargo shorts, and plastic sandals.

He turned off the water and walked to the curb, hose in hand.

Milo said, "Mr. Duke?"

"Yeah, I'm Phil." Resonant radio baritone. "Don't know what else I can tell you about the bum."

"Mr. Waters rented a room in this house."

"Had an extra bedroom, used to be my daughter's then she got married. Nice room, **including** a shower and separate exit out back. I never rented before, figured why not and put it on Craigslist. Live and learn."

"Not an ideal tenant."

"First month he paid on time, second he was late, it kept getting later."

"He pay with a check?"

"Nah, cash," said Phil Duke. "Last month he didn't pay at all. I called a lawyer, he said eviction was a real hassle, everything favors the tenant. So I tried talking to Waters. So sorry, didn't mean it, some sort of bank problem, I'll pay you by the end of the month. Instead, one night when I was out, he packed up and left. Took some of my plates and cups, to boot. Last time I do that."

"Did you file a police report?"

Phil Duke's lips did something that made the croquet wicket compress on both sides. "Lawyer said it was a waste of time unless he'd taken something valuable. The dishes were twenty, fifty bucks. Why're you asking about him? He scam someone else?"

"His name came up in an investigation."

"That doesn't exactly tell me anything."

"Sorry, sir. We can't divulge. When did Waters begin renting and when did he leave?"

"All hush-hush, huh? Figures," said Duke. "Let's see . . . begin was five—no, six months ago, leave was three weeks ago. Daughter's coming back, anyway, so it worked out." Another compression. "Divorce, never liked the guy."

"What kind of work did Waters say he did?"

"Sales and marketing. Don't know what he sold or marketed, didn't ask. Didn't even get a last-month or a damage deposit, that shows you how stupid I was."

"It could happen to anyone," said Milo.

"It could if they're stupid," said Phil Duke. "I should've listened to myself."

"Is there anything you can tell us about Waters that might help us find him?"

"Love to help you, respect what you do, a few cops in my family. But nah." He rubbed his bare head. "Honestly, not a bad guy when you first meet him. Friendly, agreeable, talked softly. No bad habits that I could see. Smoking, drinking, he didn't do neither."

"What kind of hours did he keep?"

"Normal. Out by eight, back by six or seven. Like a normal job."

"He ever entertain anyone?"

"Nah, kept to himself. Which I guess is strange, him being so friendly, you'd expect some kind of friend. But you never know with people. That's why I like plants."

He jiggled the hose. "If there's nothing else, I'm going to watch my grass grow."

◆

Driving back to the station, I said, "Superficial charm, poor impulse control, criminal history. Waters might be the reason Thalia called me. And/or his bungalow-mates."

"They show up on her doorstep, 'Hi, Auntie'?" he said. "Talk about a family reunion."

I said, "In my head it's shaping up calculated. Chapter One's a friendly drop-in. Two is returning to the hotel and checking in, asking for a nearby bungalow so they can stalk her and pick their moment. If they are kin, no mystery about motive. Like you said, they banked on being in the will. Or resented being excluded and were either taking revenge or looking for loose cash. Either way, the effort was minimal, the payout potentially high."

"For someone to expect they'd inherit, there had to be some kind of relationship."

"Maybe there was and we haven't found it."

"Or we're totally off and Waters and his pals were staying there for another reason. Like being able to three-way in privacy. The big problem is we still don't know a damn thing about Thalia. When are you gonna talk to your pediatrician buddy, whatsisname—Eagle?"

"Just did. One of Ruben's former residents mentioned his work to Thalia in passing, she walked into his clinic with a check for ten grand."

He whistled.

I said, "The following year she gave him fifty. That's been her annual donation, since."

We traveled a block. He said, "You know Eagle well."

"I do."

"Above reproach and wears a halo."

I stared at him. "Oh, c'mon."

"Hey," he said, "follow the money, gotta ask."

"What connection could Ruben have to Waters and the other two?"

"Solid citizen hires out? Like that never happens?"

"Not in this case."

"Fine, he's a saint but I still gotta ask."

"Fair enough."

"Would it be agonizing for you to do a face-to-face with him? Check out the nonverbals then maybe talk to the resident, see if Eagle's story holds up? If I'm putting you in a bad position, do a Nancy R. and just say no. And if you feel like washing your hands of the whole damn mess, no problem."

"Why would I want to do that?"

He smiled.

As we neared the station, I said, "While I'm studying Ruben's nonverbals, what will you be doing?"

"Calling cops who busted Gerard Waters and

jailers who gave him room and board, try to find out who his pals were. Maybe I'll get lucky and I.D. the cute-looking couple."

"Bravely into the past," I said.

"Where else?" he said. "When you get down to it, we're both historians."

CHAPTER

14

I drove to the hospital, parked in the staff lot, clipped on my faculty badge, and walked to the outpatient clinic on the ground floor of the main building.

Poor people often use emergency rooms as general practitioners. It ties up the E.R., makes triage a challenge, and saps hospital budgets. But doctors and nurses don't ask for financial reports when it comes to sick kids.

Ruben Eagle was Western Pediatric Medical Center's attempt to solve the problem, with nurse practitioners serving as first-line screeners and interns and residents doing much of the diagnosis and treatment. But demand always outstrips supply and at Western Peds, the result can be a human logjam.

Ruben's waiting room was filled with small humans and those entrusted to care for them. No clear pathway to the reception window but I squeezed through sniffles, coughs, and cries and finally got there. The harried-looking woman was someone I'd never met but my badge caused her to nod.

"Dr. Eagle, please."

"He's with a patient. What shall I say it's about, Doctor?"

"Follow-up on Thalia Mars."

"Miss Mars," she said, peering at the badge. "Psychology. She was your donor, too? We're all going to miss her." She pushed a button, talked, listened, turned back to me. "I was wrong, he's actually rounding on Four West. He says for you to meet him in the doctors' dining room in five minutes, he's due for breakfast."

The clock behind her read one P.M.

She laughed. "He likes breakfast food and never has time for it so they save him oatmeal."

The doctor's dining room is a pocket of oak-paneled calm tucked into a corner of the hospital basement. The rest of the floor reeks of chemicals and the morgue is steps away. No one's appetite seems affected.

The only vacant table was near the silverware bins. I helped myself to turbo-boosted coffee and sat. Ruben's five minutes turned into fifteen and I was on my second cup when the door opened and he charged in, white coat flapping, Coke-bottle eyeglasses slipping low on an aristocratic nose. He looked around, saw me, mouthed, **Sorry,** and hurried over.

Ruben's a slim, finely boned man with a wiry gray beard. His parents escaped from communist Hungary in '56. Ruben was born in L.A. but a couple of older sisters were smuggled out of Budapest in packing crates. One of them was mentally disabled from birth, and during the journey they put her on chloral hydrate.

Ruben tells the story with wonderment but no bitterness. His parents are gone and he's been Magda's primary emotional and financial support for as long as I've known him. She lives with him and his wife, a Chilean-born dentist, and the youngest two of their five children, in a far-too-small Sherman Oaks ranch house. Ruben drives a dented old Toyota and manages to look well groomed despite no interest in clothing. He runs marathons to raise money for his clinic, lifts weights on off days, and never works less than a hundred hours a week, divided between treating the poor and training student doctors. He wins teaching awards regularly. Everyone likes him. You can't not like him.

Let's see what his nonverbals had to say this afternoon.

He pumped my hand and sat down. "Alex, great to see you. Considering the circumstances, that is."

A waiter brought him a pot of hot tea and said, "The usual, Doctor?"

"Yes, please. That's oatmeal for me, Alex, I'm still making a go at breakfast. What can I get you?"

"A salad's fine."

The waiter said, "One usual, one green-s," and left.

Ruben said, "Doris told me you want follow-up on Thalia. I think I told you everything."

Calm steady eyes, the skin above the beard was smooth, the forehead unlined.

"Just trying to see if anything else came to mind."

"At your cop friend's request? Don't imagine you have time to be running around randomly."

"It's a tough one, he's trying to be thorough."

"Well," he said, "after we spoke on the phone, I did try to see if I could come up with anything that could be helpful. I couldn't, Alex. Thalia was one of our best donors but I spent very little time with her."

"She didn't need to be stroked."

"Just came by with the check."

"She could've mailed it," I said.

"She wanted some kind of personal contact? Guess so. But not more than once a year. We kept sending her invitations, anyway. Last time she showed up I asked her if getting mail from us was bothersome. She said not at all, but she didn't believe it was a two-way transaction. I said I appreciated that but if she changed her mind, we'd all enjoy having her here. She said that was unlikely, her entertainment days were over. And then she winked."

"Plenty of partying when she was younger."

"That's how I took it, Alex. Could that help?"

"Everything's got potential, at this point. Did she tell you anything about her past?"

"Other than that comment and the wink, not a hint."

"**Bring** the money and run."

He laughed. "I'm sure most division heads would consider her a dream donor. But now, looking back, I wish I'd been more assertive trying to get to know her. Not out of charity, she must've had an interesting life, don't you think? That age, all the history she'd lived through."

The food arrived. Ruben added brown sugar, milk, and raisins to his oatmeal. Put his spoon down. "The thought of someone murdering her is beyond the pale but I suppose anything's possible. Couple of weeks ago, we had a family,

Mom poisoned all four kids with windshield washer fluid in their juice. Because the father left her for another woman."

I shook my head. He ate a spoonful of oatmeal.

"We haven't located any family."

"Maybe she was the last woman standing," he said. "I had a great-aunt, never married or had kids, moved to Rome and stayed there rather than come to the States with the rest of our family. She lived to a hundred and two, crazily healthy almost to the end, alone by choice. When my mother called her, Aunt Irma made her feel she was intruding. You'd probably have a diagnosis for that. Mom said she was the last woman standing because she never caught germs from anyone."

I said, "Isolation as a wellness technique."

"It wouldn't work for me, but all types, right? Though the few times I saw Thalia she was friendly, nothing antisocial about her."

I said, "The doctor who sent Thalia to you—"

"Belinda Wojik. No idea how she knew her. Your call got me curious but I didn't try to contact her, don't want to get in the way of the investigation. If I had to guess, I'd say something to do with show business. It strikes me that Thalia could've been an actress, no? She did have a theatrical side to her—the flamboyant clothes, the easy manner. That wink? And Belinda had something to do with the movies before she became a physician."

"From screenplays to pediatrics?"

He smiled. "The opposite of what usually happens, no? All those docs think they can get rich with screenplays. Belinda went back to college for a post-bac in her forties, then med school."

"Impressive."

"She's super-smart, Alex. Did a year with me then a fellowship in cardiology over at County, I figured she'd concentrate on research. Then she had a chance to take over a practice in Beverly Hills—Simon Webster."

"Pediatrician to the stars," I said. "A showbiz connection would help scoring something like that."

He ate a bit. "Something just occurred to me. Thalia having money, Belinda working in B.H. What if one of her patients was Thalia's great-grandniece or -nephew or something along those lines?"

His pager went off. He called in, listened, stood. "A real one, I'm afraid. Whooping cough in a six-month-old, so many people aren't vaccinating, the infection vector's screwed up." Eyeing his bowl, he bent and took another spoonful. "Nice seeing you, hope you find whoever killed Thalia. I really liked her. Such a **refined** woman."

I sat there as he whooshed out of the room, wondering how he'd react about the huge money coming his way.

Assuming he didn't already know.

No reason to think otherwise, nothing I'd just seen or heard made me uneasy about him. I texted Milo to that effect, received no reply, looked up Belinda Wojik, M.D.'s office number and phoned.

Voicemail delivered in a sultry female voice offered a host of possibilities. I pushed 0 in order to talk to a human being and was entertained by the soundtrack from **Annie** before a woman with a Russian accent said, "Dr. Wojik's office."

"This is Dr. Delaware calling Dr. Wojik."

"In regard to what patient?"

"Thalia Mars but she's not a patient."

"Oh," she said. "Then what?"

"Miss Mars is a mutual acquaintance of Dr. Wojik and myself."

"It's personal?"

"Yes."

"I'll tell her but she may not be able to get back until the end of the day. What's that name again?"

Just as I got home, a text dinged on my phone.

Milo: **call me in the office.**

I said, "You got my message about Ruben."

"No. What, you just learned he's a sure-bet serial killer, we're closing the case?—ah, here it is. Nothing iffy, huh? Too bad. Reason I called is the autopsy results on Thalia just came in. Definitely asphyxia, pathologist said she was amazingly healthy for any age, let alone hers. The one new thing he found is bruising on both sides of her torso, like she got squeezed. Hard enough to crack one of her ribs. Which he described as 'pickup sticks.' Best guess is whoever covered her nose and her mouth did it while straddling her."

"Oh, man. You know what I'm going to ask."

"Nope, zero evidence of sexual assault. Pathologist also said there's a decent chance she never woke up because the bruises were faint, there wasn't a lot of stress hormone in her blood and no signs of a struggle."

"A decent chance," I said.

"You know those guys, commitment issues. Anyway, it doesn't tell us much and so far I can't find anyone from Gerard Waters's past who fits the toothsome-twosome, just a few petty miscreants and drunks locked up in local jails the same time as him."

"What about his stretch in prison?"

"Still waiting for a callback. Still waiting for lots of callbacks. So Eagle really is a saint, huh?"

"Would you settle for decent human being?"

"Guess there are a few."

I told him about Thalia's "entertainment days" comment and wink.

He said, "Sounds like she was flirting with him."

"She did have that quality."

"You, too, huh?"

"It could mean something," I said. "Belinda Wojik—the doctor who referred her to Ruben— used to work in motion pictures and now has a big B.H. practice. He wondered if Thalia had once been an actress. His other guess was that one of her great-grandnieces or -nephews was a patient of Wojik's and that's how they met."

"Our girl did the starlet thing before switching to accounting? Talk about shifting gears."

"My initial search on her pulled up nothing along those lines. Nothing, period. But if her work predated the Internet by decades and she never starred in anything, that could explain it."

"She seem the type? Beyond being flirty."

"She did have a presence," I said. "Meet her and you wouldn't think 'municipal clerk.' "

"Guess I should talk to Dr. Wojik."

"I left a message with her receptionist."

"Thanks," he said. "How about you start with her, she has anything juicy to say, let me know. I'm gonna try the prison again, someone's gotta know who Waters's K.A.'s were. All of Thalia's stuff was packed and carted a few hours ago. When the place was empty, I had a third go. No hidden cubbies, trapdoors, or buried treasure. Only thing I figure was worth much were those few pieces of jewelry and the Tiffany lamps, if they're real."

"I only saw one Tiffany, blue with dragon-flies."

"There was a standing one, too, kinda red, pretty."

Bubbled shade, to my eye, crude compared with the dragonfly lamp. Not the time for a discussion on decorative arts.

I said, "When can she be buried?"

"Ricki Sylvester just called to ask the same thing. I said it would have to wait. So would finalizing the estate. She accepted it but I was b.s.'ing, can only delay up to a point. So eventually, Dr. Big Bird and all those other charities are gonna get a windfall. Too bad he didn't twang your antenna."

CHAPTER

15

By end of day, I'd heard nothing from Dr. Belinda Wojik.

I'd used the time to research her, found an active medical license in the state of California, no complaints or violations, and four-and-a-half-star patient evaluations on two rating sites. The only carp: Dr. Wojik was always busy and sometimes waiting time was prolonged.

No trace of an Industry link or anything Wojik had done other than practice medicine.

Milo phoned at three thirty P.M. "Found another jail deputy who remembers Waters, says he was a crafty bastard. When I asked him about violence, he said, 'Naw, weasel not a wolf.'"

The federal penitentiary in Colorado had finally served up Waters's most recent cellmate but no additional information.

I said, "Good fit with the guy sharing the bungalow with Waters?"

"Judge for yourself. I'm sending you the info right now."

Seconds later, prison photos came wafting through the cloud. Henry Adam Bakstrom, thirty-eight, six-one, a hundred seventy-six pounds, sported a chiseled face blessed by crisp, symmetrical features. Strong chin, straight nose. A long, substantial neck sprang from muscular shoulders.

Life is biased in favor of good-looking people and I could see a cleaned-up Bakstrom passing at a nice hotel. Once you got past the bristly black Mohawk, the arrow-shaped soul patch bottoming moist vaguely ravenous lips, the icy blue eyes trying to stare down the camera.

Not much could be done about the eyes but they'd attract a certain type of woman as well as corporate buyers of edgy men's fashion. Pour on the grooming and he'd be ready for **GQ.**

I said, "Decent-looking guy, he'd fit."

"So would his priors. This one knows how to be aggressive."

Bakstrom's criminal history was more impressive than Gerard Waters's, with three serious prison sentences taking up the bulk of his twenties and thirties.

Assault, extortion with violence, an eight-year stretch for accessory after the fact in an armed Boulder bank robbery. The last had landed Bakstrom in the same facility privileged to house Gerard Waters.

"Years before Waters's arrival," said Milo.

"When did he get out?"

"Four months before Waters, early parole due to good behavior. Which from what I can tell from the prison website was something like going to church and classes in 'insight training,' maybe fashioning cute little plywood birdhouses for the prison gift shop."

"At least he had a P.O."

"You'd think that would help. Unfortunately, the Denver parole office is understaffed to the point where Bakstrom wasn't even assigned an officer for six weeks. He got room and board in a halfway house, courtesy of the taxpayers, but the P.O. had no idea who I was talking about and I had to bug her to pull up his file. He showed up for two visits then never again. Of course, she'd followed up, meaning going to the halfway house, confirming he'd absconded, and making note of it in the file. I called there, hoping for something. Guy who runs it said, 'They come and go, it's all we can do to stop them from stealing the furniture.'"

I said, "Where does Bakstrom hail from?"

"No ties to L.A., if that's what you mean. Born in Louisiana, spent time in Georgia and Maryland, then, from what I can tell, he drifted westward. We've got nothing on him locally but Colorado to California is a logical trajectory if he reunited with Waters."

"Go West, Young Felon."

Milo said, "Everyone wants to reinvent once they get a whiff of smog, right? My next step is trying to find out if Bakstrom filed for public assistance locally, got himself a credit card, a driver's license, a phone, or, God forbid, a legit job. Want to take bets on any of that?"

"Waters got a license."

"And nothing else that's on the records." Clicks on his end. "Hold for a sec."

Dead air, then: "That was Creech, the limo driver. He remembered something. In addition to taking Thalia out to dinner, he also took her to a cemetery in Hollywood. Couple of times a year but not for the past year. He has no idea who she visited because she always had him wait outside."

I said, "Only place I know of there is Hollywood Legends. I used to pass it driving to the hospital. Lots of Industry folk are buried there."

"Back to our girl Thalia's entertainment days?" he said.

"I'll drop by and try to find out. I've got patients tomorrow afternoon but a free morning. How about e-mailing Thalia's most recent DMV photo so I have something to show them."

"You think it's worth your time?"

"Know thy victim."

"Maybe she just visited Rudolph Valentino or some other squeeze from her era, but sure, appreciate it. In return, I can walk your pooch, clean your oven, or supply you with pricey distilled spirits."

"Chivas will do nicely," I said. "Once we make some progress, we'll toast."

"Love that optimism," he said. "Blue Label in a fancy box work for you?"

"Plain is fine."

"You ain't plain."

Know thy cemetery.

What began as Hollywood Memorial Park and Spiritual Gardens sits on fifty urban acres a couple of blocks east of the Paramount lot. Back when Hollywood was Hollywood, several studios made their home in the neighborhood, surrounding the cemetery and making it the butt of jokes.

Where do old actors go to die?

Forest Lawn if they've got cab fare, Hollywood Memorial if they don't.

Or:

The place is a drag.

How so?

Agents drag useless clients in. Then they dig extra holes for themselves and jump in.

Like the Aventura, the place had fallen into disrepair until a fire-sale purchase ten years ago. Unlike the Aventura, full up, no more rooms in the inn.

The new owner's history of developing amusement parks, and the rechristening to Hollywood Legends, fueled rumors that a "morbid Disneyland" was in the works. That sparked the expected preservationist outrage along with panic in families whose loved ones were interred in the ornate crypts, mausoleums, and granite-marked grave sites crowding the crumbling facility.

Lawsuits were filed, an arbitration board set up, compromise reached, with the purchasers assuring they had no intention of altering the cemetery's essential nature and promising to plow millions of dollars into renovation. Five years later, defects had been remedied and the families received notice that their maintenance fees were being quintupled. A second rash of suits led to Compromise 2.0: The owners agreed to double fees for five years, then tack on another twenty percent for the next fifteen, while obligating themselves to binding arbitration for any future increases. In return, they'd be allowed to offer "tasteful supplementary services on the property that maintained the dignity of this venerable, hallowed site, so rich in Los Angeles cultural history."

Examples of "tasteful" were classical music concerts and fundraisers for worthy causes.

What actually ensued was a steady stream of rock and hip-hop concerts, private parties, and filming of movies and rock videos. A gift shop memorializing the "high and mighty who chose to entrust their eternal remains to Hollywood Legends" was built. Every Halloween a cinematic masterpiece titled **Buckets of Blood** was screened, and tour buses were encouraged to make the park part of their circuit. Pathway markers directed gawkers to the graves of departed stars. The gift shop thrived.

Early outrage about rank commercialism sputtered, as it always does in L.A., profits from the "supplements" keeping the maintenance fees reasonable, everyone content.

Perfect for a city where the county coroner runs a retail website and guides driving pimped-up hearses cruise past the manors of dead rich people, doling out schadenfreude.

In L.A., death—the kind of death that attracts tour buses—is a production, no more, no less.

I got to the cemetery just after opening at nine A.M., parked on Melrose, and walked under a rococo stone arch topped by a menacing mop of wisteria. Lovely morning, warm, balmy, honey-lit.

Once you got past a Florentine fountain and a long, skinny reflecting pool reeking of chlorine, the gift shop was the first thing you saw.

The photo Milo had emailed of Thalia was as faithful as a DMV shot could be. One eyebrow arched higher than the other. Amused.

I showed it to the girl at the register, a young Latina with a gentle voice and a ready smile. To her side was a collection of coffee mugs silk-screened with the faces of film stars. A separate pyramid displayed beer steins featuring the sneering, acromegalic mien of a dead punk rocker named Billy Stink. Other wares included snow globes, T-shirts, stuffed animals, windbreakers, fuzzy hats with gravestone logos. A board game called Six Feet Wonder.

Too early to attract shoppers to all that treasure. I had the clerk's attention.

She said, "Sorry, don't know her."

"May I ask how long you've been working here?"

She hesitated.

I said, "She hasn't been here for over a year."

"Oh. Then I wouldn't see her. Ten months."

"Is there anyone who could help me?"

"Is she your grandma?"

"Great-aunt, just passed," I said. "She told me she came here to visit someone and I'd sure like to know who. Kind of a roots thing, you know?"

That confused her.

"Family research. I'm from Missouri, trying to learn about my California relatives."

"Oh," she said. "I've got cowboys from Texas in my family—maybe Pedro will know."

She got on the phone, called, hung up. "He'll be here soon."

Ninety seconds later, an older man wearing gray work clothes and a canvas hat entered.

He looked at me, then the clerk. "Tina?"

"This gentleman wants to know if his aunt came here to see anyone so he can find some family."

She held up the photo.

Pedro said, "Yeah . . . I think but not for a long time."

I said, "Aunt Thalia hasn't been here for over a year. She just passed away herself."

He was unmoved. No surprise, considering his job. "She's your aunt, you don't know your family?"

"I'm from Missouri, haven't seen the Califor-nia branch for years. Do guests sign a register or something that tells you who they're visiting?"

"Nah."

He took another glance at the photo. "You

want to look around, now's the time. Hour or so, we're going to have people looking at him."

Pointing to the Billy Stink cups. "Purple hair, green hair, they're always doing some kind of a ceremony. You wouldn't believe what they leave on his grave."

The girl said, "Ick."

I offered a conspiratorial frown.

He said, "Yeah, it's gross. Like to help you, but we don't follow anyone around, see where they go. Our rule is don't get nosy unless you see something illegal. Like the tour buses, they'll be pulling up soon, after they've seen the Chinese Theatre, Ripley's, all that junk." To Tina: "Tell him what they buy."

She said, "Mostly hats but they're always asking for food."

Pedro said, "Like this place gives them an appetite. Anyway . . ."

"Okay, thanks," I said. "I'll just walk around."

Pedro said, "I can tell you where **not** to bother with. You turn out of here you're going to see the big mausoleums, then a section that used to be a fishpond till they got rid of it to make room for people like **him**."

I said, "Dead musicians."

"Overdoses," said Tina.

Pedro said, "That crazy girl Patsy who did the

heroin and had her car painted with pills and marijuana leaves? People leave dope near her stone. I used to call the cops, they said throw it out so now I just throw it out. Is your grandma related to someone like that—are you?"

I smiled. "Not to my knowledge."

"Then you can avoid all that. After that, it's the Grand Mausoleum, which is all comedians from a long time ago, then the Regency Mausoleum, which is producers and directors and studio heads. They don't get a lot of visitors. You related to any of that kind of person?"

"Nope."

"There's also a Jewish part over by the southwest."

I shook my head.

"The Jews leave rocks," said Pedro. "The real old graves, from when we opened—1892—are out back against the back wall. You looking for something that old?"

"Unlikely."

"Okay, after that, it's up to you, friend." He plucked a cemetery map from a rack near the register, lifted a souvenir pen from a can, and circled the areas he'd listed.

Tina cleared her throat.

I said, "Happy to pay."

"Map is five dollars, pen is four."

I gave her cash.

Pedro said, "You should pay me commission, Tina."

She colored.

I said, "Thanks for the help, sir."

He leaned in, sniffed, and pretended to examine my hair. "Don't see no green or purple roots, you're not going to leave anything gross—last time it was a dead bat." He chuckled. "Unless you got some tattoos under those nice clothes."

"Not a one."

"I was in the marines, never messed with my skin even with a semper fi. Someone never fought, why would they do that?"

He left.

I said, "Some guy."

Tina said, "Tell me about it. He's my dad."

I walked by the mausoleums and a terribly wrought bronze sculpture of Billy Stink, the rocker two-handing a mike and grimacing as if his colon had corroded. The rest of the dead-musician section was small, just a couple of rows, and when I got closer I realized the markers weren't stone, they were some sort of resin. Nor did they mark actual resting spots. Jim Morrison was buried in Paris, Jimi Hendrix in Renton, Washington State, Keith Moon in Wembley,

England, all facts attested to by the writing on the memorials.

Virtual burial. Sign of the times.

When I got past all that and found myself facing acres of bona fide markers, the truth of Pedro's reservations hit me hard. Hundreds of grave sites. Unless I happened upon a **Mars,** what could I hope to achieve?

Even with that, all I'd have was the ancestor of a hundred-year-old woman.

I was about to leave when I spotted a man carrying a rake and an oversized dust-bin toward the rear of the cemetery. Same work clothes as Pedro but his headgear was a pith helmet. Younger than Pedro but not by much.

I caught up with him.

Florid, heavyset guy with a Boston terrier nose and massive forearms. "Yeah?"

I said, "My great-aunt used to come here and I'm trying to find out who she visited." I showed him the photo.

He said, "Nice lady, she always went to the same section. She tipped me for nothing. Haven't seen her in a while."

"She passed away last week."

"Oh," he said. "Sorry to hear it. She dressed nice, could walk okay for her age. Let me show you."

He looked at the twenty I offered. "This is more than she gave. You got a nice family."

He pocketed the bill, guided me to a single row toward the center of the cemetery, and left.

Well-weathered headstones, death dates ranging from the forties to the early sixties.

The tallest marker caught my eye. A good foot above the others, three plots from the end, black granite speckled with gold and topped by an exquisitely carved red granite crown.

Lemuel Leroy Hoke, Jr.
July 31, 1892–August 9, 1954
"My Kingdom Is of This World."

The gangster who'd purchased the Aventura in the thirties and turned it into a haven for gamblers, adulterers, and other seekers of entertainment before being busted for tax evasion.

I phone-googled. Hoke's name showed up in a list of pre–Bill Parker thugs. Convicted and sentenced in 1941.

Deceased thirteen years later, no mention if in custody or after release.

Four years prior to Hoke's death, the hotel had been bought by Conrad Grammar. Soon after, Thalia was a full-time resident, paying far more than a civil servant could afford.

Buying up real estate using mystery funds.

My Kingdom.

A self-styled monarch. Misspelled Monark?

Had moving Hoke's girlfriend in been **part** of the arrangement with Grammar? A sweetheart deal for a sweetheart?

In 1941, Thalia was twenty-three, Leroy Hoke, nearing fifty.

Money and power gravitating, as it always does, to youth and beauty?

Hoke's year of death reminded me of something else. I looked up the leather-bound gift book in Thalia's library.

Something Smithee . . . **Robber's Destiny.**

Published in 1953, just prior to Hoke's passing.

This guy got it. A man dying behind bars reminiscing?

Or sending a warning to his youthful paramour?

Hoke's gravestone was dusty. No flowers, no sign of a recent visit but the crown atop the grave said it all. So did the inscription inverting Jesus's declaration.

Self-proclaimed royalty.

Monark loves **Midget.**

Milo said, "Our sweet old lady really was a gun moll?"

I said, "Or at least a gangster's love interest."

"This from a gravestone."

"A grave she visited regularly until she grew feeble. The chronology fits. So does Hoke's prior ownership of the hotel and Thalia's being able to afford staying there after it was sold. He went to San Quentin but that doesn't mean he stopped doing business, and Thalia being his outside agent explains her real estate buys. Her early knowledge about foreclosures and other bargains would've been perfect synergy. And when Hoke died ten years later, she could've inherited everything, off the books."

"Hoke ever get out of Q?"

"Haven't checked, yet. Wanted to call you first."

"A gangster's gal . . . even if it's true, you see it connecting to her death seventy years later?"

"Maybe she wasn't worried about a psychopath in her family. What if Hoke's descendants paid her a visit and nosed around the topic of Great-Grandpa's dough?"

"That sounds like a scary visit," he said. "You didn't describe her as frightened."

"True, but if she was able to conceal a long romance with Hoke, she was an expert at hiding her feelings."

"Hundred-year-old siren worried about Bad Seed's bad seed," he said. "Mr. Waters and/or Mr. Bakstrom."

"Or the woman they're apparently sharing."

"Okay, it's somewhere to go, thanks. Let's see if San Quentin keeps decent records, talk to you later."

Back home, I got on the computer. Nothing on Leroy Hoke beyond a mention in a list of old-time L.A. gangsters published in an academic article on policing in L.A.'s pre- and post-Parker days. The author, a history professor at the U. named Maxine Driver.

I reached her at her office.

She said, "Hoke? No one's ever asked me

about him, he was pretty obscure. Usually, they want to know about Bugsy Siegel or Mickey Cohen."

"Hoke didn't make the big time?"

"From what I can gather he was up there in terms of criminality. But unlike Bugsy and Mickey, he avoided the limelight. Who exactly are you and why're you asking about him?"

"I'm a psychologist working with LAPD. It's a long story."

"I'm a historian, we're used to that. Can someone vouch for you at the police?"

"You bet."

She called Milo, phoned me back.

"I'm free in an hour. For an hour. Pizza Maniac in the Village."

The restaurant was a brick-walled beer joint for students, with pizza as an afterthought. I got there first, and per Maxine Driver's instructions ordered a small white pie with mushrooms and a pitcher of Bud. The beer I got to carry to a table. The pizza was served by a distracted-looking kid just as a woman's voice said, "Perfect timing."

Maxine Driver was in her late thirties, tall, lithe, Asian, with a short glossy do that evoked the Flapper Era. Clinging black slacks and a matching sweater emphasized the sparseness of her frame. She toted a huge black purse. A big diamond glinted from her left ring finger.

"Dr. Delaware? Maxine." Her handshake was strong, dry, business-like.

"Thanks for meeting me."

She peeled off a crescent of pizza and nibbled a corner. "Good timing for dinner. My husband practices gastro at Santa Monica Hospital. Colonoscopies until eight P.M."

She smiled. "Hope that doesn't ruin your appetite."

Mentioning her marital status to set boundaries? The rock on her finger would've sufficed. Then again, attention to detail would serve her well in her profession.

I said, "Worked at a hospital for years, no problem."

"Which one?"

"Western Peds."

"Kids," she said. "I couldn't handle seeing them sick." She incised another millimeter. "You're not indulging?"

"Small pie," I said. "All for you."

Maxine Driver laughed. "I have to remember about male appetites. David—my husband—could snarf three of these and claim he was dieting. Anyway, Leroy Hoke: I looked up my records, didn't find much but made you a copy of what I have."

Out of the purse came a manila envelope. Neat black lettering on the flap. **HOKE, LL.**

I thanked her, offered to pour her a beer.

She said, "Only if you're having. Food's one thing, drinking alone has a weird alkie feel to it."

I filled two mugs. She kept working at the slice of pizza, daintily but steadily. A surgical scalpel versus Milo's buzz saw.

When she finished chewing, I held up the envelope. "I'll read every word but if there's anything between the lines—"

"You want something psychological?" she said. "A personality analysis? I'm not one of those historians who think they're Freud. But even if I was, there's not much known about Leroy other than he was bad to the bone. A rawboned character. I guess in that way he **was** different."

"From other mobsters."

"L.A.'s scene was mostly urban—transplants from the East Coast. Mickey and Bugsy were both originally from New York, as were a lot of the guys who came out here to explore their options. L.A. was considered wide-open territory. Before Bugsy invented Vegas, everyone thought we were going to be the next Sodom. Wild Bill Parker eventually disabused them of that notion, but before he came on the scene, the organized scene was thriving. The movie business helped because there was a natural affinity between actors and bad guys. Any thoughts about that? Psychologically speaking?"

"Creative people like to see themselves as outsiders," I said.

"Creative people and fakers," said Maxine Driver. "That was the topic of my doctoral dissertation: posers and hangers-on attracted to the short-term gratification of crime as entertainment. My primary thesis was the more ambiguous the product, the greater the opportunity for bullshit artists and criminals to move in."

"Mobsters at Hollywood parties," I said.

"And vice versa. But it went beyond socializing. Dirty money was routinely laundered through production deals because the studios needed quick cash and took out short-term loans from questionable sources. The ultimate meld was a guy like George Raft, a gangster who actually became an actor."

She smiled. "Mob-connected crooners we won't even talk about."

I said, "Hoke was part of that scene."

"No, that's the thing, he doesn't seem to have been. In all the research I've done, I haven't picked up a single shot of him at Ciro's, not a word about his hobnobbing with the stars. When I told you he was obscure, I meant it."

"He kept out of the public eye."

"He certainly didn't play to the press like the

others. Nor have I found any association between him and other gangsters."

"Lone wolf."

"He had his own gang, you can't pull off the
jobs he's suspected of as a solo artist."

"What kind of jobs?"

"He was suspected of an armored car heist,
kidnapping for ransom, a big-time jewel theft."

"Suspected but not arrested."

"His name came up in police reports but
there was never any follow-up that I could find."

"Connections other than showbiz?"

"Who knows? He did start out in Culver City
and it was extremely corrupt over there—local
police alerting bootleggers to raids."

She picked up a second slice. "A few of his associates disappeared permanently."

"Sweet guy."

"I suppose he had his charm. They finally got
him for taxes, just like Capone."

She sipped beer. "What I find interesting, reviewing my material, is even though Leroy
doesn't appear to have associated with any other
major bad guys, he didn't inspire obvious ani-
mosity or competition. If he had, he wouldn't
have lasted as long as he did."

"Never ratted out by anyone," I said.

"Never shot at," said Maxine Driver.

"Disappearing associates would help."

"It would have discouraged loose lips but it wouldn't have stopped one of the bosses going after him, they were utterly ruthless. Bugsy earned his nickname by being a mad-dog killer, but God help you if you called him that. He still got taken out, over in Virginia Hill's house in Beverly Hills. Mickey's house in Brentwood got bombed, though he survived."

First-name basis with her subjects. The same place Milo inevitably reaches with victims.

She said, "Mickey **was** attacked while in prison. Survived and got released and died peacefully in his sleep. But as far as I've heard, no one roughed Leroy up in San Quentin. He died there."

"Where did he hail from?"

"Oklahoma."

"Classic Dust Bowl story?"

"If it was, he didn't stay poor very long. His first address was in Culver, like I said. But his second address was a big house in the hills near the Hollywood Bowl. Torn down years ago—it's all in the file."

I said, "Maybe rural roots led him to keep his own counsel."

Maxine Driver's eyes widened. "Interesting you should say that, it's another one of my themes: For all that criminals pride themselves on deviation from social norms, they're conservative when it comes to race and ethnicity. Like the gangs of today. You get occasional racial crossover but for the most part, people stay with their kind. My family's from Seoul and I've finally gotten to the point where I can study Korean gangs with detachment. Same story. People even remain loyal to their villages back in the old country. Now how about telling me why a psychologist working with the police is curious about Leroy."

"A homicide victim might have known him."

"That would have to be a cold, cold case."

"A brand-new homicide," I said.

She frowned. "Leroy died sixty years ago. Are we talking a victim who was a kid back then?"

"A young woman. Possibly a girlfriend."

She put the pizza down. "Math isn't my strong suit, but she'd still have to be pretty old."

"She was nearly a hundred."

"Wow," said Maxine Driver. "And someone murdered her? That's sick. Why do you think she knew Leroy?"

"She visited his grave regularly and his name cropped up in her personal effects."

"Leroy's girlfriend," she said. "Well, that would be a nice bit of new data. So, what, she lasts a century and someone gets her? Bizarre. But I can't imagine it would relate to Leroy."

"Probably not but the cops are looking at everything. What can you tell me about Leroy's love life?"

"Nothing. If he was married, I've never found a record of it. The same goes for consorting with party girls, strippers, actresses, the usual gangster thing. Was your victim one of those?"

"Don't know, yet."

Red nails re-tweezed the slice of pizza. "I look for interesting subjects and Leroy wasn't until now. What can **you** tell **me** about this woman?"

"Nothing more, sorry."

"Oh, c'mon."

"Ongoing investigation."

Maxine Driver frowned. "I'll accept that for the moment but when the cops do close it, you need to offer some reciprocity, I want a nice juicy publication out of it."

"Fair enough."

"More than fair. I'm serious, going to hold you to it."

She drank half a beer, took most of the pizza to go, said nothing when I paid.

Outside the restaurant, we shared a briefer, firmer handshake.

I thanked her again.

She said, "The way to thank me is to keep your word."

"Promise."

"A psychologist digging up the past for the cops, you really didn't explain that but I've got to run. One thing I can tell you, Wild Bill wouldn't have trucked with therapists. He preferred tossing mobsters off cliffs."

"Finesse," I said.

"Hey, it worked. He cleaned up the city and the mob never regained a foothold. There's always a trade-off, of course. Order versus personal liberty. My priorities shift depending on the headlines."

"Mine, too."

She said, "I really do expect you to contact me once you're able to be more forthcoming."

"Scout's honor."

Frosty smile. "I was a Brownie. And by the way, I'm also conversant with your field. Double-majored, psych and history. Hated math, all those statistics courses for psych, so I did the humanities thing."

She studied me. "Sounds like you're into the **in**humanities. Maybe we've got something in common."

CHAPTER
18

I opened the envelope in my car.

Generous receptacle, sparse contents.

Maxine Driver had included the same list I'd pulled off the Internet, with Leroy Hoke's name circled in yellow. Next came photocopies of Hoke's black-and-white San Quentin mugshot and data card. The photo showed a fair-haired man with dark brooding eyes. The hair was wavy and piled high and the stats clarified the color. **Red.** Lighter patches at the temples that were probably gray; notable freckles on forehead and cheeks.

Five-eleven, one hundred forty-six pounds fit the bony, knife-blade visage glaring at the prison photographer. Lantern jaw, off-kilter boxer's nose, narrow mouth, skimpy unamused lips.

The eyes, listed as **Black,** were narrow and accusing, set deeply and shadowed by a shelf of brow.

A scar ran diagonally across a meaty cleft chin. One ear was set higher than the other, protruded a bit and was missing a section of lobe.

Despite less-than-ideal parts, a surprising outcome for the whole. Not a bad-looking guy.

The card listed scars on chin, arms, back, and buttocks. No tattoos, no warnings of violent tendencies, just a notation that the prisoner had led a "criminal enterprise."

Aliases: **Oklahoma Red, Tulsa Red, Double-L, Okie King, Sir "H," Monark.**

The remaining contents consisted of two sheets of paper containing photocopied snippets from articles in the **L.A. Herald-Express,** the **Mirror,** and the **Times,** again with Hoke's name accented in yellow.

Each clipping reported on unsolved crimes, beginning with a broad-daylight armored car robbery on Sixth Street, downtown, that remained "mysterious" after a year of investigation. Police had looked into "criminal gangs led by 'Italians' and other mobsters" including Mickey Cohen, L. L. "Tulsa Red" Hoke, and "colored kingpin Julius 'Papa Blue' Carpentier."

Similar outcomes were detailed for a smash-and-grab jewel theft at a posh store in Pasadena, bank robberies in Culver City, Mid-Wilshire, and San Gabriel, and the "enigmatic disappearance" of a truckload of furs intended for Bullocks Wilshire.

The final felony was another jewel theft in 1938, this one in Beverly Hills, accomplished in the dead of night.

The wall separating Elena's Dress Shoppe on Rodeo Drive from Frederick LaPlante Fine Jewelers had been breached, probably with hand tools. The burglary netted "countless bracelets, necklaces and rings and other faceted female finery." An unconfirmed rumor said some of the glitz had been set aside for the tenth annual Oscars gala, held at the Biltmore Hotel.

For that one, "publicity-shy" Hoke was described as a "serious person of interest," then quoted as "denying his involvement unequivocally through a spokesman and offering an iron-clad alibi: At the time of the robbery, he'd been in a back booth at Perino's, "dining in full view of numerous citizens, including society notables."

That claim, the **Mirror** was happy to add, "was confirmed by our journalists."

No mention of Hoke's suspected ownership of the Aventura Hotel.

No photos of Monark with anyone, let alone a diminutive young moll named Midget.

I drove home and worked the computer,

using Driver's information. Nothing, until I came upon a series of photographs commemorating Perino's sixty-four-year run as an haute-cuisine hangout in 1940.

A black-and-white photo spanned three groups of diners. Film folk on both sides, the reason the shot had been archived.

It was the middle banquette that interested me.

In the center, a fair-haired, dark-eyed ectomorph in a broad-shouldered tuxedo, with a half-eaten wedge of cream pie in front of him, nursed what looked to be a cup of coffee. To his left was a hulking, pug-faced man twice Leroy Hoke's width, his beverage a crystal stein of foam-topped beer.

To Hoke's right sat a tiny blond beauty in her twenties. Nestled under the gangster's arm, delicate fingers resting near a Martini glass.

Pixie face, big eyes, darkly rouged lips. A black spaghetti-strap dress set off pale shoulders and a swan neck. Young enough to be Hoke's daughter but nothing daughterly about the mischievous half smile she beamed up at him.

Nothing fatherly about his hand dangling over her shoulder, a pinkie looped languidly around a strap.

No way to be certain she was a young Thalia. Nothing said she wasn't.

I studied the picture, thought I found familiarity in the huge, lively eyes, the subtle amusement.

My bet would be Yes. I'd take almost any odds.

I stayed at my desk for another hour and a half, searching for info on any crimes linked to Hoke. No coverage of the earlier felonies in the **Mirror** piece, but the Frederick LaPlante robbery had been a big enough deal to merit ink in all four L.A. papers. Same story as the **Mirror**, nearly word for word, which meant regurgitation of an LAPD press release.

Researching the jewelry store brought up a story about its opening four years prior to the heist, in **The Beverly Hills Monitor,** a free weekly, now defunct, with a flexible attitude toward syntax and style. The font looked as if it had been typed and mimeographed.

Fine European Jewels Flock To The Verdant Hills of Beverly.

There are considerable admirations of the gifts and talents of Count Frederick Charles Normandy Etienne De LaPlante, a post–World War I emigre from Paris, France, who has dazzled us constantly and most consistently due to his esteemed history as a noted **desinatrace de bijoux** who has formerly and prominently consulted to Cartier and other Gallic geniuses of glamour. Thus acquiring first-hand expert knowledge of both exquisitely rarified items and also Olde Worlde **haute** jewelry — artistry at the most demanding and discerning level.

Included among the Count's recent treasured acquisitions now brought to our temperate California shores under cover of discretion and taste, are a more than 15 karat flawless diamond said to have been worn by Marie Antoinette within hours of her decapitation at the hand of bloodthirsty, merciless revolters, also the massive Inca Goddess Emerald from the Andes of Peru presented in its original guanaco-lined case, an animal that only exists at the most alpine level of the Ande mountains. Eyes have glistened viewing so many others including the 57 karat Wine of the Nile ruby, said to have been excavated by daring explorers and orientalism near an ancient Egyptian pyramid.

But these are not all, Count LaPlante's sanctum of fabulous facets has items to satisfy any level of connoisseurship.

A headshot at the top portrayed a wax-mustachioed dead ringer for Errol Flynn, if Flynn had put on midlife weight.

I keyworded LaPlante's full title and name, found an article dated six years after the heist in the **New York Post.**

This one was anything but puff:

Fake-Frog Scamster Unveiled as Count-Me-Out Count

A phony French nobleman palming himself off as an art consultant to the rich, famous, and gullible, has been revealed as an all-American con-man who's coasted for years on the stupidity of the moneyed set.

Fred Bullard Drancy, born in a working class section of Boston, and convicted as a young man of numerous shams, swindles and scams, managed to go almost clean for a few years when he worked as a delivery driver for Shreve, Crump and Lowe in Beantown. A few years later, he'd moved to California, was palming himself off as a Gallic hoo-hah with the unwieldy moniker Count Frederick Normandy De LaPlante.

Police say Drancy's m.o. was to leverage his fake aristocracy in order to consign expensive jewelry from other merchants with no down payment. The items were then marked up and unloaded on hare-brained heirs and heiresses.

Though chronically late paying his suppliers, Drancy did eventually come through and the scheme worked so well that he was able to open a jewelry store on Rodeo Drive, the poshest shopping street in Beverly Hills. There, he kept raising the stakes by "investing" in progressively more expensive gewgaws that he continued to peddle to naïve West Coast celebrities. It was only when a robbery cleaned out Drancy's stock and exposed his lack of insurance that furious gem dealers began digging into his background and uncovered his shady past. Drancy hightailed it from LaLa Land, laid low for a while, then had the chutzpah to re-invent himself as an Old Masters expert in Manhattan without even changing his ersatz name.

Drancy's Gotham scheme finally met an end when a Long Island City storage unit housing paintings he'd "borrowed" was broken into and looted. Drancy is currently in The Tombs awaiting arraignment on multiple charges, though word has it that he may be able to skate because fancy-pants Upper East Side art dealers will be reluctant to expose themselves to ridicule at being shellacked by a career con-man with a sixth-grade education.

No mention of suspects in the art burglary. At the time, Leroy Hoke had resided in San Quentin.

I paired Hoke with a succession of keywords: **laplante, drancy, midget, thalia, mars.** The last pulled up gazillions of hits on the joys of astronomy and the virtues of candy bars.

The lack of anything else was consistent with Maxine Driver's characterization of Hoke as publicity-shy. If he had masterminded the LaPlante job, entrusting his legitimately employed girlfriend with the take also fit. So would using her as his agent while in prison.

Thalia's path to fortune was another nice mesh: Parlaying a cache of stolen jewelry into legal real estate purchases was Laundering 101.

A cute little city accountant could avoid scrutiny if she bought steadily and slowly. She'd certainly avoided scrutiny about living in a luxury hotel suite whose rent far surpassed her salary.

A tribute to her smarts? Or had she inherited connections from Hoke during the pre-Parker days when corruption was a municipal pastime?

If her wealth had been rooted in crime, had she come to feel guilty nearing the end of an astonishingly long life? Trying to atone with spontaneous acts of charity but, not content with that, deciding it was time to talk to someone about it?

Milo likes to say psychologists are the yea-sayers of our times. Who better than a psychologist who'd worked with the cops and knew something about the criminal mind when it came to setting a former moll's mind at ease?

Or perhaps Thalia was just fine with the way she'd lived her life and the spawn of a man whose associates tended to disappear had shown up wanting to talk about that life.

Some scion of Monark's family tree ferreting out Thalia's link to his ancestor and believing himself entitled to whatever remained of Hoke's fortune.

Scion or scions.

The Birkenhaars from Austria. Fake accent, most probably a fake name.

Assumed names, like the inflated biographies of celebrities and politicians, were often crafted to impress. Case in point: Fred Drancy aka Count Frederick et cetera LaPlante.

Was it a bud from **his** family tree that had sought to take root in Thalia's life?

Lots of possibilities, but no facts. I couldn't even be certain that the girl at Perino's was Thalia.

Monark and Midget.

I studied the photo again. Made progress convincing myself. Considered calling Milo but decided not to, no sense dumping a whole lot of what-if on him, this early in the game.

At nine P.M., Robin was reading in bed and I was playing guitar in a corner chair. The Brazilian music she likes at night, lovely meld of simplicity that lulls the listener and complexity that challenges the player. I was trying some new chord inversions on "Corcovado" when the phone rang.

Milo said, "Mr. Waters is absent no more. Oops, poor choice of words. He's here, but he's gone."

CHAPTER

19

The dump site was in Pacific Palisades, above Pacific Coast Highway, just past the Getty Villa and up a skinny bait-worm of a street.

Unremarkable houses sat on too-small lots. The air was cool and salty and expensive. Between the meager space separating the homes, glimpses of ocean flashed, starlit onyx. I drove until a cop slouching against a cruiser stopped me.

My name got me waved to the end of the block. A construction site, what looked to be the beginnings of a mega-mansion.

Block foundation, wooden framing, fake-tile roof, all of which appeared shopworn. Heaps of trash filled most of the lot. An Andy Gump with its door agape and a poorly tended rent-a-fence completed the picture: The project hadn't been worked on for a while.

The drive-in gate was chain-locked but the fence, high and topped by barbed wire, sported a man-sized hole. Milo had filled me in as I drove. Discovery of the body had been accidental, a pair of lovebirds, barely thirteen, sneaking out of their houses a few blocks east, had hurried over to the site with plans of passion amid rusted rebar, warped plywood, and rotting roof shingles.

A regular thing for the kids, as it turned out. Nice to know the girl/boy-next-door thing had durability.

This time, a stench gave them pause, curiosity surpassing true love and hormones.

Tracing the reek, the kids had discovered something rotted worse than the shingles. Horror-struck but fascinated, they'd illuminated the body with the flashlight the girl always brought because she was studying ballet and didn't want to "fall down and mess up my body in the dark."

Romeo and Juliet stood off to the side now, near an officer absently working his cellphone. Both were blond, cute, skinny, the girl taller and surprisingly composed. The boy cowered next to her, eyes hazed by huge, red-rimmed designer eyeglasses.

Milo said, "Sean and Shawna. Adorable, no? All four parents are M.D.'s and pals and were out to dinner. On their way back, now, and mightily irritated. I might need to offer the young'uns some police protection."

His smile was a grim strobe. "Little Lothario looks freaked out, no? Maybe he'll need you, as well."

I said, "Nothing like ambulance chasing. It's definitely Waters?"

"We'll verify with prints but, yeah, there's enough left to say it is."

"Where's the body?"

He pointed at one of the junk heaps. I moved toward it.

He said, "Sure, why not."

Gerard Waters's naked body had been covered with objects taken from the trash, each one tagged with an evidence marker: scrap wood, broken blocks, a sheet of black plastic tarp pocked by little jagged holes that Milo assured me were the work of Mickey and Minnie. "They chewed on him a little, too. Over here. And here."

Indicating the ragged tips of fingers. And toes. Then a pile of vomit.

"Courtesy Sean. After Shawna pulled back the tarp and exposed the face."

I said, "Tough girl."

Milo said, "Blood doesn't bother her, she wants to be a surgeon like Daddy and Mommy. They run a plastic practice in Malibu. Nip and tuck won't help Mr. Waters."

Another point: neck flesh flaccid and sloughing. A hunk of shoulder mottled like overripe cheese.

I said, "He wearing anything?"

"Stripped nude."

I bent and took a closer look. The face was bloated and decaying, folds and wrinkles filled with fluid and gas, straining like the seams of too-tight trousers. Crime lab pole-lights accentuated the damage but failed to clarify the precise color of the skin. I guessed gray. Maybe overlaid with purple. Maybe even some green.

A dark patch nearly hid the tattoo on the left calf. Degraded but I could still make it out. Daffy Duck.

I said, "A lot of decomp for how cool it's been."

"C.I. guesses he was kept warm somewhere else before being moved."

I said, "Any idea what killed him?"

"Single bullet, here." Poking the back of his own skull. "No casing, no exit wound, and our chewy friends have enlarged the entry hole. But when you poke around, the tunnel's narrow enough to say small caliber."

"You stuck your finger in there?"

"After the C.I. okayed it." He grinned and stuck out his hand. "Shake on it, buddy."

"I'll take your word for it."

"In answer to your next question, until the pathologist weighs in, best estimate of time is the C.I.'s off-the-record guess. Days, not hours."

"Soon after Waters cleared out on his landlord," I said. "He went to meet up with his partners, maybe figured they'd all be traveling, and got a surprise. If Thalia's bungalow had given up serious cash, the pie got reduced to two slices."

"Miss Hotcha-Hotcha and Mr. Handsome," he said. "That's the scene I picture. I went back to the hotel today and showed Henry Bakstrom's mug to Refugia and a couple of desk clerks. They all had trouble seeing past the Mohawk but no one said it couldn't be Bakstrom. Then I showed it to Alicia Bogomil and she said ninety percent it was him."

"Cop eyes."

"Or she's eager to please. Techs will be looking for prints on or near the body and with the bullet still in Waters's head, maybe it'll give up something."

I said, "Why dump the body here when there are trails and canyons up the coast?"

"You're thinking someone familiar with the

neighborhood. Bakstrom and Bad Girl going high-rent?"

"Not necessarily. There are cheap motels in Santa Monica and Venice. I'm suggesting this isn't random because bad guys tend to stay close to home and they've also been known to work freelance jobs, like pickup construction."

"Maybe Bakstrom was here nailing or pouring concrete," he said. "Good point, I'll talk to the contractor. Probably the former contractor, the kids say no one's worked here for a while."

"People hike in rural spots, not in junkyards," I said. "If Mr. and Ms. Cute were in a hurry to split and knew the job was abandoned, this would be the perfect dump spot. Give them a head start while decay sets in and hinders identification. Maybe they were hoping the remains would eventually end up in some recycling facility. Unfortunately for them, Romeo and Juliet intervened."

"Head start," he said. "So they're already in the wind."

"I was a criminal with a windfall, I wouldn't stick around."

Noise on the other side of the fence drew our attention. A quartet of well-dressed people in their forties passed through and converged on the young lovers. A rush of hugs was followed by angry adult oration and allegro finger-wagging.

Shawna stood her ground; Sean tried to hide behind her but his mother yanked him out by the arm and worked her mouth rapidly.

The uniform pretending to watch the kids looked over at Milo. Milo pushed his palm frontward. Permission to leave. The cop said something, the parents took the kids with them.

As the families separated, Shawna finger-waved at Sean and Sean blew a kiss.

Milo said, "Rome and Jule save the day and now they're gonna get grounded."

"Send 'em consolation prizes," I said. "LAPD flashlights for future exploration."

He laughed. "I'll walk you to your car."

I said, "Can your mental state handle some purely theoretical input?"

"I'm made of stern stuff. What?"

I told him what I'd learned about Leroy Hoke, the LaPlante/Fred Drancy robberies, the cute young blonde at Perino's nestling under Hoke's arm.

"You think she's Thalia."

"What's your opinion?" I showed him the photo on my phone.

He said, "Could be. That's Hoke, huh? Kinda country . . . who's the hulk with them?"

"No idea."

He returned the phone. "Let's assume our gal made her fortune laundering the wages of sin. How does that help solve her murder?"

"Hoke was never arrested for the LaPlante robbery and I haven't found any record of the jewels being recovered. But not long after, he got sent up for tax evasion. What if he was betrayed by an insider? Not Thalia. If she'd sold Hoke out, she wouldn't have lasted a week. But a year before he died he sent her a book about a heist gone wrong due to betrayal. 'Hey this guy got it.' That could've been a warning about another potential back-stab."

"Why warn her ten years after he got sent up?"

"Maybe because it was shortly after Thalia got active financially, until then she'd been lying low. Think about it: She'd just moved into the Aventura and was buying real estate. Maybe Hoke activated her because **his** priorities changed. He got sick, knew he didn't have long and wanted to take care of Thalia. Or just the opposite, he was figuring to get out and wanted to take care of himself. Either way, a tax felon sitting on an illicit fortune risked discovery and confiscation. So he used Thalia as a shadow investor. But raising her profile brought its own risk, so he sent her the book, with a coded message to be careful."

"Telling her to watch out for some other thug. An associate Hoke hadn't managed to disappear."

"Or," I said, "the victim of the heist, not exactly a solid citizen, himself."

"Count Whoever."

"Aka Fred Drancy."

He pulled out a panatela, jammed it in his mouth, unlit. As his jaws clenched and slackened, the cigar bobbed like a yardarm.

"Thalia couldn't have been at serious risk, Alex. She survived another sixty-plus years."

"Which supports what we've been saying: Hoke took care of the immediate threat but it crossed generations."

"Third-, fourth-generation bad seeds."

"One of whom could be lying right there. Wars have been fought based on thousand-year grudges, the same for family feuds. Maybe there's a clan that's passed down a story of being cheated out of a big score, and one of the offspring finally decided to do something about it. Thalia told me she chose me because I worked with you. Her plan was to make sure I could be trusted, then get you involved. Even at the risk of making herself an accessory to a whole lot of long-cold crimes. At her age, what could any-one do to her? Unfortunately, her timing was off."

He took out a matchbook, tore off a match, bent it, slipped it into his pocket. The cigar fol-lowed. "So all I have to do is look for some low-life who hung with Hoke in the bad old days and trace his family tree."

"Or start with Waters and Bakstrom and work backward."

"The natural history of nasties . . . lemme see that picture again."

I retrieved the Perino's shot.

"The other guy," he said, "central casting, goon, no? We find out his name was Moose Bak-strom or Biff Waters, I'll buy you a **case** of Chi-vas. Blue, green, name your color."

I said, "We could start with the original case files on Hoke's tax bust and the LaPlante rob-bery."

"Something that old won't be computerized, and paper files are dumped in some out-in-the-boonies place the department claims is an ar-chive."

"I'll call Maxine Driver tomorrow, see if she has advice."

"There you go," he said.

As we headed for the Seville, he found the

match and the panatela and lit up. "History's peachy, but I'm kinda partial to current events."

I reached Driver at ten A.M.

"You have something to tell me?"

"More like another question."

Silence. "I see."

"Once the case is resolved, you'll be the first person I call."

"You remind me of a guy I dated in grad school. Very earnest, lots of promises."

"He keep any of them?"

"A few."

"I'll do better."

"Ha. What now?"

"I'd like to email you a photo of Hoke with a man, see if you can identify him."

I pushed a button. She said, "Where'd you get this?"

"Web article on Perino's."

"Darn, wish I'd thought of that. Is the girl your centenarian victim?"

"Maybe. Any idea who the bruiser is?"

"Nope, sorry. Looks like a bodyguard."

"Is there anyone you can think of who'd know more about Hoke?"

"Doubtful, gangster-research isn't exactly a hot topic for historians," she said. "The grant money goes to gender inequality and colonialism—wait a sec, there **might** be someone. Janet Pitcairn at Princeton, I see her at conferences. She's into the East Coast mob, gets foundation dough by framing it as research on ethnic immigration patterns. Maybe she knows someone, I'll give her a call."

"Ask her about Fred Drancy—Count LaPlante's real name. He was originally from Boston but moved to New York after the robbery and got into big-time trouble."

I told her about the art theft.

She said, "Same M.O., different commodity. Maybe Drancy was a co-conspirator in the jewel thing, not a victim?"

"I hadn't thought about that but sure, why not? With the consignors cut out, his share would've been larger than if he'd operated legitimately. Excellent idea, Professor. Thanks."

"Maxine's fine and you know how to thank me—yes, I'm a tape loop."

"Persistence," I said. "Perfect for research."

"A heckuva lot more productive than spending all afternoon arranging one's shoes so they face precisely the same way. Which is not to say I wasn't an ideal child."

"I really appreciate the time, Maxine."

"I probably shouldn't admit it," she said, "but this is turning out to be fun. My parents wanted me to be an orthodontist. They still have no clue why I do what I do."

I left messages for Milo. He called in shortly after two P.M.

I told him Driver's conjecture about Drancy. "If it's true, add his offspring to the bad seed list."

"I like it," he said. "His being in on it woulda made the job a cinch. Alarm's off, safe door's unlocked. What I don't like is an expanded suspect pool but yeah, it's definitely worth considering. Meanwhile, I've got a few more facts on Hoke. He was sentenced to eleven years, came down with cancer a few months before his release date and died in the prison infirmary. Prison historian only found one visitors log, covers the last three years. One person for Hoke, Christmas, Easter, July Fourth, Labor Day. Woman who signed in as Thelma Myers, no other details. She also shows up after Hoke's death as custodian of his body. Without her, he'd have ended up in an unmarked grave on the prison grounds."

"Thelma, Thalia."

"Myers, Mars. Everyone reinvents themselves, Alex. No records that I can find, for all we know her real name's Lola Montez."

I said, "Limiting her visits to four times a year fits with keeping a low profile. So does showing up on holidays when she could get lost in a flood of visitors and wouldn't be missed at her job."

"I called Vollmer—the archive—to get Hoke's arrest file and anything on the jewel thing. Gonna take a while, only one guy handles all the requests, some wild-child who managed to slide from homicide to traffic to eating dust and mold. He said he'd search manually, maybe he even will. No luck on the dump-site contractor, either, can't get a response from the owners, property's under dispute in a divorce."

"Send me Bakstrom's photo, I'll go back and see if anyone recognizes him working there."

"Don't waste your time, Alex, we already canvassed the neighborhood."

"Let me try, anyway."

"Persistent."

"Better than arranging toy soldiers so they face the same way."

"What?"

"Send the picture. Anything on the bullet in Waters's head?"

"Too messed up for ballistics, all they can say is it's a .22. Which is kind of like saying a hit-and-run victim encountered a car. The pathologist did say she found the decomp impressive, given the date we know Waters cut out on his landlord, so he probably was stored somewhere hot and humid."

I said, "Waters being killed so soon after Thalia's murder could mean he was a pawn from the beginning."

"Mr. and Ms. Adorable are anything but? Maybe one of **them** should be worrying. Why slice the pie at all?"

"Waters and Bakstrom were cellies. If Bakstrom already knew the woman, she could be on **his** visitors log."

"So she could . . . that mind of yours, who says there's no perpetual motion machine—all right, the photo's coming your way. A better one actually, I had a tech guy Photoshop the Mohawk into oblivion. Went back to the hotel, now Refugia says probably and Bogomil says for sure. I put a BOLO out on him."

The image came through.

I said, "Perfect."

He said, "There you go, back to boosting my self-esteem."

Too late that day but the following afternoon, equipped with Henry Bakstrom's cleaned-up visage, I drove to Pacific Palisades.

Blue skies and golden sun can prettify anything but the unfinished construction fared poorly in the daylight, wood turned ashy and ragged by glare, fissures on blocks wound-like, the gouged earth soupy and arid in equal proportions.

No entry, the damaged section of fence had been replaced. But the spot where Waters had been tossed was obvious: a barren rectangle of dirt. I turned, ready to begin my door-to-door, when I spotted a woman descending the crest and heading my way. Fast pace, dictated by the small dog walking her.

She saw me and crossed the street. My waiting around made her glance at me nervously. Forties, brunette, tight body in a jean jacket, black leggings, yellow running shoes.

As she passed, I smiled and said, "Excuse me."

She kept going but the dog skidded to a halt and studied me. She tugged; grimaced as her canine boss stood its ground. Stocky brown-and-white mutt, probably heavier than its size would imply. Staffordshire terrier mixed with something low-rise like corgi or dachshund.

The woman said, "Shit, Petey! **Go!**"

Petey planted his legs and kept appraising me. I said, "He's cute."

The woman finally made eye contact. Yanking the now taut leash and cursing silently. Her glare said it was all my fault.

No sense pushing it. I began walking.

"Hold on, there!" I looked behind me. She'd recrossed the street and was charging toward me. Whipped out her phone and began jabbing buttons while in motion. Made a mistake and cursed and tried again and dropped the phone.

Petey looked amused. I retrieved it and handed it to her. She snatched it. Petey assumed an obedient sit.

"Now you behave?" Scowling and sun-creased, but not a bad face. Maybe even capable of pretty when not compressed in anger.

I said, "Is something the matter?" I flashed my LAPD consultant badge.

"What's that?"

"I work with the police."

"With? What does that mean?"

"My name is Alex Delaware. Feel free to call Lieutenant Sturgis at the West L.A. station." I recited the number.

She said, "Why should I believe you?"

"You don't have to," I said. "Call and verify." I smiled at Petey. He produced a noise that began as a low growl but ended up as a friendly purr.

I said, "Hey, there, little guy."

No aggression but no smile; Blanche is the only dog I've known who can strikingly simu-late human joy.

The woman tugged the leash for no apparent reason. Petey bared his teeth. Big teeth for a small pooch. He raised a leg and let out an impressive fart. Shook himself off with pride. I laughed.

The woman said, "I don't see what's funny. Especially not here. This is a terrible place."

"The murder. I was called to the scene."

"Hmm . . . give me your name again."

"Alex Delaware."

She stared at her phone but did nothing with it. "No one's telling us a thing and we don't feel safe. Let me see that thingie again."

She squinted at the badge. In need of glasses but not wearing them. "Behavioral science?"

"I'm a psychological consultant—"

"Oh, shit," she said. "You're profiling? There's a crazed serial killer here?"

"Definitely not. I'm here to do follow-up—"

"About what?"

"I'm talking to people who live here and might be able—"

"The police already came door-to-door. Not very polite, considering they wanted my help. Now they send a psychologist? To do what? Shrink our heads."

I sighed.

She said, "Am I causing you stress?"

I pocketed the badge, walked to the Seville.

"What?" she said. "This happens and I have to be nice about it? What's nice about someone being killed? About that piece of **shit**." Pointing to the construction.

"The project?"

"Piece of absolute shit. They tear down a perfectly nice Spanish and plan a ten-thousand-
square-foot piece of I-don't-know, everything's
lovey-dovey according to her, meanwhile everyone knows he's bringing bimbos home while she's
traveling. And when he's gone, she's going off with
the contractor. They're lowlifes. From Europe!"

"Where in Europe?"

"Sweden, Denmark, someplace like that. Don't
ask me how they made their money, what I do
know is they brought bad karma here when they
tore the Spanish down. Then someone gets murdered? Un-be-liev-able. Who was the victim?"

"No one from here," I said.

"That doesn't tell me anything."

"Sorry, Ms.—"

"Like I'm going to give you my name? Last
time I gave my name I got served with papers.
By the rat-bastard."

"Your ex."

"Don't call him that. He's nothing to me."

Petey looked up at her and let loose more
wind.

She said, "Look at this, you've delayed his
bowels, now his schedule's going to be all
screwed up."

"Could I take a sec to show you a photo?" Before she could answer, I flashed Bakstrom's image.

"Shit! **He** did it?"

"You know him."

"He was one of them, pretending to work here, mostly they're standing around the roach coach a million times a day, we have to listen to 'La Cucaracha' over and over."

I said, "What was his trade?"

"What are you talking about?"

"Was he a framer, a mason, a—"

"How would I know? I never saw him **doing** anything. He sure wasn't doing anything when he hit on me."

She waited.

I said, "Really."

"What, you think I'm making it up? I walk by, not with Petey, just power-walking for the burn, he's on the sidewalk drinking some sugar drink. Smoking." She stuck out her tongue. "Like I'd give him the time of day. He tried it the next day, also. **Hello, ma'am.** Moving his hips. Yeah, right, I'm supposed to be impressed by a sleeveless shirt? Filthy nails?"

She took another look at the image. "Lowlife."

I said, "Did he look like this?"

"It's your picture. Don't you know what he looks like? That's exactly him, thinks he's God's gift. Why're you asking about him?"

"He knew the victim, so the cops want to talk—"

"God, that creeps me out. Was it a sex crime—

they won't even tell us if it was a woman or a man, everyone's betting on a woman, women always get victimized."

"It wasn't a sex crime."

"Man or woman?"

"Man."

"Another lowlife from the job or someone innocent?"

"Sorry, I can't—"

"Blah blah blah. **Psychologist.** All questions, no answers, just like Dr. Montag and you know what we think of him, Petey?"

The dog was noncommittal.

She said, "Why do I bother with you?" and walked away.

Milo said, "Sounds like a fun chat. Got a name for this harridan?"

"Nope, but she was certain and I'm sure someone in the neighborhood can I.D. her."

"Agreed. So you got Bakstrom at the scene, muchas gracias. My next step is Manucci, Thalia's moneyman. I was going over my notes, realized he never called back, and when I try him by phone I get corporate voicemail. So I'm figuring a drop-in's called for. Care to participate? I'm thinking Monday morning."

"I'm clear."

"More like lucid."

Joseph A. Manucci, CPA, CFP, was one of twenty-three brokers operating out of the Morgan-Smith Financial Services office in Encino. Senior position, his name near the top of the list in the lobby.

The building was two stories of white marble Greek Revival sandwiched between a Jaguar dealership and a private hospital.

Milo said, "Stocks do well, buy yourself hot wheels. They tank, check into the cardiac ward."

The security guard in front of the door raised an eyebrow but kept staring straight ahead. Milo flashed the badge and asked for Manucci.

The guard made a call. Said, "Okay," to the apparatus, and "First floor, that way," to us.

A man was waiting in a warmly lit, marble-floored hallway. Late forties to early fifties, short and slight, tightly curled hair an improbable ecru. A white-on-white shirt rolled to the elbows was tucked into navy trousers. Brown loafers, pale-yellow suspenders, bright-yellow tie patterned with fat little ducks.

"Joe Manucci, sorry for not getting back to you, on the road, got a desk full of messages. Please. C'mon in."

Hard shake, soft skin, downcast expression.

He said, "Ricki Sylvester just called and told me. Unbelievable. Please come in."

He backed into a corner suite. Three windows looked out to a clutch of rubber trees, shiny green leaves nearly masking the parking lot. On the wall were a bachelor's from Cal State Northridge, Manucci's certification as a financial planner, his public accountant credentials.

A bookcase was stocked with volumes by financial savants. A sofa was heaped high with paper. No wood visible on the desktop; the space was taken up by quarterly reports, a collection of paperweights, two pairs of eyeglasses, and an alp of loose papers.

Among all that, pink message slips flashed like discarded rose petals. That made me willing to consider Manucci's sincerity.

"Sorry for the mess, guys. I like to think of it as controlled chaos."

He put on a pair of eyeglasses, blinked, switched to another pair, blinked some more. "Just got into bifocals, the optometrist gave me two options, can't stand either. I'll eventually adjust, what's the choice, no one's getting younger."

Milo said, "Thalia Mars knew about that."

"Poor Thalia." Manucci chewed his lower lip. Same expression inept dancers wear when they're trying to fake cool. "What exactly happened to her, guys?"

"Someone killed her, sir."

"I know that. Was it robbery?"

"Is there a reason it might have been?"

"I just can't see anyone wanting to hurt Thalia for hurt's sake. Do you have any suspects?"

"We were going to ask you the same thing, sir."

Manucci poked his own chest. "Like I'd know? I did investments and filed her taxes and that makes it sound more complicated than it was."

I said, "Simple account."

"Large account but by the time I began with Thalia, she'd put most of her portfolio into munis—tax-free bonds, it's a typical investment for those wishing to conserve wealth. The only other products she owned were a few blue-chip stocks, mostly preferred, which is actually closer to a bond than a stock, we're not talking lots of trades. Occasionally she'd sell something for a profit and either balance the gain against a loss or donate it to charity. What I'm getting at is there wasn't much work to speak of."

He removed the second pair of glasses. "I filed her taxes for her, as well. Gratis, no reason not to, it was basic."

Milo said, "Not much movement in her account."

"Her account was close to inert," said Manucci. "Sometimes a bond gets called and needs to be replaced but even that was simple. Thalia authorized me to buy lots up to a certain amount without consulting her."

"What amount was that?"

"Fifty thousand. That basically covered everything because she avoided owning larger issues of any single product. Eggs in one basket and all that."

"So you had carte blanche."

"I didn't view it that way," said Manucci. "I always think of the client as the boss. I got her the best product available, she never complained. Recently, she'd begun donating mature bonds to charity rather than replenishing."

"How recently?"

"Three or four years. She had no heirs, why wait until she was gone and give a massive chunk of inheritance tax to Uncle Sam?"

I said, "So she was a low-maintenance client."

"Dream client," said Manucci. "When I first began working with her, I'd visit her at home at the end of every year and give her a progress report. After a few years of that, I showed up and she said, 'Today will be the last time, Joe.' That threw me, I thought I was being fired. She patted me on the hand and said, 'I don't need a dog-and-pony show, just keep me solvent.' Then she winked and said, 'I'll know if you don't.' That sounds like a threat but it wasn't, she was referring to a previous conversation we'd had. When I started out managing her, she told me she was a CPA herself, used to do her own taxes, found it tedious."

"An informed client."

"She read prospectuses, sometimes had ideas. 'Look for airport issues, Joe, airports never go out of business.' It was a pleasure dealing with her. She had . . . an aura, I guess you'd call it. Of elegance, like from another era."

He frowned. "I guess she **was** from another era. In amazing shape for someone that old, I never imagined she'd be . . . what a terrible thing. Are you asking about her finances because money was involved?"

Milo said, "Being thorough. Any idea who'd want to kill her?"

"Of course not."

"How long was she your client?"

"Eighteen years. I'd just started here, was happy to get her."

"Because of the size of her account."

"Of course that," said Manucci. "But also because she came recommended. Intelligent, easy to work with."

"Recommended by who?"

"My boss at the time. I inherited Thalia from him after he got sick. Heart attack, right here in the office. Everyone was stunned. Fifty-seven, great shape."

"What was his name?"

"Frank Guidon."

Out came Milo's pad. "Please spell that."

"G-U-I-D-on."

"How long did Mr. Guidon work with Miss Mars?"

"All I can tell you is she was his client when I was hired."

"Your name's on all her documents."

"It would be," said Manucci. "After the companies merged—New Bank with Allegiant then Allegiant with Morgan-Smith, all the paperwork was adapted."

"Fifty-seven," said Milo. "So he probably inherited from someone else. Would anyone here know who?"

"I doubt it. At this point, I'm one of the old-timers."

Milo said, "Those house calls you used to do. After you stopped, how often did you see her?"

"If a lot of paper built up, I'd sometimes hand-deliver documents to her rather than use the mail. I live in West L.A., she's right on the way."

"What did you think about Miss Mars's living circumstances?"

"Meaning?"

"Living in a hotel."

"The place seemed a little tired but Thalia seemed happy."

"When was the last time you saw her?"

Manucci pulled an iPad out of a desk drawer, scrolled, knitted his forehead. "Bear with me . . . nope . . . nope . . . okay, here we go."

He showed us the screen. Calendar page from nine months ago. **TM** in a Monday box. Three P.M. A **BQR** notation.

"A reminder to myself," said Manucci. "Bring quarterly reports. The home office likes documentation."

Milo said, "Maybe the home office can tell us the name of Mr. Guidon's predecessor, how about trying to find out."

Manucci put on glasses, dialed a number, got someone named Rod, stated his request and waited.

Moments later: "Really? Wow."

Jotting on a pad, he said, "Go know."

From The Desk Of

Joseph A. Manucci, CPA, CFP
Vice President

Frank's predecessor: William P. Wojik.

CHAPTER
22

By the time we left Manucci's office, it was nearly five and Ventura Boulevard had clotted.

Milo said, "Wojik. The doc who sent Thalia to Eagle. Another grandpa?"

Nosing into the fuming mass without apparent care, he laughed at a chorus of honks. "Be thankful I don't put on the siren and freeze your asses in place."

Continuing to weave in and out blissfully, he said, "Sylvester, Wojik, it's like Thalia was an asset, passed down to the younger generation."

I said, "Sylvester inherited a client. I don't see a pediatrician benefiting from knowing an old woman."

"She sent a donor to the boss and earned brownie points."

"Ruben's not her boss."

"Whatever, Alex, it made her look good to the hospital. She's on staff there, right?"

He hit a clear patch, put on speed. "I'm not saying she's dirty for anything but maybe she can tell us something about Thalia's past. Where's her office?"

"Bedford Drive."

"The Gold Coast," he said. "Puts us against traffic, excellent."

Belinda Wojik, M.D.'s second-floor suite offered two waiting rooms, **Healthy** and **Sick.**

Milo said, "Bit of a stretch but I'm gonna claim Healthy."

Beverly Hills practice but a Spartan waiting room. White walls, washable vinyl floor, eight blue plastic chairs. A wall rack held back issues of **Jack and Jill, Scholastic, Sesame Street Magazine,** and Dr. Seuss books. A table stand housed brochures on the wisdom of vaccination.

Empty waiting room. Other than a weird mixture of zwieback and soiled diaper in the air, no evidence of a pediatric presence.

A cough sounded through the wall separating us from Sick, followed by a muffled female voice and more hacking.

Milo muttered, "Health's in short supply, today," and rapped on the glass doors shielding the receptionist from germs. The partition slid open and a woman said, "How could I help you?"

The Russian accent I'd encountered on the phone belonged to a woman in her thirties with cheekbones sharp enough to slice cheese and more hair than I'd ever seen on a human head. Brown-black except for magenta bangs. Tight white uniform. **Tatiana** on her tag.

Milo said, "Police, we'd like to talk to Dr. Wojik."

"Po-lize . . . Doctor's with patients."

"We'll wait."

"It could be long time."

"No problem."

"Can I ask for what it's about?"

"Thalia Mars."

"Miss Mars?"

"You know her."

"She sometimes visits—not for a while. She okay?"

"Unfortunately not."

"Oh. Really?" Blue eyes misted. "Oh, no."

"How often did she visit?"

"Sometimes," said Tatiana. "She goes for coffee with Doctor."

"When was the last time?"

"I dun know, maybe . . . months? Is she gonna **be** okay?"

"Afraid not," said Milo.

Tatiana's hand flew to her mouth. "Polize." As if the fact had just processed. "I go get her. Only one patient in the Sick room, it's a virus, fluids and rest, she'll be done soon."

The glass slid shut. Milo leafed **The Cat in the Hat.** Two more croupy coughs sounded. "Can viruses get through drywall?"

He switched to **Oh, the Places You'll Go!** Smiled faintly, as if remembering something. The door opened and a woman in her fifties shuffled out, red-eyed and sniffling.

White hair was carelessly cut in a pageboy. A white coat several sizes too large tented a gray-blue dress. Support stockings, sensible shoes, round unlined face. Not young-looking but oddly child-like.

Dr. B on her tag, along with a daisy drawn in red marker.

"My assistant said Thalia is dead." Whispery voice, curiously lacking in inflection.

"Unfortunately, Doctor." Milo held out his card.

Belinda Wojik was looking at the floor and didn't notice it. The fingers of her right hand beat a rapid tattoo on her chin. Her lips turned down. Nostrils pulsed. Cheeks began to flutter as she exhaled slowly.

"Thalia," she said. The fingers on her chin rose to her forehead, slapping softly. Then up to her hair, scratching, pulling.

She sat down heavily.

Through all of it, not a moment of eye contact. Not, I sensed, the evasion of the guilty. This was something else.

Milo said, "Could we talk a bit, Doctor?"

"You're a homicide detective," she said. "Are you Dr. Delaware?"

"I am."

"Know of you. Read your work in oncology. Sorry for not calling you back. Didn't understand why you wanted to talk about Thalia. I wanted her permission. Was going to ask her. I didn't. I'm sorry."

Clipping segments of speech like links of sausage.

She raised her head. Close-set hazel eyes struggled to find their bearings, failed, and aimed down at the floor. "Very sad to hear about this. Who's the perpetrator?"

"That's what we're trying to figure out, Doctor."

"You think I could tell you?"

"We're talking to everyone who knew Thalia."

Rapid nodding. "I knew her. Since I was a child. My grandfather . . ." She clapped a hand over her mouth. "Not relevant. After you leave, I'm going to the hospital to see a poor little thing with cystic fibrosis. Not a pulmonologist. I handle general issues in concert with a pulmonologist."

Milo looked at me.

I said, "Makes sense."

She inhaled slowly. "I know. I just sounded strange to you. I know. Give me a second. I'll explain."

Several more breaths. "I'm of ambiguous diagnosis but let's say spectrum. I like to think mild. I function well on a professional level. Not Asperger's, I'm not even sure I believe Asperger's is a bona fide diagnosis. Even if it is, not me, no obsessive hobbies, I like people, I just don't—I **love** my work, the children. They don't mind."

Plaintive expression. "Did that explain it or have I confused you more?"

I said, "You've explained perfectly."

"With my littlest patients I don't need to explain. With grown-ups, as long as the children are happy. When I'm exposed to anxiety-provoking stimuli, I have to work harder. Like now. This is anxiety provoking. I can be more conventional when I'm not anxious. This is . . . I'm in denial, first stage like anyone."

I said, "Sorry we had to tell you—"

"You have your jobs like I have mine. I can't think of anyone who didn't like Thalia."

Milo said, "Your grandfather was her money manager. How far back did they go?"

"William P. Wojik," she said. "That's how you found me."

I said, "Actually, Ruben told me you'd sent Thalia to him."

"She asked me for a worthy cause. Ruben's a good man doing good work."

Milo said, "About your grandfather—"

"I don't like to talk about my grandfather. He loved me. But he associated with criminals."

Milo and I looked at each other. Belinda Wojik continued to stare at vinyl.

"That was a long time ago," I said.

"It was," she said. "He wasn't a criminal himself. At least I don't know anything to the contrary. If there's anyone I grant analytic caution it's Grampa. He was always good to me. Even though I confused him. I confused everyone but only Grampa took the time . . . do I need to talk about him?"

I sat down next to her. "If you could, we'd appreciate it. We know so little about Thalia so any link could be valuable."

Long silence. One leg began to pump up and down. She crossed her arms.

"Thalia considered Grampa a good friend. She told me. After I told her he was nice. Even though I confused him. He was socially smart. What you'd call charming. He lived to ninety-five. Died eleven years ago in his sleep. That's a good way to go. Even when he was old, he was social. He grew a beard, looked like a thin Santa. When I was a child, he dressed up like Santa and put pillows under his costume. Because I was afraid to go to Bullocks Wilshire. Where the real Santa was. The real fake Santa."

She frowned.

I said, "Your grandfather understood you."

"It was my father who told me. My father didn't approve of his father. They didn't get along. Father and I didn't get along. Grandfather and I did get along. Grandfather always said, 'Common enemy, Belle.' Then he'd laugh and give me a candy. He gave me extra when Father said no sweets."

I said, "A rebel."

"You'd have to be," she said. "Associating with criminals."

Milo said, "Which criminals?"

She shook her head. Drummed faster. "I don't know but my father never lied. He was a dentist and very honest. He did work for the studios. Fixing stars' teeth and he didn't lie. Even though he said that business was all lies. He was religious, Presbyterian, thought of being a minister but chose dentistry. After Mother died, I don't remember her, he raised me. Dr. William Wojik, Junior. Same name as Grandfather but different. It happened because of candy. Grampa gave me some and he got angry. Pulled me out of Grandfather's house and took me home. In the car, he said, 'You think he's a great guy, Belle? He associated with criminals, okay?' And then he drove too fast."

Her hands settled in her lap. "That's how I learned about it. I was curious so I asked Thalia about it. Because she knew him for a long time. Knew me through Grampa. It was here in the office. She came to have coffee, she sometimes did if she was shopping in Beverly Hills. I finished my last patient. Asthma attack, I prescribed albuterol plus comprehensive allergy tests with Dr. Epstein, he's my consulting allergist. The patient had a Level Three reaction to horsehair and was riding horses. The reaction took a while to manifest. Allergic load had to build up but then it did and all the wheezing and constriction and congestion increased. I had her stop riding and everything was fine . . . that's the day Thalia came by for coffee. I remember it that way, Thalia-asthma. It's like a bookmark. It was also the day after the anniversary of Grampa's death. It made me sad, remembering. I told Thalia. Then I told her what my father said. He's dead, too, had an accident, skiing. Hoping she'd contradict Father and say no, Bill never did anything like that. She smiled and said, 'People have pasts, Belle. If I told you about mine, you might not want to have coffee with me.' Then she winked. The next time I saw her, she asked me for a worthy cause and I said, Dr. Ruben Eagle. He does good work."

I said, "You met Thalia through your grandfather."

"At Grandfather's house. Several times when I came to visit Grandfather, she was there. Often she had a briefcase with her. When I came in, she always said, 'I'll give you two your special time.' She smiled at me, patted my head, said I was cute, then she left. Later, when I was an adolescent, she didn't pat my head."

"A briefcase," said Milo.

Belinda Wojik knitted her hands. "Grampa was social but it was probably business. Grampa invested money for people. From his office but also from his home. He had a huge house in Hancock Park with an office full of books."

"Where was his office?"

"Encino. I didn't believe Father. But then Thalia didn't deny it and she hinted and winked about herself. That's when I started to believe it. It bothered me. But I loved him. I still don't know how to process it."

She looked at us. "Was Thalia murdered because of something Grampa did?"

Milo said, "No reason to believe that."

"I hope you're right, Lieutenant. At Grampa's funeral, Thalia came up to me and said feel free to call if I needed someone to talk to. So I called her the next week and we had coffee. I talked to her about becoming a physician. It seemed a crazy idea but I couldn't get rid of it. Thalia encouraged me. I gave up the idea, anyway. Years later I came back to it. I was forty-one and didn't think I'd get into medical school. I tried anyway because I didn't want to work anymore as a secretary for an extremely hostile movie producer, Marvin Redman."

A tear stream ran down her cheek. "I did it. I told Thalia. She kissed my cheek and we had coffee."

I said, "The cemetery you visited—"

"Hollywood Legends. It's close to Western Pediatric Medical Center. I stop in on Grampa's anniversary. I don't go other times. I might get into a habit. I have to maintain a structured schedule. By point of illustration, when you're finished with me, I'll drive straight to the hospital and see my CF patient. I'll drive past the cemetery but I won't stop."

"When Thalia told you she'd participated in criminal activities, what was her affect?"

Her eyes returned to the floor. "Discerning other people's emotions is difficult. It's like a foreign movie. Unless I'm paying strict attention and watching for subtitles, it passes me by."

"Did she seem to take it lightly?"

"She didn't laugh," said Belinda Wojik. "She didn't cry, either. She was . . . somewhere in the middle. Then she looked away. I interpreted that as wanting to change the subject. Then she said she was looking for a worthy cause. Oh, I remember something: She said she was looking for a cause because she was as old as Methuselah's wife and wished to do good with her money. May I go, now?"

Milo said, "Soon, Doctor. Do you recognize either of these men?" Showing her Waters's and Bakstrom's mugshots.

She said, "Obviously, they're criminals." She shuddered. "Their eyes are blank. They scare me. Are you saying Thalia associated with them?"

Milo said, "Not necessarily."

"You're showing me these pictures for a reason." He smiled.

Belinda Wojik said, "You're telling me nonverbally to shut up so I will. May I go now?"

As we walked out to Bedford Drive, Milo said, "That was different. How the hell does she work with kids?"

"She's nonjudgmental and kind of child-like, herself."

"Beverly Hills parents would dig that?"

"She probably has a sparse outside life and is available twenty-four seven."

"A slave with an M.D.? Yeah, that would do it," he said. "So Gramps might've moved money around for thugs and Thalia 'fessed up to being a bad girl."

I said, "This goes way back. Time to learn more about Gramps. Ricki Sylvester's, too."

He said, "Your place. Faster computer plus catering."

CHAPTER
23

Twenty minutes later, we were in my office. I expected Milo to commandeer the keyboard but he slumped on the old leather couch. "Go for it."

William P. Wojik was mentioned in several newspaper articles from 1940 and 1941, all to do with Leroy Hoke's tax evasion trial. As Hoke's "accountant" he'd been subpoenaed to testify, no record of what he'd said.

Several papers added another label: "reputed mob moneyman."

"Reputed" in order to avoid a libel suit. I kept scrolling, found no evidence Wojik had ever been charged criminally. Following Hoke's conviction, he avoided the public eye until 1975, when he, along with other alums, had been honored at a Yale Club of L.A. gala.

New tag: "esteemed financial consultant and philanthropist."

A photo from the party showed a white-haired man with a toothbrush mustache and an easy smile. A chubby girl clutched his arm and gazed up at him. Eleven or twelve, pigtails, glasses, a frilly pink dress that threatened to consume her.

The round, perplexed face of a young Belinda Wojik.

Milo said, "His dinner companion. Like he told her, common enemy."

I keyworded **jack mccandless**.

Even more coverage on him. A "mob lawyer." "Reputed" not necessary because the facts were clear. Formerly from Chicago, McCandless had defended "Capone soldiers and other organized crime figures" before moving to San Francisco, where he'd served as the "legal mouthpiece of union bosses and political figures accused of corruption."

Living in L.A. by the midthirties, McCandless had faced a "potential conflict of interest due to his work on behalf of both jewel-theft victim Count Frederick LaPlante and the chief suspect in the case, mobster Leroy Hoke. However, with no one ever charged in the heist, the necessity of making a choice was avoided."

I kept scrolling.

Similar to William Wojik, public attention on McCandless had faded soon after Leroy Hoke's imprisonment. I came across a few anniversary trial rehashes then nothing until a twenty-year-old obituary in the **American Bar Association Journal**.

McCandless was lauded, in memoriam, as a longtime ABA member who'd served on numerous committees, including several that dealt with professional ethics. Another "noted philanthropist." He'd died at age ninety-six "peacefully, in his sleep." Interment at Hollywood Legends Memorial Park, in lieu of flowers any sort of charitable donation was appreciated. Predeceased by his wife and son, Mark McCandless. Survived by his granddaughter, Richeline Sylvester, also an ABA member.

Milo said, "Mob moneyman makes ninety-five, mob lawyer goes him one year better, Thalia pushes a hundred. Maybe the good die young because they bore God."

I laughed, switched to an image search. "Well, what do you know."

Half a dozen color shots, like Wojik's, all in formal garb. Planned Parenthood benefit, same for the Dorothy Chandler Pavilion, three for the art museum, the zoo.

Even in old age, Jack McCandless had been a

forbidding presence, well over six feet tall and three hundred pounds or more, with a hairless bullet head and crushed features. Tiny porcine eyes aimed like handguns intent on demolishing the lens. Or the photographer.

One black-and-white shot, decades older, was familiar: Perino's, Hoke and a tiny blonde. McCandless the hulk we'd assumed to be a bodyguard. That one traced to an eBay auction featuring "classic L.A. restaurant images," this one peddled as "Rich folk enjoying the Beverly Hills high life."

Not quite; Perino's had occupied a stretch of Wilshire five miles from B.H. No surprise, on any given eBay day, you could bid on a five-hundred-dollar Stradivarius.

Milo said, "Even as a geezer he looked like a gangster."

I said, "That could've worked for him in court, the power of intimidation. In Hoke's case, there was an added benefit: Compared with the lawyer, the defendant looked harmless."

"Didn't do the defendant any good."

"But obviously Hoke didn't hold the conviction against McCandless. Continued to employ him, using Thalia as a surrogate the way he did with Wojik. What I find interesting is McCandless working for both Hoke and LaPlante aka Drancy."

He said, "Backs up the collaboration scenario."

"Big-time. Drancy and Hoke planned the whole thing together, the jewels got fenced or sold to other buyers with loose standards, the consignors ate the loss. If we're right about Hoke continuing to operate from behind bars, he could've been involved in Drancy's New York art scheme. The same goes for Thalia. But that one didn't work out well for Drancy, he got busted. Maybe his descendants believe he was sold out. Or hadn't gotten a fair share of the take."

"Criminal genetics," he said. "Seventy years later, Thalia pays the price."

I said, "Tying her to any of it would be tough unless you were related to a criminal insider and had heard stories about Hoke's number one girl. The person he entrusted with his fortune."

Milo walked over to the computer. "Look for a link between Drancy, Bakstrom, and Waters. That doesn't work, toss in McCandless and Wojik. Hell, do a goulash."

I tried every combination. Nothing.

"My luck," he said, "anonymous Ms. Cutie will turn out to be the killer kin . . . okay, I'm gonna lean on Lev—the guy at the archive."

"What about Bakstrom's and Waters's visitors list?"

"Still looking."

"Quentin coughs up Thelma Myers and they can't give you anything?"

"Data's 'in flux.' They got a federal grant to go completely digital and something screwed up, big surprise."

He sat back down.

I said, "Waters and Bakstrom have been in L.A. for a while but apart from Bakstrom's pickup construction job, neither seemed to have stable employment. What if they freelanced? Nothing violent. Fraud, bunco, something to tide them along while they planned the big job. Using the same name they gave the hotel."

"The Birkenhaar brothers," he said. "That's got to come from somewhere—maybe it's Girlie's real name."

"We already searched and came up with zero. But the name of a suspect in an ongoing investigation might not make it to the Web."

"I'll ask around about scams." He glanced at his Timex. "Grampas and the little girls who admire them. Dr. Wojik's an odd bird, I don't see her consorting with serious bad guys. Ricki Sylvester, on the other hand, is a lawyer, which in my book is at least one strike against her. Let's inform her what we've learned about ol' Jack, see what she has to say."

At four forty-five we took the unmarked to Ricki Sylvester's office. When we were moments away, I got a text.

Maxine Driver. **Pitcairn has no idea who the palooka is. She'll look into Drancy. Intrigued. As am I.**

Milo said, "Palooka? That's prof-speak? Okay, here we are."

Diminishing sun had altered the building's glass walls to a yellow-gray that suggested chronic liver disease. The lights in the windowless waiting room had been switched off and the bearded receptionist was gone. Milo tried the door. Locked.

He phoned Sylvester.

"This is Ricki."

"Lieutenant Sturgis again. Could you spare a few minutes?"

"Tomorrow's kind of full."

"How about now. We're outside your door."

"Oh, boy . . . hold on."

Moments later, she appeared wearing a puffy gray jacket and carrying a purse. Unbolting the door, she flipped a switch that triggered the waiting room light.

"I hope this is quick. I'm tired and kind of famished."

Milo said, "Happy to tag along while you dine, my treat."

She waved a hand. "Let's just do it right here."

She took the receptionist chair. We stayed on our feet.

Milo said, "We've learned about your grandfather."

The flush that captured her face was instantaneous and intense. "What **about** my grandfather?"

"He seems to have led an interesting—"

"Uh-uh, don't even **go** there, Lieutenant. It's hearsay innuendo and I don't have to listen to it." She stood. "You're wasting my time with ancient history? End of discussion."

"No offense intended," said Milo. "Not that I see why you're so off—"

"Of course I'm offended. You come here the first time, I do everything to help you, hand over every lick of information I have on Thalia, and you repay me by implying that one of the most important people in my life was a criminal. He was **not**. That's an ignorant way to look at it and you, as a peace officer, should know better. Grandfather provided defense to those who deserved it."

"Ma'am, I never meant to imply—"

" 'We learned about your grandfather'? Like that's supposed to alarm me. To what end? I already told you everything I know."

She smiled. "Let me guess: no progress on Thalia, so you began snooping around on anything related to her, found something about Grandfather in the documents I gave you, looked him up on the Internet. If I was trying to protect Grandfather, don't you think I'd have taken the time to remove any references to him?"

She shook her head. "The Internet is a garbage dump."

Milo said, "Sorry if I touched a nerve. Though I'm not sure why it's a sore point."

"It's a sore point," she said, "because I dealt with it a lot in law school and don't want to repeat the experience. Please leave."

I said, "What happened in law school?"

"Hearsay innuendo from a smug bastard visiting professor, some idiot named Gallico, I still remember his name because he was a total ass."

"He insulted your grandfather?"

She glared.

I said, "A lecture on stretching the moral boundaries of legal representation?"

Her mouth dropped open. "That's nearly verbatim. How the hell?"

Because I know academia.

I said, "Lucky guess."

She said, "He brought a **slide** show, showed unflattering photos. Roy Cohn, people like that. And yes, Grandfather. He singled Grandfather out. 'This one even looks like a mug.' The lecture hall erupted in laughter. A few days later, one of my idiot classmates dug up the fact that I was related to 'the mug.' So of course, that spread and became **the** hot topic. Not just students, the faculty had fun with it. Staring at me, barely hiding their amusement. I thought I'd die. Built up my courage and confronted Gallico, stupid me, thinking he'd have regrets. Instead, he told me to 'man up'—I was 'supposedly' studying to be a lawyer, not a wet-nurse. And of course, in his final lecture, he made sure to pay extra attention to Jack McCandless and kept looking at me pointedly. So you can see why I don't feel like raking that muck up, years later. Our system guarantees a right to representation for everyone and Jack McCandless represented all sorts of people. That's what criminal work's all about. You don't work with saints."

"Same for police work," said Milo.

"But you people don't get excoriated for doing your job."

He smiled.

Ricki Sylvester said, "Fine, you have your problems, all the more reason to get where I'm coming from. Grandfather doesn't deserve to be demeaned, he should be honored for serving the Constitution."

Milo said, "We're not here to demean anyone. But seeing as you inherited Mr. McCandless's practice and we've since learned that Thalia had some links to criminals, we're trying to find out if that relates to her murder."

The logical question: Which criminals?

Ricki Sylvester said, "I didn't inherit his criminal practice. He'd already switched to estate work."

Milo said, "You know about Thalia's criminal associations."

Eyeblink. Shift to the right. "I haven't the faintest what you're talking about."

"She was the girlfriend of a man named Leroy Hoke."

"Don't know him."

"He was a mobster in the thirties and forties.

Mr. McCandless represented him in a tax evasion trial back in '41 that ended up with Hoke going to prison."

"No one wins every case."

"The point is, Thalia's criminal connections, even though they go back a long time, need to be explored."

"Everything I know about Thalia was in the file I gave you. To me she was a sweet old lady— what, you think she was some kind of moll? Decades ago? How can that possibly be relevant?"

She headed for the door. "Am I being defensive? You bet. Because some things deserve a good defense. Let's go."

Milo said, "Bear with us for a few moments, please." He rummaged in his attaché case.

Ricki Sylvester said, "When you do that you look like one of those loser lawyers who hang around the courthouse."

He showed her Gerard Waters's mugshot.

"And this is . . ."

Instead of answering, he produced Henry Bakstrom's prison headshot.

"**He** looks like an over-the-hill musician. Why are you **showing** me these?"

"They're known criminals who may have had contact with Thalia."

"You think they killed her?"

"We're not saying that—"

"Whatever you are saying, I can't help you. Now if you'll be so kind and allow me to have my dinner."

"Sure. Sorry."

She switched off the lights and the three of us left. As she locked up, Milo said, "Does the name William Wojik mean anything to you?"

"Of course it does. He managed Thalia's money before Joe Manucci, his name was also in that file. What, he's got criminal associations, too?"

Milo said, "Just groping, ma'am."

"Good luck with that."

An uncomfortably silent elevator ride ended when Sylvester got out a level above us.

When she was gone, Milo said, "Not even a 'bye-bye'? I'm feeling micro-aggressed."

His pace to the unmarked was a near-jog that I matched. Speeding out of the parking lot, he positioned himself on a dark stretch of block with a clear view of the exit.

He said, "My layman's view is that was an incredible overreaction. What does a behavioral pro say?"

"An incredible overreaction."

"All traumatized about something that happened back in law school? Did you see her eyes shifting? She knows more than she's letting on and our asking about the past freaked her out."

"More important," I said, "Wojik's name **wasn't** in the file. And there was another broker between him and Manucci—Guidon."

"She knew Wojik personally, wants to keep herself out of something. Think Dr. Belinda was using all that spectrum weirdness to bullshit us?"

"My gut says no but I'll ask Ruben about her." I texted. **A few questions about Belinda W.**

His return message: **Crazy clinic. Can we talk tomorrow?**

Milo said, "Tell you one thing, getting that emotional wasn't a smart move on ol' Ricki's part. If she'd stayed cool, I'd probably have forgotten about her. You'd think a lawyer would know better."

"Her specialty doesn't demand being cool under pressure. She sits in an office, shuffles paper."

"Unlike McCandless, before he became a shuffler."

I said, "McCandless could've switched because an important client wanted it that way. Hoke had amassed tremendous wealth and knew he wouldn't be getting out of prison. So his emphasis shifted from criminal defense to wealth preservation."

"Aka laundering," he said.

"With Thalia controlling the detergent."

"Looky here, our touchy gal shows herself."

A ten-year-old, pale-blue Buick LeSabre nosed out of the lot, Ricki Sylvester at the wheel. She drove to Olympic and turned right. We followed.

By Sepulveda, she'd crossed several lanes and entered a left-turn-only slot. Three cars between her and the unmarked.

Humming "Call Me Irresponsible," Milo turned after the amber arrow had died. He tailed the Buick to Wilshire, where it drove a block, hooked left onto a side street, then left again and returned. A right took Sylvester west on Wilshire and under the odd metal arch that marks the border with Santa Monica.

Quiet section of Wilshire, most stores closed for the evening. One exception was a brick-faced bar and grill called High Steaks. Extended happy hour, prime beef, surf-and-turf special.

Ricki Sylvester scored a parking space in front of the restaurant, clicked her alarm fob, and entered.

Milo drove two blocks up and we backtracked on foot. At the eatery's front door, he said, "Wait here, let me scope it out." Moments later, the door cracked and he gave a thumbs-up.

In front was a busy bar with three TVs tuned to ESPN, separated from the dining area by a freestanding partition wall. Everything nicely dim, not much conversation from the resident drinkers. When the bartender wasn't pouring, he was washing glasses. We took stools at the far right end. He ordered a Boilermaker, I asked for Chivas on the rocks. While the drinks were being made, he got up and snuck a look around the partition. Sat back down and said, "Go for it."

Scotch in hand, I hazarded a peek.

No need to be that careful. Ricki Sylvester had positioned herself in a far booth that put the rear of her head in our view. Her attention was fixed on something green and milky in an oversized Martini glass, and a folded newspaper.

For the next twenty minutes, Milo and I alternated between drinking, pretending to watch a soccer game somewhere in Chile, and taking turns checking on Sylvester.

"Still by her lonesome," he reported. "Second glass of foamy mouthwash."

"Any food other than the shrimp salad?"

"Nope but she ate all of it so maybe she's waiting for someone before having her entrée. Let's make a pool. I say something chicken or a small steak."

I said, "Sounds reasonable."

"Don't be agreeable. You have to bet."

"I hear you and raise one specificity. Roast chicken."

He sneered. "You're not fun."

Next turn to look was mine.

I said, "We both lost, she just paid. The good news is the waiter's face. Not a happy camper."

We rotated, keeping our backs to anyone approaching from the restaurant.

The soccer match was tied at scoreless. The camera panned an arena full of bored faces. The clock said nearly an hour of nothing. Maybe that's why the game inspired riots.

Milo quarter turned. "There she goes. A coupla minutes and we chat up a disgruntled gentleman in a red jacket."

He gave paper money to the barkeep.

The guy said, "Come back anytime."

The waiter was in his seventies, squarely built, with a face shaved so impressively it glowed and a head of wavy white hair. A busboy was clearing another table and Clean-Shave had taken on Ricki Sylvester's scant leavings.

We waited until he'd left the dining room and headed to a nook that led to a glass-walled kitchen. Two men in toques and one woman sautéed away. Off to the side, several carts were piled with crockery and flatware. The waiter added to the collection. As he turned, we approached.

"Sir," said Milo, offering his best public-servant smile and his badge.

The waiter said, "Yes?" Brass name tag. **Arturo.**

"Could you spare a moment, please?"

Sudden appearance by the police but Arturo's shrug was serene. Bragging rights of the innocent. "What can I do for you, Officer?"

"The woman you just served—"

Serenity exited. Indignation walked onstage. "Her," he said. "She did something wrong?"

"She's a person of interest."

"Not to me," said Arturo. "Then again, she's a lawyer, they're capable of anything."

We laughed. He joined in. It made him look younger.

Milo said, "She's a regular, huh?"

"Not too regular, thank God. Maybe once a month. Twice, if I've offended The Good Lord."

"Not much in the way of tipping."

"Five percent?" said Arturo. "Who **does** that? Even when I started out, it was ten."

"Five," said Milo. "That **is** nuts."

"Nuts and cheap. Plus, she's boring, the same thing every time, two Grasshoppers—who **drinks** that, anymore?—and the shrimp salad."

He winked. "Frozen shrimp, not our tour de force. We got great steak, sometimes excellent fresh fish. Years ago, before I got to know her, I tried to steer her away from the shrimp. Try the Dover sole except on Sunday. No fish on Sunday, period. No deliveries since Friday. You have to have shellfish, do the crab salad, it starts out fresh, it's chilled real cold. Frozen shrimp? We defrost and throw in a bunch of spice and oil. So what does she order?"

"Not an adventurous type."

"Two **Grasshoppers,** you ever taste one of them? Even for a female, there's all these good brandies and fruit stuff, or just toss in the simple syrup. My daughters drank that crap when they were in college, it's like she's living in the old days."

He shook his head. "Five per**cent.** When did **anyone** do five? So what do you want to know about her, I can't even tell you her name, she pays cash. All these years, you'd think she'd introduced herself. I think of her as Poodle Hair."

Milo said, "You know she's a lawyer."

"She sometimes reads lawyer magazines. Or is she one a those—paralegals?"

"She's a lawyer."

"There you go," said Arturo.

"Does she ever come in with anyone?"

"Only once, a guy. I remember because it's the only time, I'm thinking, someone's stupid enough to date her?"

"Not a business dinner?"

"Can't swear it wasn't, sir, but that wasn't my impression."

"They were lovey-dovey."

"The way they talked—close to each other. Softly, keeping a big secret. Also, one time he had his hand on her thigh."

"A big secret," said Milo.

"I got five kids, I know when someone's keeping secrets. But what it was, I can't tell you."

"Who paid?"

"Him, the tip was ten, which isn't great but it's better. Also with cash. I'm thinking what, they're members of a cash-only club?"

Milo said, "How long ago was this?"

Arturo straightened his bow tie. "Months—maybe two. Or three. Not four. So what'd she do? Cheat a client?"

"Sorry, can't say," said Milo. "Can you describe the guy she was with?"

"Not really, I wasn't paying attention."

"Black, white—"

"White. Older than her, younger than me. I'm seventy-nine."

"No way," said Milo.

"Genetics," said Arturo. "And eating right. She ever gets to seventy-nine on frozen shrimp and toothpaste we'll be talking hag in a bag, right?"

"What about the guy? Good shape?"

"I honestly don't remember. You want, he comes in again, I'll call you."

Milo handed him a card and a twenty.

"You don't need to do that, sir."

"Enjoy, friend."

"Appreciate it," said Arturo. "Today, you're the lottery."

Walking back to the unmarked, I said, "Ex-spouses and disgruntled waiters, let's hear it for resentment."

Milo said, "Five percent. He's right, who does that?"

"Someone who's not big on social relations."

"In her own way, kinda like Dr. Belinda? Two social Grandpas and they end up with dodgy prodge."

"It's a gene **pool**," I said. "All kinds of things swimming beneath the surface."

We got in the unmarked. I said, "Sylvester eats by herself except for one dinner out with an older man. On the surface, not much, but you know what I'm wondering."

"A blast from the past shows up and connects with her," he said.

My phone rang. Ruben calling in response to my text.

I switched to speaker.

He said, "Yes, she's pretty unique. I didn't tell you much because I figured, let you form your own impressions." A beat. "Also, I like her, didn't want to reduce her to an odd personality."

I said, "How does she deal with patients?"

"Really well, Alex. When she was a resident, she was among the kids' favorites. Super-gentle, took the time to listen, endless patience."

"What about parents?"

"Initially, some of them thought she was odd. But she was so good with diagnosis and treatment that it faded. Also, she works harder than anyone I've ever trained. No one takes calls for her, she's available twenty-four seven." A beat. "I suppose that's easier when you're a loner. You're not going to tell me she's done something wrong, are you?"

"No."

"That's a relief. I've always thought of her as a true innocent, Alex. A savant, I suppose."

"What do you know about her background?"

"Just what I told you, something in show business. I'm really glad she's not in trouble."

I thanked him and hung up.

Milo said, "Mother Teresa with personality issues. You forgot to ask him if she tips well."

"You're not buying it."

"I'm genetically engineered to be suspicious. But if you tell me he's righteous, I'll go with that."

A block later. "Unless I learn different."

CHAPTER

25

Two more days passed with no progress. Bad for Milo, a mixed blessing for me because a legal consult came in that could be handled quickly: reviewing the case files of a nine-year-old boy who'd fallen off a defective bicycle, broken several bones, and incurred a closed head injury.

A year later, the child's tibia, fibula, and femur had mended, as had a hairline fracture of the skull. But psych testing revealed minor learning deficits and my mandate was to judge the quality of that evaluation—first-rate, as it turned out—and to offer an opinion about the durability of the problems.

The honest answer was No Way to Tell.

The judge who'd sent the case said, "You can't do better?"

"If someone else says they can, they're lying."

"Oh, boy. All right, Alex, ambiguity will have to do. But I need someone like you to provide it."

On the morning of the third day, Milo and I were reviewing Thalia Mars's far-too-thin murder book, searching for a hidden nugget of data that might energize the investigation.

An hour later: nothing.

Blanche had settled next to Milo, following the gloomy repartee with a suitably grave expression.

"Finding a lead on this is like looking for Bigfoot," he said. "You know it's hopeless but you wanna believe."

My phone rang.

The judge in the bicycle eval, saying he'd gotten my report, didn't need anything more. For the time being. But he was reserving the right to amend that. If necessary.

Blanche trotted out of the office, into the kitchen, and out to the back door, where she sat, serene and lady-like. I took her to the garden and she favored a particularly hospitable azalea bush with attention.

When we returned, Milo was on his feet. "Just got a text from the pathologist who did Thalia's autopsy. Something I should see, no details. Haven't been able to reach her so I'm going over there."

"After all this time, something on the tox screen?"

"That would be my guess. I need to see for myself."

"In the mood for company?"

"You or the pooch?" He bent and rubbed Blanche's head.

"You'll have to settle for a biped."

"If she knew how to drive, I wouldn't. Let's take the Caddy."

I brought Blanche out to Robin and we got in the car.

Milo said, "Gotta hand it to you, how long you been driving this antique and the leather still smells great."

"TLC and fidelity." I drove south to Sunset as he re-texted the pathologist. By the time I was well into Beverly Hills, there'd still been no reply.

He said, "Maybe there is a big hairy guy roaming around."

Once the sun rises, there's no smooth way to make it to East L.A. from Bel Air. The drive to Mission Road took an hour and ten minutes. The pathologist, a new hire named Laura Robaire, wasn't at the crypt. No one knew when she'd return or what the text had referred to.

We left the building, took a stroll around the parking lot. Milo tried calling and texting back, cursed, smoked a cigar, went over to the Seville and stared blankly through a window.

I walked and stretched. White vans pulled in and out of the loading area. Rapid transit for the dead.

I'd drifted away from him and was avoiding looking at a middle-aged couple trudging toward the north end of the building. The business end of the building; probably picking up a loved one's effects.

Milo waved. I jogged over.

"The sixth damn time she answered. On her way over. Allegedly."

Ten minutes later, a racing-green Jaguar S-type zoomed into a reserved slot and a honey-haired woman in her thirties got out. Five-two, maybe a hundred pounds. Lithe walk, too-young-to-be-an-M.D. face.

She flashed a quick smile. "Lieutenant?"

Milo said, "Doctor."

"Hope you haven't been waiting long."

"Just got here."

Laura Robaire wore a knit top the same color as her car, skinny jeans, and bright-green flats. Her eyes were as light as green can be without being gray. Her nail polish was the color of a pine forest at dusk. Some sort of eco-statement? Or she just liked green.

She said, "Had to give a lecture crosstown, left the room and saw all of your texts. Sorry mine was enigmatic but I wanted you to see it for yourself so you could form your own impressions. Because I'm not sure I have anything you can actually use. Still, if it was me, I'd want to be informed."

We followed her back to the south side of the crypt, took the stairs down, and ended up in the chilly, oversized closet where bodies are wrapped in plastic and stacked on shelves.

The body Robaire wanted was near the top. "I'll call Marcel, he's six-four."

Milo said, "I can handle it."

"I'm sure you could, Lieutenant, but you'll still need help placing it on the table, rules are rules and in this case they're reasonable. You know how it is once they're taken apart. With snipped tendons and ligaments, there's less internal structure, we don't want anything sagging and slipping onto the floor."

"That would be poor form," said Milo.

"The poorest." She removed a beeper from her waistband and pushed a button. "While we wait for Marcel, I'll fill you in. This one came in early yesterday, not your jurisdiction, not even

L.A., Culver City. But the moment I saw it, I knew I had to contact you."

"Who's the lead over there?"

"A Detective Gottlieb," said Robaire. "I've never dealt with him before, then again I haven't dealt with too many people here, just moved from Detroit."

"The crypt, there?"

"You bet."

"Busy place."

"You guys do okay here, but yes, I found myself quite occupied in Detroit. I lived there because my husband had a urology fellowship. Penile repair."

"Ouch."

She laughed. "Sorry. But all those gunshot wounds afforded him experience. Anyway, Detective Gottlieb figured his case as a suicide and I could see why. No external wounds, nothing on X-ray, I wasn't even figuring it for a mandatory autopsy but the age of the decedent made me consider it. Normally, I might've just run a tox. I also have an eager-beaver resident shadowing me so I let him cut. Internally, no surprises. But then, when we used the shaver—hi, Marcel."

A rangy young black man stood in the doorway. "Hey, Doc."

"I need the benefit of your superior stature."

She pointed. "Lieutenant Sturgis will help you lower it to the gurney that's right outside."

"Sure," said Marcel. "If I need help."

He didn't. Once the body was loaded, Milo said, "I'll drive," and wheeled the cart to a nearby autopsy room.

The space smelled of chopped liver, copper, spoiled produce, antiseptic. Spotless, but for a red-brown splotch near the sink that made me think of the Aventura's liverish uniforms.

Everyone gloved up. Milo and Marcel lowered the corpse to a stainless-steel table and began lifting up per Robaire's instructions as she unraveled the plastic. Heavy-duty sheeting, rolled on in multiple layers that were nearly opaque. Lifeless flesh flashed ivory through the milky sheath.

When the face was revealed, Milo said, "Oh, shit."

Kurt DeGraw would've gazed up at the ceiling if his eyes were open.

Robaire said, "You **know** him?"

"He managed the hotel where Victim Mars was murdered."

"Wow. Unbelievable. Thanks, Marcel, you can go now."

As the attendant left, Milo took out his pad.

Laura Robaire said, "He was found in his apartment yesterday morning by his cleaning woman, lying in bed with a plastic bag over his head. The bag was secured with generic packing string. Time of death estimate is sometime during the night. Lacking any broken skin and with no sign of forced entry, struggle, or ransacking, the EMTs assumed suicide and so did my investigators. The autopsy revealed pulmonary and other organ congestion consistent with asphyxia but told us nothing about manner. I was teaching my resident the importance of being hands-on, not just relying on labs. To illustrate, I palpated, and when I got to under the chin it felt swollen. So we shaved his beard."

She tilted back DeGraw's head. "Right here—bruises notably similar to what I found on your Victim Mars. Unlike Mars, there are no broken ribs or ocular bleeding so I still wasn't considering it dramatic evidence, there are all sorts of ways to get a bruise. But it did make me wonder, so I ran the tox stat and when opiates, alcohol, or any other obvious CNS suppressants came back negative, I realized suicide was a less likely scenario. At that point, I made two calls, to Detective Gottlieb and to you. Even without a link, I thought you two should be talking. I expect you'll be hearing from him. And now that you've established an actual link between the victims, I'm sure he'll be happy to talk to you."

I said, "Suicide's unlikely because people who use bags pre-medicate."

"I've never seen different, Dr. Delaware. Think about what it would entail: You don't prep with anything to make yourself fade out, just tie a bag over your head and lie there waiting to suffocate? No matter how emotionally depressed someone is, the urge to breathe would kick in. They'd start gasping and even if they tried to fight it, there's a good chance they'd rip off the bag. Have you observed otherwise?"

I shook my head.

She said, "I just don't see anyone starving themselves of oxygen for up to fifteen minutes with no sign of any struggle, let alone actually going through with it. Thank God I took the time to shave him. My judgment is he was burked, so manner will definitely be listed as homicide."

"Burked?" said Milo.

"Same as what was done to your Victim Mars."

"You didn't use that term with her."

"It's not medical, it's idiomatic," said Robaire. "On reports I stick to technical terminology."

"What is it?"

"A method of murder that originated in Scotland, the 1820s. What one of my professors called the Case of the Two Nasty Billys."

"A team?"

"A deadly duo, Lieutenant. William Burke and William Hare were a couple of Irishmen who moved to Edinburgh and made a living supplying cadavers to the university med school, during a period where there was an acute shortage of bodies. Other suppliers got naughty but only to the extent of digging up corpses that hadn't been donated to science—body-snatching. Burke and Hare took it a step further and hastened the process along in living people. They worked as a team, one guy sitting on the victim in order to immobilize, while the other pinched off the nose and held the mouth shut. They chose asphyxia because it created a fresher body that simulated common natural causes of the day—pneumonia, bronchitis, other respiratory ailments."

Milo said, "Birkenhaar."

Laura Robaire said, "That's right."

"This is something else. Birken**haar**." He spelled it. "We've got suspects who registered at the hotel under that name."

"Oh, my," said Laura Robaire. "That **is** chilling." Her pretty face knitted in concentration. She smiled. "So I really **have** come up with something."

◆

We left the crypt, stunned. Milo was the first to speak.

"Burking. They made a joke of it, the pre-meditating bastards. What, I'm dealing with students of history?"

I said, "Couple of cellies with lots of spare time? All those books in the prison library."

"Probably true crime," he said. "Convicts love that stuff."

"Thalia didn't."

"What do you mean?"

"Not a single volume of it in her collection, just fiction."

"Yeah, well, these guys are into reality. Or Pretty Woman's the reader and she told them about it."

"Team effort," I said. "Killing Thalia was a collaboration from the beginning. They did Burke and Hare one better, made it a three-way. One to immobilize, another to close off her airways, the third to search for treasure. Like Burke and Hare they wanted to make the death appear natural. A victim that old, who'd suspect? Like Burke and Hare, they failed."

"Four on the team," he said, "if DeGraw was in on it. Can you see any other reason they'd do him?"

I said, "It explains how they got in. Who better than the manager to provide a master key?"

"Asshole. Never liked him."

I said, "Be interesting to have a look at his phone records and his computer."

He phoned Culver City PD and asked for Detective Gottlieb. The receptionist said, "Patricia or Leonard?"

"Leonard."

Dead air. Then: "He's out, sir, I'll give him the message."

We got back in the car. I said, "The three of them could've assumed they'd gotten away with it until you showed up and DeGraw told them. He seemed an excitable type, being drawn into a murder investigation could've panicked him. His mistake was showing that to the others. Maybe even pressuring them for his share. So they cut him from the team. Or like we said about Waters, it was a matter of economics and DeGraw was doomed the minute he got involved."

"Pie divided two ways," he said. "Or only one if someone else bet wrong."

I drove out of the lot. He said, "This team concept could get out of hand. What about Ricki S. and her dinner companion?"

"All we know is she had shared a booth with someone."

"Yeah, but she was **way** too touchy about Gramps and maybe that was because she was also involved. What we said before. Siphoning dough out of Thalia's estate and Thalia found out."

"Thalia wouldn't have taken action?"

"Maybe she started to, Alex. Step one, she calls you and starts talking about criminal tendencies—Ricki being bent just like Grampa Jack. She didn't turn Ricki in right away because the two of them went way back, she knew Ricki as a kid. The point of hiring you was to get her own priorities straight. But what if, after your first session, she felt clarified and confronted Ricki?"

"What, then?" I said. "Ricki just happens to know a murderous trio already staying at the hotel?"

"True," he said. "That doesn't work."

"If Ricki was involved, it had to be well before the Birkenhaars checked in. If you can find something linking her to them, you'd be in great shape."

"Neither of them sounds like the guy in the restaurant."

"For all we know, that was a blind date."

"She never had another one."

"Not at High Steaks."

"Yeah . . . I'm not thinking straight . . . I'll have Sean or Moe do a loose watch on her for at least a coupla days. An older dude shows up at her doorstep, we can at least find out who he is."

◆

The return trip was automotive atherosclerosis for ten miles. A hundred minutes later, we were pulling up to my house when Milo's phone signaled another text. "Hope that's Gottlieb."

He read, took a deep breath, loosened his tie, punched a number, and said, "That's it? You're sure? Damn. Okay, thanks."

He hung up. "That was Jake Lev, the archive zombie. Nothing on Leroy Hoke except a folder on the LaPlante heist and it's thin. He's making a copy, will fax it over tomorrow."

He phoned Detective Moses Reed, asked for the tail on Sylvester and gave specifics.

Reed said, "Sure, L.T."

Click. "Great kid."

I turned off the engine. He looked at his Timex. "Enough for one day. Let me take you guys out to dinner."

"Why don't we have something here?"

"We put in a full day and I'm sure Gorgeous did, too. Name the cuisine—I can even try Rick, see if he's free."

"If Robin's up for it, sure."

As we climbed the stairs to my front terrace, he phoned Dr. Richard Silverman at the Cedars-Sinai E.R. Head-on auto crash in the Fairfax district, Rick and two other surgeons busy repairing.

Milo said, "No big deal, three of us. The Virtuous Team."

Robin was in the kitchen reading **American Art Review.** Blanche snored at her feet.

"Hi, guys. I went to Trader Joe's and bought three huge steaks 'cause I figured you'd be beat after the drive. Let's barbecue."

Blanche opened one eye and purred. Robin smiled. "We just finished a long walk, she's bushed, but I'm sure she won't mind a rib to chew on."

Blanche got to her feet.

Milo said, "She understands Culinary?"

"And a whole lot more. Alex, how about getting the grill going?"

I said, "He offered to take us out."

Milo said, "A serious offer."

"That's sweet of you, Big Guy, but I've already begun marinating and what're we talking about—putting meat on iron?"

"Think about it, kid. How often do I get generous?"

She kissed his cheek. "Like always—okay, you make a salad, Alex tackles the grill, and I'll sit here and drink a Gimlet with my girlfriend."

"Tackles? Your grill has an electric starter, it ain't exactly Boy Scout wisdom."

"Sometimes it jams," she said.

I said, "I can always find two sticks or a piece of flint."

His phone rang. "Sturgis. Oh, hi . . . yeah it is crazy . . . yeah . . . makes sense . . . when? . . . sure, thanks, half an hour tops, probably less."

Click. "Sorry, kids, gotta not eat and run."

I said, "Gottlieb?"

"None other."

Robin said, "Who's Gottlieb?"

"Culver City detective. The manager at Thalia's hotel got murdered there the same way she did."

"Someone has a grudge against the hotel?"

"I wish I could tell you—sorry about the barbecue."

"Let me make you a sandwich."

He hugged her. "You're the perfect human being."

"So Alex claims." She turned to me. "Here's where I say you go with him and you pretend to not want to. I'll make you both sandwiches."

CHAPTER

26

Kurt DeGraw had rented a small, flat-faced house on a jacaranda-shaded street off Palms Boulevard. A Honda Accord leased by DeGraw was backed by an Impala that could've been the sib of Milo's unmarked. Crime scene tape blocked the doorway but the door was ajar.

Milo called in, "Detective? Milo Sturgis."

A voice from the back said, "Hold on." Moments later a lanky gray-haired man in a precise blue suit, white shirt, and red tie appeared. A pad like Milo's protruded from a jacket pocket. Half-lens reading glasses perched on a narrow nose.

"Lieutenant? Len Gottlieb."

At first glance, Gottlieb looked more CEO than cop. Up close, a haircut slightly past its prime, flecks of stubble at the jawline, and a nasty-looking scar running down the side of his right cheek rubbed out some of the polish.

We shook hands. Milo introduced me.

Len Gottlieb said, "One of my daughters is a school psychologist. Can't say I've ever had the privilege of working with one of you."

Milo said, "You should try it."

"Like we have the budget—anyway, this is a weird one if that cute little pathologist is right about the under-the-chin deal."

Milo said, "She's definitely right, Len. Your vic knew our vic. My working hypothesis is he helped kill her."

"That so? Fill me in?"

Milo talked, Gottlieb listened.

"Almost a hundred, huh? That's a shame. So maybe to hell with my vic for being a bad guy and I should move on to someone who deserves being spoken for. Problem is, try to find someone like that. My last two were gang scum no one's going to miss."

Gottlieb pushed back a tongue of white hair. "With you guys, I don't have to pretend everyone's the same."

He looked at me.

I nodded.

Gottlieb smiled. "I didn't offend you?"

Milo said, "He's way past the point of being offended."

"You've been corrupted, Doc? Congratulations. So where do we go with this, Milo?"

"How about we share info and communicate regularly."

"Sounds like a plan," said Gottlieb. "If I go over to that hotel, am I going to learn something you don't already know?"

"Probably not, Len."

"So, no sense duplicating. Your innocent vic—and that other villain . . . Waters—you clear all that up, it's going to clear up my vic, too. Meantime, I have to look into another case, not a homicide, a missing. A good-person missing, nineteen-year-old girl goes to a club on Washington, hasn't been seen since, no activity on her cellphone, no contact with her parents. Who happen to be friends of my boss."

"See what you mean."

"The boss agrees that's the one I should prioritize," said Gottlieb. "I listen to her because she's my wife and also she outranks me—lieutenant like you. We both agree the girl's unlikely to be found alive but the parents will go nuts if they never get at least some kind of closure."

"Makes sense, Len."

"In terms of communication, all I can give you now is what I've seen. Indications are my vic lived here alone. Kind of a neat freak, which made it easier to snoop around. No security system, alarm, or cameras. Even the smoke alarms are inoperative due to dead batteries. I can see him thinking it's a safe neighborhood 'cause basically it is until it isn't. No forced entry at the front but the back door was unlocked. Whether or not he left it that way or let someone in, no idea. Entry via the backyard would be a cinch. Crappy gate, just a latch you can reach over and undo. We dusted for prints, found nothing. Same in here, nothing but the vic's. I'm sure Robaire told you—she's a looker, no? The crypt could use some dressing up—her theory. Two killers, sometime during the night, they burked him."

"You knew the term?"

"Not until Robaire told it to me. She went to Harvard, brains plus those looks?" He whistled. "My mind, someone ticking boxes like that should be married to a really rich guy, maybe she is."

Milo said, "She's married to a doctor."

"Not as good," said Gottlieb, "but not bad. Anyway, yesterday we canvassed the neighbors, no one heard or saw a thing. Some neighborhoods, they'd be pulling your leg. Here, they're probably telling the truth. This isn't Washington Boulevard, all those clubs they've got now. This part of Culver, after dark the sidewalks get rolled up."

"No local gossip on DeGraw."

"I wish, gossip's our raw material, right? Naw, he went to work, would say hello if you said it first. Couple of people said he wore some kind of a uniform jacket—we found three in the closet, this weird kind-of-maroon color, each one hung with a pair of gray pants. One lady figured him for a waiter or someone working on a cruise ship. No one ever saw him return home so maybe he worked late or he stopped for a shot somewhere. If he did, that could be a lead, I'll try to find out."

"What was he wearing when he was found?"

"His baby suit," said Gottlieb. "There is evidence of burglary—no money in his wallet, no computer, no cellphone, and something's gone that used to sit on a stand in the bedroom, has to be a TV. C'mon, I'll show you."

The house was six small rooms: living/dining area, circa-twenties kitchen, bedroom, bath, a tiny vacant space at the rear. To the left of the unused room was a laundry area but no appliances. A flimsy paneled door with a simple turn-bolt led to the back.

Gottlieb said, "This was open," and demonstrated. Outside was scant, dark space hemmed by block walls, nothing organic but patchy grass.

We returned inside and had another walk-around. Not much furniture and what was there looked rented. The bed where Kurt DeGraw had died was a double with no headboard. Crumpled linens were piled like meringue. A gray polyester duvet had fallen to the worn hardwood floor.

"Looks like a struggle but there wasn't," said Len Gottlieb. "EMTs said they found him lying there, sheet was military-tight. What you're seeing is from when they tried to work on him. I'd show you the bag around his head and the twine but obviously they're at the lab. Tech I spoke to said both are generic, no prints or DNA, so far. Bottom line: nothing evidentiary. You weren't involved, I'd probably never close it."

Milo's mouth twisted.

I put words in his mouth. **Maybe same here, amigo.**

I said, "DeGraw's housekeeper found him."

"Found him and freaked out, Doctor. Nice lady but speaks no English, she came in once a week, when DeGraw was gone, so she doesn't really know him. I had a Spanish cop talk to her to be careful. No problems with DeGraw, basically she'd do a couple of hours and leave, he left her cash. He was always neat, she said it was like no one lived here."

We moved to the kitchen. Cheap utensils and crockery for one, a few pots and pans, most unused, some still with tags. A gold-beige fridge held bottles of Stella Artois and Fiji Water. Wilted vegetables smelling of a grocery dumpster occupied the so-called crisper. In the freezer, stacks of Lean Cuisine shared space with cans of orange juice concentrate.

Less home than stopover.

I said, "Any idea how long he's been living here?"

Len Gottlieb said, "Landlord says nearly two years, paid his rent on time, no issues."

"Doesn't look as if he put down roots."

"No, it doesn't, Doctor. Maybe he bunked down in that hotel where he worked, considered that his real crib."

Milo said, "Interesting thought."

"Once in a while I come up with one. It's not much of a crime scene, right? Visually and microscopically, not a single weird hair or print. That puzzles me because a serious cleanup doesn't go with a burglary gone evil. But now that you've told me it could be something else, I can see it, if we're talking psycho murderers. Anyway, feel free to go through whatever you want, I've done it twice but I won't be offended. Anything else . . .

oh, yeah, the guy didn't read or listen to music. There's not even a, you-know, sex toy so I can't tell you if he's straight or gay or something in between. Or into nothing. My wife claims there are people like that, have no interest at all. Though I never met one."

Milo said, "Any financial documents?"

"Those I took back to my office," said Gottlieb, "but they're not much, the guy was no serious investor. We're talking salary stubs and tax returns and an Ameritrade account with twenty K in it. Where his money went, I can't tell you. He did pretty well, they paid him ninety a year."

"He was Swiss, maybe he sent it back home," said Milo.

Gottlieb frowned. "Now, that's interesting, no passport showed up. But again, maybe the serious stuff is back at the hotel."

"We'll check and let you know, Len."

"Ninety a year's not bad, but if he could cash in mega-bucks from your vic, he'd have an incentive. You think they got a big haul from her?"

Milo said, "There was three grand in her room but that could be the small pile they missed, we just don't know. She **was** mega-rich and if we're right about four people involved there'd be enough to go around."

Gottlieb said, "I've seen throats get cut for twenty bucks. Mostly back when I worked the west side of Philly, ghetto stuff. But in Brent-wood, maybe you're right, it would have to be serious dough."

He flicked the red tie. "Hundred years old, living by herself, would she leave beaucoup green lying around?"

Milo said, "She'd been there for a long time, Len. Maybe she felt safe. But like I said, it's still at the assumption stage, I really don't know squat."

"Whodunits, our curse." Gottlieb took out his pad. "Give me what you know about your three suspects."

Milo filled him in and Gottlieb took notes, printing meticulously like a draftsman. Doing it quickly, an impressive show.

When Milo finished, he said, "Prison buddies plus a chick, she's messing with both of them. Sounds like she could be the motivator." He grinned. "But maybe I'm biased, having a female boss."

"Biased or not, Len, we've thought the same thing."

Gottlieb said, "Let's face it, lookers get their way because they have goodies to distribute. My second wife was Miss Downey before she got huge and sloppy, don't ask."

"**My** big problem," said Milo, "is I still haven't identified this looker."

Gottlieb looked around Kurt DeGraw's characterless living room. "A manager setting up a guest, talk about Hotel Hell. If he did that, he's a total bastard. You ever meet him?"

"We did," said Milo. "Not Mr. Charming."

"A bastard **and** a pain in the ass? Don't like hotels, never did. Don't like to travel, period, but my wife is always doing it, being brass, conferences and the like. She can take care of herself but those places she stays at, the ones near the airport? Every time she packs a suitcase, I tell her be careful and she reminds me about who shoots better at the range. She's my third wife but I still worry about her, she's a girl, right? And a cutie."

He shook his head. "Airports always attract scum, we had time I'd tell you about Philly but we don't. Still, in Brentwood you'd expect better. At least basic safety. Anything else I should know?"

Milo said, "Can't think of anything." He looked at me.

I said, "No computer, no phone, but not burglary. Maybe it was the data they were after."

"You're right, Doctor. Burglars find you, they might shoot you or hit you over the head, they don't do that creepy culty thing with the plastic bag—remember those comet loonies in San Diego, Hale-Bob, whatever. So it bugged me.

Now it makes more sense. And you're suggesting I find out who his phone account is with. Already in the works, Doctor, I'm planning to subpoena."

To Milo. "I find out anything juicy, you'll be the second to know."

"Who'll be the first, Len?"

"Who else? Me."

CHAPTER

27

By nine A.M. the following day, we were back at the Aventura. The parking lot was even lonelier, what might've been one guest vehicle plus a limo driver sleeping openmouthed in his car.

Milo and I got out of the unmarked and he walked up to the driver.

Not Leon Creech. A young bearded Latino wearing a black polo shirt and matching jeans. iPad on the passenger seat. Angry Birds on the screen.

He snored.

Milo poked him awake gently. The guy roused, gave a wet cough, looked panicked.

Milo said, "Police, but no hassle. Just want to ask you why it's so quiet."

The driver rubbed his eyes. "Yeah, totally dead, it's like they're going out of business. Don't know why the company sent me here. Actually, I do. They got a contract, get paid a flat fee. But we get shafted, no tips, it sucks."

"Crap deal," said Milo. "How long's it been this way?"

"The guy they sent yesterday said it was the same." He looked at the pad, like a kid wanting another bite of cookie.

"Thanks, good luck to you."

"I'll need it."

As we approached the hotel, Alicia Bogomil stepped out from behind foliage, cigarette in hand.

Milo said, "Not much going on."

"Not for three days, sir. No check-ins other than three snip tucks, all women."

"Any idea why the slowdown?"

"Four days ago a bunch of Arabs marched through with DeGraw and they looked even more pissed off than usual and he looked even more stressed out than usual. Someone said they want the land for something else, the end is near. I asked DeGraw about it and he blew me off but I could tell something was bugging him."

"When was that, Alicia?"

"Morning after the Arabs were gone, so three

days ago," she said. "Listen to this: They own the place but didn't stay here. I heard some driver say he was taking them back to the Beverly Wilshire. There's an endorsement for you."

"Okay, thanks."

"One thing you might want to know, sir. There's demo notices on all The Numbers, went up yesterday. I was going to call you in case you still needed to preserve the crime scene. But then I had a look, saw everything was cleaned out, no tape, I figured you were already on top of the situation."

Her shoulders tensed.

"You got it, Alicia, nothing to preserve."

"Well, that's good. I'm thinking more about getting back into the job."

"Great," said Milo. "Speaking of DeGraw, does he keep a room here for sleeping?"

"Sure, right behind his office. I thought that was his main crib. You're saying he has another?"

"He always sleeps here?"

"Every time I've worked late, I've seen him go in there for the night. Are you asking about him because you think he was part of something?"

"Just following up, Alicia."

"Oh, okay. Want me to page him for you?"

"Not necessary, Alicia. Have a nice day, Alicia."

As we left her, Milo said, "Ignorance, bliss, why not?"

Kurt DeGraw's office was on the ground floor, through the door behind the reception desk. One liver-coat on duty at the concrete counter, a young woman we hadn't seen before. Young, acne-spotted, chopped-up blond hair streaked with pink and lavender.

A paper tag on her lapel said **Kelli** in black marker.

Milo flashed the badge and said, "We have an appointment with Mr. DeGraw."

"Sorry, sirs, he's not here, yet."

"We'll wait in his office."

By the time she said, "Um, I guess," we'd stepped behind the counter.

She trotted after us through an empty five-foot corridor. At the end was a door marked **Manager.** Milo turned the knob. No resistance. He dropped his hand, left the door closed.

Kelli said, "Um, maybe you shouldn't go in? I can page him, uh-oh, I can't, don't know his number." Perplexed.

Milo delivered one of his classic mixed messages: Looming huge while putting on his softest smile. The infrequently visiting uncle you kind of like but also fear.

Kelli opted for fear.

Milo said, "You can go."

"Um, I'm not busy," she said.

"We're fine, Kelli."

"I don't want to mess up. I'm just a **temp**."

"When'd you start?"

"Like three days ago."

"Has it been quiet all that time?"

"It's like nothing happens. It's a **hotel** but nothing happens."

"Even so, Kelli," said Milo, "you're the only one out there handling the front desk. Better get back to your station."

"If you can just wait, I can **find** his number and page him."

"Not necessary, Kelli. Like I said, we have an appointment."

She said, "Um, okay."

"We're the police, Kelli. No one will hassle you for anything."

"Really? Okay, cool."

All traces of worry erased, she bounced away.

Kurt DeGraw's office was as large as his Culver City bedroom, furnished with similar apathy. A door with no visible lock was centered on the far wall. Milo gloved up, opened it, peeked in, and shut it.

"His crash pad. First things first."

He scanned the office. An iMac on the desk brought a smile to his face. A keyboard tap brought up a demand for a password. He tried variants of Kurt and DeGraw, got nowhere and began searching elsewhere.

Landline on the desk, but no cellphone, not in any desk drawer, the compartments of a matching credenza, or a black metal three-drawer file cabinet whose doors swung open easily.

I said, "He wasn't one for security, same as his house. Maybe he did leave the back door unlocked."

"Wish there was something iffy here," said Milo. "I like it when they think they've got something to hide." He looked at the laptop.

I said, "Maybe try something with Aventura in it for the password?"

His sixth try worked. KD Aventura.

"Voilà," he said. Then, "Shit," when he encountered blank screen after blank screen. "Wiped clean. Maybe he was ready to rabbit. So where's the damn passport?"

He reopened file drawers, inspected contents, squatted at the lowest section, finally stood up rubbing the small of his back. "Plenty of work stuff but nothing juicy."

I examined the documents. Payment records and insurance info on surgical patients, nothing on guests who hadn't gotten their faces rearranged.

Milo said, "Maybe it all goes to Dubai or wherever." His smile was crooked, mischievous. "Hell, maybe he got careless about security because he's Swiss. All those centuries of neutrality you don't figure someone's gonna declare war."

Leaning against a wall, he phoned Assistant D.A. John Nguyen, caught him up, and asked for a warrant on DeGraw's office, making it sound as if he hadn't entered, yet.

After a lot of listening, he said, "There's also a room behind the office where he sleeps and that's clearly personal space, John, so let's not exclude it—"

He frowned, listened some more, offered a couple of "reallys" and several "uh-huhs," before clicking off.

I said, "John's being lawyerly."

"Per usual. The office is a no-go because it belongs to the hotel owners and contains business records not proven to be germane to my investigation. Ergo, I need to get the consent of someone able to grant it legally. Such contingencies are especially exigent because 'we're dealing with Mideast hotshots,' no way we want **that** kind of trouble."

I said, "Oops."

He cracked up. Pointed to the rear door. "But that's okay. Which is what I wanted in the first place."

"Did John recommend the cooperative judge **du jour?**"

"Better than that, he's making the call himself, I can assume a yes and go right ahead."

"Crafty, Lieutenant."

"One does what one can. Let's see if it makes a damn bit of difference."

He had me glove up, too, and we entered the back room.

Kurt DeGraw's in-house quarters were a splurge compared with his rental house. Fully equipped marble bathroom set up with high-end shaving gear, lots of hotel soap and shampoo, fluffy white hotel towels.

A good four hundred square feet of space suggesting what the so-called hospitality industry terms a "superior room."

This bed was king-sized with a brass headboard and matching footboard, skinned in sky-blue, high-thread-count cotton and covered by a peach-colored down-packed duvet with a Pratesi label.

In the uppermost drawer of a walnut-replica, deco-replica nightstand was a small, bright-red leather book embossed with a white cross.

At first glance, a mini-Bible with souped-up binding. Five lines of white lettering said otherwise.

Schweizer Pass
Passeport Suisse
Passaporto svizzero
Passapor svizzer
Swiss passport

The most recent visa stamps were dated four years ago. Dubai, Abu Dhabi, Bahrain, Hong Kong, Singapore, Shanghai.

One European trip, a year before, requiring no visa: sixty-day stay in the homeland, entry at Zurich.

"Family probably lives there," said Milo. "I'll tell Gottlieb, he can try to find them."

I checked all the dates. "No other trip lasted more than six days. Got to be work travel."

In the closet were two blue and two white dress shirts, a navy suit, a pair of liver-red-jacket-gray-slack combos. On a top shelf, two pricey silver Rimowa suitcases turned out to be empty. On the floor, polished wingtips, brown and black, and two pairs of Nike runners. A convex dresser, also mimicking the twenties, held precisely folded cashmere sweaters, Sunspel underwear from England, dark-hued cashmere socks rolled and sorted by color.

At the bottom of the dresser were two half drawers. Another "here go my knees" squat for Milo. "Where's the WD-40 when you need it?"

In the left drawer, he found a vibrator, two tubes of Good Clean Love lubricant, and a stack of Technicolor Scandinavian porn magazines dated thirty years ago. Too-bright photography, tan skin, yellow hair. Straight sex, nothing beyond the basics.

Painfully wholesome Nordic faces in situations that didn't call for goofy glee made me laugh.

Milo said, "What?"

"Back in high school this was forbidden fruit. Now it seems kind of quaint."

"Ah, youth. At least yours was predictable." He paged through. "Go for it, Bjorn and Brigitta, afterward we celebrate with herring for all."

Last stop: the right-hand drawer. "Here we go!"

A second iMac sat next to a charging cord. He removed both, found an outlet, and plugged in. Dead.

"Damn." Placing the computer on the bed next to the passport and the porn, he contemplated, put the magazines back in the drawer, glared at the Mac. "Bastard machine. Maybe our geeks can get something out of it."

My first thought was, not likely. The lack of charge suggested it hadn't been important to DeGraw. Or even in working condition.

No cellphone on the premises said the premises didn't matter much to DeGraw, anything of interest had been stashed at his off-site pad and taken by his killers.

Bad choice. He'd made a lot of them.

I kept all that to myself, and thought about the rumors of the hotel's closure. The staff had picked up on it recently but DeGraw had likely known for a while.

I said so to Milo.

He said, "Guy's job is ending so he's got an additional motive to press for his share of the take."

"That could also explain why he let them in. The meeting was expected. He thought they'd be paying him off."

I pointed to the passport. "Everything he'd need for a smooth exit is here."

Milo said, "Score the dough, come back here, pack your good duds, and split for Yodel-land. Yeah, makes sense. But their agreeing so readily wouldn't make him suspicious?"

"Big money breeds optimism," I said. "Think of the lottery."

He paced a bit, rechecked drawers and the closet, shook his head. "Idiot's banking on serious moolah and instead he gets burked. Nice verb, that. Has that hard-edged feel . . . okay if that's what happened, why no sign of a struggle when they jumped him? Like Robaire said, there were no downers in DeGraw's system, the normal reflex would be to fight for his life."

"Maybe there **was** some kind of struggle and they smoothed it over. Not a brawl, just some mussed bedcovers. Two able-bodied men using the element of surprise could've overpowered him quickly. Especially if he was being distracted. As in a vamp by Ms. Cutie. The porn says he was pedestrian and hetero. She'd be an excellent lure. Maybe she came in alone to deliver the payment, DeGraw didn't expect the others."

"Waters and Bakstrom dangle her as bait, then crash the party."

"Money and hot sex? It would've lowered his guard way below rationality. He was probably thinking he'd died and gone to heaven. Unfortunately, he was only half correct."

He paced some more. Tucked the computer under his arm, lifted the passport, wedged it between two fingers, and headed for the door.

As we passed through DeGraw's office, he said, "She's the appetizer, big money's the entrée, you're right, he'd open the door. Wide."

28

Back at the station we headed for the evidence room, where Milo filled out forms, registered the computer and the passport as evidence but didn't deposit them.

The evidence clerk said, "You're not leaving them here?"

"This you can have." Handing her the passport.

She said, "Swiss? Kind of pretty."

He said, "Be sure to ask for priority boarding."

We climbed upstairs to the hallway leading to his office. A man walked a few yards ahead of us, past the interview rooms, carrying something blue. Nowhere to go except Milo's office and a utility closet.

The man stopped at Milo's door and knocked.

"Over here, friend."

The visitor turned.

Early thirties, tall, dark wavy hair, a few days of beard stubble. He wore a long-sleeved black tee, blue jeans, and brown ventilated shoes with crepe soles, scuffed at the toes.

Good-looking despite old eyes. The vaguely dissolute air of one of those bruised **artiste** types you see hunching over laptops in coffee joints, pretending to write screenplays.

The badge and the holster on his belt said otherwise.

Detective badge, Level II.

He smiled but the effort seemed painful. "Lieutenant Sturgis?"

"That's me."

"Jacob Lev. I brought you the copy of the file you requested."

"Door-to-door service?" said Milo, taking the blue binder. "Thought you were gonna fax it."

"Fax machine broke down," said Lev. Soft voice, boyish yet deep.

"Appreciate the effort, Detective." Milo shook his hand.

Lev said, "Sorry I couldn't come up with more. You know how it is."

"Bad record keeping at the archives."

"General attitude," said Lev. "Contempt for the past."

Forcing his smile a millimeter wider, he turned and left.

Milo said, "There's a guy could use your services. D II landing in a crap job like that must've done something serious."

He unlocked his office, sat down, inspected the binder.

Blue, hardback cloth boards blemished with mold spots and rodent nips. Despite the sturdy exterior, only two sheets of paper inside, each protected by a plastic sleeve that looked brand-new.

Jacob Lev going the extra mile. When stuck in a crap job, pleasing a superior isn't a bad idea.

Milo removed both sheets and laid them on his desk. He never minds me reading over his shoulder so I hovered.

Legal-sized paper, once-white, had aged to caramel and grown shaggy at the edges. The uneven pressure points of a manual typewriter produced letters that protruded like Braille. Lots of typos, each one X'd out by the author.

His name at the top: LAPD Commander R. G. Demarest, no division cited.

The date: May 1939.

The title, off center:

The LaPlante Jewelers Jewelry Theft
of 1938: Possible Ramifications.

What followed were paragraphs of excessively worded cop prose. It's a language of its own, taught by no one and serving no function, but enduring across generations.

The choice of topic puzzled me. Why had a Beverly Hills crime been documented by LAPD? As I read on, the reason became clear.

Commander R. G. Demarest's concern wasn't the year-old burglary, itself. The department was interested in "prime suspect Hoke in a general and optimally probative manner regarding, in particular, a prior and pending SI investigation undertaken in cooperation with and with implications for communication with Federal Entities."

The tax evasion case had been set in motion well before the theft of the Oscar bling from Frederick LaPlante's safe.

Demarest repeated himself a few times, let's hear it for Roget and synonyms, but eventually, his emphasis became clear.

Theorizing about "what effect, positive or negative, would Prm. Susp. Hoke's ultimately proven suspected complicity in this high-level jewelry covert burglarly [sic] replete with allegations of nocturnal tunneling and safe-cracking of a serious 'yegg-type' level, pertain to the aforementioned investigation?"

His conclusion at the bottom of page one: "A

definitive answer is unavailable, thus risks are both high, serious, and unpredictable."

His advice: "Minimize engagement in the collaboration and intelligence data requested by Beverly Hills Police Department in re: LaPlante, Hoke, etc, so as to avoid adding undue overt prosecutorial emphasis to the LaPlante case so that Prm. Susp. Hoke will not be unduly alarmed and flee to jurisdictions unknown id est Tia Juana where he has been known to frequent or parts south below."

Milo looked up. "The department screwed B.H. in order to continue working with the feds on the tax case."

I said, "Politics as usual and it succeeded. Who got the credit for putting Hoke away? Not B.H."

He flipped the paper, found nothing on the back, turned to the second page.

A list, also poorly centered.

Prm. Sus.s Hoke' sKnown Associates
or Individuals Suspected of
Such.'

1. John J. 'Jack' McCandless, attorney at law and so-called mob mouthpiece.

2. William P. Wojik, CPA, certified public accountant and so-called mob 'money man.'

3. Thalia Mars nee Thelma Meyer, reputed girlfriend of Prm. Sus. Hoke('moll') and additionally, reputed mob courier and bookkeeper, the latter supposition being evidenced by a regiment of comprehensive accounting classes enrolled in by said subject at Los Angeles City College, 855 North Vermont Avenue Campus. Furthermore, subsequent taking of the Certified Public Accountancy exam and passed.

4. Fred Drancy aka Count Frederick LaPlante, jeweler and consignor of expensive jewelry and suspected co-conspirator in rather than innocent victim of aforementioned 'heist.'

5. Possible and potential collaborators in prior crimes with Prm. Sus. Hoke reputed to have possibly been involved or to possess knowledge of Prm. Sus. Hoke' s prior criminal activities including but not limited to aforementioned 'heist.' All such individuals to remain un-named.

No phone numbers or addresses on anyone. Listing the college's street address was an odd divergence and I said so.

Milo said, "Pencil pushers are addicted to extraneous details, Demarest couldn't go cold turkey."

"Maybe, but I think this was more. By tossing in one bit of specifics, he's saying the department has the facts but is choosing not to divulge most of them."

"Saying it to who?"

"Anyone who might come across the report."

"Ass Covering One-Oh-One."

"Why would it be different back then?" I said.

I took another slog through Demarest's verbiage. "The message is clear: Don't mess with the robbery. In fact do what you can to **retard** the investigation. The goal had been set well before the robbery: Nab Hoke for tax evasion because that had worked with Capone and other mobsters and allowed confiscation of illegally obtained assets. Recovered jewels wouldn't fit that strategy. They could be identified and open to claims by the consignors. But once the jewels were converted to cash, no way they could be accounted for. That's why the department waited until the goods had been sold. That's why the IRS let Drancy move to New York even though they knew he was dirty. He got his freedom and the government got its money. And maybe they **knew** Drancy was dirty because he was their informant."

"They turned him and he ratted out Hoke," he said.

"He and/or one of the unnamed associates in item five. The IRS fills its coffers with a nice bunch of cash, the department rids itself of an annoyingly elusive major criminal; who cares if an incorrigible con man becomes New York's problem?"

He flipped the second page over. Another blank.

I'd turned away when he said, "Hold on."

Lowering his head close to the paper, he pointed to the bottom right-hand corner.

A swirl of faint cursive in pencil, barely visible.

He squinted, shook his head, held the sheet directly under a desk light. The writing clarified a bit, the barest gray suggesting itself on old paper.

Win Ni 57

He read it out loud. "Ring any bells?"

"Maybe a scheduled raid?" I said. "A winter night, someplace with fifty-seven in the address?"

"I guess—hell, it could be Chinese takeout. Okay, back to the Drancy-as-rat scenario. You realized what that means: Official agencies fenced stolen goods and robbed legal owners of serious money."

"It's called eminent domain."

He laughed, turned serious. "Dangerous game for Drancy."

I said, "The alternative was going to prison and ending up even more vulnerable. Be interesting to know if he was convicted of the art swindle." I punched a preset on my phone.

Maxine Driver said, "Oh, hi. I was planning to call you but not with good news, I'm afraid. Janet couldn't find anything about Hoke and all she got on Drancy was an obituary."

"When did he die?"

"Hold on . . . February 1942, but there are no details."

"Could you email it to me?"

"It's important?"

"Who knows?"

"How's the case going?"

"Getting closer."

"And . . ."

I said nothing.

"That's all you can tell me."

"The promise remains, Maxine."

"Right, I'll be the first to know . . . okay, here it is."

◆

The attachment came through seconds later.

A single, small-print, paid-for line in the **Daily News.**

> Drancy, F. B., 57, mourned by family. 'You were a
> gem. May you shine forever.'

Milo said, "Daddy's a gem? Family had a sense of humor? If they'd ponied up for a second line, he'd be multifaceted?"

I smiled but wondered if a joke had been in play. Something else about a gem . . .

Nothing came to me and I sat there as Milo phoned the New York City medical examiner, learned that death records from 1918 through 1950 were maintained by the city's Municipal Archives. A clerk there informed him even law enforcement sources were required to fill out an application, though the ten-dollar fee might be waived. Or maybe not.

"How long will it take to process the application, ma'am?"

"Depends."

"On?"

"All kinds of things."

"Please put your supervisor on."

A woman named Leticia was willing to pull the file and read the summary over the phone because "my husband and both brothers are cops. But if you want a Xerox, Lieutenant, you do need to do it officially."

"Let's see what it says, first."

She was back in a moment. "You know, this one's kind of interesting." She recited the summary. Milo told her he'd definitely want a copy, would get back to her.

He hung up, wide-eyed.

Fred Bullard Drancy had suffered massive internal bleeding and blunt-force trauma due to a fall from the tenth floor of a vacant building on East 65th Street near Second Avenue. The structure had been undergoing remodeling for months, was deemed unsafe to enter except by authorized personnel. What Drancy had been doing there at night had never been ascertained. Seventy years later, manner of death remained undetermined.

Milo said, "I'm gonna go out on a limb and determine he got pushed. Jesus."

I said, "Ratting out Hoke was a risky move. And maybe being a gem wasn't family puffery, more like a bitter in-joke. They knew he was murdered."

I pointed to the date of the obit. "Not long after Hoke began his sentence. Behind bars but far from impotent."

"Long arm of the lawless," he said.

"The boss was incarcerated but his minions

were free. Including his true love, living comfortably at the Aventura, working a legitimate accounting job and managing to evade law enforcement attention. I've been assuming Thalia's concerns about criminal behavior were related to someone else. But what if she was talking about herself? Not just because of her money laundering for Hoke. What if she'd helped set up the hit on Drancy? Or knew about the contract and did nothing to stop it?"

"All this time later, she gets an attack of the guilts?"

"End-of-life introspection," I said. "It's pretty common. And her needing to atone would explain leaving everything to charity."

"Then why was **she** killed?"

"Because someone else judged **her** guilty."

He frowned. "Drancy spawn."

"The push from the tenth floor could've become enshrined as family lore. The kind of thing that can harden over time into outrage. The right spawn comes along, a decision's made to set things right and profit in the process."

He wheeled back from his desk, swerved sharply to avoid colliding with my knee. It happens all the time when we're coexisting in a space meant for a lapdog. No injuries to date; he's a master of the near-miss.

"I don't know about the introspection bit," he

said. "If Thalia **was** visited by Drancy kin, I can see her wanting to discuss felony genetics with an expert. Especially one with police contacts."

"You could be right," I said. "But looking back to her mood when we spoke, there was no extreme fear. At the most, curiosity with an edge, and maybe not even that."

"It was enough of an edge to make you wonder what she was really after, amigo. Let's say this particular bit of Drancy DNA came across non-threatening. Like a good-looking chick claiming to just wanna learn more about Grandpa Fred. But Thalia was no dummy, she knew what had happened to Grandpa Fred and it put her guard up. So she thought a bit, decided to groom you as a chat-buddy. Bide her time, if things got scarier, you'd connect her with me. Problem was, everything moved too fast and she was caught off guard."

He stood, stretched, sat back down. "Whatever the case, there's still the big question: Why wait so long to get even? Unless the D-clan learned something new."

"Confirmation of Thalia's involvement in the hit."

"Or a heavily sweetened pot, Alex. I can't let go of the profit motive, nine times out of ten a case like this revolves around money. What if Cutie showed up at Thalia's bungalow after learning about—or just suspecting—a serious cash stash?"

He re-read Demarest's report, placed the two sheets back in the blue folder, looked up the archive online application form, and printed it.

Muttering, "Waste of time but dot the t's. Let's get some coffee."

We were ten steps closer to the stairs when his phone rang. Still on speaker.

"Milo? Len Gottlieb."

"Hey, what's up?"

"Something actually," said Gottlieb. "Sometimes a guy gets lucky. And I'm such a saint, I'm gonna share."

CHAPTER

29

We retrieved the unmarked from the lot, drove west to Centinela, then south, just past Jefferson, to a block of tired-looking small businesses, restaurants, and bars.

Len Gottlieb was waiting on the sidewalk, smoking a cigarette and bouncing on his heels in front of a block-faced tavern called the Wind-jam.

Milo said, "What, they ran out of letters?"

I said, "Maybe they're into music. Heavy-metal oboes."

We got out, were greeted by Gottlieb's fist-bumps. "Guess how many places I tried before I found this dive?"

"Five."

"One. This was number two."

"Unbelievable, Len."

"Maybe God really does love me. That's what my name means, God-love." He inhaled smoke. "Maybe He'll even protect me from the results of this filthy habit. Anyway, this is where De-Graw watered himself after work. Regularly and pretty heavily, bartender says they had to cut him off several times, the fact that he was driving made them nervous."

"All that spit and polish," said Milo, "and turns out he was a sloppy drunk."

"Not sloppy-aggressive," said Gottlieb. "He never caused problems, would just fall asleep and they'd have trouble waking him up."

I said, "What did it take to get him to that point?"

"Meaning?"

"Did he need to be stressed to drown his sorrows? Did he ever express himself?"

"Hmm," said Gottlieb. "Let's find out."

No sailing motif inside Windjam. Nothing musical, either. The starkest drinking-dive I'd ever seen north of downtown: a single anorexic room that was mostly lacquer-top bar, the sides diamond-stitched black leatherette glued unevenly.

Bolted-in stools were wood-grain and blue vinyl. Vats for well-booze took up more space than bulk bottles of low-priced spirits. On the opposite side, a couple of tables, unoccupied.

No pool table, no jukebox, no stage, nothing on pine walls aged a better bourbon color than the bottles. Vintage Beach Boys sputtered through tinny speakers perched in two corners. "Don't Worry Baby" deserving better fidelity.

The two beer-hounds at the far end of the bar didn't seem to mind the ambience. A slew of empty bottles and foamy splotches said the corpulent barkeep's work ethic had flagged.

As we approached him, he saluted and motioned us away from the drinkers. Sparse hair, small Buffalo Bill beard under which two supplementary chins flourished. He wore a tan work shirt, sleeves rolled to the elbows.

One of those hard-fat guys, tightly packed, with powerful shoulders and ham-hock forearms. Tattoos on both arms: **Semper Fi,** a bald eagle, Uncle Sam wanting someone, **Mom** in a winged heart. Tradition flourished.

Len Gottlieb said, "This is Stan, he's been real helpful."

Milo said, "Appreciate it, Stan."

Stan said, "Swissair gets himself killed? Only thing to **do** is help you guys."

"Swissair."

"Never knew his name, sir, but when I asked him where he was from he said Bern. I thought he was being an asshole, telling me to put lighter fluid on myself or something. I almost kicked his ass out. I guess he didn't like the look on my face so he told me it's a city in Switzerland, that's where he's from. So I started calling him Swiss-air, that's their airline."

Not for a decade. No sense getting picky.

Gottlieb tapped the bar. "Stan says DeGraw's been coming in for around two years. Off and on but when it's on, it's like three, four times a week, always evenings."

"Looked to me like an after-work deal, we get a lot of those," said Stan. "He'd be wearing this maroon jacket and a tie. Couple of shots, the tie would come off. Bunch more, his head would go this way."

One hand mimed a slow descent. "I didn't want one of those lawsuits so I kept an eye on him, told my wife to do the same when she was tending. We worked out a system. The tie comes off, he gets three more, tops. He never argued. Never said much of anything, just sat by himself and put it away."

"What was his pleasure?" said Milo.

Stan said, "Scotch."

Gottlieb said, "Here's the main thing: De-Graw always came in alone until three weeks ago when he had a companion."

"Really," said Milo.

Stan said, "Oh, man." Thick arms shaped an hourglass figure.

Milo said, "Cute, huh?"

"More than cute, juicy. I'm thinking, what's he doing with something like that?"

"They get all lovey-dovey?"

"Nah," said Stan. "But he tried to impress her. Before, he never ordered a brand, this time he wanted Crown Royal. Waste of time, she wasn't into brown, ordered Stoli."

Gap-toothed smile. "What they got was Canadian Mist and Smirnoff. And no hoochie-coo, all they did was drink and talk."

"About what?"

"How should I know? I'm here, they're there."

Gottlieb said, "Stan says she wore a blond wig."

"I could tell it was a wig 'cause it was too perfect. Like back-in-the-day-Farrah, those wings and things?" He exhaled, wiped his hands on his shirt. "Some body on her, what's Swissair doing with that? But then I could see they weren't like that."

I said, "Nothing physical going on."

"Nah, they just talked and he waved his little book around, then she left and he did his usual slop till you drop."

Gottlieb said, "What book?"

"This little book," said Stan. "Red. He's showing it to her, she looks at it once, then she leaves."

Milo said, "Maybe a passport?"

Stan shrugged. "Beats me, I never had one. They're red? That's kind of communist."

Gottlieb said, "Ours are blue." He looked at Milo.

Stan's attention had wandered to the men at the bar. "Something?" he called over.

Head shakes.

Gottlieb said, "Anything else you can say about this hot thing, Stan?"

The barman outlined another hourglass. "What looked like real tits, nice and high. Confident tits, ya know?"

Milo said, "How about if we bring a sketch artist over."

Stan picked at his chin. "Never done that before."

"Maybe it's time for an adventure, my friend."

"Hmm. Sure, why not, live dangerously. But I'm not swearing to nothing. I coulda seen her topless, I'd remember a whole lot better."

"No need to swear, Stan. Just do your best." To Gottlieb: "Okay if I use one of my Rembrandts?"

"Better than okay."

"I'll give him this." He fished out a business card, showed it to Gottlieb.

Gottlieb said, "Be my guest, he's already got mine."

Stan pocketed the card without reading it.

Milo said, "Hot Stuff shows up again, please call Detective Gottlieb or me. And if you can catch a license plate, you'll be a hero."

"She's bad news, huh?"

"She interests us."

"Hot Stuff, yeah, that's her," said Stan. He licked the back of his hand. Drew it back and said, "Sssssss."

We left the bar.

Gottlieb said, "With DeGraw taken care of, why would she come back here?"

"Hope springs eternal, Len."

"Maybe in your world. Anyway, at least we got the confirmation: DeGraw was in with your suspects and wanted out. She came here to discuss it, he shows her his passport, assures her he'll be leaving pronto once he's paid off. She says it's a deal, they arrange a meet at his place, she distracts him, I don't even want to know how. When he's not paying attention, your other two walk in and off him."

Milo said, "He becomes just like Swissair. No longer in business."

"Tough shit for him," said Gottlieb. "Do that to an old lady." He lit up another cigarette. "So. We got confirmation of our theory but, again, I don't see any clear path to my case until you close yours and maybe someone talks."

"Agreed, Len, I'll carry the ball. But if you do learn something—like you did today—"

"Sure," said Gottlieb. "But the thing you need to know is I've got vacation time coming up. Assuming the Boss Wife can keep her schedule clear. So I may be out of commission for a couple weeks."

"Where you headed to?"

"Mexico, maybe Cabo," said Gottlieb. "Maybe Puerto V. Best-case scenario, a beach with Hot Stuffs in bikinis who don't want to kill anyone."

We watched him drive away. I said, "He just disconnected from the case."

"That's okay, he's right, it does all depend on me." Rubbing his face, Milo checked his phone. "Moe watched Ricki S. last night, she went home, stayed there. Sean's on tonight, let's see."

"Keep that eternal hope going."

"Thanks for not laughing, talk about a true friend."

He slapped my back lightly, returned to his phone. "Let's see if Maestro Shimoff has time to do a drawing."

Detective II Alex Shimoff, a Russian-trained painter and the man Milo calls "the other Alexander," was working a commercial burglary case in the toy district.

He said, "Culver City doesn't have anyone who can do it?"

"Anyone else is at the stick-figure stage, you're a master."

"Right," said Shimoff. "When do you need this?"

"Sooner would be better than later, kiddo."

"Of course . . . okay, we just moved to West-chester, Culver's basically on my way home. This bartender work late?"

"You could do it tonight?"

"Probably."

"Lemme ask him."

We returned to the Windjam. The pair of drinkers had added to their bottle collection and the bar-top remained splotched. The music had changed, though. Sammy Hagar, poor fidelity giving him a lisp.

Stan, eyelids drooping, sat fooling with his cuticles. When he saw us the lids remained lowered but the spheres behind them rolled upward.

Milo asked him.

He said, "Probably."

"Any way you can switch that to a yes, Stan? If I have Detective Shimoff give you an hour's notice?"

"Detective? He's a cop, also draws?"

"Multitalented," said Milo.

"Got a kid who draws. Does crap in school but makes these comic books, crazy stuff. They say he's good. You think this detective could talk some sense into him?"

"Let's aim for that, Stan."

"Then, yeah. What time?"

Milo redialed Shimoff. To Stan: "Between eight and nine."

"I'll be here," said the barkeep. "Get the kid over, maybe bring a comic book he done. He likes to stay in his room, I'll drag him over."

Back outside, Milo reached Shimoff again. "Appreciate it, Czar Alexei. Also, the witness might bring his kid to watch you work." He explained.

Shimoff said, "So now I'm a career counselor?"

"You've always been good at multitasking."

"Walk and chew gum, eh?"

"I owe you."

"You always do."

The following morning a screen shot of the drawing was in my email. Shimoff to Milo to me, no topic heading.

Beautifully rendered portrait of a generic gorgeous blonde. Monroe, if you squinted. A bit more angular if you didn't.

I couldn't see much value in it, kept that to myself and sent a text: **Binchy see anything last night?**

Instead of replying in kind, Milo phoned. "Nada. Speaking of Ricki S., the crime lab's asking when I'm gonna get Thalia's stuff out of storage and talk to her executor. They have it in an auto bay, someone crashes while shooting or being shot at, they'll need the space. Given who the executor is, I obviously want to hold off. Meanwhile, I'm heading back to the hotel, see if anyone has a story to tell about the cute blonde."

"Good luck."

"I was figuring to bop by and pick you up."

"Sure," I said.

"No sandwiches necessary, had a big breakfast."

Alicia Bogomil said, "Yup, that's her. Probably. Only saw her a couple of times. With the dudes and then by herself. She was walking in front, that's a switch. Had a bod, showed it off." Forming two balloons on her own flattish chest.

I said, "Tight clothes?"

"Tight clothes and posture." She stood up straight, arched her back, accentuated her torso. "Bod-confidence, you know? Like she liked being looked at."

Milo said, "A performer."

Bogomil said, "Hmm. Yeah. So maybe she's an actress or something."

"Maybe."

"You're saying she—they—definitely had something to do with it?"

"Not yet," he lied. "You ever see her with De-Graw?"

"No, why?"

"He just got murdered."

Her mouth dropped open. "No shit! Oh, man, so **that's** why he hasn't been around. You're kidding—crap! How?"

"Can't get into it, sorry."

"Whoa," said Bogomil. "Another one bites it. Rumors have been circulating that he got fired by the Arabs, the place is definitely closing down. Shit. It's like this place is Heartbreak Hotel."

Milo said, "Let me ask you something else. Thalia's lawyer, she always show up alone?"

"The sad-looking, dumpy blonde? Yup, every time I saw her, she was flying solo." Her face tightened. "You're saying she's also—"

"I'm not saying anything."

Bogomil looked at him.

"I wish I **could** say, Alicia. This is a damn whodunit."

"Got it. Sorry," she said. "But the place **is**

closing down, right? Like I told you before, no new guests, and now the snip tucks have tapered off."

"I have no facts on that but it sounds logical."

Her hands clenched. "Damn, I got to start looking. Probably have to settle for another boring private thing so I can pay bills. But that's temporary, working with you showed me I need a real badge again. Preferably you guys. If I can't get that, San Diego, Santa Barbara, something with a warm climate and real cases."

"What I said holds true. Once you apply, let me know, Alicia."

"You can count on it, Loo, thanks." Her arms began what might've been a hug, but dropped down. "Meanwhile, I'll stick around long as they pay me, keep my eyes open for you. Not that I expect anything, place is a tomb."

Same temp at the desk—Kelli. No sense showing her the drawing. We found Refugia vacuuming the hallway of the original wing, pushing the machine around in slow arcs and looking defeated.

She studied the rendering. "Yes, that's the one in Cinco."

"What can you tell us about her?"

"She looks like this—maybe a little narrower, here." Pointing to the left jawline. "She's a bad person?"

"We're still investigating, Refugia."

"She wasn't nice."

"How so?"

"I came in to clean, she was leaving, I said hello, she walked by me. I know she heard. She was making like I wasn't there. Sometimes they're like that."

"Guests."

"Rich people," she said. "Not everyone, I know some nice ones. But you know."

"She came across like a rich lady."

"Nice clothes," she said. "Chanel purse."

"That so."

"Could be fake Chanel, I don't know."

"What color?"

"Black silk, this thing." Shaping a diamond. "This pattern sewn into it."

"That time," said Milo, "was she by herself?"

"Yes, and the place was very messy. Bottles, glasses, food, messed-up bed. Also the pull-out."

Her color deepened.

I said, "Big mess."

She looked away. "It smelled. The bed and the pull-out."

"Of . . ."

"You know," she said. "Like it happened there? Doing it all over the place?"

"Sex."

Quick nod. She fooled with the handle of the

vacuum cleaner. "They're saying we're losing our jobs."

Milo said, "Who's saying?"

"Everyone. Also, DeGraw's not here, there was something to do, he'd be here but they're saying he quit. Is it true, sir? Should I look for another job?"

"Don't know the facts, Refugia, but it might be a good idea."

Her shoulders dropped. "I thought so. Not another hotel, I want to take care of an old person. I like old people."

Her eyes filmed. "I liked Miss Mars."

CHAPTER

30

I drove home and worked the computer, searching for any kind of familial link to Fred Drancy. No success in his birth state of Massachusetts, same with New York and California. The people I talked to in a few neighboring states were baffled. My last call was to a man in Berlin, New Hampshire, who said, "Are you from that magazine outfit with the big check?"

"Sorry, no."

"Who cares, I don't read, anyway."

I was trying to figure out a next step when Robin came in, hair tied back, T-shirt flecked with sawdust. Behind her bounced Blanche wearing a frosting of wood shavings.

Robin ran her fingers through my hair, trailed them down to my neck, kneaded.

"No progress, huh?"

"My neck tells you that?"

"All of you tells me that."

"We've got a good idea about motive and a couple of dead suspects. The problem is finding the live ones."

I told her about DeGraw.

She said, "Another one? These people are relentless and greedy. You think they got away with a huge amount of Thalia's cash?"

"That's what it looks like."

"Okay," she said, adding pressure to her fingertips.

"You don't think so?"

"I'm on the outside, honey, but why would someone in her situation keep substantial cash around?"

"Milo found three thousand."

"That, I can see," she said. "Tips, gifts, shopping. But you said she'd stopped going out and her basic needs were taken care of by the hotel. You didn't describe her as a hoarder or any other kind of eccentric. She'd been investing successfully for years, wasn't one of those under-the-mattress types."

The value of a fresh eye.

I said, "It's a good point."

She pushed down harder. Muscles I hadn't realized were tight began to slacken.

"The other thing, Alex, is once upon a time she had a boyfriend who stole jewels. What if he left her a souvenir or two? Something really valuable but small, that a thief could stick in a pocket and walk out with?"

I said, "Unbelievable."

"Doesn't make sense?"

"It makes total sense. **You're** unbelievable."

"Did you find any jewelry in her room?"

"A couple of decent pieces. An amethyst ring."

She said, "Semi-precious—that's what some women do. Leave the cheaper stuff out, hide the good stuff. If there was major-league bling, that's what I'd go for."

I turned. She smiled. "If I was criminally inclined, that is. Were the jewels from the Beverly Hills robbery ever recovered?"

"There's no record of recovery. But we suspect they were cashed and the money was taken by the IRS with a possible share going to the department."

I told her about the Demarest report.

She said, "Even with that, Hoke could've left his babe a bauble or two as tokens of his affection." Wider smile. "You were a hood and I was a moll, I'd expect it."

"You're brilliant." I got up and kissed her.

She said, "That was my commission for being smart?"

"A down payment." I found my notes on the case, came upon what I was looking for. Read and sat back down.

"Oh," I said. "You're a genius!"

No reply. I swiveled again.

Just me in the office.

From the kitchen came the singsong Robin glides into when discussing topics of substance with Blanche.

Return yip. The rattle of kibble on the porcelain of a dog-bowl.

I went in, waving a piece of paper. "Look at what you've wrought, Einsteinia."

She resealed the food bag and grinned. "Appreciate the sentiment, but it's been a bad-hair day, maybe you can come up with a girlier analogy?"

"How about Ada Lovelace?"

"Sounds like a porn actress."

"She was Lord Byron's daughter, a math genius and probably the first computer programmer."

"Now we're talking—how do you **know** these things?"

"Malignant curiosity."

"Ha. Okay, what have I wrought?"

I showed her the **Beverly Hills Monitor** puff piece on Count Frederick LaPlante, pointed to the last two lines.

She said, "Wine of the Nile? The pyramids?"

"A big ruby's one helluva motive."

"Sure, but why're you focusing on this one and not the others?"

"Because of a pencil notation on the back of that LAPD report. 'Win. Ni. 57.'"

"Wine, Nile," she said. "You think she got to keep the ruby?"

I pointed.

"Ah," she said. "Fifty-seven carats, that's some boulder."

"What if Demarest made a note because it was never recovered?"

"The one that got away? Because Thalia kept it all these years?"

"Diversified investment," I said. "Let's see if we can find a picture of this trinket."

Easier than I'd expected. The ruby was listed in the holdings of an Egyptian banker named Adel Fawzi Sayed, whose collection had been loaned to the British Museum for a 1929 exhibit titled **Treasures of the Pharaohs.**

The tit-for-tat: Sayed's knighthood a month before the show opened. Soon after it closed, Sir Fawzi sold much of his cache and used the proceeds to buy a mansion in Belgravia.

Fuzzy black-and-white photos included a shot of "a 57 carat, oval, pigeon-blood ruby said to have been unearthed in one of the Pyramids of Giza. However, the Burmese origin of the gem and the nineteenth century style of cutting casts doubt on that assertion. Nevertheless, it is a jewel of uncommon size, beauty, and rarity."

"Nice," said Robin. "I'm thinking brooch. Something falling right above the cleavage."

She demonstrated.

"Now you're distracting me."

"Me? Never."

I stayed distracted all the way to the bedroom. Achieved focus without trying.

Afterward, lying on the bed, as Robin showered, I replayed my time with Thalia. Had trouble conjuring images. Then they came to me, as if a mental drainpipe had been snaked.

So did a snip of conversation.

The lapidary reference that had escaped me.

Thalia asking me about criminal tendencies, then expressing dismay.

I was hoping for better. Would still like to think of our planet as an evolutionary gem.

And again, moments later, describing images taken by the Hubble telescope.

I was cheered. The universe seemed . . . jewel-like.

Playing games? Or rehearsing a story she planned to tell me later.

There hadn't been a later.

Robin began humming as she dried off. Warren Zevon's "Carmelita."

I returned to that first time in the bungalow. Nearly snagged an image but lost it—one of those tip-of-the-mind frustrations.

I gave up. Sat up. It came to me, clear as a digital photo.

Robin walked in, wrapped in a towel. "Hi, babe . . . are you waiting for something? Love the passion, but if you don't mind—"

"Honey, I think I saw it."

"Saw what?"

"The ruby." I told her where.

"Crafty," she said. "Now, **that** could be a motive."

I got dressed and phoned Milo. "You're not going to believe this."

"At this point I'm open to all kinds of beliefs, including ecologically justified cannibalism. What religion do you want me to convert to?"

"The Church of Cautious Optimism." I filled him in.

He said, "Win. Ni."

"Fifty-seven carats, that's got to be it."

"You just came up with this?"

"Robin led me to it." I repeated her logic.

"That's some smart girl you've got."

"Lord Byron would be proud."

"What?"

"Never mind. Why don't you call the crime lab and find out?"

"No call, something like this, the evidence chain needs to be solid, I'll check it out personally. Can you meet me in front of the station, say immediately?"

"I'll be there sooner."

CHAPTER
31

LA. County's Hertzberg-Davis Forensic
Science Center is six stories of white punc-
tuated by red brick and glass, perched at the
mouth of the Cal State L.A. campus.

The ride on the 10 East took the unmarked
where tourist buses don't venture: a sixty-five-
mph drive-by of big-box discounters, car lots,
and purveyors of industrial grit.

Once we got off the freeway and drove up a
hill to campus, all was sunny and crisp. None of
the ivy-clad antiquity of the city's Big Two, here.
This was unpretentious functionality spread
across gently rolling terrain.

After nearly a decade, the crime lab still sparkles. This morning, a sky scrubbed blue by hot
dry winds added extra wattage. Parking was

ample. A few students and staffers strolled. The view to the west was crystalline, the Hollywood sign visible thirty miles away.

Pleasant place; you'd never know death paid the bills.

We checked in at the glassed-in reception desk and waited. White-coats and cops in blue or tan uniforms passed by. L.A. crime is handled by a pair of goliaths: LAPD tends to the four million people living and misbehaving within the city limits, the sheriff has dominion over the eight million who reside in the remainder of the county.

At Hertzberg, that leads to a curious accommodation: Labs and offices are divided up and demarcated by green and blue nameplates. Two evidence rooms, separate microscopes, but some facilities are shared. The potential for chaos seems obvious but everyone seems to get along. These are scientists and techs who take the job seriously.

The lab's commanding officer, a trim blonde named Noreen Sharp, came out to meet us.

She said, "You're here to arrange transfer of the Mars property. Thanks."

Milo smiled and did that shambling aw-shucks thing. "Actually—"

"You're not," said Sharp. "What's going on, Milo?"

"Noreen, I swear I'll do it soon as I can, but

right now I need to check a specific piece of evidence."

"In the Mars bunch."

"Yes."

"Like what?"

He explained.

Noreen Sharp said, "I wish someone would've told me, we'd have logged it separately."

"Someone didn't know."

She smiled. "Got it. Well if it's not here, it never arrived. I supervised the initial loading myself due to the volume of objects and my code's the only one that unlocks the bay. What exactly is it worth?"

"Don't know yet, Noreen."

"But obviously we're talking huge. Lucky for you I've held on to my moral compass."

We took the elevator down and entered a white corridor. Quiet as a Trappist monastery; the entire facility was. Any time I'd been there, it was like that. Shrine to Science.

Noreen Sharp picked up a video camera and walked us past darkened labs and the gun library to the auto bays. Stopping at one, she used her left hand to conceal her right as she punched a code into a numbered grid. Hiding the combination but doing it casually. No offense, business as usual.

The door clicked open. The interior was the

size of a double garage with a high ceiling, block walls, a cement floor, and a hydraulic lift stored in a corner.

Chilly. Noreen Sharp said, "Yup, nippy, be nice for wine." She pointed to a rear door. "You know where that leads."

Milo said, "The loading area."

"Got to get the cars in somehow," she said. "Have you ever been back there?"

"Nope."

She walked over, pushed a similar grid on the far wall, and the back door opened. Daylight over asphalt, a lot big enough for a fleet.

"Completely fenced, guys. No one gets in unless we want them to. I'm telling you this so no matter what you find, there'll be no misunderstanding. Ms. Mars's property arrived on one of our trucks that stopped just outside as the contents were unloaded."

She closed the door. "Okay, all this is cataloged but it's not arranged in any order, so you'll have to look."

"All this" referred to a mass of shapes in the center of the bay, wrapped in heavy-duty plastic that brought to mind bodies in the crypt, and secured by duct tape. Along with that, several cardboard boxes were marked **Mars, T,** along with a case number, date of death, and a stick-on label stating **Deceased Personal Effects.**

The sizable objects were a couple of sofas, a mattress, and a deconstructed bed canopy. Even with them, Thalia's possessions took up a pitiably small space.

A century of life memorialized in less than half of a cold, gray room.

Milo turned to me. "See it?"

"Right there." I pointed to a vertical package sandwiched between the cartons and what I recognized as an end table.

"Can he go over there, Noreen?"

"Sure." She hefted the camera. "But given what we're looking for, I'm going to video you, Doctor. For documentation."

I made my way to the upright form. Floor lamp with a glass shade. What Milo had called a Tiffany but I knew to be improbably crude for such.

The shade, a dome studded with bubbles of red glass.

The last time I'd seen it, it had sported a red finial. Oval, faceted, of a size that made me assume cut glass.

"Can I touch it?"

Noreen Sharp said, "First point, then touch."

I prodded the top of the shade, pushing down on taut plastic to make sure.

No need to unwrap. I'd felt and seen enough.

Where the finial had sat, just a socket.

I said, "It's gone."

Noreen Sharp exhaled and talked to the camera. "Dr. Alexander Delaware, a police consultant, has just identified what he feels is an absent component of what appears to be a floor lamp. The lamp in question was delivered to us wrapped precisely as it is now, as were all of Victim T. Mars's personal effects. No one has been in this storage area since the arrival of those objects and the subsequent locking of the auto bay in which we currently stand."

She swung the lens toward Milo.

He said, "This is Lieutenant Milo Sturgis, LAPD Homicide, West L.A. Division. I was present at the crime scene of victim T. Mars and personally oversaw the wrapping and carting of all personal effects of victim T. Mars."

Sharp said, "Now we are going to unwrap the object in question to verify Dr. Alexander Delaware's perception."

She pulled out the lamp, used a penknife to deftly snip the tape, took her time unwrapping as Milo held the base for stability.

Perception verified.

Noreen Sharp put the camera down. "Obviously some defense attorney can always say one of your guys or one of our guys stole it. I think we're looking pretty solid, that's why I always play it by the books. But you know how it is post-O.J."

"One way to avoid that bullshit, Noreen, is for me to find the damn ruby and solve the damn case. So let's keep this quiet."

"Something like that missing?" she said. "I need to file papers."

"I know that but keep them in your desk until I tell you."

"For how long?"

"Wish I knew."

"Hmm."

"Please, Noreen."

She took in the room, shook her head. "I'll do what I can. And both of you will need to fill out incident reports, plus we've still got the other problem: What if I need the bay for an actual car?"

"Can you find another place for the stuff?"

"Probably, but it might have to be divided up. And given what's happened, we're adding another layer of complication."

"Let the chips fall, Noreen. I'll make sure it's my problem, not yours."

"Appreciate the sentiment, Milo, but it's not always up to people at our salary grade. Meanwhile, I'm changing the code to the bay. Going to find my deputy and have him witness it and video that, too."

She phoned an extension. "Bay Three, Arnie, A-sap." Unflappable blue eyes scanned the space again, settled on the bubble-glass lamp. "We need some idea about what we're dealing with in terms of value, so if you could get an appraisal? I realize it would be without an in-person inspection and less than sterling, but it's important to document on at least a theoretical level."

"You read my mind, Noreen."

"A clairvoyant?" she said. "We haven't established that division, yet."

Reports written and signed, we got in the car and headed back to the freeway.

Milo said, "She's right, we could use an appraisal." Looking at his Timex. "Not exactly my field of expertise."

I said, "I know a guy."

He looked at me. "You always do."

Elie Aronson sold high-quality diamonds and custom jewelry from a vault-like office in a building on Hill Street, downtown. A judge who loved his wife had referred me to Elie as a source for "When you really mean it, or have to atone."

I'd bought a few pieces from him for Robin. Last year, we'd done an insurance appraisal. Everything from Elie had appreciated.

We were approaching downtown when I reached his cellphone. He said, "What are you looking for?"

"Information." I explained.

"I'm having lunch, when do you want to come?"

"I can be there in ten."

"Fifteen, I'll be finished with my shawarma, drive slow. Then we need to go fast, in twenty-five I got an appointment. I wait for you out front, okay, and we do it **chick-chock**."

He stood to the right of the building's guarded brass doors, wearing a white shirt, pressed jeans, and red calfskin loafers. Muscular Israeli in his fifties with an unlined face, a luxuriant mass of wavy gray hair, and piercing black eyes. No trace of bling on him, not even a digital watch.

Milo pulled to the curb and I stuck my head out the passenger window. Elie looked around and got into the backseat of the unmarked.

"A police car," he said. "Looks like I'm being arrested. How you doing, Doctor?"

"Good. You?"

"Can't complain. Wouldn't help anyway."

He looked at Milo. Traffic zipped by as I made the introductions.

Milo said, "Appreciate the consult, sir."

"Hey," said Elie, "you guys protect me, I shouldn't help you? Okay, show me the picture of this thing."

I handed him the black-and-white from the museum show.

He glanced at it briefly, handed it back. "Can't tell from that."

Milo said, "Can you give a general idea?"

"I give you something but I don't promise, too many iffies. First thing, is it genuine? Second, is it Burmese? Was it heat-treated? Do you got serious inclusions? Even with that it's a tough thing. Something that size, it gets complicated. But . . . real, Burmese, no problems . . . it's millions. How many?" He shrugged. "Could be two, could be eight, could be ten, could be twenty, if the color and clarity are super-good. But then there's the market, another complication."

"The market's unstable?" said Milo.

"There's fluctuations," said Elie. "Also the larger the stone, the pool of customers gets small, there's no standard, everything's negotiable. Top of that, if it's stolen, it's gonna go cheap, like ten percent of value. But still, this size, a real Burmese . . . I don't see it not being millions."

I said, "What about the provenance?"

"Some guy showed it at a museum a hundred years ago? Big deal. Unless you get a collector of historicals who also has the big money. No one cares about a hundred years, these things are billions of years old."

Milo said, "Any guess where it might end up?"

"If I'm betting, I'm putting my money on Asia, number one, an oil state, number two, Russia, number three. Maybe Russia is even two, they got oligarchs, want everything big and flashy for the twelve girlfriends."

Milo said, "No buyers in the States?"

"I'm not saying no, Lieutenant, but that wouldn't be my bet. Someone buys a stone this big and hot and wants to keep it here, they going to have to hide it. No way the girlfriend can go to the party with it dangling from a chain. Asia, Abu Dhabi, Russia, they don't care."

"Meaning it could already be gone."

"I wish I could give you good news but that's my other bet. Who belonged to it?"

"An old lady who got murdered."

"Oh." Elie shook his head. "That's terrible, I'm sorry for her. You want, I can ask around but I don't think I'm gonna learn anything."

Milo said, "We'd sure appreciate anything you can do."

"You bet." He reached for the door handle. "Murdered for a piece of carbon. Same old story."

As we approached West L.A., Milo said, "Millions of bucks at stake makes me jumpy. Ergo hungry. Feel like pizza?"

"Whatever you want."

"How do you do it? Control the appetite."

For most of the ride, I'd been thinking about Thalia being snuffed out. Visualizing the details. An excellent suppressant.

I said, "I'll eat, I just don't care what."

A mile later, he said, "Forget pizza, too festive. Something Irish would be appropriately morose—soda bread and boy-yald poday-dos, ey? Then again, that's why my ancestors left the old sod, so how 'bout Mexican for a compromise?"

I said, "Olé."

◆

He sped past the Overland exit for the station, got off two ramps later in Santa Monica, and pulled into the parking lot of a fake-hacienda called El Matador. Big, mostly empty room, warm air ripe with cheese and beans and corn chips. Heavy fixtures of not-quite wrought iron, tile floor, clumsy Tijuana furniture. Bullfight posters on the walls—there's a shock, for you.

We settled in a corner booth. Milo said, "We were right near Boyle Heights, coulda had something authentic, my timing's off."

A sweet-faced waitress took our order. Bottle of Tecate and the combo special for him, iced tea and beef fajitas for me.

She said, "With fajitas the pan's super-hot— legally, we have to warn you."

I said, "Skillet-chasing lawyers."

That confused her.

Milo said, "At least someone's looking out for us."

She flashed a puzzled smile and left.

He said, "I need to regroup, let's lay it out. Hoke left Thalia the ruby and maybe other stuff from the heist and she got killed for it decades later."

"Maybe there wasn't other stuff," I said. "The only item noted on Demarest's report was the ruby. The fact that it was scrawled on the back might mean it wasn't discovered until after the report was written. Hiding one stone would've been easy. Conceal too much of the take and they'd have come looking for it."

"You're being therapeutic, right? Telling me there's only one blingo-o to worry about."

"No, I mean it."

"Fine . . . so the feds got most of the haul and Thalia got to keep the ruby. So, what, she hid it in plain sight, all these years?"

"My guess is she stashed it away, brought it out years later when she felt safe."

"Something to remind her of Lover Boy."

"She was a woman with a sense of humor." Then I thought of something. "Either that or she viewed the ruby as something special. We know she was in charge of Hoke's burial. On top of his gravestone is a red marble crown. Kind of jewel-like, I saw nothing like it on any other marker. Hoke was a redhead but I'll bet she was commemorating something else."

Our drinks came. He drained half his beer. "Goddamn finial on top of a goddamn **lamp**."

I said, "Screwed into the fixture. A custom job that someone had to fashion and install."

He put his glass down. "So, what, I ask around for a hundred-year-old felonious craftsman?"

I fished out my phone, switched to speaker.

Tatiana at Belinda Wojik's number said, "Doctor's office."

"This is Alex Delaware, I was there with Lieutenant Sturgis—"

"Doctor's busy."

"Put her on, anyway."

"She's busy—"

"We can come down or she can answer a quick question over the phone."

"Hmnh."

Moments later, a flat voice: "Hello, this is Belinda."

One advantage of her personality quirks: no need for small talk. "It's Alex Delaware, again. Did your grandfather have any hobbies?"

"You think he did something wrong," she said. "I guess it would bother me if he did. Or maybe not. He was always wonderful to me."

I said, "Not at all. Did he have any hobbies?"

"Like stamp collecting or pinning butterflies." A beat. "I used to catch bugs and pin them on a corkboard. Grampa told me it was cruel so I stopped."

I said, "So no outside interests."

"No collections," she said. "He tinkered with antiques, does that count?"

"What kind of antiques?"

"His father was a furniture refinisher so he

knew how to fix up furniture. Does that qual-
ify?"

"Sure. Anything else?"

"Grampa was very handy," she said. "He
could cane a chair, put patina on metal, fix handles. He had a shop out back. Am I allowed to
ask why you're inquiring?"

"Just what I said, rounding—"

"Things out. I guess that means something to
you, it doesn't to me."

"Sorry, but until we learn who killed Thalia—"

"You must be careful. Now that I'm remembering, Grampa also worked with leather. He
made me a nice belt. A leather hat for himself
and he used to bind his own books in leather.
He kept pots of glue and hides in his shop, they
smelled. Father wasn't handy at all."

I thanked her and hung up.

Milo said, "What made you think of Wojik?"

"I figured it would have to be someone Hoke
and Thalia trusted. Jack McCandless was an
equally good choice but what's the chance Ricki
Sylvester would talk to us?"

"You knew Wojik would."

"She's artless and pretty much a pure soul," I
said. "Honest because she doesn't know any
other way. What she said doesn't help much but
it does firm up the picture."

"Thelma and the others plotting in Hoke's best interest," he said. "There's a charge for you: aiding and abetting, by way of tinkering."

He pulled out the British Museum photo. "In this it's a blob. What's it like in real life?"

"Big, red, shiny. I assumed it was glass so I didn't pay attention. No one did until recently."

"Fifty-seven carats in plain sight. So how would the bad guys know where to find it?"

"Knowing what it looked like would've made it easier. An inside person would've made it a cinch."

The food arrived. He ate fast, without obvious pleasure, finished his beer, wiped his mouth hard enough to redden his lips, looked at the photo again. "Some Drancy spawn goes looking for revenge plus a mega-payoff, locates Thalia, verifies this **thing** is in her room through an inside person."

"Theoretically," I said, "it could be anyone who'd been in the bungalow."

"Any hotel staffer but probably DeGraw," he said. "Bastard verifies the location of the ruby, walks over to Cinco, tips off the bad guys, and gives them a key. They spend a day or two watching Thalia, knowing her schedule. Come back after dark, snuff her, unscrew the damn thing, and check out."

"Without paying their bill."

"DeGraw was full of outrage about that. Duplicitous asshole."

"All that planning," I said. "If they'd just settled up with DeGraw, they would have attracted less attention. Same for the show they put on in Creech's car. But that's psychopathy. Low impulse control and thrill-seeking."

I took a few bites of hazardous fajita. "DeGraw would've been a good source for the key but I'm thinking someone with deeper knowledge from her grandfather. Who got real defensive after you brought him up."

"Sylvester. Still got my guys on her, nothing."

"Wouldn't surprise me if she's got a safe in her office."

"The ruby's with her? Good luck getting access to that."

Several bites later, he said, "The same itch is still bugging me. If we are talking long-standing family lore and mega-bucks, why take so long to act?"

"Could be changing life circumstances," I said. "Someone got poor. Or was released from prison and decided to go hunting. Lockup can lead you to all sorts of research. The Internet raped privacy a long time ago."

"Idle hands," he said. "So who's the avenging devil, Waters or Bakstrom?"

"Could be either," I said. "Or neither and the Drancy descendant is someone who knew a con comfortable with violence about to be released."

"Blondie and Bakstrom," he said. "Bonded to Bakstrom more than Waters because ol' Henry's better-looking and still alive."

I put my fork down. "Another changing circumstance would be the arrival of a family member actually willing to do something about it. It's like terrorism. An entire village might nurse a grudge but not everyone's ready to wear a suicide vest."

"Blondie, again," he said. "What I need to do is find an actual connection between her and either of the cons. Problem is our federal pals in Colorado. The latest is there is no visitors list anymore. Nothing goes back further than a month, ye olde computer glitch."

He finished his beer, called for another. "You know what really bothers me? Thalia, so helpless, thinking all her needs are being taken care of. It's like the damn hotel is an accomplice."

We finished, paid, walked back to the unmarked. As he slid behind the wheel, his phone jangled a text.

He shrugged. "Well, **this** is possibly not futile." His arm swung, showing me the screen: **Could maybe have something on the h.c. Mel.**

"Mel Howe," he said. "She's one of our sex crimes D's."

I said, "H.c.? Your hard case?"

He laughed. "Good guess. Hot **chick**. That's what I've been calling Blondie when I asked them to check."

"Possibly not futile" was enough to get him speeding back to the station.

Detective II Melanie-Anne Howe worked in the big room where every D but Milo operated. Her desk was in the center, neatly organized, as was she: a medium-sized brunette around forty with a round, freckled face, Cupid's-bow lips, and brown eyes slightly blurred by black-rimmed hipster eyeglasses.

She said, "Sorry for not getting back sooner, I was on vacation, just caught up with my messages."

"Have fun?"

"Disney cruise with Bob and three kids? Entire week, I got to have two Margaritas and one I couldn't finish because the baby started throwing up right after she went to bed."

She wrinkled her nose, picked up a blue folder lying next to her computer.

Thin file; too bad. Milo frowned.

Howe said, "Yup, not much unfortunately— it's too loud in here, let's find a place."

◆

A place was out on the sidewalk where Howe lit up a cigarette. "Basically, I quit. Basically, I cheat. As in three puffs and you're out, Mr. Winston."

She demonstrated, dropping the smoke on the sidewalk and grinding it dead with the toe of a medium-heeled pump. "When I got back I found your note and thought maybe. Even though my case never went anywhere and we're talking two months ago."

Her hands flexed. "My victim's memory was hazy in the first place and she was no angel. Officially that doesn't matter but yadda yadda, we know how it really is, try finding a D.A. wanting to put a stripper on the stand in a he-said-she-said. Top of that, the second time I talked to her, she'd changed her tune completely, shut down and refused to cooperate. I tried a third time and she went AWOL, dead phone, not at her home address or at work."

I said, "Voluntarily?"

Howe's eyebrows rose. "Yes, she's alive and kicking. Literally. Switched from a club in Commerce to one near the airport but I'm not pursuing it."

Milo said, "New job, new phone. Think she shut down 'cause she's scared?"

"She is scared, Milo, but not the way you might think. I was gentle with her, woman-to-woman, she was totally into filing charges if it got that far. Then, no dice and she told me why. Something she'd neglected to mention at the beginning: She has a rich boyfriend, some computer geek she gave a lap-dance to, knows nothing about it. In between interviews, she moved in with him, is petrified he'll find out."

Milo said, "Lap-dance leads to true love and he thinks she's a choir girl?"

Howe said, "With a geek, who knows? They can be like raw meat to girls in the know. You've probably got a technical term for that, Doctor."

I said, "Raw-meat-itis."

Melanie Howe laughed. Then she told us the story.

Vicki Elena Vasquez, twenty-two, performing, variously, as "Fatima," "Selena," or "Madrilena," had arrived in L.A. thirteen months ago after a youth misspent in Texas and Louisiana. Arrests for DUI, shoplifting, and petty theft, but clean since she'd turned Californian and began earning decent money taking off her clothes in sweaty dumps mislabeled as gentlemen's clubs.

A little over two months ago, after a double shift at the City of Commerce skin-palace, she'd driven to a hipster bar west of downtown called Brave Losers, a place she'd been once before with **"other girls, I don't remember who or when."**

Two Zombies into the early-morning hours, she'd struck up a conversation with a **"hot blond chick and a hot dude,"** neither of whose names she could recall ever knowing.

Nor could she remember leaving with the couple.

"They roofied me or something."

She'd woken up in an unknown place at an unknown time, tied to the posts of an unfamiliar bed, with the man's penis up her anus and the organ of **"a fat dude sitting on me"** in her mouth. At the same time, the blond woman performed cunnilingus on her **"but did it rough, like teeth, she hurt me. All of them did. I thought I was gonna die."**

At that point in the narrative, Melanie Howe's notes documented, **"V is crying and exhibiting signs of extreme anxiety: twitching, blinking, scrunching her face."**

As Vasquez realized what was happening, she tried to protest and was slapped hard in the face. Then someone's hand, she couldn't be sure whose, grasped her neck and exerted pressure until she began to lose consciousness.

"I didn't want to die so I let them do what they wanted."

The triple rape continued **"for a long time,"** until the assailants got off her and told her to forget them if she didn't want to die. The good-looking man then slapped her face several times, the woman pinched her nipples, and the fat man smacked her rear and said, "Nice place to visit but I wouldn't wanna live there." She was then blindfolded tightly and pulled into a shower where several hands scrubbed her, **"poking and rubbing deep inside everywhere. It hurt."**

Her vision still obstructed, she was dried off. A piece of cloth landed on her shoulder and she was ordered to get dressed. The cloth was the black Zara micro-dress she'd worn to the bar and after much effort she managed to get into it. Her underwear, stockings, and shoes were left behind as she was dragged outside and shoved into the backseat of a car. A silent ride of unknown duration ensued until the vehicle stopped and she was shoved out onto a hard surface.

She lay there woozy, stunned, and terrified until she heard the car drive away and managed to remove the blindfold—her own black stockings. She was in an alley. Her purse lay a few feet away. Two hundred dollars, her share of the cash tips she'd earned that evening, was gone, but her credit cards and cellphone were in place.

"Considerate rapists," said Milo.

I said, "Smugness. They're telling her, go ahead, call for help, we couldn't care less."

Melanie Howe said, "It did puzzle me, why leave anything? But now that I'm hearing it, you're probably right, Doctor. Anyway, she 911'd and because it was an alley it took a while to find her."

Milo said, "Alley, where?"

"That's the thing, she didn't know. Dispatch finally got her to use the phone and GPS. East Brentwood, apartment district, Westwood, just north of Wilshire. She got taken to the health center at the U. I was on that night, by the time I got there the rape kit had been done. Totally negative for semen, foreign blood, any kind of fluid. So they used condoms or the shower did the trick. That was a letdown but I was encouraged because initially she seemed to be a good victim, able to describe them enough to work up sketches. Also, the modus was pretty specialized, we don't see many mixed-gender gangbangs. Between that and how calculated and callous it was, I figured a similar would show up somewhere. Fortunately, the drawings got done. Unfortunately, she changed her mind."

She opened the file, showed us three faces.

Crude and ill-defined renderings, way below Shimoff-quality and in another context, probably useless. But once you'd seen Gerard Waters's and Henry Bakstrom's photos, the connection was easy.

The female suspect was another story, just another proto-blonde. Not as pretty as in Shimoff's rendering. This artist had drawn her slightly off kilter, probably unintentionally.

Milo showed Howe the mugshots.

She said, "Oh, God. If I'd had these to show her she might've stuck with me. Then again, with Geeky in the background, probably not."

"Think showing them to her now could pull up more info, Mel?"

"Maybe, if you can even get to her, who knows where she's at psychologically? Any suggestions, Doctor?"

I said, "No harm trying."

Milo said, "That's what I like about him, practical."

Howe said, "If you think it would help, I'm happy to go with you. But I think it could hurt, she associates me with real bad memories and the second interview didn't go well. Not that I pushed her but she got really hostile, like I was the enemy."

"After she went AWOL, how'd you find her?"

"She let slip the boyfriend's first name, Charlie, and figuring he'd been a regular at the club in Commerce, I talked to the owner. Guy didn't come in anymore, so he was happy to oblige. Charles Ruffalo. DMV shows a face like a spaniel but he drives an Aston Martin and has a house in the hills, the address is in here. Whether or not Vicki's still with him, I can't say. If she is, I'd be careful about ruining her relationship, so you might want to make sure the Aston's not there. So do you want me to tag along?"

Milo said, "I see your point, think I'll try by myself."

"Either way," said Howe. But she sounded relieved. She pulled out a pack of Winstons, bounced it on her thigh.

Milo said, "Thanks, Mel. Maybe it'll work out for both of us."

"Appreciate the thought, Milo, but I'm out of it. Vicki's lack of cooperation, the passage of time, any bruises are healed. Even if I did have my suspects, defense could always claim it was a consensual party. Especially given her occupation and level of intoxication."

I said, "Even with being dumped on the street?"

"That's her story. They'll say they dropped her off and she was fine, wandered into the alley and got mugged."

"She drove from work to the bar. What happened to her car?"

"Nowhere to be found. If it ever got that far, a prosecutor could threaten to add GTA to the charges but no way that would happen. Defense counsel would say no car, no evidence of theft, plus, losing jurisdiction of her own wheels just proves how intoxicated she was. And guess who the judge would agree with? She really **was** hammered, guys. Blew a .24 at the hospital with no evidence of any other drug in her system, including Rohypnol. If they roofied her, it could've worn off but her vulnerability could've come purely from way too much booze."

I said, "She met them in a bar. Bartender have anything to say?"

"Busy night, loud, crowded, he **maybe** remembered seeing Vasquez but not the other three. I don't doubt her, I'm sure it happened, poor thing. And I don't hold anything against her, it's her life."

She studied the mugshots. "Murder suspects. She doesn't know how lucky she is. So now you get to look for three really bad people."

"Two," said Milo. "Found the ugly one." He described Waters's crime scene.

Howe said, "The Palisades? Where they dumped Vicki isn't super close to there but it's not that far, either. The fact that they picked her up on the Eastside and dumped all the way west was interesting. Now I'm finding it fascinating."

Milo said, "Their crib is in our jurisdiction."

"Lucky us," said Melanie Howe. "Good luck. I'd say give my regards to Vicki but that's not going to help you."

We left her staring at a second cigarette, walked back inside the station and up the stairs. When we reached the corridor leading to Milo's office, he said, "Gottlieb distances himself, she does the same. I'm starting to feel like a leper."

"Take it as a vote of confidence," I said. "With you in charge, why bother?"

He groaned. "Oh, man, there's friendship and then there's pathological enabling."

"What am I enabling?"

He shook his head, unlocked his door, settled in his chair hard enough to threaten its integrity. Placing his palms together, he gave a small bow. "Please, Dr. Therapist Sir, no more questions, my head's gonna explode."

Leafing through the Vasquez file, he said, "What's the chance Vicki will supply any relevant info?"

I kept silent.

"I said no questions, amigo. Answers are fine."

I smiled.

"Monty Lisa," he said. "Just what I need."

CHAPTER 33

A call to Smooth Operator Gentleman's Club in City of Commerce confirmed Vicki Vasquez no longer danced there. A call to Brave Losers Cocktail Lounge west of downtown elicited stuporous ignorance of her patronage from three separate employees.

Milo phoned Charles Ruffalo's residence on Credo Lane. Out of service. Same result with Vasquez's cellphone.

"For all we know he moved her up to Silicon Valley." He stood. "Only one way to find out."

GPS'ing Credo Lane, he studied the map.

"High up. At least we can catch a view."

I said, "There you go," but the street-grid on the screen meant more to me than a random attempt to find a witness.

Little more than a jog from the home of an actress whose shattered mind had led me on a search for a missing child last year.

Milo saw me staring. "What?"

"Zelda."

"Oh, yeah, that. Something about Hollywood, the hills, huh?"

"People think they can hide up there."

"We know better."

Charles Ruffalo, "an independent IT Consultant and Data Manager," according to his LinkedIn page, lived at the apex of an axle-tormenting road that skinnied as it unraveled north of Sunset.

We zipped past the Chateau Marmont as if the hotel was an afterthought. Celebrities had partied and died there. Ordinary people, too, but who'd know or care?

The hospitality industry was based on a strange concept when you thought about it. Foster homes for adults that were seldom homey. Pledges of comfort and security impossible to guarantee.

I was still turning that over when Milo parked near the house. Charles Ruffalo's chrome address numerals were placed just off center on an eight-foot wall of gray stucco. Stress cracks sprouted from the bottom and spidered upward.

The low flat roofline of a house barely cleared the barrier. Off to the left was a wide gate made of plastic trying to pass as glass.

Chrome for the front door, same finish for the keypad.

Milo said, "Tight little fortress, can't even check if the Aston's there."

"I had one of those, I'd garage it."

"If she's in there with or without Geeko, and I say who I am, what's the chance she'll open up?"

Noise from behind saved me from the sad, truthful answer. Big mass of brown, chugging up the hill.

UPS truck. It rumbled just past us, motor idling as the driver jumped out with a package, laid it down in front of the door, pushed the button, and dashed back behind the wheel. After effecting a jerky three-point turn that maimed part of a neighbor's shrubbery, he sped off.

Before the sound of the truck engine had wiffled to silence, the chrome door opened and a woman came out, rubbing her eyes. Young, pale, and chesty, wearing a black top with a hood that flopped on her back and hot-pink yoga pants striped with silver. Hair a half foot below her waist was curled at the ends like a pageant queen's do. White-blond on top, mahogany in the center, black on the bottom. A cosmetic parfait.

She bent and picked up the package. By the time she'd finished reading the label, we were there.

Even with dual smiles and Milo's softest, "Ms. Vasquez? L.A. police, nothing to worry about, we'd just like to touch base," Vicki Vasquez reacted with the purest terror I'd seen in a long time.

Tight-throat wheeze followed by a gasp. Electric eyes bouncing as her already wan complexion lost color.

She backed away from us, trembling hands letting go of the package. I caught it. Something addressed to C. Ruffalo from Net-a-Porter. From the size and the rattle, probably shoes.

Vicki Vasquez said, "My Jimmy Choos," and burst into tears.

I said, "Here you go."

Instead of taking the box, she crossed her arms. "I—I—I . . ."

"So sorry to barge in," said Milo. I'd never seen him more avuncular. That and his badge offered subtly did nothing to calm her.

She said, "I **don't** want to **talk** about it."

I said, "We don't want you to, either."

She gaped. Nice teeth. Even with the chattering.

I chanced inching closer to her, kept my voice low and soothing, my speech slow and rhythmic.

Hypnotic induction voice. Back when I was helping kids deal with pain, I could do ten inductions a day, leave the hospital sleepy and serene.

Vicki Vasquez didn't seem impressed but a second later, she did reach out for the box. Hugged it to her bosom and maybe that was enough temporary comfort because she stopped retreating.

I said, "There's absolutely no need to talk about what happened to you, Vicki. This is something different."

She continued staring. Finally: "What?"

No sense being abstract. "The people who assaulted you are suspected of murder."

Milo's arched eyebrows said, **That's psychology?**

Vicky Vasquez said, "Charlie's right."

"Charlie—"

"My soulmate. He says I'm lucky."

"He's right, you sure are."

"Who did they murder?"

"Someone involved in a business deal," I said.

"Nothing to do with me."

"Absolutely nothing. But if we could show you some photos—"

Vicki Vasquez looked down the road. "Out here?"

"If you'll allow us, we're happy to come inside—"

"Let me see that badge again."

Milo complied, showed her his card, as well.

She said, "Homicide. Okay, that's not my problem. Come in."

The house was more gray stucco inside and out, the flat roof white pebbly stuff. The interior was one sprawling space backed by glass and floored in slate. A few randomly placed pieces of bright-red and blue furniture carved from foam coexisted with molded-resin tables. Italian contemporary, probably uncomfortable, probably expensive.

The glass let in sky and hillside and the real estate dreams of homeowners lower down in the hillside pecking order, most content with postage-stamp lots. Altitude reduced patio furniture to matchsticks. Lawns and swimming pools were colored mosaic tiles.

Vicki Vasquez crossed halfway across the room, placed her package on one of the tables, refolded her arms across her chest. No art, no books, no cooking implements visible in the kitchen. A seventy-inch flat-screen took up the largest masonry wall, wires dangling. A single photograph was propped on another table. Vasquez in the merest black bikini standing next to a skinny guy in his forties wearing baggy swim-trunks. Ruffalo had thin dark hair, gray temples, a hangdog face unrelieved by a Bucky Beaver smile so wide it threatened to bisect his head.

Moving back inside seemed to shore up Vicki Vasquez's confidence. She tossed her hair, clamped her hands on her hips, turned so her body formed an hourglass framed by glass.

Panorama drama.

She said, "Show me what you got."

Gerard Waters's and Henry Bakstrom's mugshots narrowed her eyes. She flipped the bird, made a raking motion with her other hand.

"Motherfuckers. Catch them and kill them."

Milo showed her Alex Shimoff's drawing of the blonde.

Her nostrils flared. A screech escaped from somewhere deep inside her.

"You know her, Vicki?"

"Duchess. Fucking bitch, I hate her the worst."

"Duchess."

"That's what they called her."

"What'd she call them?"

"I never heard none a their names."

"But the men called her Duchess."

"That's no name, anyway," said Vicki Vasquez. "Right? That's like a . . . a . . ."

I said, "A title."

"Yeah, a fucking title. Like she's a queen or

something. Fuck that, she ain't. She's a fucking bitch."

I said, "You especially hate her because—"

"She's a **girl**. She should be on **my** side."

That let loose a storm of obscenity and a quick march across the picture window and back. When she returned, Milo said, "What else can you tell us about them?"

"You didn't find my car?"

"Not yet."

"I don't give a," she said. "It was crap, Charlie's buying me a Mustang."

"Good for you. Anything else you remember?"

"They need to **die**." She stabbed air. "Charlie knows kickboxing, he could smash their fucking brains and shove it up their asses."

"Glad you have someone to protect you."

"Charlie loves me."

"Is there anything you can—"

"If I knew something, I'd tell it. I want you to catch them." She grinned. "So you can do what **you** do."

Milo said, "What do **we** do?"

"You **guys**?" she said. "The **po**-lice? You find 'em, you shoot 'em." She flashed a gang sign. "LAPD. Baddest homeys in the hood."

We left her posed in the doorway, drinking a can of Fresca and playing with her hair.

As we passed out of earshot, I flashed the same sign. "Yo, Homey."

Milo said, "Nice to be appreciated. Maybe she was on to something. Blondie's in charge, sees herself as royalty."

We got back in the car.

I said, "The way they assaulted Vasquez has similarities to burking, no?"

"Three-on-one teamwork, a helpless body." He stuck out his tongue. "All the stuff I've seen and you can still creep me out." He started the engine. "Yeah, you could be right."

"Teamwork," I said, "but no team spirit. First Waters got cut from the roster, then DeGraw. The Duchess and Bakstrom are the core—directing and producing. The others were likely expendable right from the beginning."

He pulled the same three-point turn as the UPS driver but avoided landscape assault. "Same old story. The good-looking popular kids rule."

CHAPTER
34

As we passed through the Strip, Elie Aronson called my cell.

"No one's talking about a big ruby, Doctor,
stolen or legal. But that doesn't mean nothing, if
they took it out of the country fast. I talked to
an Armenian, specializes in colored stones. He
says the same thing I told you. That size, unless
it's garbage, for sure millions."

"Thanks, Elie."

"The Armenian," he said. "He says he could
handle something like that, you ever find it and
it's legal to sell it."

"I'll keep that in mind, Elie."

"Just passing it along."

◆

Forty minutes after leaving Vicki Vasquez, we were back in Milo's office. He tossed his jacket on the floor and speed-rolled his desk chair to his keyboard.

Several "Duchesses" in the moniker file, all young gang girls, except for a six-foot-six career burglar named Clarence Bearden inexplicably nicknamed Duchess C.

NCIC and other rosters gave up a couple dozen more pretenders to nobility but none came close to fitting Blondie.

Milo said, "What you said before, it's a production. Maybe I'm looking for bad in all the wrong places. How about an actress?"

"No shortage of them on the Westside."

"Especially the ones that don't make it and get real hungry."

No shortage of stage productions and movies with "Duchess" in the title or roles featuring noblewomen. An old English play, **The Duchess of Malfi,** was saturated with violence but bore no obvious link to the case.

One contemporary actress popped up, Duchess Ella, a star in the industry known as Nollywood.

Nigerian cinema. Not a blonde.

Milo said, "That's what I love about my job, learn something new every day."

He rechecked his notes and his messages. Sean Binchy had watched Ricki Sylvester last night, was off for the day, at his daughter's class party.

Nuttin. She went to work at nine.

Leaning back in the chair, Milo clasped his hands behind his head and stretched his legs. Even phony relaxation didn't mesh with his mood; he rolled his shoulders, flipped open Thalia's murder book, and studied the old photo of the ruby.

"A gazillion bucks of red carbon. Your jeweler pal's right, that kind of payoff, Ken and Barbie could be sunning themselves in Abu Dhabi." He shut the file. "Stuck on a lampshade and illegal. Good luck proving it was there in the first place."

I said, "Maybe the ruby was part of why Thalia called me. She was ready to cash in and leave it to charity, along with everything else. I'm obligated to confidentiality and have links to Western Peds. She could've hoped I'd help her work out a plan to gift it without attracting too much attention."

"That sounds like sucking you into a criminal conspiracy," he said. "Shrink as laundry consultant. The psychopath talk really **was** about her?"

"Her, Hoke, the life they shared years ago. Not guilt, necessarily. She was lighthearted, manipulative. More like tiptoeing into the past in order to rationalize."

"The wages of sin going to a good cause. If it had gotten that far, what would you have advised her about the ruby?"

"That I was out of my element."

"So no risk to her," he said. "Yeah, I can see that. She's old and adorable, out to help sick kiddies, who's gonna bust her, let alone prosecute her after all these years?"

"I'm not sure anyone could be prosecuted," I said. "All Thalia had to say was it was a gift, she had no idea. And once the department started digging and found Demarest's report, I'm guessing they'd err on the side of discretion."

"How would they find it?"

"You, being a peace officer, would give it to them."

"Would I?" He smiled. "I think she wanted more from you than help with a donation."

"Like what?"

"What we all want. Absolution."

He yawned, closed his eyes and opened them. Shook himself off like a wet dog and shot to his feet. "No more oxygen in here, I need to kickstart my metabolism."

We left the station and walked west on Santa Monica Boulevard, heading for coffee brewed anywhere but in the big detective room. The first place we found was a block up, jammed with stubble-faced idlers in their twenties and a homeless guy who'd cadged enough for a latte. A couple of blocks later, we scored lukewarm something-brown at a place that specialized in high-fat ice cream. No effect on my metabolism but a coconut vanilla cone and a tall cup seemed to replace Milo's lethargy with green-eyed fury.

As we headed back, he crushed the empty cup and kept up the pressure, as if trying to obliterate every molecule of paper by sheer dint of will.

As we passed the first café, the homeless guy was sitting on the sidewalk, grinning toothlessly and holding out a grimy hand. "Panini for a gourmet? I like truffles."

Milo's glare shut him up. The five Milo handed him nearly crossed his eyes.

We picked up our pace.

He said, "What bothers me the most is Sylvester, if she was involved. No matter how cagey you are, you have to trust someone. Your own lawyer sells you out . . . maybe ol' Ricki didn't freak out because of law school. Raking up memories of the past scares the hell out of her because she knows what she really is."

"All those house calls," I said. "Lots of opportunity to spot the ruby. But something she said when you informed her Thalia was dead makes me wonder if she knew the extent of the plan. Along the lines of 'never believed something like this could happen.' Maybe I'm overparsing but 'I never believed' is different from 'I can't believe.'"

"She knew something would happen."

"A burglary, not a murder. Easier to rationalize, with Thalia being rich and obviously not needing the ruby."

He tossed the now unrecognizable cup into a trash bin. "Maybe, but still. All that righteous talk of not charging for executor services? More like **execution** services. For all I know, she has money issues of her own and got the ball rolling."

We turned the corner on Butler. As the station came into view, he said, "Let's have another go at Ricki. Wait here, I'll get my stuff. Your turn to drive, I wanna think."

Jared the bearded receptionist wore a turquoise polo shirt and a leather bolo tie and sat busying himself with his phone, his teapot and cup resting on a madras-print towel.

Ignoring us as we walked up to the plastic desk. Pretending to be surprised when we arrived. "Oh, hi."

Milo said, "Tell the boss we're here, please."

"Love to do that, but she's not in."

"When's she due back?"

"Wish I knew, sorry."

Milo took the phone from his hand. Jared looked as if he'd had a limb ripped off. "Why would you do that—"

"Same question, friend."

"And same answer, sir. I'm not hiding anything, she wasn't here when I arrived and she's still not here. I've called her several times and she's not answering."

"Is that typical?"

"No."

"Does it concern you?"

"No. She's an adult."

"So she does take time off."

"I've only worked here a few months. She's always here but people change, right?"

"Has she seemed different, recently?"

"No. Why are you asking—"

"When did you show up this morning? Jared, right?"

Nod. "Around ten."

"When does the boss typically get here?"

"Before me, like nine thirty. She likes to have quiet time for herself."

"Meditation?"

"I don't know what she does in there. Can I have my phone back? Don't you need a warrant?"

"Only if I read your messages and they go viral."

Jared flushed. Milo said, "Just kidding," and put the phone on the desk. Jared snatched it up and held it to his chest. Nestling a tiny, electronic infant.

"Jared, tell her to call when she does arrive."

"Sure."

Outside, Milo said, "We didn't even get offered tea."

As I drove away, he put his speaker on conference and called Binchy.

"Sorry to interrupt the party, Sean."

"It's over, Loot. What's up?"

"What time did Sylvester enter her parking lot?"

"Around ten, but I didn't exactly see her enter, Loot. You said loose surveillance, don't get mad. I followed her until she was right at the lot and kept going."

"Okay."

"Did I screw up, Loot?"

"Not at all, Sean. Have a nice day, go kiss the kid."

"Really, Loot. Did I mess up? If you want I can go up there, pretend to be a delivery guy or something and ask if she's in."

"She's not, I was just there."

"Oh," said Binchy. "I did screw up."

"You didn't, Sean. Her parking lot has cameras, if I need to, I'll look at the footage."

"Darn," said Binchy. "I should've looked back. I just—"

"It's okay, Sean. Give me her home address."

"All right . . . looking for it . . . darn, Loot."

Binchy read it off. Milo copied. "You want to really upset me, Sean?"

"God forbid, Loot."

"Then no more apologies and keep your self-esteem up. Kiss the wife, too."

He hung up.

I said, "Impressive therapeutic skills."

"I must be slipping." He examined what he'd written. "Not far from here. But I'll put in a fuel voucher for you, anyway. Drive, Jeeves."

CHAPTER
35

Ricki Sylvester lived in a mustard-colored two-story house on the eastern edge of Santa Monica, south of Wilshire. The block housed a couple of original structures like hers, the rest McMansion replacements.

Flaking stucco blemished the walls, window-sills were in need of paint, the brown composite roof sported patches of missing shingles, landscaping was a scraggly lemon tree devoid of fruit and a lawn reduced to gray fuzz.

Shabbiest address on the block. The place neighbors whisper about.

Milo said, "Maybe she's planning to cash in, figures it'll be torn down, anyway, no need to keep it up. I'm thinking a bunch of cats and maybe a hoard of crap, inside."

We got out and walked to the front door. A bell-push was followed by silence. So was Milo's steadily intensifying cop-knock. We walked around, peering through windows. Most were covered by shades. Those that weren't revealed no hoarding, just the opposite.

Minimal furniture, a monastic simplicity.

No cats aroused by the presence of a stranger, inside or out. An untrimmed eugenia hedge walled more gray earth. Where a garage should've stood, a patch of cracked cement bore oil-stains.

I said, "Not much estate for an estate lawyer."

"A piece of that ruby could change everything."

I said nothing.

We returned to the car. He said, "I'm wrong?"

"She's practiced law for years, could live a lot better than she does so I'm not sure the issue is economic."

"What, then?"

"There's a depressive element to her. A man shows up, takes the time to woo her, she'd be vulnerable. Someone like Bakstrom would be perfect for the assignment but he doesn't fit the description the waiter gave."

"Another member of the team we don't know about."

"Or more than one other person," I said. "Like we've been saying, this could be a family project."

"The clan strikes back." He glanced at Sylvester's house. "Think something bad happened to her? More culling?"

"They do have that track record."

He put a BOLO on Sylvester and the Buick. "Now what?"

I said, "The prison in Colorado has to be key. Bakstrom and Waters were cellies and Duchess had some sort of relationship with one or both of them. Maybe one of those pen-pal things or she has a criminal record of her own."

"She murders, she rapes," he said. "Unlikely this is her virgin outing. But without a name, what am I supposed to do? Fly to Colorado and beg? Even if they wanted to help, their system's totally screwed up."

I said, "Why not work from the bottom up? Forget wardens and data managers, find a guard who'll talk."

"Power to the people," he muttered. "How the hell do I do that?"

"The old-fashioned way."

"Aw, Jesus."

The two of us sat in the Seville as he began the call-fest, bypassing prison administration and beginning with the lowest-ranked person listed on the website, a guard captain named Potrero.

He was out but his secretary obliged with Potrero's nearest subordinate. And so on.

The closer prison staffers were to hands-on, the more cooperative they were. Even with that, Milo contended with numerous delays and being kept on hold.

All that frustration and the weather kicked up the heat in the car. As he fumed, I got out and strolled up the block.

Three properties north of Ricki Sylvester's house, a young, long-haired man in snug charcoal velvet sweats picked leaves out of a boxwood hedge. Fronting the hedge were fragrant gardenia bushes. Then, a velvety lawn, a matched pair of red-leaf plum trees, and half a dozen massive sago palms that cost hundreds of dollars each.

The structure behind all that was a peach-colored Spanish retro-hacienda that tried to look authentic but didn't come close. Too many architectural tweaks applied too exuberantly. What you see when young girls put on makeup for the first time.

As I passed, the plucker stopped and watched me with suspicion. That level of vigilance plus the landscaping and the meticulous abode said potential busybody. I backtracked, he tensed up.

I showed him the out-of-date LAPD consultant badge.

He said, "There's a problem?" Mediterranean accent.

"We're looking for one of your neighbors as a possible witness."

"Which neighbor?"

"Ms. Sylvester. The mustard-colored house."

"Her. Bleh. She up to something?"

"You've had problems with her?"

"The house is the problem. She has no money? Fine, sell and let someone make it nice."

"She has money. She's an attorney."

"No way."

I nodded.

"Crazy," he said. "My husband's an attorney. Why would she live like this?"

"Who knows? Anything else I should know about her, Mr.—?"

"Massimo Bari."

"Where in Italy are you from?"

"I'm from Malta," he said.

"Ah—so is there anything about—"

"Her? Nothing. She doesn't talk."

"Not friendly."

"I say hello, nothing, Robert says hello, nothing. She gets in that dump-car and drives away. Robert and I wondered where she went all day. An attorney? We figured she sits in the park."

"She's got an office."

"Unbelievable."

"She have any social life?"

"Who's going to want to be social with that?"

"How about visitors?"

"Nothing—oh, yeah, one time, long time—months—there was another car, Robert and I said, maybe we get lucky and she's moving out."

"A car in her driveway."

"In back of hers, she parks all the way in," said Massimo Bari. "Then it happened again, few nights later. Robert and I are so happy, finally. But then it's gone, never comes back, nothing changes, she's still here ruining the block."

"How long was the other car there?"

"Don't know, all I can tell you is in the morning it was gone. "There is something to worry about? More than an ugly house?"

"Absolutely not. What kind of car?"

"Minivan, they all look the same."

"Color?"

"Darkish." He grimaced. "I'm into color, but it's at night, I'm not paying attention. Darkish."

"Did you notice who was driving it?"

"Never saw no one, just a minivan, Robert and I were hoping for a nice family moving in. **Is** there something you're not telling me, sir? She **did** something criminal?"

"There's nothing to worry about, Mr. Bari. It's just what I told you."

"She's a witness. To what?"

"Nothing you should worry about."

He studied my face. "You look honest, I hope you are. It's a great neighborhood, that's why we put the money in. Robert and I were thinking. Maybe we should start a Neighborhood Watch. Like we had when we lived in the Valley. What do you think?"

"Can't hurt."

"You could help with that, no?"

"I can refer you to someone."

"Great! Have your people call me." He reached into a pocket of his sweatpants, fished out a bill-fold, extracted a business card from a wad of cash and credit cards. Stiff cardboard, matte black, peach-colored lettering.

Design by Massimo
Fashion and Lifestyle Consulting

Gmail, no phone or street address.

He said, "I build gorgeous formal and business casual menswear. Are you married?"

I shook my head.

He appraised me head-to-toe. "You have decent taste, easy to fit, okay, I give you a discount."

"Appreciate the offer."

"I mean it, sir. Get married, I fix you up gorgeous. Dressing up's a good way to start a relationship." Another glance at the mustard-colored box. "You want me to keep an eye on her?"

"That would be great." I patted my pockets. "Don't have a card of my own, could you spare another of yours?"

"You bet."

I wrote Milo's name, title, and number on the back, returned it to him.

He read. "Lieutenant." Sly smile. "For you, I could design something with a little bit of the uniform vibe, you know?"

"Keeping it official," I said.

"Fun, Lieutenant. It's all about fun."

Milo had exited the car, too, but he hadn't strayed from the passenger door.

From the look on his face, no fun had transpired.

I said, "More stonewall?"

"North Korea's got nothing on these guys but some progress."

He got back in. I started up the engine.

He said, "I finally got the name of a guard who worked that particular visitors area for the past few years. Of **course**, they can't promise he knows anything. Of **course**, he's on vacation. I called, left a message. Let's get back to the office, maybe I can find some more info on him and interrupt his recreation. What were you doing?"

"Impersonating a police officer."

I drove past Massimo. He waved.

"I leave you alone for a minute and you make a new friend?"

"Maybe a useful friend. The Maltese Mynah." I told him about the van in Sylvester's driveway. "Months ago fits the waiter's time line."

"The old guy's wheels. Okay, one baby step closer. If it means anything. Thanks."

A block later, he said, "Mini but still a van. You know what I'm thinking."

"Ideal for transporting bodies."

"But let's not be morbid." A beat. "On the other hand, let's."

The guard's name was Herman Montoya. His Facebook page advertised eighteen pals, all family members. Thirteen of whom were vacationing with him in Sedona, Arizona, in celebration of the eighty-fifth birthday of the matriarch, Montoya's grandmother, Estrella.

Details of the trip were courteously laid out.

Milo said, "Now everyone on the planet knows their houses are vacant. He works with scumbags all day and gets this careless?"

Everyone also knew the Montoya family's mode of transportation from Colorado to Arizona: a caravan of rented RVs, scenic stops along the way.

Arrival date, yesterday. One of Montoya's daughters was kind enough to list the mobile home park hosting the caravan as well as the creature comforts it provided.

Snackbar and even WiFi hookups!!! for streaming
Orange is The New Black for Patti and
Lorna and me, Breaking Bad and sports for the guys
Nick for the kids!!! Yeah!!!.

Milo said, "If the information age keeps growing, detectives will be redundant."

"You'll always be needed," I said. "Personal charm and all that."

He grunted and phoned the desk at Red Rock RV Lodge.

The manager was an agreeable woman, had no problem walking over to check Herman Montoya's patch of asphalt. After being reassured by Milo that none of the clan was suspected of anything.

"Salt of the earth," he said. "He's in law enforcement."

"Awesome," she said. "We love law enforcement. Okay, shouldn't take long, I'll get back to you."

Five minutes later, Milo's cell played a Sousa march.

A soft, wary voice said, "Herman Montoya. This really LAPD?"

Milo repeated his name and rank and Montoya said, "Okay, what's up?"

"Thanks for calling back. Sorry to interrupt your vacation."

"Vacation," said Montoya. "How much red rock can I look at? Also, the jewelry's outrageous but of course they all have to have some. You got me curious. What can I do for LAPD?"

Milo told him.

He said, "Sure I remember her. Name was DeeDee, last year or so she was there every couple months to see Bakstrom."

"Not Waters."

"Just Bakstrom."

"DeeDee what?"

"Hmm . . . those were her initials, Dee something, Dee something . . . sorry, that's what I remember, she called herself by the initials. Hi, I'm DeeDee. Cheerful, like that. She'd get all wiggly, the hips, you know? Had a pair of boobs on her, whoa. But like I care. What I **care**, honey, is you don't slip him something that's going to hurt me."

"Bakstrom was violent?"

"No," said Herman Montoya. "Just talking generally, every visitor's a potential problem. But she was okay, except for too friendly with the staff. I don't like 'em too friendly, usually means they're hiding something."

"Friendly and wiggly."

"God gave her a bod and she sure used it," said Montoya. "Premium bod. Face, too. **Good**-looking chick. Not what we usually get." He laughed. "By that I mean she had all her teeth. Dee . . . what the heck was her name . . . ?"

"Something with a 'D,'" said Milo. "How about Drancy?"

"Nope."

Too-quick answer. Milo sagged. His lips formed a silent obscenity.

Herman Montoya said, "Dee . . . I'm having a senior moment . . . maybe Diane, maybe Deena . . . Debbie. Something with a darn 'D.'"

Milo said, "Duchess?"

"Ha," said Montoya. "Now you're kidding me. It was a while back, sorry."

I said, "Demarest?"

Milo stared at me.

Herman Montoya said, "Who was that?"

Milo said, "My colleague, you're on speaker."

"Oh. Didn't hear what he said."

"Could the last name be Demarest?"

"There you **go**! Demarest. **Now** I remember. **Damn** I'm **losing** it. I used to make a joke to myself when she'd flip the hair, wink and wiggle and tell me I didn't need to bring a female guard to search her. I'd tell myself, 'Give it a **rest, De**-marest. I don't care how cute you are, honey. My deal is getting out by end of shift **not** on a gurney."

Noise piled up in the background. Montoya said, "Hold one sec."

A few seconds of dead air before he returned. "Wife and sister and daughters and granddaughter have jewelry to show me. Anything else I can help you with?"

"Did DeeDee visit anyone else but Bakstrom?"

"Just him. His cellie, Waters, no one came to see him. The two of them were always discussing something. Bakstrom and Waters."

"Any idea about what they talked about?"

"You know cons," said Montoya, "too much spare time. For all I know they were setting up a political party and planning to run for office."

"Any discipline issues for either of them?"

"Nope," said Montoya. "They did their time and piled up the behavior points and now **you** guys have to deal with them—**Deandra! That's** her first name, it just hit me."

"Deandra Demarest."

"Yup, D and D."

"Terrific, Officer Montoya. Thanks a ton."

Montoya said, "So what'd these jokers do in L.A.?"

"Killed a bunch of people."

"Killed? A bunch? Geez," said Montoya.

"Killed . . ." Soft whistle. "Nothing like that with us, like I said, no problems with either of them. But we're like a separate society, the smart ones figure out the rules and adapt. Then they get out and break **your** rules."

Deandra Katrine Demarest, thirty-nine, had two arrests that showed up in NCIC.

Age nineteen, armed robbery, in Louisville, Kentucky.

Age twenty-nine, writing bad checks in Ossining, New York.

I said, "Every ten years. She was due."

"Those are the two she got caught for," said Milo. He looked up the details, read, printed, passed over the info.

The robbery, of a jewelry store, had been committed by two ex-cons. One, Demarest's boyfriend, had done the gun-waving and the looting, the other drove the getaway car. Deandra, sitting in the backseat, claimed she'd known nothing about the vehicle being stolen or plans to rob. She'd pled down to accessory before the fact, got a year in prison, most of which was consumed by time served.

The bad check earned her probation and community service at a local preschool, due to "the absence of prior arrests and exigent circumstances."

Milo said, "Her and toddlers, there's a smart move."

I said, "Isn't Ossining where Sing Sing is?"

"Sure is. Another con-romance, huh?"

"Good bet," I said. "With Louisville on her record, why no priors, there?"

He said, "Shitty record keeping, no one talks to each other. Also 'exigent circumstances' is D.A.-speak for 'I'm letting you off, honey.' Maybe she got wiggly and impressed some prosecutor. Preschool. Brilliant."

He pointed to the pair of mugshots. "She does have the equipment to impress."

Mugs bring out the worst in their subjects; even movie stars come across desperate and eroded. Deandra Demarest's smile said the booking process was just another modeling session.

Both times she'd held her head up high, rotated her face to create a flattering contour, squared her shoulders, flashed perfect teeth. Her smile was a strange mix of wholesome and sinful.

The kind of blitheness that comes with getting away with too much for too long. In her case, biology helped: perfect oval face, cute cleft in her chin, widely spaced blue eyes with enormous irises that would make her appear appealingly confused when she was anything but. All of that crowned by a creamy sweep of wavy hair—brunette at nineteen, blond at twenty-nine.

They say eyes are the true mirrors to the soul but Deandra Demarest's eyes projected a softness that did nothing but lie. The kind of earnestness and implied vulnerability that could sell anything.

The photos offered no view of the body she'd worked to impress Montoya but the stats said plenty: no change in over a decade: five-five, one hundred nineteen, "slender build."

A lithe structure free of scars, tattoos, or distinguishing marks. Eschewing ink because she knew what she had, wanted to keep it pristine.

Milo said, "In both shots she looks younger than her age."

I said, "Easy to preserve yourself when others are doing the dirty work."

"No aliases or nicknames, she must've added the Duchess bit later."

He ran a DMV search; no license or registered vehicles. No employment history, per Social Security. "Guess preschools don't report."

I said, "For all we know she's doing the same thing here under an assumed name."

He shook his head. "DeeDee Demarest. So much for the Drancy hypothesis."

I said, "Wrong family but the correct theory. I wonder how she sprouted on a cop's family tree."

CHAPTER
37

Information on LAPD Commander Raynard Gordon Demarest was easy to come by.

In 1951, at age fifty, the former "high-ranking police official and one-time driver for Mayor Frank Shaw" had been arrested, tried, and sent to prison the next year. Every local paper had covered the story.

Milo said, "A tree with rotten roots."

A ragout of charges had been leveled at Demarest, creating a legal tsunami that washed him to San Quentin on a thirteen-year sentence. Notable lack of character references, pre- or post-conviction, including by family members.

No mention of family, period, and recently appointed Chief William Parker's characterization of Demarest as "exactly the kind of morally degenerate character we're striving to eliminate from our midst" hadn't helped.

Neither had a parade of victims with grievances stretching to Demarest's early days as a Central Division patrolman and chauffeur for Shaw, the most corrupt mayor in L.A. history.

"Numerous business owners" recalled how Demarest had strong-armed them for protection money. "Citizen witnesses testifying behind barriers for fear of recrimination" remembered being physically threatened and intimidated. Several "colored and Mexicans" accused Demarest of racially motivated beatings.

Violence didn't appear in any of the indictments but as an assemblage they were damning. Larceny, fraud, perjury, obstruction, false report by peace officer, false affidavit, peace officer misconduct, contempt of court, conspiracy.

I said, "Appealing all that would take years. Someone wanted him gone."

"Classic Bill Parker," said Milo. "Upright and merciless. Shaw represented everything he hated and Demarest having anything to do with Shaw made him an obvious target."

I said, "The kind of degenerate who'd go along with a jewel-grab."

"Easily."

"Demarest was probably chosen to write the report because he was involved in the confiscation. The handwriting on the back could've been a note he wrote to himself because the ruby was missing and he intended to look for it. First step would've been pressuring Thelma. Luckily for her and unfortunately for him, Parker went after him first."

He said, "If the bastard did go looking, he was out of his element."

"How so?"

"Too much time strong-arming, not enough learning how to detect."

The final article on Demarest covered the day he was shipped off to San Quentin. Identical LAPD photo in every paper: tall, broad, fair-haired man in jail clothes, head-down and cuffed, escorted by two plainclothesmen to the van that would transport him to Northern California.

Shortly before Christmas of 1952. Some holiday.

Milo said, "Let's find out what happened to him."

County records told that story.

Not Marin, where the prison sat. L.A., where the body of Inmate Raynard Gordon Demarest had been shipped to a mortuary in Boyle Heights.

He'd served less than a year of the thirteen before expiring in the prison, due to "cranial injury following a fall."

I said, "Prison showers can get slippery. Especially when it's the prison housing Hoke. If Demarest was behind the jewel confiscation and tried to pressure Thalia, it wouldn't have sat well with her true love."

"The long arm of Leroy," said Milo. "Yeah, I can see that."

"Shades of Drancy's tumble off that building."

"But his clan didn't care about revenge. Or the ruby."

"Or he had no family to speak of. But Demarest's relatives passed down a fable: Grandpa wasn't a corrupt bully, he was a knight errant on a quest for a priceless jewel who'd been railroaded. Marinate it over enough generations, they'd start believing they were entitled to the ruby as reparation."

I tapped Deandra Demarest's mugshots. "Like I said, it took until now for the right descendant to come along. Even with that, Deandra needed to ripen criminally. She also had to track down Thalia. Not easy—even if she did have a copy of Demarest's report, she'd be looking for Thelma Myers. Things fell into place once she learned the name of Hoke's lawyer. That led her to Jack McCandless's granddaughter, who either succumbed to pressure or was recruited willingly."

He re-read Deandra Demarest's arrest record.

"Her first bust. Back at nineteen she had a thing for jewelry."

I said, "And she did that with a pair of cons who ended up bearing the brunt. Sound familiar?"

"On the other hand," he said, "the bad-check thing was a solo act."

"So she's versatile. Or the records are inaccurate. Either way, she's developed a talent for manipulating men and discarding them."

"No bets on Bakstrom's longevity, huh?"

"Not an insurance policy I'd write. The same goes for Ricki Sylvester. We saw how emotional she can get and that makes her unreliable. If she complained to Deandra that you'd come by again and displayed anxiety, she might already be gone."

He said, "Manipulating men . . . the older guy Sylvester had dinner with. He could turn out to just be a blind date or he is another piston in DeeDee's engine. This femme is way past fatale."

He went out to the hall, paced up and down, came back. "Now I'm visualizing Cutie Pie all by herself on that Gulfstream to Arabia. Hell, she could have her sights on some emir—oh, man, the owners of the hotel. You think the plan could include them? Who better to buy a rock like that?"

I thought about it. "Doubt it. There'd be no reason for them to risk murdering an old lady for a gemstone when they could just buy one. That doesn't eliminate an under-the-table sale. But DeGraw's behavior—sneaking around, preparing to leave the country—says he was going behind his bosses' backs. He knew he'd be out of a job soon, was trying to augment his severance pay."

"Hope you're right, amigo. The case expands to potentates, I'm cooked. Unlike Duchess, who'd like to think she's a poobah but is eminently arrestable."

That made my head throb. "Who goes with a Duchess?"

"A male poobah—"

"A Duke."

"I don't get it."

"Waters's landlord, Phil Duke. An older guy. Maybe I'm reaching but—"

He swiveled so fast his chair tipped and he fought to keep it stable. Pounding the keyboard with big, white-knuckled hands, he said, "Oh, my."

CHAPTER
38

Philip Demarest Duke fancied himself an actor.

That, despite no film credits and only a scatter of community playhouse roles, none more recent than ten years ago. In the eighties, he had appeared on episodic TV but, again, the crop was thin: a few cameos in pilots that never went to series, one walk-on in a forgettable police drama.

"He does have the voice," I said.

Milo said, "Does he?"

"Stentorian."

"I'll pay closer attention when I've got him in a small, windowless room."

The résumé Duke included on his Facebook page listed a birthdate that made him sixty-four years old. DMV records added two years, Social Security, six.

Social Security also provided his employment record. For the past forty-five years, he'd worked in long-distance trucking, insurance sales, unspecified retail sales, real estate management, swimming pool maintenance, construction, landscaping. All that topped off by stints at big-box nurseries and building supplies emporia.

For two years, he'd been living on Social Security and disability. One piece of real estate, the house in West L.A. where we'd met him. Where we'd had no reason to doubt his account of Gerard Waters's movements.

His registered vehicle, a 2003 gray Ford Windstar minivan.

Milo said, "Gotcha! Think he's DeeDee's daddy?"

I said, "The age fits and he did mention his daughter was moving back in."

We returned to Phil Duke's social network. More like asocial: no friends, followers, or family.

A headshot atop the anemic acting history showed Duke looking around forty and dressed in costume. The production, **King Lear,** a non-profit playhouse in La Habra. Duke had played "a Knight of Lear's Train."

He'd chosen a shot that made him look like a

comical send-up of the bard, himself: puffy red velvet tunic, oversized ruff that appeared fashioned from cardboard, glued-on handlebar over what looked like a real Vandyke, atop his head a goofy skin cap simulating baldness and fringed with shoulder-length scraggle.

Milo said, "A star is born. This is the best he could do?"

I said, "Living in the past. And now he's expecting wealth and eternal bliss."

He logged on to the assessor's page and found the record of purchase of Duke's house. Initial purchase, thirty years ago. A quartet of near-foreclosures, all forestalled at the last minute.

Milo sniffed the air. "What's that wafting? Oh, yeah, Eau de Loser."

I said, "The cologne or the handy-dandy aftershave?"

"More like toilet water. Okay, let's firm up the I.D. on this prince—scratch that, duke."

He phoned High Steaks. Arturo wasn't working but the manager gave up the waiter's full name and number.

"None of that do-you-have-a-warrant crap," said Milo, "I must be getting good at this." He punched buttons. "Mr. De La Cruz? Lieutenant Sturgis. We talked the other day in the restaurant about the lady who tips five percent."

"You got her for something?"

"I was wondering if I could show you a photo, see if it matched the man you saw with her."

"Sure, c'mon over."

"Where do you live?"

"Reseda," said De La Cruz. "Traffic's going to be brutal but I'm not leaving."

Milo said, "How about I email it to you?"

"I don't have one of those phones gets emails."

"Do you have a computer?"

"My wife does but she's out."

"How about I lead you through it?"

"Hmm, I guess," said Arturo De La Cruz. "Second most exciting thing happened all month."

"What's the first?"

"Last week some guy was choking, I got to do the Heimlich."

"Good for you."

"Better for him. Okay, I'm walking over to her sewing desk, that's where she keeps it, no more sewing since she got into the yoga."

Guiding De La Cruz through the finer points of electronic transmission took a while. Once the image arrived, the waiter's verdict was instantaneous. "Yup, that's him."

"No doubt at all, sir?"

"Never forget a face, Lieutenant. Actually, that's a lie, I forget plenty of faces and a lot of other stuff, to boot. Like names, places, why I come into a room. But **him** I remember. 'Cause he was the only person I ever saw with **her**."

"Got it," said Milo. "Really appreciate it."

De La Cruz said, "So what'd the two of them pull off? Some kind of lawyer scam?"

"Don't have the whole picture yet."

"But they did pull off something. I knew something was off with her. You ever feel like telling me, I won't argue. Who knows, it could knock the choking guy down to number two."

Milo reached Sean Binchy at home in Long Beach. Kids' voices in the background.

"Still doing daddy stuff?"

"The party's finished but the girls are having fun, Loot. I was just about to shoot a few holes, but not important if you need me."

"How long will it take you to get here?"

"I'll try for an hour."

Binchy arrived in forty-three minutes.

Milo said, "Hello, Lead-foot."

The young detective grinned. He'd gelled and spiked his rusty hair, put on his usual work clothes: dark suit, blue shirt, and tie. Spit-polished Doc Martens, the sole reminder of his pre-cop days as a ska-punk bassist.

Milo said, "We're in the big room, down-stairs, let's go meet the others."

"Not just Moe, a team?" said Binchy.

"This one calls for it."

During Binchy's drive-time, Milo had talked personnel with his captain, his case made easy by the possibility of a mountain of victims. The three of us walked downstairs to a conference room he'd commandeered, complete with a long, impressive table and a whiteboard. On the table, a pointer, a case folder, and half a dozen two-way radios.

No one else in the room. Binchy examined the photos taped to the board. Grimaced when he came to Ricki Sylvester.

"Loot, it still bugs me—"

He cut himself off, realizing Milo was back on the phone.

First call: Moe Reed's desk in the big D-room. Two additionals: a couple of rookies released by the captain and waiting on stand-by.

Patrol officers Eric Monchen and Ashley Burgoyne arrived together, wearing black rock-concert tees, jeans, and sneakers, and looking nervous. He was twenty-two, she a year older. Both of them were cute enough to be models for a wholesome product. Both had requested plain-clothes assignments, despite skimpy and fruit-less experience with stings. Monchen's, a dope surveillance near the U. that went nowhere; Burgoyne's, a Pico-Robertson prostitution sting, equally futile. They didn't know each other but looked as if they belonged together.

Reed was the last to arrive, apologizing for the delay, an armed robbery call that had taken time to palm off. Blond, crew-cut, baby-faced, and built like the power lifter he was, he wore a white shirt with short sleeves that fought to contain his biceps, a gray wool clip-on tie, black jeans, and black cop oxfords shined glossier than Binchy's Docs.

Both young D's mostly worked their own cases, primarily assaults and robberies because of late Westside murders were in short supply. When Milo beckoned, it often meant lots of sitting around and watching, a gig few detectives enjoy. Binchy and Reed never balked and both excelled at remaining sharp over long, tedious stretches.

Who says the younger generation has no attention span?

Without bothering to introduce me to the rookies, Milo stepped up to the board, pointer in hand. "This is a nasty one involving multiple murder and there's no guarantee surveillance is gonna pay off but we have to try."

Directing the preface to the rookies. They sat up straight and stared directly ahead.

Milo tapped Deandra Demarest's and Henry

Bakstrom's photo enlargements. "These are the faulty citizens we're after."

He embarked on a quick, efficient summary, starting with Thalia's murder and progressing to those of Gerard Waters, Kurtis DeGraw, and possibly Ricki Sylvester.

Next topic: the ruby. The mention of fifty-seven carats and the image of the gem got all four of them wide-eyed.

Sean Binchy said, "Super-bling, it's like a movie."

Milo said, "Funny you should say that, **this** guy thinks he's an actor." Tapping Phil Duke's ten-year-old DMV shot. "He's involved on some level but the specifics are unknown beyond romancing Sylvester. What we do know is he's related to Deandra and is the right age to be her daddy. However, no kids or marriage show up in his records."

Moe Reed said, "He romanced Sylvester in order to get her to play along?"

"That's the working hypothesis, Moses." He recounted Sylvester's role as executor, her frequent house calls, the role her grandfather had played in Leroy Hoke's criminal enterprise. "In general, she's privy to tons of insider information relating to Thalia."

Reed said, "And now she's parts unknown. So either a rabbit or bad news for her."

Milo nodded. "DeeDee and Henry like to clean house, there's logic to either possibility. Any other questions, so far?"

Head shakes.

"Onward to the surveillance, kids." Tap tap on Phil Duke's house.

Milo read off the address.

Binchy said, "That's real close to here."

"Fifteen minutes, tops. That's the good news. The bad news is if you could pick a surveillance target, this one would be way at the bottom of your list. Respectable low-crime neighborhood, quiet, not a lot of trees or any other kind of cover, and the parking regs work against us: no street parking during morning drive-time— seven to nine—then again from six to eight P.M. After that, there's a brief okay-period from eight to nine P.M. Why they bothered I don't know because at nine it reverts to no overnight until five a.m. Obviously, we can't risk a sit-by, so we're limited to drive-bys and we can't be conspicuous."

He returned to the head of the table and sat down. "Cruising past in the same vehicle over and over is going to attract the wrong kind of attention. Don't even think about walk-bys. And even though Phil Duke's dirty, he's not our priority, at least not yet. So if he does appear—and he probably will, like tending to his gardening, he's picky about his front yard—we make a note of it but keep going. He's an anchovy, we're trolling for sharks."

Pulling sheets of paper out of a folder, he dealt them like playing cards.

I got one, too, but no need for education, I'd helped put together the contents.

Surveillance schedule arranged in a grid. Two observers per two-hour shift, driving serially with several minutes between them, each pass requiring a change of vehicle.

The motor pool, twelve forfeitures rushed over from the West L.A. lot.

Milo drank coffee as the four young cops read. When everyone looked up, he said, "Anyone not drive a stick?"

Head shakes.

"Good, we've got a Ford truck with a three on the column. The teams are Detective Reed and Officer Burgoyne, Detective Binchy and Officer Monchen. That's in reverse order, after the lead team finishes, which is myself and Dr. Delaware."

My title sparked Burgoyne and Monchen's curiosity. They studied me.

Milo said, "You heard me right. Doctor. Psychology, he's our behavioral consultant and too highly educated for this kind of thing. But you know the staffing situation and he offered and years ago he took a race-car course, so I'm sure he can keep up."

Binchy said, "Do you get to use your Caddy, Doc?"

The rookies' eyes widened.

I said, "I wish."

Milo said, "Okay, you all just read the drill but now I'm going over it. When it's your turn to drive, you leave here on one of three predetermined routes to the target and cruise past at medium speed—no hot-rodding, no dawdling. You see DeeDee or Bakstrom you radio in immediately but keep going. You see nothing, you return here, your partner takes off, you pick up a new set of wheels and take another of the three routes. What we're aiming for is a steady but not obvious stream of observation. Got it?"

Nods.

"Your shift lasts for two hours, during which you'll probably complete seven to nine circuits. After that, you're off for two hours and another team takes over but you stick around here, just in case things get interesting and backup is called for. Sticking around includes grub and water but no personal phone calls, you're on call and can't afford to miss a message. Obviously, we're not talking a twenty-four-seven regimen, unless any of you have figured out a way to survive without grub and water and sleep."

Sean Binchy said, "I heard there's a guy, MIT or something, working on stretching human capacity with hormones."

"If he wasn't in Boston, Sean, I'd ask him to join us."

Nervous laughter from the rookies, a wee smile from Moe Reed.

"Given our mortal limitations," said Milo, "I'm starting with a fourteen-hour surveillance period. I'm not saying there's anything magical about that time period but we need to prioritize and bad guys like darkness and this is the best I've come up with, courtesy of Dr. Delaware's input. A couple of days of this proves useless, maybe I'll change my mind and switch to something completely different. Questions?"

Silence.

"You'll each get a two-way and wear your issued firearm. Communication will remain open between all of us. When I'm not driving, I'm the command post. When I am driving, Detective Binchy and Detective Reed will take over."

"It's kind of an algorithm," said Ashley Burgoyne, poring over the grid.

"Dr. Delaware informs me a whole bunch of combinations are possible over the long run. Right now, I'll settle for no one getting made or hurt."

CHAPTER

39

Day 1, shift 1, four thirty-five P.M.

Milo, leading off in the Ford truck, spotted Phil Duke walking around from the back of his house.

By the time I cruised by there in a malodorous Audi, Duke was picking leaves out of his flower beds. Same **Catalina Jazz Club** T-shirt, baggy shorts, rubber thongs. Limited wardrobe? Waiting for the big score before going couture?

I slowed down enough to snag a look at his face. Bland, nothing furtive. Maybe he was a cold bastard. Maybe we were wrong about him.

By the time Milo made his second circuit in a Toyota Tercel, Duke was gone.

◆

No further sightings until the end of my third shift at five A.M.

Milo said, "Tomorrow, you go last, so take your time getting here, say seven thirty."

I drove home, tried to empty my head and catch some sleep. When I got to the conference room the following evening at six thirty, Reed and Binchy were out driving and the rookies sat at the far end of the table, watching videos on their phones.

My greeting was met by slow, dispirited nods. Monchen and Burgoyne looked like they were about to take a test.

Milo pulled me aside. "They're bored. It keeps going this way, they'll probably switch careers."

"Find something more exciting," I said. "Like sitting in a tollbooth."

He switched on his radio. Moe Reed's calm voice did nothing to attract the rookies' attention.

"Sean and I both saw him for a full hour but he went back inside, the van's still there."

Milo clicked off.

I said, "Out gardening?"

"Seems to be his favorite thing. Maybe this is a waste of time and the worst thing he does is overwater."

I spent the next hour and a half polishing evaluation reports on my iPad, picked up my new ride, a nice black Camaro, just before eight, waited until Milo returned in a barely breathing Datsun at eight thirty.

Circuit one, nothing. Same for two.

By the time I began three, at nine thirty-five, I was wondering if having a scotch or two when I got home would help or hinder sleep.

A full-sized van driving slowly up Phil Duke's street caught my attention. Lettering on the back said **Rapid-Rooter** was available 24/7 for plumbing emergencies. Toll-free number, cartoon of a beaming, bow-tied man who could've been Ward Cleaver's cleaner-cut brother.

The van stopped and started.

I notified Milo.

He said, "Sounds like something we'd do. God help me if there's some other agency involved and we're crossing wires."

The van stopped again. I held back. Suddenly, it sped up, lurched forward several houses past Duke's, and pulled into a driveway. A man carrying a tool case walked up to one of Phil Duke's neighbors. A pretty young woman in a T-shirt and shorts greeted him.

Genuine emergency.

I told Milo.

He said, "Or someone's shooting a porn movie."

I laughed. "No cameras in sight—okay, I'm coming up on Duke's place."

"Yawn yawn."

I drove past the lovely lawn, ready for a whole lot of nothing.

Instead, I got something. The front door was open. Two figures stood in the doorway, one partially hid by the jamb, the other totally visible and backlit.

Female contours. Big mop of hair. One leg crooked. Languid wrist.

Sparks tumbled. Flicking her cigarette.

Taken by surprise, I pulled an amateur move and lifted my foot off the gas. The figures in the doorway didn't seem to notice. Standing close to each other. Facing each other.

I drove on, passed the plumbing van. Lights on inside the house with the clogged drain. At the end of the block, I radioed in.

Milo said, "Really," and broke his own rules, gunning a battered Dodge Ram and arriving sooner than scheduled.

"Got it! Shapely blonde."

I said, "I'll go back, make an extra circuit."

"No, hold on—who's up, guys?"

Moe Reed said, "Sean and me, the toddlers were yawning so we sent them to get coffee. I can take the next one."

"Do it, Moses."

By the time Reed drove by, the door was closed.

◆

The next morning, the team reconvened at seven A.M.

Milo and the young D's were in fresh clothes and had shaved. The rookies arrived slightly late, wearing backpacks and looking bleary.

Milo said, "Everyone knows about last night. Can I prove the female's the lovely Deandra? Not yet and the male was partially hidden, no idea if he's Bakstrom or Duke, they're about the same size. But I'm declaring success and trying for warrants. Any thoughts?"

I said, "As far as we can tell, she never left the house. That sounds more like hiding out than just bunking there."

"Or," said Moe Reed, "she attends to her business during the day and we missed her."

Milo said, "It's possible, Moses, though I don't see why she'd do that when nighttime would give her better cover. Either way, we're shifting gears and switching to a daylight routine, with you two kicking it off."

Indicating the rookies.

Eric Monchen said, "Same drill, sir?"

"A little different," said Milo. "It'll be drive-time, so you go with whatever the flow is but obviously don't call attention to yourselves—gawking, doing anything a commuter wouldn't do. Part of my warrant application is gonna include sticking a GPS on the bottom of Duke's van, with installation tonight. You ready?"

Monchen: "Always, sir."

Ashley Burgoyne: "Yes, sir. Who goes first, me or him?"

"Flip a coin."

The two of them looked at each other and headed for the door. Burgoyne stopped. "Sir, do you foresee eventually breaching the premises?"

"Are you asking if you'll finally get to do something exciting?"

"No, sir—" Slow smile. "Actually, yes, sir."

"Breaching would be the goal, Officer Burgoyne. In the meantime, stay safe while you're doing the uninteresting stuff."

CHAPTER

40

At nine twenty-three A.M., Phil Duke left his house, got into his minivan, and backed out of his driveway. Reed and Binchy were on by then and Milo told Binchy to follow, Reed to keep circling.

The rookies had just returned from their shift looking eroded.

Eric Monchen said, "Damn, just missed it."

Ashley Burgoyne said, "Maybe next time we'll see the bitch."

Milo had put together a stash of trail mix, donuts, and bottled water. "Nutrition, kids."

Monchen said, "Um, sir, is there time for a healthy kinda protein breakfast?"

"Sugar and oil doesn't work for you?"

Monchen's up-and-down appraisal of Milo's physique was rapid but telling. "I'd prefer something protein, sir."

"Big T-bone."

"Too fatty, sir, I was thinking an omelet, there's a place up the block."

"I know the place," said Milo. "Sure, if you can ingest and digest and be back in forty-five minutes."

"Thank you, sir."

Ashley Burgoyne said, "I'm totally okay with what you got here, sir." She picked up a bear claw, took a big bite, wiped her mouth.

I'm the good kid.

Monchen shot her a nervous look, glanced at the trail mix. "I guess I could stick with nuts and get protein."

Milo said, "Have your omelet, Officer."

"Sir—"

"They make a humongous Denver over there, son. Just about the size of Denver. Also, a thing with chili con carne. Think of me when you're eating."

"Sir—"

"Vaya con huevos, kiddo."

Monchen screwed up his mouth and left.

When he was gone, Burgoyne said, "He'll probably do egg whites."

◆

Binchy followed the van to a Ralph's on Olympic. Phil Duke got out with three empty fabric shopping bags, went into the supermarket, and emerged twenty-four minutes later. Three full bags went into the rear of the vehicle. Nothing else inside.

Milo said, "His own bags, eco-sensitive. Touching. What's his demeanor, Sean?"

"Normal."

I said, "At least we know there's no body in there."

"Three bags," said Milo. "He could be shopping for one or two or who the hell knows how many. Stay on him. How about you, Moses?"

"Driving by the second time," said Reed. "Nothing. Plants are nice in the sunlight."

Ten minutes later, Reed radioed in, again. Duke's second stop was a nursery on Sawtelle where he purchased three large yellow plastic sacks of what appeared to be topsoil. Those ended up on the van's rear seat.

Next: a McDonald's a few blocks south on Pico. Purchase in the drive-through. Two small bags.

Milo said, "Same question, grub for one, two, or three?"

Moe Reed broke in. "I see her, L.T. Smoking in the doorway. Relaxed—kind of posing, like she knows she's hot. It's **definitely** her."

"Anyone watching her pose?"

"Not that I could tell, L.T."

I said, "It really wouldn't matter. She's out to please herself."

Phil Duke got back on Olympic and made a fourth stop at a Union 76 station where he put gas in the van and squeegeed his own windshield.

"Like a regular guy," said Binchy.

Moe Reed said, "Just passed the house. Door's closed, no sign of her. Can't swear she went back in but she's not visible on the street."

I said, "Not a homebody, this is definitely a hideout."

Milo said, "Bow out for the time being, Moses. Sean'll stick with Duke."

Ten minutes later, Binchy sounded like a kid at his own birthday party. "He went home, had his hands full with the bags and **guess** who opened the door for him? I took a chance and slowed, hoping they wouldn't notice. I'm sure they didn't, they were too busy, Loot. Making out, right there in the open. He's standing there with the McDonald's, she's wearing like a black bathing suit top and Daisys and she's full-on sucking his face, Loot. Want me to do another go-round?"

Milo said, "No, hand it off to Moses and come back here."

To me: "Father–daughter, indeed." Then: "God, I hope not."

I said, "Maybe they're kissing cousins."

Ashley Burgoyne looked up from her glazed donut. "Gross."

"Excellent," said Milo, punching air.

Burgoyne stared at him.

"Not the gross part, Officer. The her-not-being-nervous part. Know why?"

"No, sir."

"We like when bad people get all comfy."

CHAPTER

41

Despite targeting an easygoing judge named Ronald Marquette, getting a warrant to search Phil Duke's premises proved problematic. Nothing close to evidence on Duke for anything, let alone multiple homicide.

"Judge—"

"He gardens and shops? That's prosecutable, I'll have you arrest my wife."

"The woman living there—"

"From what you just told me, there's nothing on her beyond being sexy. Why're you coming to me with thin gruel? This isn't like you."

"It's been a tough one, Judge."

"If this is the best you come up with, it'll stay tough," said Marquette. "Sorry, they're taking a closer look at every scrap of paper we sign. I am not going to be one of those fools gets reversed for obvious error. Get me more and come back."

"Judge, I'm willing to submit rape as my primary charge. Suspect Deandra Demarest was clearly I.D.'d by the victim, as was Suspect Bakstrom. It was a gang rape, extremely brutal, and the victim was a hundred percent on the identification."

"Give me the details. Quickly, I've got a case in an hour."

Milo began relating Vicki Vasquez's story.

"Why didn't you tell me this in the first place? Woman raping another woman like that? Even the lefties will find it repellent, try finding a friendly jury. She'll get put away for a long time, the murder doesn't work out, be happy with that."

"I'm happy, Judge."

"No, you're not. You never are. Fax it within fifteen or I'll be unavailable until lunch recess. During which I'll be eating and not taking calls."

CHAPTER 42

Faxed, signed, returned. For all his pee-vishness, Marquette had approved a broad search.

Next step: how to get in there and do the job, safely.

The amended plan: the rest of the day and part of the evening, drive-bys of Phil Duke's house would increase in frequency but be carried out at a greater distance: four cars cruising serially up the street perpendicular to Duke's.

Too far and too distant to make out details but close enough to keep tabs on the core issue: Was Duke's van in place.

If Duke or anyone else got into the vehicle and left, they'd be followed by the nearest cop while the three others continued visual surveillance.

Given no additional drama, entry to the house would take place at nine P.M., the team supplemented by two veteran patrol officers Milo had finally cadged from his captain. Both had SWAT experience but this would be more stealth than combat mission. Yes to vests and all-black clothing, no to helmets, heavy artillery, or a BearCat rumbling up the quiet street and panicking the neighbors or, worse, alerting the targets.

"This day and age," said Milo, "it'd be on YouTube before we got to the door."

He continued laying out the details.

Three armed and dangerous suspects were assumed to be in the house: the couple everyone was calling the kissing cousins since I'd thrown out the term and Henry Bakstrom, even though he hadn't been spotted.

So far, no clarification of the relationship between Philip Demarest Duke and Deandra Demarest had surfaced beyond sharing a surname.

Milo finished and called for questions.

Moe Reed said, "With her making out with Duke like that, you really think Bakstrom's still part of it? Especially in view of what happened to Waters."

Milo said, "Maybe he isn't, but romance alone doesn't tell us a thing. Think about the three-way on Vicki Vasquez."

"Hmm. Good point, L.T."

"The major point—what I want you **all** to bear in mind—is that no matter how many people we find in there, assume every one of them to be murderous and unpredictable and be prepared for the worst."

The rookies looked at each other, Monchen fidgeting, Ashley Burgoyne pleasantly animated.

Sean Binchy said, "With Ricki Sylvester still off the radar, there could be four suspects or another victim."

Milo said, "That's why we're gonna do it like I just told you."

No one argued.

CHAPTER

43

At nine thirteen P.M., Moe Reed, dressed in United Parcel Service brown, drove a UPS van to the curb and parked illegally. Retrieving a cardboard box, he checked the Glock in his jacket pocket, exited the driver's door, paused again to study Phil Duke's front door before walking up and ringing the bell.

I was in the back of the van's empty cargo section, along with Officer Eric Monchen and one of the veterans, a three-striper and former Cal State Long Beach running back named Tyrell Lincoln.

The three of us wore radio earplugs. Monchen looked distracted and uneasy. I felt antsy and confined, sat still to hide it.

Tyrell Lincoln was equally inert but seemed

genuinely serene, sitting up against the sliding cargo door that faced the street.

Milo, Binchy, Ashley Burgoyne, and the other vet, a bearish man named Marlin Moroni, had snuck around to the back of the house, aided by the absence of outdoor lighting and a sliver moon smirched by night-haze.

Reed's body-mike transmitted his footsteps, the rumble of one passing car then another. Tyrell Lincoln sat up an inch straighter but remained expressionless.

Nothing for several seconds.

Then: a woman's voice, barely audible, muffled by the wood of the door. "Yeah?"

Reed: "UPS."

Creak. Louder clearer voice: "Well, hi, there. Kinda late for you boys to be out." Throaty voice, syllables stretched, friendly. More than that. Creamy.

Lincoln's eyebrows rose. He looked amused.

Reed: "Delivery, ma'am, needs to be signed for."

"Wow. What time is it?"

"Nine fifteen, ma'am."

"They workin' you guys hard?"

"Ain't that the truth. I don't mind."

"Bet you don't." Giggle. "Who's it for?"

"Um . . . says here P. Duke."

New voice, male. Stentorian. "Who's there, baby?"

"UPS for you, Daddy."

"I didn't order anything from UPS."

Reed: "Are you P. Duke? Shipment from Zappos?"

Duke: "What the hell's Zappos?"

Deandra Demarest: "That's clothing, Daddy. They got cool stuff."

"I didn't order any clothing."

Reed: "Says here this address, P.—"

Duke: "I know what it **says** but it's not **mine**."

Reed: "Are you rejecting the shipment, sir?"

"I sure as hell didn't order any—"

Deandra Demarest: "Why don't we see what's in it, Daddy? Maybe it's a cute shirt or somethin'."

Another giggle.

Phil Duke, softer: "You got me a shirt?"

"We-ell . . . don't you like surprises, Daddy?"

"I mean sure, baby, but—"

Reed: "Sir, if you could just sign here on this screen, I've got a whole bunch more deliveries."

"Yeah, sure, but I'm not paying for something I didn't order."

"Sir," said Reed, "like the lady said, it could be a gift."

Tyrell Lincoln's head rose, as if his neck had

been elevated by a mechanical hoist. He rose to a crouch. One hand took hold of the door handle.

Waiting for the code word.

Duke: "Where do I sign?"

Reed: "Right here, this little machine."

Duke: "Everyone's got a stupid computer—hey, where you going, baby? We got to see if you actually—"

"I need something to open it, Daddy."

Reed: "Sign here, too, please, sir."

"You need two?"

"Yes, sir."

Grumble. "Like I need a **shirt**."

"Hey, sir," said Reed. "Think of it as early **Christmas**."

Lincoln bolted the van.

Monchen and I hurried to the front, squinting as we shared the passenger window.

Too dark to see much but the earplugs told plenty, spitting out a grunting, panting scuffle.

Duke: "Hey—wha—the—"

Deandra Demarest, using a new voice, shrill as a screech owl. **"Let go of him, you fuck! Let go you you fu—Daaaa-deeee!"**

I rolled down the window.

Monchen said, "Is that okay? Don't you need to be authorized?"

Talking right at my nostrils. Full-on taco breath from his food-truck dinner.

More than a desire for fresh air led me to stick my head out.

Monchen edged closer, muttering, "Oh, man, it's happening."

Tyrell Lincoln had positioned himself five feet from the front door, half crouched, hands out, as if ready to receive a pass.

Inert, as he watched the manic ballet in the doorway.

Moe Reed grappling with Phil Duke. Short struggle. Reed's massive right arm clamped on Phil Duke's wrist, flinging a good-sized man outward with the ease of someone flicking a dandelion.

Duke's body beelined to Tyrell Lincoln's left hand. Lincoln, without shifting any other part of his body, snagged Duke like a relay runner grabbing a baton. In a breath, Duke's arms had been bent behind his back and he was facedown on his perfect lawn, cuffed.

Reed, no longer visible, had entered the house.

From his wire: "Police! Freeze! Police! Don't move!"

"Go away!"

"Put that down **now**."

"You're a gangster, **fuck you!**"

"Put it down—"

"Fuck you—"

"Put it down and don't move—no don't come closer."

"Gangster! Liar! Motherfucker!"

"Put that down! Freeze!"

A new sound intruded. Wall of noise that clarified as multiple voices. No words ascertainable, just a sawmill buzz of speech, growing louder.

Night of the locusts.

Reed's voice louder: "Drop that now!"

"Fuck y—"

The roar separated into shouting. Reed, Milo, Deandra Demarest.

Reed, the loudest: "Drop it! Drop it! Drop it now!"

"I'll fucking cut—"

Clap of gunshot.

Five more.

Milo: "Shit."

Silence. Scratchy noise.

Reed: "She's gone?"

Milo: "Yeah."

Marlin Moroni's basso: "For a box cutter. Stupid bitch."

Binchy: "That's what the 9/11 terrorists used. Main thing is you're okay, Moe."

A long stretch of audible breathing.

Milo said, "Who shot?"

Silence.

Then, a new voice. Girlish, tremulous.

Ashley Burgoyne said, "Did I do the wrong thing?"

CHAPTER

44

I got out of the van.

Eric Monchen said, "Hey, hold on," but he followed me.

We passed Tyrell Lincoln standing over Phil Duke's prone form.

Duke whined. "My arms hurt like a bastard."

No concern about **Baby**.

Lincoln said, "Just hold it together, man."

Monchen said, "Need me to watch him, Sergeant?"

"I'm fine."

Monchen and I continued toward the front door. He said, "I don't get how you're authorized to do all this."

I said, "Luck and interpersonal skills."

◆

Moe Reed stood in front of the doorway, big arms dangling, impassive.

He said, "Sorry, Doc, no entry, they're still clearing room by room."

Monchen stepped in front of me. "I'll help clear."

Reed didn't move. "Not necessary, everyone's got a gun out, we don't want surprises."

"Oh," said Monchen. "So what should I do?"

"No one's called it in, yet. You know the code, right?"

"Sure," said Monchen. Far from certain. "Should I call from the van?"

Reed said, "Good idea."

"Ashley actually shot her?"

"She did."

"Damn," said Monchen. "That's heavy."

Reed looked at the van.

"Roger," said Monchen. Saluting, he ran off.

Reed said, "Tomorrow it's going to hit him. Not to mention her."

The obvious question: What about you?

The obvious thing to say: nothing.

Maybe Reed was being considerate, maybe he shifted his weight to the left unconsciously. Either way, the space he created allowed me a view of Deandra Demarest's body.

Mercilessly lit by an overhead fixture, she lay facedown on a brown carpet stained with red.

Wearing what Binchy had described earlier: a black top that could've come from a bikini but might've been a bra, and cut-off denim shorts revealing crescents of butt-cheek. Bare feet. Clean feet. Blond hair fanning. Black polish on her fingernails. Not even a chip.

When I leaned in a bit closer, Reed didn't stop me. Details seeped in.

Red sump at the base of the skull.

Five additional blood blossoms grouped near the center of her spine.

Rookie or not, Ashley Burgoyne was a crack shot.

Everything on tape, justification for the shooting seemed obvious. Though the damage situated on the back might prove problematic if someone complained.

I heard footsteps from the rear of the house, shouts of "Police, show yourself." Then: "Clear here."

"Clear."

"Clear."

A black-and-white had pulled behind the UPS van. Tyrell Lincoln led Phil Duke away.

Reed shook his head. "I was trying to keep her alive, Doc. Even with the cutter, I could've handled her."

I said, "Tough decision on Ashley's part."

"If she actually made a decision."

"Reflex move?"

"Happens. She'll have to deal." He looked over his shoulder. "L.T. let her clear. Maybe therapy, huh?"

Burgoyne stepped from the rear of the house, looking far too young and dispirited.

Reed said, "You okay?"

"Uh-huh." Shaky voice. "Um . . . totally all clear. I'm supposed to wait in the van, now."

"Then that's what you do."

She looked at Reed, lower lip trembling.

"Thanks for backing me," he said.

Fighting back tears, the girl who'd shot a woman ran to the van.

"There we go," said a voice nearly as deep as Phil Duke's. Marlin Moroni came forward, holstering his Glock. "I'm keeping watch, here. Milo says you should meet out back, he thinks he found something, didn't say what."

Reed said, "Maybe a big ruby."

"A ruby? Like a gem?"

"Yup."

"Really," said Moroni. "Any chance of buried treasure, also? Commission for a dedicated public servant?"

"If only," said Reed.

"It's always if only," said Moroni. "That's called real life."

◆

Reed and I headed down the driveway. A few steps took us to a tiny backyard. Exterior lighting fixtures shaped like tulips on stalks were in place but not in use. The sole illumination was the narrow, bouncing beam of Milo's flashlight.

He said, "Can't figure out how to turn the fixtures on," and ran the beam across a fusebox on the wall, then over to a meager square of lawn. As perfect as the grass in front and backed by precisely cut beds overflowing with flowers.

Behind all that, reached by a brief brick pathway, was a greenhouse that spanned the entire rear of the property. Impressive wood-and-glass structure, a good eight feet tall, with a pointed finial adorning a shingle roof. More ornate than the house, far too large for the space.

Dim light and not much sound made for sensory deprivation. But a third sense was on full alert.

The reason Milo had called us back was clear.

The smell you never forget.

Moe Reed's hand shot to his nose. "Oh."

Milo's nose was unprotected as he washed the panes of the greenhouse with his torch, highlighting smudges of condensation on the inner surface of the glass, dirt speckles, the contours of vegetative things pressing against panes like curious children.

Further scanning revealed flowers grayed by

night. A pulpy-looking blossom so intensely orange, the color forced its way through nocturnal retinal cells.

Meanwhile, the reek grew, invading my sinus passages, climbing into my head, overtaking my brain. Then my gut.

The vile stink, something beyond rotten. Cooking and boiling over.

I suppressed a gag.

Moe Reed, habitually stoic, looked as if he was ready to hurl.

Milo turned to us. "Far as I can see the damn thing's shut tight and it's still getting through."

Reed stepped back, managed speech. "Pretty rank, L.T."

"You're a master of understatement, Moses. Okay, I'm seeing two choices. The easy way is call the crypt and leave all the fun to the C.I.'s. Or, on the off chance there's someone in there who needs saving, we go take a look ourselves."

"Ricki Sylvester," said Reed. "Saving a lawyer."

Milo laughed. "Don't tell anyone, Moses."

Reed dredged up a smile and stepped back farther.

Milo whipped out a handkerchief, folded it double into a wad that he pressed against his nose.

Cotton seemed flimsy protection; he usually

carries mentholated ointment for coating his nasal passages.

All the planning, you can't think of everything.

He said, "Let's try not to breathe," and walked toward the greenhouse.

I bunched my jacket and pressed my lapel to my nose, decided that was awkward and worthless and pinched my nostrils shut with my fingers.

When I stepped forward, Moe Reed said, "You really want to, Doc?"

But he didn't stop me and a few seconds later, I heard the sound of his footsteps, trailing.

CHAPTER
45

I was right behind Milo when he flung the greenhouse door open. Letting loose humid heat and putrescence that would've repelled Satan.

"Oh, God, the things I do for God and country," he said as he stepped in.

The floor was brick, a central walkway between rows of wooden tables.

The reek seemed to have acquired solidity, jellying the air as it poisoned.

A whole lot of visual beauty made matters worse, though I couldn't tell you why.

Pots on the tables, glossy and patterned intricately, housed palms, ferns, bromeliads, and other pineapple-like things. Plants with fleshy

leaves, spoon-like leaves, spiky leaves, others fil-
amentous and delicate as corn silk.

I spotted one of those red, heart-shaped things
they sell in Hawaiian souvenir shops. The orange flowers I'd seen through the window belonged to a squat, spreading thing with hairy,
leathery leaves.

A plant that resembled a bird's head.

A vine that reached for the ceiling, sucker-
like appendages gripping glass, an herbaceous
octopus.

Something that resembled nothing I could
classify.

Everything healthy, lush, thriving.

As we trudged slowly, a squirt of fragrance hit
my nose. Sweet, exotic, tropical, facing up to the
stink but dying quickly.

Another burst: gingery. That, too, lost out to
the ambient toxicity.

Milo stopped, retched, coughed. Bent a bit,
straightened, resumed the slog.

I found myself teetering. Reached out for the
support of a wooden table, thought better of it
and forced myself to keep going.

No one behind me. I half turned, saw Reed's
fleeing form. I sympathized but found perverse
pleasure in that. Good to know something could
get to him.

Milo took another couple of steps. His flashlight found something and he stopped, pointed, covered his entire face with the handkerchief then dropped it just enough to undrape his eyes.

At the far wall of the greenhouse, several large yellow bags were neatly stacked.

The potting mix Binchy had seen Phil Duke bring home from the garden supply house.

To the left of the bags was a massive heap of loose dirt. Five feet high, shaped like a first-grader's clumsily drawn mountain.

Oddly messy for this precise herbarium.

The flashlight searched, floundered.

Found something.

Sprouting from the top of the pile. Melon-shaped.

Large melon.

We got closer. The stink beat us mercilessly.

Melon with eyeholes . . . wet, sloughing rind.

So much bloat and rot that a first glance told you nothing.

A second glance refined the perception.

What had once been a human head. The mouth degraded to a black O, the eyeholes tiny caverns leading to nothing.

Milo retched. "I'm losing it." He ran past me and out.

What possessed me to stick around for a few more seconds, I'll never know.

Something was wrong with this Gehenna.

Then it came to me: the silence. No flies. No maggots destined to be flies.

All at once, the silence was gone, replaced by a clanging in my head, metallic, insistent.

I took one last look at the head and walked out. Slowly, deliberately.

In control. Nothing was going to rush me.

When I got out, Milo was at the top of the driveway, sucking air.

I did the same. Thinking about Gerard Waters's body, kept in a warm, moist place before being dumped in the Palisades.

Milo recovered enough to talk, but his voice was weak. "C.I.'s and techs on their way. I warned them. Go hazmat."

"Considerate," I said.

"See something like this, you aim for any virtue you can snag."

CHAPTER
46

Phil Duke got stashed temporarily in the West L.A. holding jail, Tyrell Lincoln completing the paperwork and going home with Milo's blessing. Marlin Moroni stood guard at the house, saying, "I don't mind, got the next four days off, gonna drive to Laguna Seca for two-wheel day, run my Indian around the track."

Moe Reed drove the brown van back to the station, both rookies the passengers. Ashley Burgoyne would be answering questions, soon. We all would.

The crime scene army would take a while to arrive, busy with three other murders, one in Lancaster, two in South Central.

Milo and I gave Duke's house another go-round, searching for the ruby with no luck.

"Like you said, Ricki's got a safe. For all we know, she's the big winner, took it and split."

I said, "You see her as the mastermind?"

"I don't know what I see, other than that . . . thing in the mulch has to be Bakstrom. Meaning everyone else is dead and she might not be."

We went outside where he smoked a cigar and I let my thoughts settle.

I said, "I'm still seeing Deandra as the boss. The ruby was important to her. She might've kept it close."

"Meaning?"

Moroni had shut the front door. I pointed at it.

"What?" said Milo.

"On her person."

He puffed hard. Walked to Moroni who stepped away and let him open the door. Staring inside, he returned, got on the phone to the night desk at the crypt. "Pedro? Milo. What's your investigator's ETA? Can you see if they can snap it up a bit . . . I know, but what're you talking about, coupla gang thingies, mine's **way** more interesting . . . we've **all** been doing it a long time, Pedro. It can still happen, something you never saw before, trust me."

Twenty minutes later, the white, blue-striped crypt van rolled up with two drivers, ready to do the usual sit-by until the C.I.'s okayed transport. A few minutes later, a larger van, the mobile crime lab.

Last to arrive was a blue sedan bearing two investigators, one I knew as Gloria, a former nurse, one I learned was Tish, a former respiratory therapist.

Both wore knit tops, jeans, and sneakers. Gloria said, "Where's the decomp situation?"

Milo said, "Out back, a greenhouse. First do the one in the house, she's clean."

He told them what he needed.

Tish said, "Pedro said it could be interesting. I might start thinking he's credible."

They approached the body the way experienced C.I.'s do. Gloving up and taking time to observe, then recording the scene orally and visually, Tish using her cellphone to snap pictures, capturing every wound, Gloria speaking into a mini-recorder.

She counted the shell casings from Burgoyne's service gun, said, "That'll be fun for the techies."

Back to the wounds. "Not much mystery about cause."

Down to the shorts. "Not much by way of clothing and I don't see any bulges in the pockets but let's give it a go."

She patted the garments as Tish continued to film.

Nothing in the four pockets of the short-

shorts, same for the cups of the top, which turned out to be a bra from Trashy Lingerie.

"Nope, sorry," said Tish. "Any reason we shouldn't tell the guys to transport?"

I said, "Is it okay to take off the shorts, right here?"

Everyone looked at me.

I reiterated the logic I'd given Milo.

He said, "Oh."

Tish said, "You think it could be **up** her? Yick."

"Just a thought."

Gloria said, "Protocol is to disrobe them back at the crypt." A beat. "Why not, better than something falling out and we don't see it."

Tish said, "Hey, we're all grown-ups."

Down came the shorts, sliding fluidly after an initial tug.

No panties.

A thin gold chain belted the widest part of Deandra Demarest's lovely, flaring hips. Tugged down at the center by a bit of weight.

A red stone the size of a large cocktail olive dangled at the precise center of a vertical strip of dyed-blond pubic hair. Partially concealed by the hair but the harsh overhead light zeroed in on the ruby and set off sparkles.

"Whoa," said Tish. "We'd have seen that back

at the crypt, we'd figure fake, one of those strip-per deals, we'd probably stash it in some locker."

She looked at me. "You're a smart man. Or you understand women." Crooked smile. "Both possibilities scare me."

The ruby was photo'd, logged, placed in an evidence envelope, and handed over to the crime scene techs. After a call to Noreen Sharp from Milo, delineating precisely.

She said, "Over to us, huh?"

"Safest route."

"Only route, Milo. I'm driving over there now, find the right place for it."

It didn't take long for Deandra Demarest's body to be bagged, gurneyed, and wheeled to the blue-striped van.

The C.I.'s left.

One of the techs said, "Now what?"

Milo said, "The dirty work. Sorry."

"We do plenty of hazmat."

"I asked for two extra masks."

"Got them, too."

"God bless you."

"We hear that all the time," said the tech.

"You do?"

"Not."

He and his partner laughed.

Whatever helped.

The airtight greenhouse had prevented the entrance of flies and the compression of the soil heap had partially preserved the body. But you can't stop nature, and bacteria and tiny mites migrating from the plants did their thing, albeit at a far slower pace than blowfly maggots.

Decomp had spread downward, concentrating on the exposed head, leaving the legs below the knees and the feet pristine. The arms and hands were somewhere in the middle of the spectrum, with all ten fingers still able to serve up decent prints.

ID was verified, along with the route the male victim had taken to eternity.

Two bullets had entered the occiput of Henry Bakstrom's brain. Later that day, a ballistics match was obtained at the crime lab: The same weapon had killed Gerard Waters. Never to be located.

Milo came by the house and filled me in. "Dirty end for a dirty guy."

I said, "How long was Bakstrom in there?"

"Best guess, a week or so."

"He was also expendable from the beginning."

He nodded. "DeeDee and Phil's mulch pile. Not that Duke's admitting anything. Lawyered up after I asked him a few questions. I did learn his relationship to her. Distant cousins, third or fourth, he wasn't really sure. He barely knew her when she showed up and told him a story."

I said, "Before or after seducing him?"

"Who knows? Not that going mute is gonna help him, stick a body in your greenhouse and let it molder, even an L.A. jury will get it. The other news is no news on Ricki Sylvester. Not at home or in her office, so she's either another stashed corpse or flown the coop."

I said, "That about sums it up."

But we were wrong.

Shortly after ten P.M. a call came into the West L.A. station. Milo was off-service but the desk sergeant was smart enough to remember and phone him.

He reached me at home and we arrived at the Aventura simultaneously. Chain-link fencing blocked the drive but a car-wide gate hung with a condemnation sign had swung open.

The hotel had its own odor: an arid, musty aura of desertion. Like a sauna gone bad.

One vehicle in the lot, a Saturn bearing the signage of a private security firm. Two black-and-whites parked near the mouth of the loggia leading to The Green. The windows of The Can were black, the landscaping spots as inoperative as those in Phil Duke's backyard. But the lobby was brightly lit and exposed by glass walls.

A uniformed rent-a-cop sat behind the counter, middle-aged, paunchy, playing with his phone.

Milo said, "Wait here," went in, and talked to the guard.

Brief chat. "He's the one found it, routine patrol."

I said, "He seems unscathed."

"Twenty years on the job in Pittsburgh, says he's seen it all. He's looking at nudes on his phone, couldn't care less."

Both cop cars were unoccupied. Their roof bars strobed the pathway red and blue.

After the first turn, we came upon four uniforms.

One said, "All the way at the end."

"Thanks for preserving the scene."

"Sure, sir. Nothing out here except bugs."

Milo and I gloved up.

The cop said, "Let me know when you're ready, sir."

◆

It hadn't taken long for Uno to acquire the look of abandonment, screens removed from the porch, front door ajar and off kilter, window shutters splintering.

The steps to the porch deck mewled in protest. The deck was littered with leaves and dust and scraps of paper. Milo looked at each one of them, said, "Trash," and turned to the right.

Looking at the big rattan peacock chair where Thalia had sat the first time I met her.

No Sydney Greenstreet bulk taxing the cane, no wispy centenarian dwarfed by the curvaceous throne.

Something in between.

A chubby woman with unfashionable curly yellow hair wearing a too-tight floral dress that had ridden up as she'd slid downward, revealing dimpled knees and feet turned away from each other, clumsy and duck-like.

Ricki Sylvester's head lolled. Her skin was green-gray. A dry drool trail striped her chin.

On the floor to her right was an empty bottle of Svedka vodka. Next to that, a small amber pill bottle. Childproof cap.

Rules say you wait until the C.I.'s clear the body. Milo cupped Ricki Sylvester's chin and lifted her face gently.

Nearly shut eyes, a sliver of gray glass barely visible.

Slack mouth, tongue drooping to the right.

He lowered her, still gentle. Crouched and shined his flashlight on the pill bottle's label.

Sixty tabs of Percocet, legally prescribed by an M.D. in Santa Monica.

"All that and a bottle of booze," he said. "Not exactly a cry for help."

I said, "There's an envelope wedged at her side," and showed him.

"Protocol says wait for the C.I.'s. I already bent the rules."

"You bet."

"Hell," he said, and fished out the envelope. "Anyone asks, we found it on the floor."

Just to make sure, he rubbed it on the floor, picked up grime.

Business-sized envelope, with Ricki Sylvester's name, degree, and office address at the top.

Closed but not glued. He lifted the flap.

Same information on the single piece of paper folded inside.

Below the letterhead, graceful handwriting in burnt-orange ink.

"Custom color, looks like a fountain pen," he said. "Haven't seen that in a while."

We read together.

To whoever chances to find me, I'm doing this willingly and with peace. There's always

been pain but now it's risen to another level and I need to leave.

Thalia Mars was dear to me and I let her down. Worse, I let myself down, getting swept away with emotions that turned out to be hollow. Philip Duke is an evil, manipulative murderer. He pretended to care about me and led me to a dark place where I did the unthinkable. Though I had no idea, absolutely NONE that it would go as far as it did. (Details are available in the bottom right-hand drawer of the desk in my office, the address of which is listed above.)

My last will and testament is also in that drawer, as is a list of referrals to other attorneys for my wonderful clients whom I leave with profound regrets.

But this needed to happen.

Warmly, Ricki.

CHAPTER

48

It took until the following day to gain access to the drawer. Milo notified Jared that his services would no longer be required.

The receptionist said, "What are you talking about? You can't fire me."

Milo explained.

Jared gathered up his teapot, his phone, the pleather jacket he'd draped over his chair, and hurried out.

Milo turned to me. "Onward, we know the route."

The will was right where Ricki Sylvester said it would be.

No fountain pen but for her signature. She'd

computer-typed concisely and clearly. The kind of lawyer you'd want if you could trust her.

For most of her life, she began, honesty had been her "byword. A tradition handed down by my grandfather, the noted attorney John E. 'Jack' McCandless."

The grand exception to her moral stance had taken place during an "intoxicated state." Agreeing to look for and eventually verifying the presence of a "57 carat ruby" in Thalia's room.

At the request of her "seducer" Philip Duke.

I will not lie and say I expected nothing
to happen vis a vis the gem. Philip Duke
was clear about his belief that it belonged
rightfully to his family and that he was
going to own it. But I did turn down his request to actually take the gem during one of
my house calls to Thalia.
I suppose I knew he'd attempt to acquire
the ruby by stealth, however I rationalized
that as only a minimal loss to Thalia, seeing
as she'd left it in plain sight for decades and
had never included it in her estate when she
enumerated such to me, as her executor. In
fact, it was only after Phil Duke alerted me
to the visual characteristics of the gem that
I was able to locate it, serving as a finial
atop a lamp, a use that I chose to character-

ize as Thalia's humorous belittling of the stone.

I am not offering an excuse, however I am emphasizing that in no way did I expect my transferring the information about the stone to Philip Duke to lead to homicide. When I learned of Thalia's death, I was as shocked as anyone. Thalia was dear to me. It took a long time for me to integrate the terrible facts and to make sense of them. I finally realized that someone as callous as Philip Duke was likely to attempt to effect a similar end upon me. Frightened, I traveled to the Ojai Valley Inn where I spent two days contemplating my future.

Eventually perceiving that future as dim and hopeless, in addition to having lived with neuralgia and other sources of physical pain for years, and in the spirit of full atonement, I have decided to set my own punishment as capital punishment. In that same spirit, being of sound mind and body and lacking any natural heirs, I hereby bequeath my entire estate to the identical charities benefited by Thalia Mars's estate, in identical proportions.

Sincerely,
    Richeline (Ricki) Sylvester, J.D., Esq.

Below that, a description of her estate. Stocks, bonds, real estate. Not dissimilar from Thalia's. Smaller but still substantial.

"Six mil," said Milo. "Big Bird's gonna be soaring."

Harold Saroyan looked at Elie Aronson. Elie looked at Milo and me. Both men wore the sad expression of parents forced to punish a usually well-behaved child.

Saroyan, a white-haired, mustachioed man in his eighties, bought and sold colored gemstones from an office in Elie's downtown building. He'd come to the meeting in a tailored black suit, flawless white shirt, and extravagant yellow cravat, carrying a black leather case from which he drew out a jeweler's loupe and a stereoscopic zoom microscope.

The meeting was in a high-security room in the crime lab's property area, accessed by Noreen Sharp's coded card. Noreen wasn't there, called moments before to one of the loading docks where two cars, battered and blood-soaked due to a fatal crash on the 101, had just come in.

Just Milo, myself, and the gem dealers, arranged around a plain, gray table. In the center, a gleaming bit of gorgeous, faceted red sat atop a black velvet bag supplied by Noreen. ("Shows off the color, no?")

Saroyan had begun by holding the ruby up to the light and turning it between his fingers. Following up with the loupe, then the scope, before placing the ruby back.

He sighed. Looked at Elie, again.

Elie said, "Something to tell? Tell."

Saroyan faced us. "I apologize for having to say this to you. It's a spinel."

Milo said, "Which is . . ."

Elie said, "Not a ruby."

"It's a fake?"

"If you tell someone it's a ruby, it's a fake. But it's not glass, it's another stone, called a spinel. S-P-I-N-E-L."

Harold Saroyan said, "I knew the minute I held it up but to make you feel better, I had a look inside. No doubt."

I said, "What did holding it up do?"

"Showed me it has no pleochroism—doesn't break up light the way a ruby does. Rubies are double-refractive, the light divides at two different speeds. Spinels are single-refractive, you don't get a prismatic effect. The look inside said the same thing. Spinels have eight-, sometimes twelve-sided crystals. Rubies have six. This one has twelve."

Milo said, "What's it worth?"

Saroyan: "Nice spinel, this size? A few thousand dollars. Maybe you could get five."

"Thousand."

Elie said, "That's the point. Not millions."

Milo sat back in his chair. He'd lost color. I knew what he was thinking.

All those lives for this.

He said, "Obviously, the British Museum wasn't conned, so it was probably switched with a ruby sometime later."

Saroyan tugged at the knot of his tie. "Not necessarily, Lieutenant. Dealers in Asia caught on a long time ago but Europeans took longer to get educated. Years ago, a nice blue stone was a sapphire, a nice red stone was a ruby. There's a big spinel in the British Imperial State Crown that everyone thought was a ruby. Many other situations like that."

Elie said, "Czars and kings thought they knew what they were getting. They didn't."

Saroyan lifted the gem, rubbed it between his fingers. "A little softer than a ruby, seven and a half, eight on the Mohs scale instead of nine for a ruby, but that's still pretty hard. Making it more confusing, spinels are found where rubies are. They're actually rarer than rubies. So why aren't they more valuable?"

He shrugged. "That's gemstones, it's all about mystique. Like with women—models. Photographer wants a blonde, pretty brunettes don't get hired."

Milo said, "But sometimes brunettes are called for."

Saroyan said, "True. But so far, the market wants only blondes."

I said, "So there wasn't necessarily a substitution."

"I looked at the pictures of the museum exhibition, sir. No way to know for certain from an old photograph, but I took my time going over it and found facets that are identical to this stone. If I had to bet, it's the one the Egyptian owned."

Milo said, "No one would know different until they tried to sell it."

"Maybe even after they tried to sell it, Lieutenant. Sometimes people aren't careful. Sometimes they lie."

"Okay, thanks, gentlemen," said Milo. "Appreciate your coming down and sorry it was a waste of time."

"Not a waste," said Saroyan. "It's an interesting story. My age, you start to collect stories more than money."

The four of us exited Hertzberg together. Saroyan got into a gleaming black Mercedes S300, Elie into an equally pampered silver version of the same model.

I said, "So many opportunities for a swindle. Whoever sold it to the Egyptian and who knows how many before that, then onward to the jeweler who consigned with Drancy, Drancy, Hoke, Thalia."

"Not Demarest," Milo said. "Idiot. You think Thalia stuck what she thought was a fortune on top of a lamp?"

I said, "That's the assumption I want to live with."

"Why?"

"Her having a sense of humor."

We reached the car. I asked him when I could go public.

He said, "What the hell, nothing to hide anymore."

"Then hold on for a sec."

I punched a preset on my cell. Maxine Driver answered at her office.

"Oh, hi," she said. "About to start office

hours. Whining sophomores wanting their grades changed."

"Keep 'em waiting in the hall, I've got a story for you."

I gave her the basics. Surprisingly short tale.

She said, "That was **definitely** worth waiting for. You've restored my faith in humanity."

I hung up without comment. But as I drove out of the crime lab parking lot, I thought: What a wrong way to put it.

CHAPTER
50

Nearly a year after the murder of Thalia Mars, I was invited to a celebration at the Outpatient Division of Western Peds. Normally, I beg off that kind of thing. This time I put on a suit and tie and asked Robin to keep me company.

For the past eleven months, I'd tried to put Thalia behind me with pretty good success. After I'd arranged transfer of her tiny body from the crypt to the mortuary at Forest Lawn in Burbank, I'd selected a hillside plot with a view of a major TV studio, movie lots, and low-rise sprawl.

Scoring her a place near the love of her life would've been a nice touch but no room at Hollywood Legends.

No gravestones in this place, so I didn't need

to order one. Everyone got a generic brass plaque installed flat on the emerald turf.

I had composed the text, kept it simple. Name, dates of birth and death denoting an incredibly long life, a quote from Lord Byron. Because he'd sired a genius and was as good a poet as any.

I knew it was love and I felt it was glory.

And that was that.

"Good cause," I told Robin. "Also, there's seeing you in that red dress."

She said, "What makes you think I'll wear the red dress?"

"Why not?"

She laughed. "Why not, indeed. I do look hot in it."

The party had been postponed several times, held up for months as Thalia's estate was fine-toothed by the IRS and the state Franchise Tax Board. Every charity listed in the will vetted repeatedly and repetitively, in the hope of finding something unkosher and open to confiscation.

Ricki Sylvester had done a fine job as an estate lawyer but her implication in the murders gave both agencies an additional excuse to comb the will for symptoms of impropriety. Then there was the matter of Sylvester's will and her instruction that both documents needed to be considered as "an entity." After that, meetings, memos, a whole bunch of head-scratching at progressively higher levels of government authority.

I knew nothing about the logjam, was enjoying a bottle from the case of Chivas Blue that Milo had sent me right after closing the case, when Ruben Eagle called.

I'd held on to Milo's gift card. Inscribed **Early Christmas.**

With him, it never stops.

Ruben's call was about getting a neuropsych referral for a child with hard-to-categorize seizure disorder. I gave three names of great people, then asked how it felt to be well funded.

He said, "Not yet."

"What's holding it up?"

"No idea."

I phoned the hospital's chief lawyer for development, gave him a rundown of the Drancy robbery and the likely illegal federal confiscation of privately owned bijoux.

"That might be something I can use," he said. "I assume you don't want to be quoted."

"Good guess."

"Hmm . . . well I'm not sure how I can use it . . . but thanks."

Two weeks later, the funds were released in full. Including the spinel, which sold to a gem broker in Atlanta for forty-five hundred dollars.

What happened to it after that, I have no idea.

Same for whether or not my call actually had anything to do with freeing Thalia's estate.

What I did know was that Phil Duke, claiming he'd never fired a weapon in his life and that Henry Bakstrom had shot Gerard Waters and been shot, in turn, by Deandra Demarest, had been allowed to plead down to voluntary manslaughter.

Eighteen-year sentence. At his age, that could turn out to be life.

His sole request: a prison "where they have a theater program."

Robin and I arrived at the party ten minutes late.

Cake, soda pop, bottled water for the virtuous, everything set up in a room near the hospital chapel.

Ruben Eagle, a fine doctor and sterling human being, was no orator. But what his speech lacked in dynamism it made up for in sincerity. His eyes moistened as he held up the giant check facsimile created by the hospital's public relations office. Impressive thing, full of zeros, Thalia's signature a faithful reproduction.

Ruben spoke a little longer than he needed to, informing the audience—members of the hospital board, development honchos, the pediatricians who worked for him, residents and fellows not on call, a few med school deans, Robin, Milo, and myself—what a blessing Thalia had been for the department. How that blessing would grow in years to come. How this changed so much.

Several children—long-healed patients—had also been invited, along with their parents. Personalizing the good works the Outpatient Division did every day. They stood to the side, intimidated by suits and white coats.

But two of the kids, a boy and a girl, got to hold the giant check and a second girl was in charge of hoisting an enlarged photo of Thalia.

Black-and-white image, shot at Perino's.

Leroy Hoke and Jack McCandless. A Martini glass cropped out, leaving the unlined, bright-eyed pixie face of a beautiful, happy young woman.

About the Author

JONATHAN KELLERMAN is the #1 **New York Times** bestselling author of forty-one crime novels, including the Alex Delaware series, **The Butcher's Theater, Billy Straight, The Conspiracy Club, Twisted,** and **True Detectives.** With his wife, bestselling novelist Faye Kellerman, he co-authored **Double Homicide** and **Capital Crimes.** With his son, bestselling novelist Jesse Kellerman, he co-authored **The Golem of Hollywood** and **The Golem of Paris.** He is also the author of two children's books and numerous nonfiction works, including **Savage Spawn: Reflections on Violent Children** and **With Strings Attached: The Art and Beauty of Vintage Guitars.** He has won the Goldwyn, Edgar, and Anthony awards and has been nominated for a Shamus Award. Jonathan and Faye Kellerman live in California, New Mexico, and New York.

jonathankellerman.com
Facebook.com/JonathanKellerman